## Praise for
### *New York Times* bestselling author
### Brenda Jackson

"The only flaw of this first-rate, satisfyingly sexy tale
is that it ends."
> —*Publishers Weekly*, starred review,
> on *Forged in Desire*

"[Jackson's] signature is to create full-sensory
romances that deliver on the heat, and she duly
delivers.... Sure to make any reader swoon."
> —*RT Book Reviews* on *Forged in Desire*

"Leave it to Jackson to take sizzle and honor, wrap it
in romance and come up with a first-rate tale."
> —*RT Book Reviews* on *Temptation*

"Brenda Jackson is the queen of newly discovered
love... If there's one thing Jackson knows how to do,
it's how to pluck those heartstrings and stir up some
seriously saucy drama."
> —*BookPage* on *Inseparable*

"This deliciously sensual romance ramps up the
emotional stakes and the action.... Sexy and sizzling."
> —*Library Journal* on *Intimate Seduction*

"Jackson does not disappoint... First-class page-
turner."
> —*RT Book Reviews* on *A Silken Thread*, 4½ stars,
> Top Pick!

"Jackson is a master at writing."
> —*Publishers Weekly* on *Sensual Confessions*

CH

# BRENDA JACKSON

## Love in Catalina Cove

HQN™

HQN™

ISBN-13: 978-1-335-00564-9

Recycling programs
for this product may
not exist in your area.

Love in Catalina Cove

To the man who will always and forever
be the love of my life, Gerald Jackson, Sr.

To my readers who are cruising with me to Aruba
in 2019, this story is for you.

To my sons, Gerald Jr. and Brandon.
You guys are the greatest and continue to
make me and your dad proud.

To Brenda Woodbury and Connie Moore.
Thanks for all the things that you do
in keeping my readers informed.

Happy 65th birthday, Jackie Johnson!
You are more sister than cousin,
and I appreciate having you in my life.

"For there is nothing hidden that will not be
disclosed, and nothing concealed that will not be
known or brought out into the open."
—*Luke* 8:17

# Love in Catalina Cove

# Part 1

"Life is a journey that must be traveled no matter how bad the roads and accommodations."
—Oliver Goldsmith

# *CHAPTER ONE*

*New York City*

VASHTI ALCINDOR SHOULD be celebrating. After all, the official letter she'd just read declared her divorce final, which meant her three-year marriage to Scott Zimmons was over. Definitely done with. As far as she was concerned the marriage had lasted two years too long. She wouldn't count that first year since she'd been too in love to dwell on Scott's imperfections. Truth be told there were many that she'd deliberately overlooked. She'd been so determined to have that happily-ever-after that she honestly believed she could put up with anything.

But reality soon crept into the world of make-believe, and she discovered she truly couldn't. Her husband was a compulsive liar who could look you right in the eyes and lie with a straight face. She didn't want to count the number of times she'd caught him in the act. When she couldn't take the deceptions any longer she had packed her things and left. When her Aunt Shelby died five months later, Scott felt entitled to half of the inheritance Vashti received in the will.

It was then that Vashti had hired one of the best divorce attorneys in New York, and within six weeks his private investigator had uncovered Scott's scandalous activities. Namely, his past and present affair with his boss's wife. Vashti hadn't wasted any time making Scott aware that she was not only privy to this information, but had photographs and videos to prove it.

Knowing she wouldn't hesitate to expose him as the lowlife that he was, Scott had agreed to an uncontested divorce and walked away with nothing. The letter she'd just read was documented proof that he would do just about anything to hold on to his cushy Wall Street job.

Her cell phone ringing snagged her attention, the ringtone belonging to her childhood friend and present Realtor, Bryce Witherspoon. Vashti clicked on her phone as she sat down at her kitchen table with her evening cup of tea. "Hey, girl, I hope you're calling with good news."

Bryce chuckled. "I am. Someone from the Barnes Group from California was here today and—"

"California?"

"Yes. They're a group of developers that's been trying to acquire land in the cove for years. They made you an unbelievably fantastic offer for Shelby by the Sea."

Vashti let out a loud shout of joy. She couldn't believe she'd been lucky enough to get rid of both her ex-husband and her aunt's property in the same day.

"Don't get excited yet. We might have problems," Bryce said.

Vashti frowned. "What kind of problems?"

"The developers want to tear down your aunt's bed-and-breakfast and—"

"Tear it down?" Vashti felt a soft kick in her stomach. Selling her aunt's bed-and-breakfast was one thing, having it demolished was another. "Why would they want to tear it down?"

"They aren't interested in the building, Vash. They want the eighty-five acres it sits on. Who wouldn't with the Gulf of Mexico in its backyard? I told you it would be a quick sale."

Vashti had known someone would find Shelby by the Sea a lucrative investment but she'd hoped somehow the inn would survive. With repairs it could be good as new. "What do they want to build there instead?"

"A luxury tennis resort."

Vashti nodded. "How much are they offering?" she asked, taking a sip of her tea.

"Ten million."

Vashti nearly choked. "Ten million dollars? That's nearly double what I was asking for."

"Yes, but the developers are eyeing the land next to it as well. I think they're hoping that one day Reid Lacroix will cave and sell his property. When he does, the developers will pounce on the opportunity to get their hands on it and build that golf resort they've been trying to put there for years. Getting your land will put their foot in the door so to speak."

Vashti took another sip of her tea. "What other problems are there?"

"This one is big. Mayor Proctor got wind of their offer and figured you might sell. He's calling a meeting."

"A meeting?"

"Yes, of the Catalina Cove Zoning Board. Although they can't stop you from selling the inn, they plan to block the buyer from bringing a tennis resort in here. The city ordinance calls for the zoning board to approve all new construction. This won't be the first time developers wanted to come into the cove and build something the city planners reject. Remember years ago when that developer wanted to buy land on the east end to build that huge shopping mall? The zoning board stopped it. They're determined that nothing in Catalina Cove changes."

"Well, it should change." As far as Vashti was concerned it was time for Mayor Procter to get voted out. He had been mayor for over thirty years. When Vashti had left Catalina Cove for college fourteen years ago, developers had been trying to buy up the land for a number of progressive projects. The people of Catalina Cove were the least open-minded group she knew.

Vashti loved living in New York City where things were constantly changing, and people embraced those changes. At eighteen she had arrived in the city to attend New York University and remained after getting a job with a major hotel chain. She had worked her way up to her six-figure salary as a hotel executive. At thirty-two she considered it her dream job. That wasn't bad for someone who started out working the concierge desk.

"Unless the Barnes Group can build whatever they want without any restrictions, there won't be a deal for us."

Vashti didn't like the sound of that. Ten million was ten million no matter how you looked at it. "Although I wouldn't want them to tear down Shelby, I think my aunt would understand my decision to do what's best for me." And the way Vashti saw it, ten million dollars was definitely what would be best for her.

"Do you really think she would want you to tear down the inn? She loved that place."

Vashti knew more than anyone how much Shelby by the Sea had meant to her aunt. It had become her life.

"Aunt Shelby knew there was no way I would ever move back to Catalina Cove after what happened. Mom and Dad even moved away. There's no connection for me to Catalina Cove."

"Hey, wait a minute, Vash. I'm still here."

Vashti smiled, remembering how her childhood friend had stuck with her through thick and thin. "Yes, you're still there, which makes me think you need your head examined for not moving away when you could have."

"I love Catalina Cove. It's my home and need I remind you that for eighteen years it was yours, too."

"Don't remind me."

"Look, I know why you feel that way, Vash, but are you going to let that one incident make you have ill feelings about the town forever?"

"It was more than an incident, Bryce, and you know it." For Vashti having a baby out of wedlock at sixteen had been a lot more than an incident. For her it had been a life changer. She had discovered who her real friends were during that time. Even now she would occasionally wonder how different things might have been had her child lived instead of died at birth.

"Sorry, bad choice of words," Bryce said, with regret in her voice.

"No worries. That was sixteen years ago." No need to tell Bryce that on occasion she allowed her mind to wander to that period of her life and often grieved for the child she'd lost. She had wanted children and Scott had promised they would start a family one day. That had been another lie.

"Tell me what I need to do to beat the zoning board on this, Bryce," Vashti said, her mind made up.

"Unfortunately, to have any substantial input, you need to meet with the board in person. I think it will be beneficial if the developers make an appearance as well. According to their representative, they're willing to throw in a few perks that the cove might find advantageous."

"What kind of perks?"

"Free membership to the resort's clubhouse for the first year, as well as free tennis lessons for the kids for a limited time. It will also bring a new employer to town, which means new jobs. Maybe if they were to get support from the townsfolk, the board would be more willing to listen."

"What do you think are our chances?"

"To be honest, even with all that, it's a long shot. Reid Lacroix is on the board and he still detests change. He's still the wealthiest person in town, too, and has a lot of clout."

"Then why waste my and the potential buyer's time?"

"There's a slim chance time won't be wasted. K-Gee is on the zoning board and he always liked you in school. He's one of the few progressive members on the board and the youngest. Maybe he'll help sway the others."

Vashti smiled. Yes, K-Gee had liked her but he'd liked Bryce even more and they both knew it. His real name was Kaegan Chambray. He was part of the Pointe-au-Chien Native American tribe and his family's ties to the cove and surrounding bayou went back generations, even before the first American settlers.

Although K-Gee was two years older than Vashti and Bryce, they'd hung out together while growing up. When Vashti had returned to town after losing her baby,

K-Gee would walk Vashti and Bryce home from school every day. Even though Bryce never said, Vashti suspected something had happened between Bryce and K-Gee during the time Vashti was away at that unwed home in Arkansas.

"When did K-Gee move back to Catalina Cove, Bryce?"

"Almost two years ago to help out his mom and to take over his family's seafood supply business when his father died. His mother passed away last year. And before you ask why I didn't tell you, Vash, you know why. You never wanted to hear any news regarding what was happening in Catalina Cove."

No, she hadn't, but anything having to do with K-Gee wasn't just town news. Bryce should have known that. "I'm sorry to hear about his parents. I really am. I'm surprised he's on the zoning board."

For years the townsfolk of the cove had never recognized members of the Pointe-au-Chien Native American tribe who lived on the east side of the bayou. Except for when it was time to pay city taxes. With K-Gee on the zoning board that meant change was possible in Catalina Cove after all.

"I need to know what you want to do, Vash," Bryce said, interrupting her thoughts. "The Barnes Group is giving us twenty days to finalize the deal or they will withdraw their offer."

Vashti stood up to cross the kitchen floor and put her teacup in the kitchen sink. "Okay, I'll think about what you said. Ten million dollars is a lot of money."

"Yes, and just think what you could do with it."

Vashti was thinking and she loved all the possibilities. Although she loved her job, she could stop working and spend the rest of her life traveling to all those places her aunt always wanted to visit but hadn't, because of putting Shelby by the Sea first. Vashti wouldn't make the same mistake.

THE NEXT MORNING, for the first time in two years, Vashti woke up feeling like she was in control of her life and could finally see a light—a bright one at that—at the end of the road. Scott was out of her life, she had a great job, but more importantly, some developer group was interested in her inn.

*Her inn.*

It seemed odd to think of Shelby by the Sea as hers when it had belonged to her aunt for as long as she could remember. Definitely long before Vashti was born. Her parents' home had been a mile away, and growing up she had spent a lot of her time at Shelby, especially during her teen years when she worked as her aunt's personal assistant. That's when she'd fallen in love with the inn and had thought it was the best place in the world.

Until...

Vashti pushed the "until" from her mind, refusing to go there and hoping Bryce was wrong about her having to return to Catalina Cove to face off with the zoning board. There had to be another way and she intended to find it. Barely eighteen, she had needed to escape the town that had always been her safe haven because it had become a living hell for her.

An hour later Vashti had showered, dressed and was walking out her door ready to start her day at the Grand Nunes Luxury Hotel in Manhattan. But not before stopping at her favorite café on the corner to grab a blueberry muffin and a cup of coffee. Catalina Cove was considered the blueberry capital in the country, and even she couldn't resist this small indulgence from her hometown. She would be the first to admit that although this blueberry muffin was delicious, it was not as good as the ones Bryce's mother made and sold at their family's restaurant.

With the bag containing her muffin in one hand and her cup of coffee in the other, Vashti caught the elevator up to the hotel's executive floor. She couldn't wait to get to work.

She'd heard that the big man himself, Gideon Nunes, was in town and would be meeting with several top members of the managerial and executive team, which would include her.

It was a half hour before lunch when she received a call to come to Mr. Nunes's office. Ten minutes later she walked out of the CEO's office stunned, in a state of shock. According to Mr. Nunes, his five hotels in the States had been sold, including this one. He'd further stated that the new owner was bringing in his own people, which meant her services were no longer needed.

In other words, she'd been fired.

## CHAPTER TWO

*A week later*

VASHTI GLANCED AROUND the Louis Armstrong New Orleans International Airport. Although she'd never returned to Catalina Cove, she'd flown into this airport many times to attend a hotel conference or convention, or just to get away. Even though Catalina Cove was only an hour's drive away, she'd never been tempted to take the road trip to revisit the parish where she'd been born.

Today she took the time to recall the day she'd left fourteen years ago for college. Since this was the closest airport to Catalina Cove, her flight had left from here. Her parents and Aunt Shelby had been there to see her off and the parting had been bittersweet.

To this day she often wondered if her parents had forgiven her for the embarrassment she'd caused them when she'd gotten pregnant. They had thought sending her to that home for unwed mothers would have her coming around to their way of thinking, until she'd informed them she had no intentions of giving her baby up for adoption. That had caused a huge discord in the family. It seemed the only person who'd been in her corner had been Aunt Shelby. Vashti hadn't caved in to her parents' demand to know the father of her child. To this day, they still didn't know. The only person who knew her secret was Bryce, and she knew her friend would carry the information to the grave with her.

"Welcome to *Nawlins*. Need help with your luggage, ma'am?"

Vashti smiled at the baggage handler. "No, I'm fine. I didn't check in any luggage." She just had her carry-on since she intended only to stay a couple of days.

As she headed toward the car rental counter she thought how different her life had become in a week. She was still absorbing the shock of having been fired from her job. Fired. There had been five of them in all—all part of the executive team—that had been given their pink slips.

There hadn't been any warning, not a single word around the office that Mr. Nunes had had plans to sell off any of his hotels. No one had suspected a thing. The new owner hadn't even let them linger. They'd been escorted out the door in the time it had taken to clear her desk and grab her purse. The only good thing, if you wanted to call it a good thing, was that Mr. Nunes had been awful generous with their severance and had even offered some jobs at his other hotels if you were inclined to move out of the country. Some had jumped at the offer. She had not. So here she was, in New Orleans and about to rent a car to drive to the town she thought never to see again.

With no job and more time on her hands than she really needed or wanted, in addition to the fact that there was ten million dollars dangling in front of her face, she had returned to Catalina Cove to attend the zoning board meeting and plead her case, although the thought of doing so was a bitter pill to swallow. When she'd left the cove she'd felt she didn't owe the town or its judgmental people anything and likewise, they didn't owe her a thing. Now fourteen years later she was back and to her way of thinking Catalina Cove did owe her something. The right to sell her land to whomever she wanted and for them to build whatever they wanted on the land.

"Welcome to New Orleans. What kind of car would you like to rent today?"

Vashti smiled at the young college-aged woman behind the counter. "Umm, what do you have?"

"A couple of sedans, some midsize vehicles and a couple of SUVs. And if you feel like being daring, we even have a two-seater sports car."

"A sports car?"

"Yes, a candy apple red Corvette. It was ordered for one of the NFL players who had to cancel his flight."

"A Corvette..." That was her dream car. She didn't need a car to get around in New York since she lived in the city and the subway worked just fine for her. But she would love getting behind the wheel of a 'vette. "And it's red?"

The young woman smiled. "Yes, and a convertible. It's a beautiful March day to have the top down while cruising. I give you fair warning. My father is a police officer and he said red cars, especially convertibles, stick out like a sore thumb. You're liable to get a speeding ticket if you even go one mile per hour over the speed limit."

Vashti chuckled. "Thanks for the warning but I have no intention of speeding."

"PLEASE, DAD..."

Sawyer Grisham drew in a deep breath, wondering at what point he would be able to give his daughter a firm no and truly mean it. She had the ability to wrap him around her finger and he had a feeling she knew it. With this particular request of hers he knew that he needed to turn her down, but...

"I'll think about it, Jadelyn." She knew whenever he called her by her full name that meant there wouldn't be any more discussion on the subject until he decided to have it.

"Thanks, Dad. You're the greatest. Love you."

He shook his head, grinning when he clicked off the phone. Of course she would have to end the call like that. Like he'd already given his permission for her to get a job this summer. She could spend her summer doing volunteer work at either the hospital or animal shelter, but as far as he was concerned she didn't need a job. He gave her a weekly allowance and a pretty darn generous one. All she needed to do was continue to make good grades in school. She would have plenty of time for employment later in life.

Sighing deeply, he pushed back the seat in his patrol car and stretched his legs out. This was the part of his job that he didn't mind doing since it got him away from behind his desk and out of the office. He loved this expanse of highway that connected New Orleans to Catalina Cove. The picturesque scenery made the drive one of the most pleasant he'd ever known. Giant oak trees lined both sides of the highway and through the low hanging branches you could see the sea marshes.

The closer you got to Catalina Cove, the highway merged from four lanes to two and even more tall oaks were perfectly strung along the roadway, providing a countryside effect. In this particular area that he loved, a cluster of the huge tree limbs joined to form a canopy. This was the spot where he would park under the shade of huge trees, hidden from sight off the highway to clock speeders. On occasion he would steal away here just to clear his mind, think about important matters and to put a number of things in perspective. Right now the main thing on his mind was that his daughter would probably start dating soon. So far she hadn't mentioned anything about it and he definitely was not going to put any ideas in her head.

He needed to call his office to remind Trudy Caldwell, his office manager, to make sure the Miller file was on his desk when he got back, which wouldn't be too long. So far he'd issued six speeding tickets and had been here only a few hours. Didn't anyone feel compelled to abide by the speed limit anymore? And some of the excuses they made while trying to talk their way out of a ticket were just downright ridiculous. As sheriff he expected people to operate within the confines of the law and not the other way around.

It was hard to believe he'd been sheriff in Catalina Cove for four years already. When he'd accepted the job and relocated here, Jade had been twelve. Not once had she complained about moving from their home in Nevada to Louisiana, although she'd left her friends behind. They'd decided to look at the move as an adventure. Thankfully, because of Jade's outgoing and bubbly nature, she'd quickly made new friends.

Leaving Reno was necessary in order to move on with their lives after losing Johanna. Cancer had claimed her exactly three months to the day she'd noticed the discoloration of a mole on her thigh. He would never forget the day he'd gotten that call at the FBI headquarters where he worked as an agent. In a teary voice Johanna had told him the results of the biopsy. It had come back as cancer, already at stage four. It seemed once the diagnosis was made the condition worsened, and he had buried his wife on the day that would have been her thirtieth birthday.

He pushed from his mind thoughts of Johanna. Even after over four years they were too painful to dwell on. He was about to reach for his phone to call Trudy when a car sped by. The driver was clocked doing sixty in a fifty-five-miles-an-hour zone.

Pulling his patrol car onto the highway, he flipped on his flashing red-and-blue lights and siren as he took off behind the speeding red Corvette convertible.

VASHTI HAD THE radio on full blast while singing along with Beyoncé, belting out her newest hit. This was a perfect day to drive with the top down. March was about to roll into April with spring-like days. The midday sun wasn't too hot and the breeze was just right. She loved the feel of her hair blowing in the wind, and wished somehow her problems could be blown away as easily. If she had to return to Catalina Cove she might as well make the drive fun. She would admit this car had a lot of power. Already she'd made it to the outskirts of town and should be reaching her destination soon.

She glanced in her rearview mirror and saw the flashing red-and-blue lights and immediately turned down the volume on the radio. That's when she heard the siren. Where had the police officer come from and how long had they been following her? She pulled to the shoulder of the road and he pulled off the road behind her.

Vashti wondered why she'd gotten stopped. Annoyed, she tapped her hand on the steering wheel and when the police officer reached her car, she looked at him. OMG. She was convinced she was staring up into the most handsome face she'd seen in a long time. And on top of that, a snap of sexual awareness she hadn't felt in years rocked her to the bone.

He was so tall and she thought there was something magnetic about those dark brown eyes that were staring back at her. It took her a minute to notice his lips were moving, which meant he'd been talking. What on earth had he said? She'd been too busy concentrating on the shape of his lips.

"Excuse me, Officer. Could you repeat that?"

He gave her an irritated look. "I asked why you didn't stop when you heard my siren?"

"I didn't hear your siren probably because I had the radio on full blast. Sorry about that."

"Your license please."

"Sure." She then went into her purse and pulled out her driver's license, wondering who had ruined his day. It was obvious he was in a bad mood. She handed him her driver's license. "And why was I stopped?" And why was she noticing how the shirt of his officer's uniform seemed to stretch across a broad chest and over muscular shoulders?

He didn't answer her. Instead he returned to his patrol car. She was tempted to hang out the window and check out his rear end but quickly talked herself out of doing so. Mr. Not-So-Nice-Cop had one redeeming quality. He was definitely a hottie. But regardless of his sexy attributes, he could have answered her question before walking off.

A good ten minutes had passed before he returned

and handed her license back to her. "And why was I stopped?" she asked him again.

"You were speeding."

"Speeding?"

"Yes. You were going sixty in a fifty-five-miles-an-hour zone."

Had she? She knew that was a possibility. More than once she'd had to ease her foot off the pedal when she'd discovered she'd been going faster than she intended. He handed her a ticket to sign and she felt a tingling sensation in her stomach when their hands brushed in the process. She looked up at him. "Is this a real one?"

He lifted a brow. "A real what?"

"Ticket."

"What other kind is there?"

She frowned. "A warning ticket."

"I don't give out warning tickets."

She looked at the ticket and then back at him. "Two hundred dollars!"

"Yes. That's forty dollars for ever mile you were going over. Forty times five would be two hundred dollars."

"That's a bit much."

He lifted his brow again and she wished he wouldn't do that. Each time he did she was captivated by the beauty of his eyes. "You think so?"

"Yes."

"I don't. You broke the law."

"It wasn't intentional."

"If you say so. Here's your driver's license back." Again their fingers brushed and Vashti felt that tingling sensation.

"I take it you're headed to Catalina Cove," he said,

pushing his hat back from his face to reveal even more of his features.

"Yes, why do you ask?" she asked, noticing that besides being handsome, the man was broad-shouldered and fit.

"No reason. Just make sure you drive within the speed limits while you're there. Looks like this little toy you're driving might get you in trouble."

She looked at her ticket before looking back up at him. "Looks like it already has."

His mouth formed a smile and she felt a fluttering in her stomach at the sensual curve of his mouth. No man should have the ability to have such an effect on a woman...especially when he'd just made her two hundred dollars poorer.

"Do you have family in town or are you just here to enjoy all Catalina Cove has to offer?" he asked her.

No need to tell him why she was there. It really wasn't any of his business. "I'm here to enjoy all Catalina Cove has to offer."

He nodded. "Well then, enjoy your stay. Good day."

Watching in her side-view mirror as he walked back to his patrol car, she also thought he looked good from the waist down and appreciated the way his slacks fit a pair of masculine thighs and long legs. And his backside was pretty darn nice, too. It was only after he'd gotten in his vehicle did she allow herself to breathe again. As far as she was concerned, he'd provided her with the best view she'd seen since arriving back in Louisiana.

Starting her car, she pulled back onto the highway.

SAWYER WATCHED UNTIL the little red Corvette was no longer in sight. What the hell had happened when their hands had accidentally touched? Hell, even now he could feel a burning sensation. It had taken all the control he could muster to maintain his professionalism and give her that ticket. He had not been that attracted to a woman since Johanna.

According to her driver's license her name was Vashti Alcindor and she lived in New York City. Since she wasn't wearing a wedding ring he assumed she was single. The car was a rental and he wondered what had brought her to the cove. He'd tried asking her in a roundabout way, but she hadn't told him anything. That was okay. Everybody had the right to keep their business to themselves. He of all people understood the need for seclusion and privacy at times. Well, unfortunately because of her inability to drive within the speed limits, this trip just became two hundred dollars costlier for her.

"You there, Sheriff?"

Trudy's voice intruded through the car's intercom. "Yes, I'm here."

"I put that Miller file on your desk."

"Thanks, and I'm on my way back to the office."

"Okay."

He started the ignition in the patrol car, and as he pulled onto the highway he couldn't help wondering if his path would be crossing with Ms. Vashti Alcindor's again.

A FEELING SHE hadn't anticipated washed over Vashti when she entered the city limits of Catalina Cove. It wasn't the resentment she'd expected but a sudden sense of coming home. Of belonging. How was that possible when she'd left here fourteen years ago without looking back, thinking this town would never be her home again? She could only assume because there was a time she thought she had belonged. After all, she'd been born here, in that house on Higgins Lane. It had been the only home she knew…except for those months her parents had sent her away to Arkansas to have her baby. She had felt all alone then, housed with other girls in the same predicament and whose families were determined to take control of their lives.

She had refused to let her parents take control of hers. She'd made plans. She would keep her baby, quit school, attend classes at night for her GED. In her mind, that was better than nothing, and her aunt had said she would watch the baby at night while she was at school.

Returning to Catalina Cove without her baby had been hard. *Get over it because things happen for a reason. Consider losing the baby a blessing. It would have ruined your life.* Her mother's words had cut to the core. There had been no compassion and no regret with either of her parents.

Vashti had finished her last year of school and had been accepted to NYU to start during the summer semester instead of waiting for the fall. She had caught a plane to New York a week after high school graduation. Other than Aunt Shelby and Bryce there hadn't been anyone left in the cove that she truly cared about…at least not anymore.

Well, there had been K-Gee but he'd left town two years before she had, the night he'd graduated from high school in fact. And besides Bryce's parents, there had been Ms. Gertie. Gertrude Landers was a midwife who'd probably delivered every baby that had been born in the cove over the past fifty years. Ms. Gertie had always been a loving soul and one of the kindest people Vashti knew while growing up in Catalina Cove. She'd always had a kind word to say about everybody and had been one of her aunt's dearest friends. And like her aunt, she'd stuck by her when Vashti had gotten pregnant. To this day Vashti thought of Ms. Gertie as the grandmother she never had.

It had been Vashti's desire for Ms. Gertie to deliver her baby since she'd taken care of her during the first months of her pregnancy instead of the doctor in town. But when Vashti began showing, her parents decided to send her away to have her baby. Those months had been the loneliest of her life.

Bringing her thoughts back to the present, Vashti drove through the historic part of the city and was reminded how the town got its origin. It was required history in the Catalina Cove school system.

Vashti knew that the parcel of land the cove sat on had been a gift to the notorious pirate Jean LaFitte, from the newly formed United States of America for his role in helping the thirteen colonies fight for their independence from the British during the American Revolution. There were some who actually believed he wasn't buried at sea in the Gulf of Honduras like history claimed but was buried somewhere in the waters surrounding Catalina Cove.

For years because of LaFitte, the cove had been a shipping town. It still was, which was evident by the number of fishing vessels she could see lining the piers as she drove through the shipping district. The Moulden River was full of trout, whiting, shrimp and oysters. Tourists would come from miles around to sample the town's seafood, especially the oysters. The cove's lighthouse-turned-restaurant was the place to dine and you had to make reservations weeks in advance to get a table.

She came to a stop at a red light at the intersection of Adrienne and Sophie, the streets reputedly named for two of LaFitte's mistresses. The entire downtown area was a close replicate of New Orleans's French Quarter, a deliberate move on LaFitte's part. The cove was where the pirate would return to when he and his team of smugglers needed some down time with their women. And if the naming of the streets was to be believed, he'd had several of them, she thought, making a turn on Margaux Lane.

Her thoughts shifted from Jean LaFitte to the man who had pulled her over earlier. That was something that had definitely changed in the cove. It appeared police officers were no longer middle-aged, potbellied men who looked like they'd eaten one blueberry muffin too many. The man who'd given her a ticket was so fit one would suspect he spent a lot of his time at the gym. He was definitely pleasing on the eyes. She hadn't felt this much interest in a man since finding out what a scumbag Scott was. It was then she'd sworn off men. Nothing had changed, although she had gotten a jolt between the thighs, a sort of reminder of what she hadn't had in over two years now. At some point she and Scott had begun engaging in what she called courtesy sex and then months later she'd decided not to bother at all. It hadn't been worth the effort. It hadn't seemed to bother him any, and now she knew why. His boss's wife had been his sidepiece.

Reaching Adele Street meant she was entering the historical residential district. Stately older homes, most of them of the French Creole style, lined the streets with pristine manicured lawns. She'd always liked this style of house and recalled that a number of the same style were scattered around New Orleans. That was another deliberate duplication the pirate had taken from there.

It was a known fact that New Orleans had the largest French Creole population in the country. Catalina Cove was next. What a lot of people failed to realize was that being a Creole had nothing to do with your race. It didn't matter what your skin color was. It had everything to do with your cultural heritage. Her father, a Creole born in Catalina Cove, had met her mother at Grambling University. They had returned here to live after they got married. As a child, Vashti remembered her paternal grandparents, and how her grandmother had told her about the rich Creole history and culture. To this day Vashti was proud of her Creole heritage.

She came to a stop in front of one of the stately looking houses. Bryce had purchased her house three years ago and this would be Vashti's first visit. Her best friend had visited her many times in New York and Bryce had also joined her in New Orleans whenever Vashti happened to go there on business.

Vashti sat there a minute after turning off the ignition. It was a nice home, and she thought the two-story structure was perfect for her best friend. The previous owners had approached Bryce about being their Realtor and she'd ended up buying it herself.

The minute she got out the car, the front door opened and a smiling Bryce stepped out in the sunlight. Vashti felt her smile grow wide in return.

"Where did you get that thing?" Bryce asked, coming down the steps to meet her and giving more than an admiring glance to the Corvette convertible.

"A rental. It was ordered for an NFL player who had to cancel his trip at the last minute so I thought I'd take it."

Bryce gave her a hug and she gave her one back. "Glad you got here in one piece."

"Me, too, but not without a little bit of drama," she said, opening the passenger door to retrieve her carry-on.

Bryce raised a brow. "Drama? What kind of drama?"

Vashti looped her arm through Bryce's. "Come on, let's go inside and I'll tell you about it. And I'm dying to see your home."

## CHAPTER THREE

SAWYER CLOSED THE file he'd been reading and leaned back in his chair. For some reason he couldn't get the woman driving that red Corvette out of his mind. When he'd returned to town he took the route he usually traveled as a shortcut to get back to his office. That's when he saw that same vehicle parked in front of the house where Bryce Witherspoon lived. The woman had definitely been a looker, even with all that wind-blown hair from driving with the top down. And there had been something about those soft brown eyes of hers and well-defined lips that enhanced her honey-brown skin. He figured her age to be in her late twenties, and evidently, she had a flare for flashy stuff, that rental Corvette convertible being one of them. But then she was a New Yorker. He'd dated a woman from New York once while stationed in New Jersey and the one thing he remembered about her was that she'd been a party girl who never took anything seriously. It was all fun and games. He wondered if Vashti Alcindor was the same way.

He looked up when he heard the knock on the door. "Come in."

Trudy came in with purse in hand, which meant it was time for her to leave. Was it five o'clock already? It was a wonder Jade hadn't called. She'd decided to try her hand at learning to cook and since he hadn't gotten a call yet from the fire department he could only hope she hadn't burned up the place.

"I'm calling it a day, Sheriff."

He smiled. She always did at exactly five every day. Trudy, who liked to claim she was only fifty-five, was probably a good ten years older than that and should have retired years ago. But she was good at what she did and he was convinced she could work better and faster than a woman half her age. He hoped she wouldn't bring up the issue of retiring anytime soon. Having worked for the previous sheriff, she was someone Sawyer had come to depend on. She was efficient and well liked by all.

"Okay, Trudy. I'll see you tomorrow."

"Don't work too late. Jade is making beef strudel tonight."

He lifted a brow. "And how do you know that?"

Trudy smiled. "Because she called for my recipe. There's nothing like a teenager who prefers going home from school to cook instead of hanging out at the Livewire."

Sawyer nodded. The Livewire was a hangout spot for the teens in town. It was a decent place that provided a safe environment for them to play arcade games and fill up on hamburgers, fries and milkshakes. There was even a quiet corner in the back for those who wanted to get an early start on their homework. Jade went there some days but she mostly preferred going on home, especially since she was trying her hand at cooking now.

"I can't wait to try it out." Okay he was lying. He could wait. The last recipe she'd gotten from Trudy was for a lemon cake, and she hadn't thought the recipe called for enough lemon flavor so she added more. A lot more. He was certain he'd walked around with puckered lips for a week.

"Oh, by the way, Sheriff. I was logging in the speeding tickets you issued today and noticed you gave one to a Vashti Alcindor. I didn't know she was back in town."

*Back in town?* "She's been here before?"

Trudy grinned. "Heck yes. Vashti used to live here. Born and raised."

Sawyer frowned. "I asked if she had family here and she said no."

"She doesn't anymore. Her parents moved away years ago, and her aunt Shelby Riggs passed away a few months ago."

Sawyer sat up straight in his chair. "Ms. Shelby was her aunt?"

"Yes, her mother's sister."

Sawyer nodded. He'd liked Ms. Shelby. When he first moved to Catalina Cove she had been one of the first to welcome him and Jade to town. He'd even stayed at her inn overnight when he'd arrived in town to interview for the sheriff position.

"I guess she's here to finalize the sale of Shelby by the Sea. I'd heard her aunt left it to her and there's a buyer already. While growing up here Vashti loved that inn as much as Shelby did. I hate that she's decided to sell it. I was hoping the inn would get her to move back. But in a way, I can't too much blame her, what with the way some of the townspeople treated her."

Sawyer had never been one for town gossip, but for some reason anything dealing with Vashti Alcindor interested him. "Why?"

"Teenage pregnancy at sixteen."

He lifted a brow. "Are you saying people in this town stopped being nice to her because of that?"

"Pretty much. Before that she'd been a popular girl at school, straight-A student, head majorette of the school's marching band and had won a lot of awards while a member of the school's swim team. But I honestly think the reason some of the townsfolk turned on her had more to do with her refusal to reveal the identity of the guy who fathered her child."

"It wasn't their business." That was the one thing he disliked about living in a small town. There was always a group of people who felt it was their God-given right to know everything about you. What time you woke up in the morning. The kind of toothpaste you used. If you wore underwear or not, and who you were having sex with or if you weren't getting any at all.

"No, it wasn't their business," Trudy agreed. "But they felt it was. She didn't even tell her parents. No one knew Vashti even had a boyfriend. Rumors began flying as to whose child it might be. It had gotten so bad it was probably unbearable for that young girl here."

Sawyer shook his head. "Why didn't the guy who got her pregnant step forward and claim the baby as his?" He would never forget when Johanna told him she was pregnant with his child. He hadn't wasted any time marrying her. And to this day he never regretted doing so. Johanna had been a good wife and a wonderful mother to Jade. They had made their marriage work. Listening to Jade's heartbeat for the first time was something he would never forget.

"I don't know why he didn't come forward," Trudy intruded into his thoughts by saying. "I think he should have. That led people to speculate the guy wasn't anyone from here but was probably some teenager in a family passing through who'd stayed at the inn one summer. Vashti hung out at the inn a lot helping her aunt. That would make perfect sense. Young love happens quite a bit at sixteen."

As the father of a sixteen-year-old, he hoped it didn't happen to Jade, he thought, tossing a paper clip on his desk. Luckily, Johanna had had the period talk with Jade before she'd died. But they'd had some crucial father to daughter talks, too, and she had listened attentively and asked questions and he'd found himself having a more in-depth conversation with her than he'd intended. The birds and the bees had become the roses and thorns. That open and frank discussion had established their future father and daughter talks, and she felt comfortable enough to ask or tell him anything. He was proud of their good relationship and he hoped it stayed that way. He had made sure that she understood he was not her friend but her father and there was a difference.

He glanced up at Trudy. "So what happened?" he asked.

"When she began showing, her parents sent her to one of those homes for unwed mothers. It was out of state. They wanted her to put the child up for adoption but those close to Vashti said she intended to keep the baby. I heard her parents threatened to disown her if she did, but she intended to defy them and keep it anyway. Her parents might have disowned her but she knew her aunt Shelby never would."

"So in the end did she keep the baby or did she give it up for adoption?"

"Neither. Although the baby was born alive, it later died of complications."

A part of Sawyer went still. "God, that's awful."

"It was and what was even sadder was that when she returned to town to pick up her life, there were some who made it hard for her. They were still upset about her not revealing the identity of the baby's father. Her only true friends in town were Bryce Witherspoon and K-Gee Chambray. Somehow Vashti weathered the vindictiveness and when she left for college she swore she would never come back and she kept her word."

He nodded. "I didn't see her at Ms. Shelby's memorial services."

"No, but I imagine she attended the funeral services held for her in Connecticut where Ms. Shelby was from. Shelby always said she wanted to be returned there for burial when the time came." Trudy sighed as she glanced at her watch. "I'm leaving. Let me know how dinner turns out."

"Trust me I will." Sawyer glanced at his own watch. His deputies for the evening shift had arrived and he could leave knowing things were in their capable hands. Anderson and Minor knew how to reach him if anything crazy went down. Things never did in Catalina Cove. He would admit it was a nice town and the perfect place to raise a family. He was glad of his decision to accept a job and move here.

His thoughts shifted back to what Trudy had told him about Vashti Alcindor. He hoped the townspeople now saw the error of their ways and would make her homecoming a lot different than when she'd left.

"You really got a ticket for speeding?" Bryce asked as they sat in her kitchen enjoying blueberry muffins and iced tea.

Vashti shrugged. "Hey, I wasn't speeding intentionally. In fact, I honestly hadn't realized I was doing so," she said in her defense. "That Corvette has more power than I realized. Besides, it was only five miles over the speed limit."

"And you couldn't talk your way out of it? Or get the patrolman to go easy on you with just a warning ticket? You used to be good at doing that when you first started driving."

Vashti remembered those days. Back then she'd been deliberately speeding. All the teenagers in town considered that stretch of road as the Indianapolis 500. "No, this cop wasn't friendly. In fact, he seemed like he wasn't in a good mood, and when I asked him about a warning ticket he got all huffy and said he didn't give warnings." She took a sip of her tea. "The only good thing in his favor was his looks. Definitely eye candy."

"Did you get his name?"

"Yes. His name tag said S. Grisham."

"I figured you were talking about Sawyer, and he's not a patrolman. He's our sheriff."

"Whatever happened to Sheriff Phillips?"

"He finally retired, and after his son was killed while hunting, there wasn't another Phillips to pass the badge to, thus ending the dynasty."

There had been a Phillips enforcing the law in Catalina Cove since the beginning of time. It had become a foregone conclusion that if a Phillips ran for sheriff he would win. "When did sheriffs begin staking out speeders? I've never known Sheriff Phillips to come out of his office to do anything, other than to show up at your parents' restaurant every day around three for his blueberry muffin and cup of coffee. His deputies did all the work."

Bryce chuckled. "You remember those days, do you?"

"Can't forget them."

"Well, Sheriff Grisham is nothing like Sheriff Phillips. He's a hands-on sort of sheriff. He gets out of his office a lot and will do anything he'd ask of his deputies, which includes setting speed traps. He's strict when it comes to enforcing the law but is very approachable. He doesn't act like he made the law the way Sheriff Phillips used to do. Like he thought he was King Phillips or something."

She and Bryce spent the next hour sitting at the kitchen table, eating blueberry muffins and drinking tea while reliving the past; at least the fun days when she'd thought the cove was the best place in the world to live and she would never leave. Life was good. The people were great. The natives stuck together and it took a while for any outsiders to be accepted.

"So, what's the story with Sheriff Grisham?" Vashti finally asked. During her and Bryce's stroll down memory lane, she'd kept pushing thoughts of him to the back of her mind. For some reason she couldn't forget the moment she looked up into his face. She'd been mesmerized.

"He's ex-military and ex-FBI. Moved here from Reno, Nevada, four years ago after being offered the job. It's just him and his daughter, Jade."

Vashti nodded. "No wife?"

"He's a widower. His wife died of cancer around five years ago. I heard they buried her on her thirtieth birthday."

"How awful."

"I don't remember her, but she was the Smithfields' granddaughter who'd lived in Texas."

"I remember her. She spent a few summers here visiting them," Vashti said. Herb Smithfield had been a federal judge, and he and his wife, Lora, had been members of her church while growing up. She remembered them as a nice older couple.

"Well, she grew up and married Sawyer Grisham. When the Smithfields passed away they left their house to her, but she never moved here to live in it. Instead she had it rented out as one of those Airbnb places and was making pretty good money off it since it was always occupied by honeymooners. I guess Sawyer Grisham decided to put it to good use when the sheriff position came open."

Vashti remembered the Smithfields' house at the end of Meadowbrook Lane. It sat on three acres of land with a small portion of the cove in the back, and she could see how it would be a perfect honeymoon getaway.

"With Sawyer Grisham looking so good and all, I bet most of the single women in town are clamoring for his attention," Vashti said.

"You wouldn't believe how ridiculous they are," Bryce said, grinning. "Although he's friendly enough, he's a private person and pretty much stays to himself. He and K-Gee are good friends, though. I guess their friendship became close since they're both ex-marines who'd spent a lot of time in Afghanistan."

"Does he date much?" She could see women standing in line to go out with him.

"So far he hasn't dated any woman in town, and it hasn't been for lack of trying on any of their parts, trust me. Like I said, things got downright ridiculous. You wouldn't believe all the blueberry pies left at the police station for him and the mass of dinner invitations I heard he got. Even Rachel Libby tried catching his eyes."

"Rachel Libby? You've got to be kidding me? Isn't she a lot older than him? I would put his age to be at thirty-four or thirty-five."

"He's thirty-six and she is older, about ten years older to be exact. But she's been acting the part of a cougar lately. An aggressive one at that. She began acting all crazy and wild ever since Mr. Libby died a few years back."

"So he hasn't dated anyone in town since moving here?"

"No, not a single feminine soul. Rumor has it that he's involved with some woman living in New Orleans. I don't know if that's even true and if it is, I don't know how serious it might be since he's never brought her to town to attend any of the local events. All we know is that he is a good sheriff and a great father to Jade."

Vashti took a drink of her tea. "How old is his daughter?"

"Jade turned sixteen earlier this month and is a real cutie and extremely friendly. She's popular in town and well liked by all."

So had she been at sixteen, Vashti thought. Until she'd gotten pregnant. Then all the townsfolk hadn't wasted any time kicking her off that pedestal they'd placed her on. Being popular and well liked by all in Catalina Cove wasn't all it was made out to be as far as she was concerned.

Not wanting to seem too interested in the sheriff,

Vashti asked, "So why didn't you mention K-Gee had moved back to town? And don't hand me that BS about me not wanting to know what was going on in this town. Any news about K-Gee would have been an exception to the rule and you knew that."

She watched Bryce stiffen and knew this was one subject she didn't want to talk about, so Vashti asked, "Why, Bryce?"

Bryce set her glass of iced tea down and looked at her. "Because eventually that topic of conversation would have led to others about K-Gee that I wasn't ready to talk about. I'm still not, Vashti." She paused a moment and then said, "You're not stupid. I'm sure you've figured out something happened between us during that time you were away in Arkansas. And it continued even after he left town. And by the way, he prefers going by Kaegan now. No nickname for him anymore."

Vashti nodded. "Okay, I got that and I understand. A grown man still being called K-Gee is a bit much. So, what questions would I have asked that you didn't want to answer? And you're right, I've always suspected something went on between you two, but you didn't talk about it and I didn't push it. I had my own problems to deal with, but I hope you know I would have been there for you. You're my best friend. So tell me, are the two of you seeing each other now?"

Bryce got up from the table and poured more iced tea into their glasses. "No. K-Gee hasn't talked to me much since returning."

"Why?"

Bryce sat back down in her chair and took a drink of her iced tea before saying, "Long story. And please don't say that you have time to hear it because I don't

have time to tell it. Not only is it long, but it's also drain-
ing and I don't need to deal with that today."

Vashti knew her friend well enough to know when to
back off. Whatever the issue was, Bryce wasn't ready
to let her in on it…like before.

"Well, whatever the problem, I hope the two of you
work it out. I love you both. It's been years and there
are some things that happen in the past, that are best
left there. In the past."

"You're a fine one to talk. You haven't left the things
that happened here behind you, Vashti. Look how long
you've been gone. The only reason you're here is to
sever one more tie by selling your aunt's property."

Vashti couldn't dispute what Bryce had just said.
That meant she was a fine one to think she could give
anyone advice about letting go and moving on. "You're
right. Today is not a good time to talk about anything.
I want to shower and take a nap. Then what can I do
to talk you into preparing some of your crab bisque?"

Bryce smiled. "Consider it done."

"Thanks. Since the zoning board meeting isn't meeting until tomorrow evening, I think I'm going to get up
in the morning and go visit Ms. Gertie. Then I'm going
to Shelby by the Sea and check out the place."

"Get prepared, Vash. Ms. Gertie has dementia pretty
bad. Her family put her in that nursing home on Silas
Lane after she kept wandering off. Don't be surprised if
she doesn't recognize you or if she thinks you're somebody else."

Vashti didn't want to see Ms. Gertie in that condition, but she had to see her before she left town. "Getting old sucks."

"Yes, it does. By the way, I took the time off to spend

tomorrow with you. We'll take my car and I'll do the driving."

Vashti raised a brow. "Why?"

Bryce grinned over at her. "I'm trying to save you from getting another ticket while you're here."

"So, Dad, what do you think?"

Sawyer wondered if his child really wanted to know. He placed his fork beside his plate and glanced at her. Her smiling face showed she was in good spirits and he knew his words could be a setback and wipe that happy look right off her face. She was expecting positive feedback and this was where his "truth-time" habit had to be done in a way that wouldn't hurt her feelings…at least he hoped not.

"It tastes different than the one Trudy makes." It tastes a lot different.

"I know," she said, smiling. "I changed the recipe."

You most certainly did, he thought. "May I ask you why?" he asked standing to take his plate to the kitchen.

She followed him. "I thought it needed more than what was on the recipe."

After placing his plate in the sink he turned and leaned against the counter. "Then why bother following a recipe? It's no different than following a road map. If you want to get to New Orleans and I gave you directions as to how to get there, but you choose to change those directions, you might end up anywhere."

Her smile faded. "Are you saying I should have followed the recipe?"

"I think when Trudy gave it to you she expected that you would and not experiment. How do you think she's going to feel tomorrow when she asks me how the beef strudel turned out and I tell her you changed the recipe? She'll think you thought the original recipe wasn't good enough for you."

"It was good, but…"

"But what, Jade?"

"I thought I could make it better."

Evidently. "Well, I'm going to be honest with you, Jade. You didn't. I'm not saying some good things can't be improved on because they can, but it often takes a lot of work and trial and error."

"I guess I blew it tonight, huh, Dad?"

He reached out to tweak her nose. Lord, how he loved this kid. Whenever he looked at her he was amazed that this incredible child was made by him and Johanna. "No, you didn't blow it, but can I make a suggestion?"

"Yes."

"Follow any recipe you get the way you should. Then if you think it can and should be improved try it, but know why you're doing it. Ask yourself what's your goal and what you're trying to achieve."

He knew that look. She was thinking and that was good. "Take the beef strudel recipe for instance," he said. "You got carried away with certain ingredients so it didn't taste so hot. If you're really serious about learning to cook, how about taking a cooking class? I understand there're several good ones in New Orleans. If you'd like, I'll see if they offer Saturday classes."

Her smile came back and it brightened her entire face. "You would do that for me, Dad?"

He smiled at her. "Don't you know that I would do just about anything for you, Jade?"

She nodded and then flung herself into his arms and

hugged him. "Yes, I'd like that and you are the best dad ever."

*And you*, he thought, *are my pride and joy.*

## CHAPTER FOUR

THE NEXT MORNING after breakfast, Vashti and Bryce went to Berkshire Nursing Home to visit Ms. Gertie who didn't recognize either of them. Bryce had tried preparing Vashti, but seeing the older woman in such a state tore at her. She tried engaging in conversation with Ms. Gertie but the older woman became annoyed and told them she didn't appreciate being interrupted while watching CNN.

According to Bryce, Ms. Gertie's son, daughter-in-law and grandson didn't visit her often because it bothered them when she didn't recognize them. Vashti thought that was a poor excuse. Whether Ms. Gertie recognized them shouldn't matter. The important thing was that she wasn't left alone, and that they recognized her and remembered her importance in their lives.

"When you visit her tomorrow it might be a different story," Bryce said as they left the nursing home. "She might remember you."

"Unfortunately, I'm leaving first thing in the morning." And what she didn't have to tell Bryce was that she didn't plan to come back.

Bryce gave her a look that told her exactly what she thought of that, but let it be. "We'll stop by the folks' place before driving out to Shelby by the Sea. Mom and Dad would love to see you."

"Alright." Vashti wanted to see them as well. Vashti would admit to being surprised at how friendly two of her former classmates had been when she ran into them at the nursing home, almost as if they were glad to see her. She had once considered Charlette Hansberry and Mavis Green to be her good friends, until she'd gotten pregnant and they'd become scarce. Their mothers had probably ordered them to stay away from her, but still it hurt. She'd needed more of her friends during that time, not less of them.

It turned out Charlette owned the nursing home, having taken over for her parents when they decided to retire and move to California to be close to their only son and grandkids. Charlette was divorced with a six-year-old son. Mavis was the head nurse on staff. She had married her childhood sweetheart, Hugh Green. Like a number of men in town, Hugh worked at the blueberry factory and the couple had two kids.

"I was surprised Charlette and Mavis gave me the time of day," Vashti said, getting into Bryce's car and buckling the seat belt.

"Why wouldn't they?" Bryce asked glancing over at her before starting the car.

"Do I need to remind you of how things were for me here, back then?"

"No, but that was back then, Vash. Years ago. People change and ideas they might have had change, too. I'm sure they look back at that time with regret about how they treated you. If I remember correctly, it was their parents forbidding them to have a friendship with you and not them doing it on their own."

"Your parents didn't forbid you to hang out with me," Vashti reminded her. Once she'd gotten pregnant, the parents of some of her friends acted like pregnancy was catching. However, she knew what they were really worried about was that since she'd been sexually active that made her a loose girl and they didn't want their daughters around anyone they thought lacked morals.

"My parents weren't your typical parents," Bryce said.

"Yes, that's true." It had been rumored that back in the day when he'd graduated from high school here, Chester Witherspoon had fled to Canada to avoid fighting in the Vietnam war. It wasn't that he'd been a coward; he just didn't feel the country needed to go to war. At least he hadn't at first. A year later he returned with a wife and baby in tow. It was then that he'd decided to do his patriotic duty and enlist, leaving Bryce's mom and three-month-old brother in the care of his parents.

After returning home from the war, Bryce's parents had another son before Bryce, their only daughter, was born. Although Bryce never said and Vashti never asked, if you did the math of the date the Witherspoons celebrated their anniversary and the close proximity to Bryce's oldest brother's age, her mother was pregnant before her parents had married. Both of Bryce's brothers, Ryan and Duke, lived in Catalina Cove and were partners with their parents in the family-owned café.

"I honestly think Mavis and Charlette were glad to see you again," Bryce was saying, interrupting Vashti's thoughts. "If you give Catalina Cove a chance, I think you'd find people aren't the same."

Vashti chuckled. "Oh, they feel they can change but they want the town to stay the same?"

"Pretty much. I don't have a problem with some change here but I don't want too many developers coming in here and changing things. You recall what I told you about Allen Heart."

Yes, she remembered. Bryce had family who'd lived in Allen Heart, South Carolina, years ago when it had just been a small town with no name recognition. A mass of developers came in and all but ran the locals out when property taxes soared. Most of the residents had been forced to sell homes and land that had been in their family for years when they couldn't pay escalated taxes.

Vashti glanced over at Bryce. "Are you saying you don't want the Barnes Group to buy Shelby by the Sea? Do I need to remind you how much commission you'd make with the sale?"

"No, you don't need to remind me. I was thinking about what I would do with all that money. It would be nice but it won't buy me happiness, Vash."

Vashti thought about that then asked, "And what would make you happy, Bryce?"

They had stopped the car at a traffic light and Bryce glanced over at her. "I'm thirty-two and have never been married so to start off, a husband would be nice."

"Don't wish for things you're better off not having, Bryce."

"And please don't think every man is a loser like Scott," Bryce begged. "I want to believe my soul mate is still out there."

"Still reading those romance novels, are you?" That had been Bryce's favorite pastime. She had been reading them long before her mother discovered she'd been doing so.

Bryce chuckled as she moved the car forward. "And what if I am?"

Vashti shook her head. "Because they are filled with unrealistic expectations and are a real disservice to women."

"I beg to differ. They provide some of us with hope."

Vashti decided not to counter. If that's what Bryce believed then she wouldn't try bursting her bubble, but personally, she knew better. There was no such thing as that much passion and desire. And most of the time it was the woman who worked at the romance part. A man was out for what he could get. He had needs.

*But then so did women.*

She hadn't thought much about those needs until yesterday when she'd been pulled over by the town's sexy hot sheriff. She would admit that for the first time in years...possibly ever, she'd felt attracted to a man. Really attracted to one. At least the encounter had let her know her libido was still alive after being dormant for a couple of years. She had Scott to thank for that and since she now knew about his sidepiece, she wouldn't complain, although she would admit it bothered her to know he'd been getting some when she hadn't. Lust, she thought, was a bitch. But yesterday she'd concluded that for a short while, lust had been given a name. Sawyer Grisham.

She doubted she would ever see the man again. At least she hoped not. One ticket was enough.

"And you're sure I can't convince you to hang around a few days?"

She glanced over at Bryce when they'd come to another traffic light. "I am positive. If it wasn't for my needing to go before the zoning board I wouldn't be here now. New York is my home and it's where I belong."

"Is it? Do you? You don't have a job there anymore."

No, she didn't and although she'd submitted her résumé to several places, nobody had called. But then, she couldn't lose sight of that. If she could sell Shelby she wouldn't have to worry about a job or anything else for years or ever. She could travel the world. Heck, she could even buy her own hotel or maybe buy into a franchise.

"That's why I need to sell Shelby, and you never did answer my question. Do you not want the Barnes Group to buy Shelby by the Sea?"

"You want my honesty?"

"Of course."

"Then no. Even with all the money I could make off the sale."

"Why?"

"Because I want you back here running your aunt's inn, Vash."

Vashti shook her head. "It's not happening."

"Will you ever forgive this town?"

She frowned over at Bryce. "It's not a matter of forgiveness, Bryce. It's a matter of what makes me happy. Honestly, I don't even think about Catalina Cove until you call. Then I remember my connection and after that the memories come, which aren't flattering. I'm no longer a small-town girl. I love big-city New York. The bright lights. Broadway. The subway. The Hudson River. I tried to get you to come live with me for a while to experience it for yourself but you weren't interested."

"I like it here."

"Because you haven't seen what other places have to offer. I have."

"I still think you belong here."

After all this time Vashti wondered why Bryce would

think so. She decided not to ask her now as they pulled up in front of the Witherspoon Café. But she would ask her later.

SAWYER PRESSED THE button on the intercom. "Yes, Trudy?"

"K-Gee is on the line."

He smiled. "You mean Kaegan, don't you?" He was well aware Kaegan Chambray had instructed the towns-people to drop the nickname K-Gee and call him by his birth name when he'd returned a couple of years ago after having been gone for close to fourteen years. Most of the people in town had followed his directive…except for Trudy.

"I mean K-Gee."

"Okay put him through." When he heard the click signaling the connection, he said, "What's up, Kaegan?"

Even Sawyer had been surprised at how easily he and Kaegan had struck up a friendship. Other than his marine buddies, he'd never had time to develop other friendships. Sawyer had been sheriff two years when Kaegan had returned to town and they'd bonded quickly because they'd had a lot in common. They'd both been marines who'd served multiple tour duties in Afghani-stan. Although their paths never crossed they'd figured out they'd been in the same area about the same time. They'd enjoyed sharing war stories over beer at Col-lins Bar and Grill.

"Just a reminder that the zoning board has a meet-ing today at five."

Sawyer released a deep sigh. He'd forgotten about that. "Thanks for reminding me." He glanced at the cal-endar on his desk. Although he'd forgotten to write it down he recalled Kaegan telling him about the meeting a couple of weeks ago. He often wondered why he'd let Kaegan talk him into being Henry Smith's replacement while the old-timer was out recuperating from hip surgery. "I'll be there."

"Okay, see you later."

After Sawyer clicked off the phone and while it was fresh on his mind, he texted his daughter letting her know he would be home late. She was at school and wouldn't see the message until the end of the day since the school's policy was to have all phones turned off during the day.

Glancing at his watch he saw it was close to noon. Usually he worked through lunch, but since he would be eating dinner late he might as well go out and grab something to eat. As usual he'd gotten up at six and cooked dinner. By the time he'd taken a jog around the neighborhood, showered and dressed the food was ready to slide into the refrigerator. On those days when he was detained, Jade could eat without him. He tried making it home at a reasonable time so they could eat dinner together but being sheriff meant things didn't always work out that way. On those days he did arrive home on time he looked forward to sharing meals with his daughter. It was important for him that they use that time to talk. He was always interested in knowing how her day went and how things were going at school.

Since joining the zoning committee he'd discovered you never knew what to expect until you got to the meetings. To him the Catalina Cove Zoning Board was nothing more than an overgrown version of a home-owners' association. The residents of the cove had to get practically everything approved before any exterior changes were made to the structure or look of any home or building. That included painting, replacing windows or doors, removing trees from your yard, adding a fence or something as simple as switching out a mailbox.

Walking out of his office, he glanced over at Trudy. "I'm leaving for lunch and will be back in an hour."

"Okay. And I meant to ask how the beef strudel turned out?"

"She altered the recipe," he said, grabbing his hat off the rack on his way out. He knew he didn't need to say more than that. It hadn't been the first time Jade had murdered a recipe Trudy had given her.

"I offered to send her to cooking classes," he said as he headed for the door.

"Not a bad idea. Especially if she seems interested in learning."

Sawyer thought his daughter seemed more inclined to experiment with recipes. Hopefully cooking classes would offer directions. When he walked out the door he glanced up at the sun that was shining bright in the sky. Hard to believe it was spring already. In a couple of months school would be out and he would have to deal with kids getting bored during the summer months and getting into unnecessary trouble.

He hadn't decided what he planned to do over the summer this year. Usually he would take two weeks off in June and take Jade somewhere. Last year they had spent a week in Orlando visiting all the theme parks there. Then they'd spent a week in Miami South Beach. Usually for spring break every year and the week after school ended he would put her on a plane to visit her godmother in Waco, Texas. Erin Daniels had been Johanna's best friend since high school.

But this year Jade wanted a summer job. She wanted a car and felt she should contribute toward the down payment. A part of him felt he should appreciate her wanting to do that, but he still wasn't gung ho on her working.

A short while later he was getting out of the patrol car to go into Witherspoon Café, one of his favorite eating places. They served the best omelets for breakfast and the soup and sandwiches on their lunch menu were tasty as well. Every once in a while he would dine here for dinner on those days when Jade had to stay after school or was involved with something at church.

He entered the café. Lunchtime was less formal, and just like a fast-food place you ordered your food before sitting down. For the dinner crowd there was someone who waited on your table. "Afternoon, Sheriff, what can I get for you?"

The man behind the lunch counter was Chester Witherspoon. He was a robust man, probably in his middle sixties with bushy brows over a pair of dark eyes, and a bald head. Sawyer had never known a time when the man hadn't had a friendly smile. Walking up to the counter, he said, "I think I'm going to have one of your juicy hamburgers and a large order of fries today, Chester." Since he wasn't sure how long the zoning board would be meeting he might as well make sure his stomach was full.

"And what would you like to drink?"

"Iced tea is fine," he said, putting a few bills on the counter. "And grab me a few of Deb's blueberry muffins to take home to Jade." His daughter loved them and Deb's were the best.

"How's Jade? I haven't seen her in a while."

That's the one thing he had to get used to in a small town. Practically everybody knew each other. "She's fine. Finishing up her sophomore year of high school and already looking forward to the fall when she'll be a junior."

"Boy. I remember when the two of you first moved to town. Hard to believe she'll be leaving in a couple of years for college."

He didn't like to be reminded of that, especially since he knew Jade planned to attend school in Reno. That was the deal they'd made when they'd moved here. When it was time for college she could return to Nevada.

A few minutes later he sat down with his food in hand. By habit he rarely sat with his back to any door and selected a table that faced the entrance. He figured it was the former FBI agent in him. This particular table suited him just fine because he had the ability to see whoever entered long before they noticed him.

A short while later he stopped eating when Bryce Witherspoon walked in with the driver of that little red Corvette, Vashti Alcindor. He had a feeling Kaegan and Bryce had history. He'd derived that assumption from their body language whenever they were within a few feet of each other. Kaegan never said and he'd never asked.

He took in both women but his full concentration quickly moved to Vashti Alcindor as his gaze swept over her from head to toe. In the very spot where she was standing, while the brilliance of sunlight shined directly on her, she looked simply gorgeous. It had been a long time since he'd bestowed such a description on any woman but he would in this case. She deserved it.

While she was sitting in that car yesterday he'd only seen so much of her. Now he was seeing it all and he liked what he saw. He couldn't take his eyes off her. So he didn't, although maybe he should. No woman since Johanna had held his attention like Vashti was doing now.

Both women were wearing shorts and tops, and his gaze sharpened as it roamed over her legs. They were a long and sleek pair that was perfect with her curvaceous hips and thighs. She was well toned and he knew a body as shapely as hers was the benefit of an active physical regime. More than likely she had a membership in one of those fitness centers in New York. You didn't get a figure like hers just eating and sleeping.

Unlike yesterday when her hair had been down and flying in the wind, today it was pulled back in a ponytail and the style made her look younger. She could easily pass for a college coed instead of the thirty-two-year-old that he knew that she was.

His gaze went back to her face, an image he'd thought about after he'd gone to bed. A first for him there as well. He had been married to Johanna for twelve years and during that entire time hadn't looked twice at another woman. Why was he trying to make up for lost time and why with this woman?

He watched her smile as she hurried across the floor when Chester came from behind the counter to engulf her in a huge bear hug. Even from where he sat Sawyer could see tears forming in her eyes and had to momentarily look away from such an emotional reunion. If what Trudy had said was true, and he had no reason to believe it wasn't, this was Ms. Alcindor's first time back to the cove in fourteen years. That was a long time not to come back home. Hell, at least she had a hometown to return to if she'd chosen to do so. He didn't.

He drew in a deep breath, not wanting to think about his childhood. His birth certificate claimed he'd been born in Dallas but he had been sent to live in a foster home with a family residing in Waco before his first birthday when his unwed mother had given him up for adoption. He recalled being sent from one foster home to another, even crossing state lines to do so. At sixteen he'd been taken in by a good Christian couple. John and Edith Fairchild had been too old to even think about raising a teenager. But they had and he would always appreciate their good deeds. To repay them for their kindness he got good grades in school and worked hard to stay out of trouble.

He had gone straight from high school to the military. He hadn't been enlisted a year when he'd received word that Mrs. Edith had passed away in her sleep. He had returned home for the funeral only to have Mr. John die the following year from pneumonia.

When he'd come home for Mr. John's funeral, he'd had to deal with the man's long-lost brother who'd shown up to claim everything, and make sure Sawyer didn't get anything. He'd gone to a bar the night of the funeral to drown his sorrows and he'd met Johanna.

Laughter made him look back to see Ms. Debbie and her two sons rush from the back to give Ms. Alcindor huge hugs as well. It was obvious everyone was glad to see her, which meant not everyone in town had thought ill of her. Hearing her story had made him think of his biological mother. He'd heard she'd also had him at a young age and had given him up for adoption. Only thing, the adoption never happened. He'd been born with a severe breathing disorder and had to spend a lot of time in the hospital before finally outgrowing it. No one had wanted what they thought to be a sickly baby.

He wasn't sure why Vashti Alcindor chose that moment to glance over in his direction. When their gazes connected a sudden jolt of heat vibrated between them. He felt it and knew she had to feel it as well. The surprised expression on her face indicated as much. It also revealed she was just as stunned by it as he was.

He wanted to break eye contact with her but for some reason he couldn't. Not when a ripple of desire rushed through him, making him glad he was sitting down. Had he been standing he would have felt weak in the knees. What he was feeling was another first. He'd never felt an intense longing for a woman just from looking at her. As if breaking from the spell surrounding them, she returned her attention to the people around her. Shaking off whatever had passed between them, he drew in a deep breath trying to get his mind back on track. He fought the temptation to steal a look at her as he finished eating.

A short while later, temptation that had been gnawing at his insides made him glance across the room to see she was sitting at a booth with Bryce. Standing, he cleared the trash off the table while thinking he didn't like being attracted to her. He didn't like it one damn bit.

He tossed the trash away before strolling to the door. Without his consent, his eyes looked to Vashti Alcindor again and the moment his gaze connected with hers, he couldn't stop the half smile that curved his lips when he tipped his hat at her before walking out of the café.

# CHAPTER FIVE

VASHTI SLOWLY DREW in a deep breath while trying to ignore the flutter in her stomach as she continued to stare at the door Sheriff Sawyer Grisham had walked out of. If a half smile from him could cause her body to react the way it had, she didn't want to think what a full smile would do.

Damn it. Why did he have to look so good even with a gun and holster around his hips and a badge of the law on his chest? Just knowing he'd given her a speeding ticket yesterday should have made him a total turnoff, but instead she'd found him a total turn-on.

And hadn't Bryce said the hot sheriff was already involved with someone? A woman living in New Orleans? On top of that, she would be leaving Catalina Cove in another day. She would be leaving tomorrow if Bryce hadn't made her feel guilty and talked her into staying another night. She had changed her flight to Friday to accommodate her best friend's plea.

"I guess now that Sheriff Grisham has left, I can claim all of your attention," Bryce said, as a corner of her mouth teased into a smile. "I need a fan to cool things off."

Vashti had to laugh since she knew exactly what Bryce was referring to. That hot stare he'd given her had certainly heated things up.

"Sorry about that," she said, taking a sip of her iced tea.

"No need to apologize. Sheriff Grisham is the hottest thing in town and has been for the four years he's been here. But I am surprised he was checking you out as much as you were him. I saw that look the two of you gave each other before we sat down."

"Surprised?"

"Yes, like I told you, he's never shown any interest in a woman living here before."

"I don't live here and he really didn't show interest. He was probably trying to figure out where he remembered me from."

Now it was Bryce who laughed. "You don't believe that any more than I do. You are a woman no man could easily forget, Vash. There's no reason for me not to believe the sheriff doesn't have a good memory. Besides, that look was a man-interested-in-a-woman look."

Was that true? As if Bryce had read her thoughts, she said, "Sometimes I wonder about you, Vash."

Vashti lifted a brow. "Wonder about me how?"

"When will you accept the fact that the two men who let you down didn't deserve you and that you can do better? I believe one day you will do better."

Vashti didn't say anything as she ate her sandwich. She knew what two men Bryce was talking about. The only two men she'd ever loved. The guy who'd fathered her baby and Scott. Her baby's daddy had let her down when he hadn't stood by her when she'd needed him the most. And Scott, well, she was convinced he truly never intended to do right by her.

She glanced up to find Bryce staring at her and knew she had to address what her best friend had said if they intended to finish lunch. "It doesn't matter with me anymore, Bryce. I've given up on men completely. That doesn't mean I can't appreciate a good-looking man when I see one. It means I don't plan to become involved with one anytime soon."

"Why deny yourself happiness?"

"I'm not denying myself happiness. I'm *assuring* myself happiness. I've discovered men have a way of bringing you down instead of lifting you up. I couldn't handle another heartbreak."

Vashti hoped she hadn't said anything to ruin Bryce's belief of one day finding someone for herself. To make sure she hadn't, she said, "I guess you can say I've had bad luck when it comes to men, Bryce. But that doesn't mean things will be that way for you. In fact, I'm sure they won't."

Bryce was about to say something when her phone rang. She quickly pulled it from her purse. "Excuse me, Vash. This is a call I've been hoping to get," she said, sliding off the seat with her phone in hand.

"No problem," Vashti said as Bryce hurried to the back where it was less noisy. She took that time to pull out her own phone to check her messages. So far she hadn't gotten any feedback on the résumés she'd submitted to a number of job opportunity sites. She wouldn't have to worry about a job if she could convince the zoning board to let that developer do what they wanted on that land. She could certainly understand the developers not wanting to go through with the sale if there were restrictions.

She glanced at the door and her thoughts shifted to the man who'd walked out of it earlier. Sheriff Sawyer Grisham was a good-looking man. No doubt about it. She could see why the women in town were vying for his attention. He'd been smart not to become involved with anyone locally and if he was seeing someone living in New Orleans, that was a good move on his part. She of all people knew how some of the people in the cove felt it was their God-given right to know every blasted detail of your personal business.

She could still feel the look he'd given her before leaving. His eyes had shone with male interest and when he'd shot her that half smile, a small dimple had appeared in one of his cheeks. She felt a stirring in the pit of her stomach whenever he looked at her.

"I have some good news and I have some bad news," Bryce said, returning to the table and interrupting her thoughts.

"I prefer hearing the good news first," Vashti said, taking a sip of her tea.

A huge smile touched Bryce's lips. "The good news is that I have a buyer for a house I've been trying to sell for almost a year."

Vashti returned her smile. "Bryce, that's great. Congratulations."

"Thanks."

"So what's the bad news?" Vashti then asked.

"The buyer wants to close the deal right away. Today if possible. He's leaving town later today for an extended trip out of the country, and I need to get back to my office to get the papers processed. That means I won't be able to go with you to Shelby by the Sea."

Vashti shrugged, smiled. "No worries. I know how to get there on my own. Just drop me off at your place to get my car and I'll be fine."

Bryce seemed to mull that over for a moment and then said, "I was hoping to go there with you."

Although Vashti had said *no worries*, she knew Bryce would worry. She and Bryce had talked about it last night. This would be Vashti's first time back to Shelby since leaving town fourteen years ago. The hardest part was knowing that her aunt wouldn't be opening that door with a welcoming and understanding smile and giving her a huge hug. Her aunt had always been there for her. She had understood her even when her parents hadn't. Vashti had made sure her aunt left the inn at least a few times each year by bringing her to New York to visit or by going on cruises together.

"I know, Bryce, but I can handle it. I'm a big girl."

Bryce nodded. "And what about that little red toy car? You won't get another ticket, will you?"

Vashti chuckled. "No, I won't get another ticket." She wouldn't dare admit that the thought of getting pulled over again by Sheriff Grisham wasn't so bad. "I won't be at Shelby's for long. I plan to be at the zoning board meeting on time and need to shower and change clothes first."

She stood. "Come on," she said to Bryce. "You have things to do and so do I."

"How was lunch, Sheriff?" Trudy asked when he passed her desk.

"Delicious as usual," was his reply as he made his way to his office. The food had been delicious but he had concentrated on other things while eating it. Namely, another person.

Before returning to the office he had driven around town to give himself time to get his thoughts back on track and to ponder what there was about Vashti Alcindor that captivated him. She was a good-looking woman, but he'd been in the presence of good-looking women before and none had ever gotten a reaction from him like she had.

The story Trudy had told him about how the towns-folk had mistreated her just for getting pregnant had pulled at him because he knew how it felt to have people you cared about let you down. Like the Connors who'd taken him in at twelve, only to return him to social services a year later. He had liked them and their two children. He'd thought he had finally found a home. But then when money started missing from Mrs. Connor's purse he had immediately become the guilty person. No one thought to question their oldest teenage son who Sawyer had known had a drug problem. But then he knew that episode with the Connors wasn't why he was attracted to Vashti Alcindor. The attraction began before he'd heard the story. He clearly remembered picking up on it when he'd issued her that ticket yesterday.

He was sitting at his desk and grabbing a stack of papers to go through when his cell phone rang. He recognized the number and smiled. Leesa was calling. Leesa Reddick was an old friend from the days they'd served in the Marines together. She hadn't reenlisted after she got married and he and Leesa had lost touch. They had reconnected when he'd discovered through mutual military friends that she was living in New Orleans with her thirteen-year-old son. She had relocated there from Cincinnati after her husband, Todd, had gotten killed in a car accident three years earlier.

Leesa was a wonderful person and someone he called a good friend...as well as an occasional lover for the past year. Leesa was the first and only woman he'd slept with since losing Johanna and he'd been her first after Todd's death. They had a lot in common. Both ex-marines. He was a widower and she a widow. More importantly, neither of them planned to ever fall in love again and marry. What they shared was nothing more than what they referred to as RS, recreational sex. They were good friends who were convenient lovers for each other whenever the need for sexual fulfilment became overpowering for either of them.

They had their own private getaway, a beautiful hotel in the New Orleans French Quarter. He'd never invited her to his home in the cove and she'd never invited him to hers. They preferred things that way. And because they both had kids, they'd never spent the night away from home. A few hours together during daytime were all they wanted and they didn't feel the need to become enmeshed in each other's lives. He liked the arrangement and so did she, with the understanding that in the interim if either of them met someone, they could end things with no hard feelings.

He clicked on his cell phone. "How are you doing, Leesa?"

"I'll be better once I see you. We're still on for Friday?"

"We sure are." They preferred meeting when their kids were in school. Stealing away during the summer months would be difficult.

"Just name the time," he said, forcing an image of Vashti Alcindor to the back of his mind.

"How about noon? We can order room service."

He nodded. "I like that idea."

"Great! I'll see you then."

After clicking off the phone he smiled thinking how his relationship with Leesa, although mostly sexual in nature, had helped him through those teenage woes with his daughter. Whenever he and Jade had a major disagreement it was Leesa who would help guide him through how the young female mind worked.

Likewise, Leesa claimed he helped her as well. When her son, Nelson, had been going through what seemed to be the beginning of the unmanageable teen years, Sawyer had been there to offer her advice on how to not only cope but to rein him in so he wouldn't be lost to her forever.

He glanced at his watch. He had a few hours before leaving for the zoning board meeting and there were a lot of items he needed to clear off his desk before then. Rolling up his sleeves he began working.

VASHTI TURNED THE little red Corvette onto Buccaneer Lane, the tree-lined street that led to Shelby by the Sea. Moments later she pulled into the long driveway of the large historic mansion with the well-manicured lawn that sat on the gulf. Years ago, as a registered nurse, her aunt Shelby had been the caretaker of the mansion's owner, Hawthorn Barlowe.

Vashti didn't remember Mr. Barlowe but others in the community did. She recalled the stories of everyone saying he was a mean, crabby and wealthy old man who didn't get along with anyone. Especially his neighbors who bordered his property, the Lacroixes. Evidently her aunt was able to break through the old man's meanness because when he died with no living relatives, he had bequeathed the mansion and all the land surrounding it to Aunt Shelby.

Her aunt decided to make the twenty-guestroom mansion, built in 1905, into a bed-and-breakfast and named it Shelby by the Sea. Vashti was told that within a year the inn had become so popular, newlyweds would come from all over the country to spend their honeymoon there and married couples checked in to reignite the flame in their marriage. Vashti brought the car to a stop and as she stared at the huge structure she swallowed her misgivings and was surprised she had any at all. But then how could she not? She had considered this place more her home than her parents' house.

Vashti had talked to her aunt often and hadn't known how run-down Shelby by the Sea had gotten until Bryce had told her. The inn had been close to shutting down and her aunt had only a bare-bones staff with few reservations. Whenever she asked, her aunt would tell her all was going well, but after Aunt Shelby's sudden death of a heart attack and Vashti'd gotten Bryce to put the inn up for sale had she only found out the truth.

Shelby by the Sea, which had once been one of the premier places in the cove, had fallen in more despair than Vashti had known. After Bryce checked the books it was discovered over the past couple of years there had been fewer and fewer reservations. Why? How? And why hadn't her aunt told her?

Vashti had used her aunt's life insurance money to give the few employees left, some of whom had been with her aunt for years, a severance package. She'd felt it had been the decent thing to do. According to Bryce, the majority of the people had found other employment elsewhere in town.

In the past her aunt had depended on word of mouth advertising of the inn's reputation to build and retain business. She had a feeling her aunt had never embraced the social media age or the idea of brand ambassadors with the use of a marketing firm.

Even with the obvious needed repairs, the inn was more impressive than she remembered. It was massive, stately and beautiful. It held so much of Catalina Cove's history since it had been in the Barlowe family for generations. Some claimed Mr. Barlowe's great-great-grandfather had been one of Jean LaFitte's right-hand men and LaFitte had awarded the man the land the mansion sat on for his loyalty.

Vashti couldn't imagine anyone tearing it down to build anything else here and in a way she understood the town for trying to block it from happening. A part of her knew her aunt would probably not want it to happen either.

She quickly pushed that thought from her mind. The structure no longer belonged to her aunt. It was hers to do whatever she wanted with and she wanted to sell it. Even if she entertained the thought of keeping it, she didn't have the money it would take to bring the inn back to the grandiose place it had once been. Besides, her life was in New York now. Convincing the zoning board to remove their restrictions was her top priority and what the buyer decided to do with it was no concern of hers. But still…

She remembered the good times she used to have here. Shelby by the Sea had once been her lifeline. When she and her parents hadn't seen eye to eye during her pregnancy, it had been her home. Aunt Shelby had always been her champion. Someone who'd understood her when her parents had not. And this inn had given her an escape when she had needed it most.

And she'd never forget that the property adjacent to

the inn was where her child had been conceived. At sixteen she was convinced she was in love and the thought of sneaking around behind her parents' backs seemed like no big deal at the time. It had been first love. Innocent love. Until one day during a picnic in the marshes by the sea, at what they thought of as their private place, things had gotten out of hand, passion had overtaken good sense and neither of them had been prepared for it. Nor had they been prepared for how their lives had changed afterward.

Pushing those memories to the back of her mind, she opened the door to get out of the car. Even with the For Sale sign posted near the street, it was hard to tell the inn was vacant. It had that open-for-business look. Vashti glanced at the huge wooden front door, expecting it to swing open and for her aunt to step out, directly into the sunlight with a huge smile on her face and a welcoming glint in her eyes. But she knew that wouldn't happen. Shelby Riggs was no longer here.

She glanced down at the ground a moment, feeling her aunt's absence more deeply now than when she'd gotten the call from her parents that her aunt had died. It had been a shock since Vashti had just spoken with her the night before. It was their usual routine to talk to each other every Saturday night and the topics of conversation were to be anything other than the cove. That was why Vashti hadn't known about the town's new sheriff or that Kaegan had returned home. So they discussed other things like fashion, her work, the inn, movies and when they would take their next trip together.

Vashti missed those calls. Now more than ever she appreciated the times she and her aunt had managed to spend together over the years. It was sad that she and her mother had never developed that same closeness. It was as if after getting pregnant her mother couldn't stand being around her at times. She knew she had let her parents down, had caused them embarrassment in town, but she hadn't expected them to blame her for everything. Her father had wanted the name of the boy who had gotten her pregnant, and when she'd refused to give it to him all hell had broken loose in the Alcindor household. That's when they began making plans for her, although she hadn't agreed with any of them. Nothing she said would change their minds. Even Aunt Shelby tried reasoning with them and offered to take care of the baby while she finished school. But her parents didn't want to hear anything. She had agreed to go to the unwed home, but she never signed any papers to give her child up for adoption. Her baby had been born a few weeks early and due to complications at birth, her son hadn't lived.

Lifting her head up, Vashti looked into the sky as the sound of the gulf filled her ears. The sky was a beautiful blue and the few clouds she could see appeared a snowy white. A part of her believed at that moment her aunt was looking down at her smiling. Or was she? Did Aunt Shelby have anything to smile about knowing Vashti had decided to let someone destroy the home that had meant so much to her?

Vashti bristled at the thought, reminding herself that at no time had her aunt asked her to not sell the place. But still, there was that niggling thought that wouldn't let her be now that she was here. Was it something her aunt just assumed she wouldn't do?

She rubbed a hand down her face, hating she'd begun second-guessing her decision. Especially when ten million dollars were at stake. That was the only reason she had returned to the cove and no matter what, she must not forget it. Nothing else would have brought her back here.

Turning, she moved toward the steps, taking them two at a time like she'd always done. Bryce had given her the code to the Realtor lockbox and within seconds she was opening the door to go inside. Although the house had been closed up for a while, the scent of gardenias was in the air. It was a good smell and one she remembered. It came from all the gardenia bushes planted around the side of the house. Magnolias were another of her aunt's favorite flowering trees and you would catch their scent when you walked in the backyard toward the gazebo.

Vashti stepped from the foyer into the living room parlor and glanced around. All the furniture was covered. Now that she knew if the Barnes Group did buy the inn they would tear it down, she hoped they planned to sell all the furnishings. Most of it was costly and were original pieces.

"Stay focused," she told herself after seeing how run-down the place looked. Paint was peeling off the walls and there were brown stains on the ceiling that indicated some type of water damage. The inn had been vacant for about six months. At least it hadn't been vandalized or anything and she was grateful for that. She headed for the stairs, deciding to check out the kitchen and dining room later. "Whatever the developer decides to do is not your business. Remain detached from this place," she muttered to herself.

When she reached the landing to the second floor everything looked the same. Like downstairs, paint was peeling off the walls and she noticed a number of items needed to be placed on a "to be repaired" list. In addition to the bedrooms downstairs, there were ten bedrooms on the second floor, five on the third floor, and two huge studio-sized bedrooms on the fourth. The majority of the bedrooms faced the cove and provided a panoramic view of the gulf. From there you could see the boardwalk that led to the beach. She recalled when that boardwalk had been constructed with steps that led down the marshy path to the cove. In the evening lanterns were timed to come on at dusk to light the path. Vashti remembered how she would sit on those boardwalk steps for hours to stare out at the gulf.

She took the stairs down to the living room. Too many feelings were crushing down on her, but she refused to give in to emotions she wasn't ready to deal with.

Squaring her shoulders, instead of moving toward the front door, she turned toward her aunt's bedroom. She stopped in the doorway and drew in a deep breath. The room didn't smell of gardenias but of vanilla, her aunt's favorite scent. Vashti was convinced the aroma had seeped through the floors and walls. Inhaling it now reminded her so much of her aunt and so many cherished memories.

She'd always loved her aunt's bedroom with the massive bed and complementing furnishing. The triple windows provided a beautiful view of a number of oak trees covered in Spanish moss. There was also the gazebo where many weddings had been held over the years. With the gulf as a backdrop, it was the perfect place for such celebrations. Leaving her aunt's room she saw the guestroom that had been Vashti's. Same furnishings, same decor and noted repairs needed.

She glanced at the trophy rack her aunt had bought to hold all the trophies Vashti had received in baton twirling. There were a number of them for all the years she'd aced the competitions and had once even gone on to win the national championship before finishing high school. Funny, she hadn't twirled a baton in years. She knew somewhere in this room she would find her baton.

Vashti smiled when she saw it hanging on a rack on the wall. She was not surprised her aunt had kept it and her trophies. When the inn was officially sold, she wasn't sure what she would do with them. She could donate the trophies to her high school since she'd represented them at all the competitions. The baton was hers. It had been a gift from her aunt on her tenth birthday along with six months of baton-twirling lessons. Her instructor had convinced her parents she was a natural and should continue the lessons and so they had.

Leaving the bedrooms, she crossed the living room and entered the section of the inn where the dining hall and kitchen were located. The inn was always filled to capacity on any day of the week. Some reservations were made a year in advance, especially from those planning their weddings and wanting to come here for their honeymoon.

There were visible scratches on several tables in the dining hall and several chair backs needed repair. The floor could also use a good polishing. There were ten tables neatly arranged. Each was covered in a white netted tablecloth. A set of double French doors opened to a beautiful rose garden. It was obvious her aunt's prized roses hadn't been tended to in quite a while. That made her wonder if perhaps her aunt hadn't been feeling well lately but hadn't mentioned it to anyone.

She had asked her mother if she'd suspected anything wrong with Aunt Shelby's heath in case Vashti had missed something during her and Aunt Shelby's weekly talks. Her mother said she hadn't suspected a thing, but then her mother and Aunt Shelby didn't talk often. Vashti had a feeling the sisters had had a disagreement about something and when she broached the subject with either of them they'd said she was imagining things. Vashti wasn't so sure about that and knew for a fact they weren't as close as they used to be.

Leaving the dining room, she entered the kitchen. This was where she had spent a lot of her days helping her aunt assist Daisy, her aunt's prized cook, while preparing meals for all the guests. That was another plus in booking a room at Shelby by the Sea. You got to eat Daisy Blanchard's delicious food. Everybody living in the cove and beyond knew Daisy had been the best cook anywhere.

A stroke last year had left Daisy paralyzed on one side and her children had moved her to live with them in Baton Rouge. Her aunt hadn't truly been satisfied with the cooks after Daisy.

It was obvious to Vashti that all the appliances—all industrial-size—needed replacing. She wondered why she was thinking about that. She had told Bryce to sell the inn as is. The buyer, she'd assume, would make any necessary repairs, changes or updates. Now if she were able to sell it to the Barnes Group, appliances or anything else wouldn't matter since they planned to tear it down.

Dear heaven, why was the thought of that suddenly

troubling her? Why was she letting it? She wanted to cut this last tie to Catalina Cove, but she had a feeling that coming here and seeing the place for what would be the last time had not been a good idea. Deciding to leave well enough alone, she turned and left the house. After relocking the front door, she got into her car and drove off and refused to look back.

## CHAPTER SIX

SAWYER ENTERED THE meeting room and glanced around. It was full. Evidently there was something on the agenda that piqued a number of people's interest. Trudy had printed the agenda for him before he'd left the office, but he hadn't had a chance to look at it.

"Evening, Sheriff."

He looked at Reid Lacroix, the man who owned the Lacroix Blueberry Plant and who was the largest employer in town. "Evening, Reid," Sawyer said, moving toward the vacant chair at the head table beside Kaegan.

"What's going on? Is someone giving away free lottery tickets?" he asked Kaegan when he took his seat.

Kaegan grinned over at him. "I take it you didn't look at your agenda."

"Nope, didn't have time."

Kaegan nodded. "The Baxters want us to reconsider letting them put up that privacy fence on the back of their property. I think he and Josh Guyton finally reached an agreement about it and just need our approval. However, I figure most of the people are here because of the developer who wants to build that tennis resort."

Sawyer lifted a brow. "Some developer wants to build a tennis resort in the cove?"

"Yes, and I heard they're willing to offer the locals

free membership at their facilities for the first year and free tennis lessons for the kids."

"You think the town is going to let them come in and build?"

"I doubt it. Reid Lacroix is totally against it and most people follow his lead. He hates change, although not all change is bad. Membership in that resort will give our young people something to do after school and over the summer months. For all we know there might be another Serena or Venus Williams living in the cove. Besides, work at the resort will bring new jobs."

"And where do the developers want to build this resort?" Sawyer asked.

"At the site of what is now Shelby by the Sea. It's been up for sale since Ms. Shelby passed and I knew it was just a matter of time before some developer showed an interest in it, especially since it's right there on the gulf. However, I think a lot of the townspeople were hoping Ms. Shelby's niece would move back and reopen the inn."

"Vashti Alcindor?"

Kaegan raised a brow. "You know Vashti?"

"Not personally. I pulled her over two days ago on Highway 63 and gave her a ticket for speeding."

Kaegan grinned. "She couldn't talk you out of it?"

"She didn't even try, although I think she expected to be given a warning ticket instead of an actual ticket."

"I can understand that. Back in the day, unless the locals were speeding excessively, tickets were rarely given out."

"I discovered that fact when I became sheriff. I told Ms. Alcindor that I don't give warning tickets."

"Well, I'm glad she's back in town, even if it's just for a little while. It will be good to see her again today."

There it was, that odd sensual pull at his gut when Kaegan mentioned Vashti. "She will be at the meeting today?" he asked to make sure. He hadn't expected to see her twice in the same day.

"Yes. I understand that Vashti and the developer will try to convince the board to lift zoning restrictions. Otherwise, the sale will fall through. I heard she's been offered a lot of money for the place."

Sawyer looked at his watch. "The meeting is about to begin, and I hope we're not here too late this evening." He liked being home to help Jade with any homework she might need his help with.

More people filed in and Sawyer finally got a chance to read the meeting's agenda. There was Vashti's name and the name of the developer, both slated to speak, no doubt to sway the board their way. Good luck on that. Just like Kaegan said, Reid Lacroix carried a lot of weight in this town and if he didn't want anything to come to the town, it didn't come. After living in the cove for four years, Sawyer had learned that about him. He liked the man. He had no reason not to as long as Lacroix operated within the confines of the law. But he knew the man was a staunch conservative who didn't believe in change.

Sawyer agreed with what Kaegan said about some change being good. He would admit one of the things that had drawn him to Catalina Cove, other than the fact he'd inherited the house Johanna owned here, was the small-town atmosphere. He liked it. After living in large metropolitan cities, the small-town environment was what he felt he needed to raise his daughter. He had no complaints. Today, he would keep an open mind and vote accordingly.

"Hello, Sawyer."

He glanced over at the woman who'd taken the seat next to him. He inwardly cringed. There was only so much he could take of Rachel Libby. The woman had done whatever she could to garner his attention. She couldn't get the fact that he just wasn't interested. It had nothing to do with her being ten years older than him since she did look good for her age. It had everything to do with her assumption that just because she was interested in him he should fall in line. Someone failed to tell her that the laws of sexual chemistry didn't work that way.

"Hello, Rachel."

She leaned in a little too close and he thought whatever perfume she was wearing was almost stifling. "Would you like to come to my house for dinner later?"

"No, thanks. I've cooked already. Besides, I have a daughter waiting at home for me."

"She's a big girl. I'm sure she can take care of herself."

He almost told her the worst thing any woman could tell him was her thoughts of his daughter. "Maybe. But then that's why I'm her father. I decide when she can take care of herself, as well as what's best for my daughter. I don't need anyone else suggesting otherwise."

Evidently she had picked up on the annoyance in his voice that he wasn't trying to hide. "Sorry, Sawyer. I didn't mean to upset you."

He fought back the urge to tell her she was of no significance to upset him. Instead he said, "You didn't."

He went back to reading the agenda, letting her know

as far as he was concerned, their conversation was over. He was glad she had the good sense to take the hint as she eased away from him to sit up straight in her chair and look over her own copy of the agenda.

Moments before the meeting was to start Vashti walked through the door. Sawyer felt a tightening in his groin as he looked at her and noticed several people had turned to peer in her direction as well. Some were smiling and there were several others who were whispering. Her return to the cove certainly was arousing interest with folks.

As she crossed the floor to take a seat, he couldn't help checking her out. She had changed out of her shorts and tank top and was wearing a black pencil skirt and white blouse. He thought the skirt did a lot to emphasize her shapely figure and long gorgeous legs.

Her hair was not in the ponytail she'd worn when he'd seen her at the café, but was flowing down her shoulders in what appeared to be a bevy of soft curls. She was wearing makeup, but not enough to make her look made-up. It looked more natural on her and he thought it enhanced her radiant beauty.

Several older people approached her, and all but pulled her from the chair to give her hugs. He could tell by her expression she was surprised by the interchange. That made him wonder if perhaps she thought that even after fourteen years people would still concern themselves with the identity of her baby's father. There was no doubt in his mind that there were some who might, but he would think most people would have the sense to move on and accept that although they had acted like asses before, they wouldn't now.

He discovered how wrong he was in his assumption

when Rachel leaned over to him and said, "If you're wondering who she is, her name is Vashti Alcindor. Poor thing, she left the town in shame years ago when she got pregnant. She kept the baby's father's identity a secret, and of course, that made a lot of tongues wag."

He had a feeling hers was one of those tongues. He glanced over at her. "Really? I never knew keeping your business to yourself was a crime. Besides, I'm sure she wasn't the only person in this town keeping secrets." There was no need to tell her that he'd been enlightened about a few of hers.

Again, she had the good sense to ease away from him. It was then the chairman of the board called the meeting to order.

VASHTI LEANED CLOSE to Bryce, who'd made it to the meeting just before the doors closed. "Why didn't you tell me Sheriff Grisham was on the zoning board?"

"It's just temporary while Henry Smith recuperates from hip surgery. Besides, I didn't think it mattered."

Vashti wanted to think it didn't but each time she looked at the head table where he sat it seemed his gaze was on her. Or was she imagining it? No, she was certain she wasn't. It might seem to others like he was looking out over the crowd, but she was convinced he was not. What other reason could there be for the way she felt like she was on fire, burning from the inside out? Or the way every single hormone in her body seemed to sizzle? More than once she tried breaking eye contact with him but as if with a mind of its own, her gaze unerringly went back to him.

"You and the developer are up next," Bryce leaned over and whispered. "Good luck."

Vashti felt she would need it, although she'd been surprised at the number of people who'd come up to her before the start of the meeting, saying how glad they were to see her and to welcome her back home. Evidently the reason she'd left meant nothing to them anymore. In truth, she'd left to go off to school. The reason she'd never come back was another matter, one they seemed eager to forget.

"Next on the agenda is Vashti Alcindor and a representative from the Barnes Group," Larry Stillwell, chairman of the zoning board, who owned the only drugstore in town, said, his voice sounding loud through the microphone.

Drawing in a deep breath, Vashti stood and strolled toward the front of the room where she was joined by the man she'd met when she arrived, Palmer O'Connell of the Barnes Group. The entire room was quiet. Typically, Vashti wouldn't be nervous speaking before a crowd of any size since she was used to doing so as part of her profession. However, knowing that some of these townspeople would be looking at her with a critical eye was somewhat unnerving.

She tried convincing herself whatever they thought about her back then didn't matter and what they thought of her now didn't matter either. She had property she wanted to sell, and she preferred they not get in the way of her doing so. But then, what unnerved her more than anything was that even if she'd imagined Sawyer Grisham's gaze on her before, it was definitely on her now.

She was handed the microphone and was about to speak when Reid Lacroix stood. "I have something to say."

Vashti's heart began pounding. She wondered what

was going on. Reid Lacroix's opinion about anything still carried a lot of weight in this town since his blueberry plant employed a number of people living in the cove. He was not someone you wanted as your enemy. She also knew Mr. Lacroix was completely against change of any kind and over the years he'd been instrumental in keeping developers out of the cove. There was no reason for her to think this time would be any different. By him wanting to have his say now might mean there would not be a need for any vote later, so she and the developer would be wasting their time.

As far as she was concerned, his request was out of order; however, she knew that there was no one here who would tell him that. Instead the chairman of the board took the microphone from her and passed it to him with a huge smile. "Yes, by all means, Mr. Lacroix."

She met the older man's gaze, expecting the worst. "I heard you'd returned to town, Ms. Alcindor, and I want to join in with the others and say, welcome home. We're glad to see you back, regardless of whether it's permanent or temporary. It always does our heart good whenever one of our own returns."

Vashti stared at the man, stunned. That was definitely not what she had expected him to say. As she looked into the depths of his dark eyes, she saw a sincerity in them that surprised her. In a public place he had welcomed her back. His opinion mattered and he'd effectively made it clear to everyone that she was welcomed back and if anyone felt otherwise they would be going against him. Why? Was he letting her know that he knew the truth about who fathered her child?

"Now, Ms. Alcindor, you may continue." Mr. Lacroix, smiling, passed the mike to her.

"Thank you, Mr. Lacroix. I truly appreciate that," she said. And she truly meant it.

"VASHTI DEANNA ALCINDOR. It's been a while."

Vashti smiled at the man who engulfed her in a huge bear hug. She needed it as the prospect of getting ten million dollars from the sale of Shelby by the Sea was gone. She had said her piece, asking the zoning board to consider the advantages that bringing a tennis resort could bring to the cove, before introducing the developer. He'd done a great job explaining to everyone how the proposed tennis resort could benefit the town and the boost it would give to the local economy.

Everyone seemed to show interest and had even asked questions—more positive than negative. However, in the end, no matter how excited the residents of the town seemed, the decision belonged to the zoning board. In the end there were eight board members voting against the resort and only two for it: Kaegan and Sheriff Grisham.

"Kaegan, it's so good to see you," she said, when he finally released her. She stared into his face. He looked the same, just older. More mature. Still handsome as ever, even more so. And he still had more hair on his head than she did. "I understand you took over your family's business. I was sorry to hear about your parents."

"Thanks."

"And you're on the zoning board. I think that's great and thanks for the yes vote."

"For all it's worth, I agree with that developer. A tennis resort coming here would boost the economy. But I don't have to tell you some people are satisfied to let things stay as they are. Then they wonder why their kids grow up and move away. Only a few return."

Vashti nodded again as she glanced around. "I was going to thank Sheriff Grisham. I'm surprised he voted yes."

"I'm not," Kaegan said. "Sawyer moved here from a progressive city. Besides, he has a teenage daughter and that resort's perks, especially the free tennis lessons, were great. I just hate you're losing the deal. I heard they had offered you a lot of money for the place."

"They did. More than I had dreamed of getting, but I guess it wasn't meant to be."

She glanced around again. "I don't see Sheriff Grisham."

"He left as soon as the meeting was over."

"Oh, I see," she said, trying to keep the disappointment out of her voice. She had really wanted to thank him, like she'd thanked Kaegan. She was glad they had voted their conscience and not the way Reid Lacroix had wanted them to.

"Mr. Lacroix didn't seem upset that you and the sheriff didn't vote with him."

Kaegan shrugged dismissively. "Lacroix is used to it. He knows both Sawyer and I will speak our minds and not sugarcoat anything either. I honestly believe he respects us for it." Kaegan didn't say anything for a moment and then he said, "To be fair to Reid Lacroix, he's the one who encouraged me to join the board."

"He did?"

"Yes. He's changed, Vashti. For the better. I heard he hasn't been the same since his wife and son passed away within six months of each other."

Vashti looked away when memories she'd put to rest

years ago suddenly surfaced. At that moment she felt pain. Real pain. And it was pain she didn't want to feel.

"He sure did take a stand tonight where you were concerned."

Vashti glanced back at Kaegan. "What do you mean?"

"That speech he gave to welcome you back to town. It will put an end to any negativity toward you while you're here. Heck, you saw the crowd surrounding you after the meeting, following his lead and welcoming you back like the Great Oz had not only spoken, but had given his blessings on your return. I wonder why he did it."

Vashti refused to look away again. Instead she looked at Kaegan and shrugged. "I have no idea. I guess he was being nice. And it really wasn't necessary since I'm leaving town on Friday."

"You just got here."

"Yes, but I've stayed longer than I intended to do."

He nodded. "Did you go by Shelby's?"

"Yes. It brought back a lot of good memories."

"Yet you were okay with that developer tearing the place down."

It wasn't a question but a statement and she heard the censure in his voice. "Yes, I need closure, Kaegan."

He looked at her for a long moment before asking, "What are your plans for tomorrow night?"

"As far as I know I don't have any. Why?"

"Tomorrow will mark the second anniversary of my return to the cove. I've invited a few friends over for beer, fried fish, crabs, oysters and shrimp. Sort of an old-fashioned seafood roast. How about dropping by my place around eight? I'm still at my parents' home but building my own place next door. I'd love to show you what I've done so far."

"And I'd love to see it."

"So will you come?"

She looked down at the floor and then she looked back at him. "That invitation extends to Bryce, right?"

She watched his chin tighten. "Sure. Why not?"

"You tell me, Kaegan."

"Why don't you ask her?" he said gruffly.

"I did, but she won't tell me anything."

He chuckled derisively. "Funny. I remember a time when she would tell you everything. I learned that people have a tendency to change on you, in a blink of an eye."

Vashti bristled at his words. If he was insinuating something against Bryce, then she would take offense to it. "What do you mean by that?"

"Nothing. So, will you come?"

"Only if Bryce agrees to come with me."

He seemed to weigh her ultimatum, then said, "Fair enough. Now let me walk you to your car. I heard you got a ticket the other day."

She started to say something flippant like was it possible for anyone to have any secrets in this town, but immediately she knew the answer. Yes, it was possible. Hadn't she been harboring her one and only secret for years?

## CHAPTER SEVEN

USING THE SPARE key Bryce had given her, Vashti entered Bryce's home to find her sitting at the kitchen table drinking a glass of wine. "I can't believe you left, Bryce."

Bryce, who'd changed into a comfortable-looking sleeveless flowing caftan, shrugged, causing one to notice how the material rested perfectly against her *to-die-for* breasts. Vashti remembered how she and Bryce were ecstatic at the prospect of having breasts when they were preteens. They would often stand in front of a mirror to see whose were growing faster than the other. Bryce was always the winner. Even before their thirteenth birthdays it had become obvious that Bryce would have a perfect pair. It had taken Vashti's pregnancy to show what she called major improvement to her breasts, which ended when her pregnancy did. Her girls were alright, and Scott had never complained, but she always thought compared to Bryce's she was underdeveloped.

"You had your own transportation and I knew you were okay. Besides, after the meeting a crowd descended on you like the prodigal daughter, thanks to Reid Lacroix. What do you think that was about?"

Now it was Vashti who shrugged. "I don't know but if you're wondering about it, others will do the same."

"They might, but even if they are, they won't whisper those thoughts out loud for fear it will get back to Mr. Lacroix. For some reason you're on his good side, even though you were trying to bring a developer into town. That alone should have placed you at the top of his shit list."

Vashti nibbled on her bottom lip. "Do you think perhaps he found out?"

Bryce took another sip of her wine. "I honestly don't know, Vash. If he did I would think his attitude toward you would be just the opposite and your name would not only head his shit list but would end it as well. But then I'd be the first to admit his attitude changed in a lot of ways after Julius and Mrs. Lacroix died."

Vashti nodded. "That's what Kaegan said." She noticed Bryce's reaction when she'd said K-Gee's name.

"So he did manage to find his way over to you, did he?"

Vashti frowned. "Is there a reason Kaegan should not have?"

"No, I guess not."

"Bryce, I wish you would tell me what's really going on with you two."

Bryce shook her head and Vashti saw a tear fall from Bryce's eyes. She quickly moved toward Bryce and captured her hand in hers. "What is it?"

Bryce shook her head as more tears flowed. "I'm just not ready. I want to enjoy this time while you're here. Can we please do that? I promise, someday I'll share, but not today." Bryce's eyes implored her to let it go, and Vashti didn't want to cause her friend any pain and Bryce was asking her only to respect her wishes, like Vashti had done fourteen years ago when she had left town and mandated that she hadn't wanted to know anything about the happenings in the cove. She'd preferred not knowing.

Bryce had broken that rule only once. That had been seven years ago when she'd called to tell her about Julius's death. Vashti had mourned the loss of the guy who'd fathered her child and the first and only man she'd loved. For years she had hated him for not accepting his part in her pregnancy and when he'd died she had let go of her dream that one day he would show up in New York for her. Or to at least explain why he'd done what he had when she had truly believed he'd loved her. That just goes to show that you couldn't trust your heart.

"Okay," Vashti said softly. "When you're ready to tell me, you will."

Bryce sighed with relief. "Let's talk about something else. Like how you managed to get on Sheriff Grisham's good side and he voted in your favor? And don't think I didn't notice how he was looking at you."

So she hadn't imagined it. "I'm sure the only reason he cast his vote my way was because he has a teenage daughter who could benefit from the perks the resort was offering."

"Well, I guess we can kiss the ten million goodbye," Bryce said, taking another sip of her wine. "Even after giving that heartwarming speech welcoming you back to Catalina Cove, Mr. Lacroix still voted against those developers."

"Did you think he would do otherwise? He might have changed in some ways but when it comes to Catalina Cove, it's not in his makeup to change. Besides, if he had sided with me on the issue, it would have really given the townspeople something to gossip about."

"I guess you're right about that."

Vashti released Bryce's hand. "I'm going to change. And then we're going to open another bottle of wine." She smiled at her friend, her heart aching for the remnants of pain she saw in Bryce's eyes from just the mention of Kaegan. She wasn't sure what was going on between them but believed when Bryce was ready to tell her, she would.

"I CAN'T BELIEVE you let the old people in this town have their way to do whatever they want to do. It should be against the law."

"Voting your conscience is not against the law, Jade."

"It may not be against the law but it isn't fair to the young people in this town. Don't we get a voice, Dad?"

Jade had lit into him the moment he walked through the door. A door she'd opened the moment she'd heard his footsteps on the porch. He'd known from the look on her face that she was fired up. He had left the zoning board meeting to come straight home. News certainly traveled fast.

"First of all, I didn't *let* them do anything. I'm not the only member of the board and everyone has the right to cast their vote as they see fit. There were more members against that tennis resort coming here than for it. And as far as your having a voice, no, you don't have one yet. You're not old enough to vote. Even if you were, your vote would not have counted. Only members of the board could vote."

"Well, every member of the zoning board should be fired…except for you and Mr. Kaegan," she said, following behind him as he headed for his bedroom to lock his gun, holster and badge in the safe and take a shower. "I heard the two of you were the only ones with the good sense to do the right thing."

He thought she'd heard a lot and didn't mind voicing her opinion on the matter. "The others felt they were doing the right thing as well. The right thing to preserve the integrity of this town," he said. In all honesty, he thought the perks would have been good for the city, not to mention a boost to the economy with new jobs. That's why he'd voted for it.

"That resort would have done a lot for this town and those eight people should not have voted against it. That's why I love you so much, Dad. You're the best. You're your own man. You think for yourself. One day I intend to be the mayor of this town and when I do I'm going to bring as many resorts here as I can."

*Mayor?* That was a new one on him. He hadn't heard of that aspiration before. "Mayor?"

"Yes, mayor. And besides the resorts I plan to bring in a Walmart, a McDonald's and Pizza Hut. It's a shame we have to go to New Orleans for fast food."

Before opening the door to his bedroom he looked over his shoulder to find her right there on his heels. "If I recall, you plan to return to Reno and go to the university there. Stats have shown most kids who go away to school rarely return to the town they grew up in."

"Well, I'm coming back and I'm—"

"Going to be mayor and bring in Walmart, McDonald's and Pizza Hut," he said, interrupting her. "I got it. Now be a good kid and warm up my food while I'm in the shower." He entered his room and closed the door.

Of course that didn't stop her from continuing the conversation. The sound of her voice carried through the wooden door. "I really feel bad for the lady who wanted to sell that land. I heard she could have made ten million dollars off it."

Sawyer reopened the door. "Who told you that?"

"Mitzi Perry's mother."

Sawyer had heard that as well and didn't have to wonder how Ms. Perry got wind of it. The gossip train was at work. "Things don't always work out the way we want them to, hon," he said.

"I heard she was pretty."

He lifted a brow. "Who?"

"The lady who can't sell her land. I heard she also drives a real sporty car. A red convertible."

He wondered where she'd heard that from and decided not to ask. But however she came about her information it was the truth. As far as he was concerned Vashti Alcindor was more than just pretty. She was gorgeous. If he wasn't sure of it before he was definitely certain of it now. "I'm going to take a shower, Jade."

"I was hoping to work at the resort one day, Dad. It was going to be my summer job. And I was going to take advantage of those free lessons and the spa and all the cute tennis players that would have come to town to stay there."

She'd had him feeling a little sorry for her until she mentioned the cute tennis players. This was the first time she'd hinted at being interested in boys. Big boys. Tennis-playing boys. Older and conceited athletes who wouldn't waste any time seducing an innocent sixteen-year-old. "Don't forget to warm up my food," he said, then closed the door again.

"That Mr. Lacroix thinks he owns this town. People always go along with what he wants. That's going to change when I become mayor." Her voice was coming in loud and clear through the door.

"I hear you," he said, yelling loud enough to make sure she knew he had responded but not giving the impression he was agreeing with what she said, although she was partly right about some of the townspeople going along with whatever Reid Lacroix said.

Like tonight for instance. He didn't know the man's motive, but for Lacroix to officially welcome Ms. Alcindor to town in front of everyone assured that the people in town would welcome her as well. If anyone still had an issue about her before, they wouldn't now.

All was quiet, which meant Jade had moved away from the door. Finally. Good. She'd been on a roll. Not that he thought it was over but for now she'd run out of steam. Tomorrow when she got home from school she would be refueled again after discussing it with her friends. And now she was thinking about returning to the cove after college in Nevada. Imagine that.

He knew not to count on it because his daughter was just in the moment. After college she would go wherever opportunities knocked. That would be the smart thing to do and he wasn't raising a dummy. She wanted to be a doctor so he couldn't see her coming back here working at the cove's small hospital while alternating at the mayor gig. He smiled at the thought of that.

As he stepped into the shower beneath the spray of water he thought about Vashti Alcindor and what his daughter had said about her. Tonight he hadn't been able to take his eyes off her and more than once she'd caught him staring and stared back. If eyes could talk he wondered what theirs would have said.

Lathering his hair, he knew it was crazy. He was

still attracted to the woman. How could he think of her in a sexual way when day after tomorrow he would be spending the afternoon in bed with Leesa. He'd never left her arms disappointed and doubted he would. But…

He turned off the water and stepped out of the shower stall and as he dried himself off, it wasn't Leesa's features he was seeing in his mind but those of Vashti Alcindor. Tonight while sitting there he had studied them, every single detail. He'd been in Catalina Cove long enough to know all about the Creoles in the area, specifically in the cove. They made up over ninety percent of the town's population. He had to admit that the cove was the most diverse group of people he'd ever known.

Before taking the job he had read everything he could about the Louisiana Creoles. He knew how both white refugees and free people of color found sanctuary in the bayous. Some lived peacefully among the Native Americans. A mixture of French, Spanish and African heritages. They had come together, united to create their own culture: the Louisiana Creole. They still considered themselves as one cultural unit, although their legacies were different. It was obvious Reid Lacroix had French ancestry while Trudy liked to boast of her Spanish birthright. He would bet Vashti Alcindor was a mixture of all three—French, Spanish and African. He would even throw part Native American into the mix.

She had soft brown eyes, long eyelashes, high cheekbones, shoulder-length dark brown hair and skin the color of rich mocha. Her full lips were a total turn-on and he thought her nose was the perfect shape and size for her face.

He'd noticed all that the day he'd given her a ticket,

so why had he concentrated on them at the meeting and why was he thinking about her features now? He could be having an attack of lust, but surely he was too old for such ailments. He'd gone three years without a woman after Johanna, and probably would have gone longer had he not hooked up with Leesa. Sex was never something that had driven him even during his bachelor days when he'd dated his fair share of women. He'd been more into a career in the military than anything else. After marrying Johanna they had enjoyed a good sex life because more than anything they were always making up for lost time. He was convinced returning-home-from-deployment sex was the best kind.

During the first six years of their marriage he was active-duty military. The hardest thing was being shipped off for a year and leaving Johanna in her fourth month of pregnancy. When complications arose and Johanna was ordered bed rest until after the baby was born, he appreciated her best friend, Erin, staying with her during that time. He had returned home to a very healthy six-month-old daughter.

Sawyer had fallen in love with Jade the moment he'd seen her, and he'd known what total happiness was. He, who never had a family to call his own, had finally gotten one. On that day while holding his daughter for the first time, he had promised Johanna that he would be the best father any child could ever have.

*That's why I love you so much, Dad. You're the best.*

As he got dressed he took comfort in the words Jade had spoken tonight, knowing he was keeping his promise to Johanna. He was taking care of their little girl and trying to be the best father she could ever have.

REID LACROIX DIDN'T know the words to the song playing on the stereo system. The only thing he knew was that it had been one of Roberta's favorites and she played it often. He recalled the song had been playing somewhere in the house the night she'd died. He was sure of it. After Julius's death she had tried stopping her chemo treatment but he wouldn't let her. He'd convinced her to finish all her sessions by saying that's what Julius would have wanted. But he hadn't been able to coax his wife into fighting for her life. The chemo really hadn't done her any good because she'd given up the fight.

It was times like these when he sat alone in the living room parlor with the music playing that he wished he could turn back the hands of time. He wished that he could have gotten wind of what his life would be like now. Then he would have asked to be taken first. Being last and left all alone in a house too massive for one was a torture he endured nearly every night of his life now.

Working late at the office didn't help because he had to come home eventually. He'd figured by the time he reached sixty Julius would be married with kids. But things didn't work out that way. At twenty-five Julius died in a car accident while driving under the influence of alcohol.

Reid had not known what had changed his son. Why had he begun drinking and become a man who couldn't stand anyone…not even himself? He and Roberta had reached out to their only child, had tried to get him help, counseling, but none of it did any good. There were demons he fought and they were winning.

When he'd gotten word Julius had been taken by lifeflight to a hospital in Baton Rouge, Reid was grateful that for once he hadn't been away on a business trip. He had arrived at the hospital moments before his son had taken his last breath. In that final moment, his son asked him to make a death-bed promise after a startling confession that explained so many of the changes in him.

Now after all these years she was back. Vashti Alcindor had returned and she had no idea that he knew her secret. Julius had told him everything. And every day following that, Reid had to accept his part in what had happened, why his son felt the need not to stand up and be a man but rather let a young woman face a difficult time alone. His son had never gotten over that period of weakness. When he should have stood by the woman he'd loved, he hadn't. He hadn't enough spine to do so for fear of what Reid and Roberta would say.

Since Roberta was having chemo treatment that day she hadn't been at the hospital. In fact she hadn't known Julius had died until he'd returned home from the hospital and told her. She hadn't been the same after. There hadn't been anything he could do for the two people who'd meant the most to him.

But there was something he could do for the woman who'd meant everything to his son. The woman Julius had died believing he'd let down. Instead of going to her and expressing both his love and guilt, he'd nearly drunk himself to death instead.

He recalled his son's words like it was yesterday… *Please, Dad, promise me that you will let her know I did love her, so much, and that I wanted to stand by her. Let her know how ashamed I was for not doing so and I will never forgive myself for being so weak that I turned my back on her when she needed me. And if she ever needs you, be there for her…something I didn't do.*

Reid knew how it felt to be consumed with guilt

about something. Maybe more than most, because like his son he'd once fallen in love and married a woman who over the years he'd neglected. A woman he hadn't known just how important she was to him until it was too late. Roberta would have given him the world, she had tried, but in the end building the company into something his father and grandfather were proud of had become more important to him.

Now he was alone. No one would know how he felt when Julius had confessed to getting Vashti Alcindor pregnant and to being afraid to come forward because of the scandal it would cause the family's name. A name Reid had constantly reminded him to uphold and protect. To never do anything to bring shame to the family.

He mourned the grandchild he hadn't known the woman had been carrying. Legitimate or illegitimate, that child would have been his grandchild. Reid vaguely recalled the scandal involving Vashti Alcindor's pregnancy. He hadn't paid much attention to it because at the time he felt it hadn't concerned him. Years later on his death bed, his son had enlightened him as to how much it had concerned him. Anything involving the Lacroix family concerned him.

And the death-bed promise he'd made to his son still concerned him, all these years later. He had promised if Vashti ever returned to Catalina Cove that he would do right by her, and Reid intended to keep that promise.

"KAEGAN IS HAVING a seafood roast at his place to celebrate taking over his family's business and having a successful harvesting season. We were invited," Vashti said as they sat in Bryce's kitchen while drinking glasses of wine.

Bryce rolled her eyes. "I'm sure you were invited, not me."

"We're both going and he knows it and is fine with it."

"Only because you probably talked him into letting me come. No, thanks."

"If you don't go then I won't either."

"You have to go, Vash. If you don't, he'll think it's because of me."

Vashti laughed. "It *will* be because of you."

"It shouldn't."

"But it will since I have no idea what's going on between you two. But like I told you, I'm here when you're ready to talk about it. Besides, you have to go."

"Why?"

"I've forgotten how to get on that side of the bayou." Vashti hadn't really, but if that little lie would get Bryce to come with her, then so be it. And because she knew how Bryce's mind worked, she quickly said, "And no, you won't be giving me directions. I don't do well with directions and you wouldn't want me to get lost, would you?"

Bryce rolled her eyes. "You won't get lost, Vash."

"I won't take any chances, Bryce. You will be going with me."

# CHAPTER EIGHT

*Sacramento, California*

KIA HARRIS ROLLED her eyes as she clicked on the phone. "Mom, I'm leaving school now. I'll be home in a little bit."

"Just be careful driving, hon. You're a relatively new driver and the roads are slick from the rain earlier."

Kia waved at the new guy at school as she walked out the doors to the parking lot. He returned the wave and smiled. She smiled back while thinking that he was kind of cute. His name was Trace Nichols. A senior who had moved from somewhere in Florida. He was tall and built like the athlete he was. She'd heard he was a member of the football team. That meant she would get to see a lot of him since she was now a majorette.

"Kia, are you still there?"

For a moment she'd forgotten her mother was on the phone. "Yes, Mom, I'm still here."

"Remember, no texting while driving."

How could she forget when her mother drilled that into her every time she left the house? The car had been a gift for her sixteenth birthday from her parents and she was elated to have gotten it but could honestly do without the phone calls from her mother before every time she got behind the wheel. "Okay, Mom, no texting while driving. Got it."

Changing the subject she asked, "When is Dad coming home?" Her father was a chemical engineer who worked for Anderson Pharmaceutical Company. Her mother had been a chemical engineer as well at the same company, but a few years ago had decided to go back to school and get her PhD. Now she was teaching engineering at California State University. Her father had been in Boston all week attending a seminar.

"He's flying back tonight. Why?"

She shifted her book bag to her other arm. "I miss him."

"Me, too, kiddo. I'm picking him up from the airport around eight. You can go with me if you'd like."

She knew at sixteen she should probably dis the idea of fawning over her parents. Some of her friends would think it was so uncool. But she didn't care. She knew she had wonderful parents. They were the best. Even if her mom did call her more than she needed to and reminded her of stuff she didn't need to be reminded of.

"Great. I should be finished with my homework by then."

"Good. And Nana has prepared you something special for dinner."

A smile touched Kia's face followed by sadness when she recalled why her grandmother was visiting. Her grandfather had passed away two years ago suddenly of a heart attack and none of them had quite gotten over it…especially Nana. The two of them had been married over thirty years.

"I can't wait, Mom. Tell Nana I love her."

"I will."

"I got to go, Mom. I've made it to my car and I remember. No texting while driving. Love you, bye." Then she clicked off the phone.

Throwing her book bag on the back seat, Kia got into the car and automatically buckled up. Before turning the ignition to her car, she inhaled. Her car still smelled new. How many sixteen-year-olds can boast of getting a brand-new car for their birthday? It wasn't the two-seater Tesla she dreamed of owning one day, but it was hers. Given with love from her parents and Nana.

As she left the parking lot she couldn't stop thinking how grateful she was for her family. Her parents had met and fallen in love while attending Massachusetts Institute of Technology. They'd gotten married after college. They weren't in a hurry to have kids and instead concentrated on their careers. When they did try to have a baby, it turned out they couldn't.

Kia knew she'd been adopted. She would never forget the day her parents told her. It was after coming home from school in the sixth grade and crying her eyes out because she couldn't understand how two people with such a high proficiency in math and science could have a daughter who detested both subjects.

That's when they had told her the truth. She had been adopted at birth. That revelation had been a shocker and then it explained a lot. Things she had wondered about but had dismissed from her mind. Like how her chocolate-skin-tone parents could have such a daughter with caramel-colored skin. But as she got older she figured nothing was strange about it after all since she and Nana were of the same complexion and Gramps had been even darker than both her parents.

And then both her parents were left-handed and

so was Nana. But she'd dismissed that as well since Gramps had used his right hand like she did. They had thought she would be upset about it, but she wasn't. For a minute, though, she had been disappointed to learn she'd been born to a parent who hadn't wanted her.

Her parents hadn't been able to tell her much about her birth mother other than she knew she couldn't take care of a child properly and had given her up for adoption, where she'd felt her baby could have a better life.

Kia didn't know what type of life her birth mother had lived, but she would admit for her, being adopted by Percelli and Alma Harris had been for the best. She knew her parents had provided a good home for her and there was never a time she doubted their love.

She recalled her mother asking her if she thought when she got older she would want to find her birth mother and her response had been a resounding no. She had no reason to ever want to meet the woman who'd given her away, no matter the circumstances.

She shifted her thoughts from her parents to that new guy at school, the one who'd smiled at her. Yesterday in the cafeteria she'd gotten close to him, but not close enough to say hello and introduce herself. But she had seen he had a gorgeous pair of dark eyes and a perfect set of white teeth. How a guy's teeth looked said a lot about him in her book.

She knew the only problem her parents might have with him was that he was a senior, which meant he was already eighteen or close to it. That was no biggie for her but it probably would be for her parents. Besides, she knew they were hoping she would finally show interest in Josh Matthews, the son of friends of theirs. Josh was her age and attended a private school in town.

Unfortunately, there was a lot about Josh his parents and hers didn't know. Like he was sexually active and sleeping with any girl who let him. And because his parents had money, most girls were making it easy for him. Kia knew about it since one of the girls, Nicole Lansford, had come back to school bragging about the fact she'd been one of them…like that was something to be proud of.

As she turned the corner toward home, she wondered what Nana was preparing for dinner.

"COME IN."

Vashti walked into Bryce's bedroom smiling while eyeing her up and down. "Wow! Don't you look good? Trying to impress anyone tonight?"

"Nope, just hope to have a good time."

"And there's no reason you shouldn't," Vashti said. She then twirled around. "Well, what do you think?"

Bryce rolled her eyes. "What is there to think? You always look good. You have that New York chicness about you."

Vashti laughed. "New York chicness?"

"Yes, like you'd be put together even if you were wearing tops and slacks that don't match."

Vashti looked down at herself. "Well, they do match so I'm good. You can't go wrong with jeans and a top. I see we both had the same idea and it was the right one."

"I agree."

"Who's driving?" Vashti asked.

"Doesn't matter, but I've yet to ride in that red little toy with you."

"Then consider tonight a done deal."

"Great! Besides, there's something I want to talk to you about."

Vashti wondered if Bryce would finally tell her what was going on with her and Kaegan. "I'm all ears."

Bryce nodded. "We'll talk in the car."

When Vashti had driven halfway to Kaegan's place and Bryce hadn't said anything, she decided to ask. "So what did you want to talk about?"

Bryce glanced over at her. "Shelby by the Sea."

Vashti lifted a brow. Not the conversation she had expected. "What about it?"

"Since the Barnes Group pulled their offer after the zoning meeting, what do you plan to do?"

"What else can I do but put it back on the market and hope next time the potential buyer is someone Reid Lacroix will approve of?"

"There is another option, Vash."

"And what option is that?"

"That you move back here and reopen the inn yourself."

"What! You got to be kidding. Why on earth would I want to do something like that?"

"Because this is your home, it's obvious the towns-people won't treat you the same. You don't have a job and running the inn would be a no-brainer for you because of your experience and education. That's what you went to college for. And last but not least, I think your aunt Shelby would have wanted that."

Vashti shook her head. "I'm not sure she would have, Bryce. You were right about the inn needing repairs. That takes money that I don't have. And I have no de-sire to leave New York and move back here. I feel confident I'll get another job eventually in New York. I like living there."

"It was just a thought. One I think you should consider. I hear all the reasons you wouldn't want to move back, but I think no one is going to do justice to Shelby by the Sea but you."

She heard what Bryce was saying but she disagreed. There was someone out there who would bring the inn back to life, but it wouldn't be her.

RAISED IN ONE big city after another his entire life, Sawyer originally had a hard time adjusting to small-town life in the cove, but he'd done so. However, he wondered if he would ever get used to this. Life on the Louisiana Bayou where Kaegan lived.

First he would have to get used to the wildlife that roamed the shores and swam the waters, namely the raccoons, coyotes, gray wolves, beavers, otters…and he mustn't forget the alligators. Then because of the swamp, there were mosquitoes that were almost as big as humans, which was why Kaegan had several lit mosquito torches lining the area. So far tonight Sawyer hadn't been bitten once and according to Kaegan, these torches, whose flame emitted some type of repellent, would assure that he wouldn't.

He knew to the people who braved the elements and lived on the bayou there was no place better. It was a culture of their own and was a mixture of just about every influence from Spanish to French to German to African and Irish and, in Kaegan's case, Native American. There were those with predominantly French ancestry, some who still spoke the language, and who made up the foundation of the Cajun culture.

Kaegan had explained a lot about the culture of the people Sawyer was duty bound to protect. The first and foremost was to respect their heritage and culture and not fall victim to stereotypes. For instance, there was more to the Cajun people than how they spiced their foods. Sawyer believed above all else, the most important thing he'd learned was about the bayou itself, and its importance to the habitat and inland areas, mainly against coastal erosion. That's why in a way he understood the environmentalists who fought to keep out developers and those who didn't understand and appreciate its contribution, and to preserve as much of the bayou as they could.

"Here you go."

He glanced over at Kaegan as a beer bottle was placed in his hand. "Thanks. And everything looks good and smells even better."

Kaegan chuckled. "There's nothing better than bayou living and eating. You won't believe the size of the catfish I caught this week just for tonight."

"I can imagine." He recalled the times he'd been able to grab a few hours with Kaegan out on the bayou to fish. He'd never known an area that had such an abundance of crawfish and catfish.

"How's Jade?"

Sawyer smiled. "She's fine, although I left her in a bit of a tiff when she found out she wasn't invited tonight. I had to explain to her that turning sixteen didn't mean she got to go to grown folk's functions."

"Good. I wouldn't want her to be mad at me the next time I see her."

Sawyer smiled. "Jade would have gotten over it by then, trust me. She told me last night that she plans on trying out for majorette next year but thinks she needs lessons. I have to start researching to see if anyone in the area offers baton-twirling classes."

Kaegan nodded. "I guess she's forgotten about those cooking classes you suggested she enroll in."

"For now, but you never know when it might pop up later. Just like I'm hoping this majorette thing is a phase."

"Maybe. Maybe not. Catalina Cove High School is known to rank high in the baton-twirling competition every year." Kaegan took a sip of his own beer before adding. "Too bad Vashti doesn't live here anymore. I know a lot of young girls who could benefit from her expertise. She's still reigning champ."

Sawyer recalled Trudy saying something like that. He could see a young Vashti Alcindor out on the football field doing a dance routine while twirling a baton in her hand. The thought made him smile.

"She might be able to tell you where she took her classes. I know it was around here somewhere. If the place is still in business then you might be in luck. You can ask her tonight."

Sawyer tried downplaying the spike of heat that flashed low in the gut. "She'll be here?"

"Yes. I expect her any minute."

Anticipation seemed to suddenly thicken the air Sawyer was breathing. What on earth was wrong with him? Instead of reacting this way to the news that Vashti Alcindor would be here tonight, he should be thinking about tomorrow and the time he would spend with Leesa. There was nothing like a quiet hotel room with the curtains drawn while their naked bodies were underneath silken sheets. As far as he was concerned he should be getting aroused at the thought of only one woman and it shouldn't be Ms. Alcindor. Only Leesa.

He and Kaegan talked about a number of other things before Kaegan left to welcome new arrivals. Sawyer knew his friend had a reason to celebrate. Returning to town and taking over a floundering family business hadn't been easy, but Kaegan had done it. Now Chambray Seafood Unlimited employed a number of residents. Some who had been with the company for years could now boast of getting paid a lot more than minimum wage. No doubt Kaegan's company was adding to the town's economy in a positive way. People appreciated the fresh catch Kaegan provided.

Sawyer was mentally debating whether to grab another beer when suddenly sexual tension seemed to fill his every pore. He was in a group talking to Ray Sullivan, a guy who had moved to the cove a year ago and had quickly advanced as Kaegan's right-hand man, and another one of Kaegan's employees by the name of Manuel Gillespie. He turned his head and saw her. Vashti Alcindor had arrived.

# CHAPTER NINE

"THANKS FOR COMING."

"Thanks for inviting *us*, Kaegan," Vashti said, placing emphasis on the word *us*, just in case he'd conveniently forgotten the invitation was meant for both her and Bryce. She felt that little bit was needed since he'd looked directly at her when he'd stated the welcome as if Bryce wasn't there. Under no circumstances would she allow him to be rude to Bryce when she'd talked her into coming. However, their attitude toward each other made Vashti only wonder even more what in the world was going on. What had happened between them to make what used to be close friends so hostile toward each other?

Evidently Kaegan got Vashti's message because he glanced over at Bryce and said, "I'm glad you came as well, Bryce."

Now that was a lot better, Vashti thought, and gave Kaegan a radiant smile, although she knew the one he returned was fake as hell. "You said it would be a gathering of a few. There are a lot of people here."

"Most are my employees," he said. "They played a huge role in helping to turn the company around and make it successful. I couldn't celebrate without them."

"The house looks great from here. When you find the time tonight we want a tour of the inside," Vashti said.

"I'll make sure I do that before the party ends. Excuse me while I welcome the other arrivals."

"Sure."

He headed toward the dock where some people had come by boat.

"I feel like I'm being forced on him. I hope you realize he hated to include me in anything," Bryce said.

"If that's true he will get over it," Vashti said, glancing around the yard, her gaze landing on Sheriff Sawyer Grisham. He was standing in a group with a beer bottle in his hand and staring at her. There was something in that look that made her totally aware of him like he seemed to be totally aware of her. Fine. Let him stare. So would she. She quickly decided she liked the way he filled out a pair of jeans. She also liked the way his shirt fit his shoulders and sculpted abdomen. Any woman would appreciate the raw masculinity that seemed to be simply him. And she was a woman.

"Hmm, I see the sheriff is here tonight," Bryce said, cutting into her intense study of the man.

"I see."

"I see that you see. I also see that he sees as well. Wouldn't you know, there's a couple who frequents my parents' restaurant standing over there. I think now is a good time for me to say hello," Bryce said, smiling.

Vashti broke eye contact with Sawyer and glanced at Bryce whose sneaky smile wasn't fooling her any. "And what am I to do while you're saying hello to that couple?"

"You don't need an answer to that, Vash, but since you asked, I suggest you go say hello to the sheriff. For the two of you to stand across the yard and stare each other down is a waste of sexual chemistry." Bryce then sauntered off.

Vashti turned her attention back to Sawyer Grisham and walked toward him. He was still looking so she decided to give him something to look at with the intentional sway of her hips. She shouldn't be doing this but the intensity of the eyes looking at her sent a restless throb through her veins. At that moment temptation thundered through her and she was well aware of the sexual vibes flowing between them. But the big question was why. What was she doing? What were *they* doing?

He stepped away from the group of men he had been in and toward her, and when she finally reached him she tilted her head back to look up at him. Sensations she'd never experienced before had her pulse pounding. "Evening, Sheriff."

"Ms. Alcindor."

"Don't you know it's not nice to stare?" she asked him.

His lips creased into a smile. Not a half smile this time but a full one. The result was too devastatingly sexy. "I could ask you the same thing," was his reply.

Yes, he could ask and if he did she would be honest and say he gave her a lot to stare at and she appreciated it all. It had been a long time since she'd given a man a second look. "Touché. I looked for you after the meeting the other night."

"You did?" he asked tilting the beer bottle up to his mouth to take a gulp.

Why did his doing such a thing heighten the pounding of her pulse? "Yes, I wanted to thank you for voting in my favor."

He held her gaze. "That developer's presentation was pretty enlightening. Unfortunately, this town isn't ready for anything of that magnitude."

"Do you think they will ever be ready?"

He shrugged massive shoulders. "I don't know. You grew up here—what do you think?"

"I was hoping things would have changed over the years, but as long as Reid Lacroix carries a lot of weight in this town then, no."

Instead of addressing that, he said, "What are you drinking?"

When she said she'd take a beer, he nodded. "I took you for someone who'd prefer wine coolers."

"Typically, I do, but tonight I'll take a beer."

"One beer coming up."

She watched him walk to a huge tub on ice. Her gaze followed his trek, again appreciating how good he looked in a pair of jeans. Nice tush, especially. And when he bent that tush over to pull a beer bottle out of the tub, she was convinced her heart skipped a beat.

He moved back toward her and he was looking at her, at all of her. She felt her body warm under his penetrating stare. "Here you are, Ms. Alcindor."

"Vashti. Please call me Vashti."

"Okay and I'm Sawyer."

He unscrewed the cap and handed her the beer. "Thanks." She took a sip and then looked at him and asked, "So, Sawyer, what's going on between us?"

SAWYER TOOK A sip of his own beer. He could deny there was anything going on between them, but that would be a bald-faced lie when it was obviously clear that there was. Even if no one else had picked up on it, the two of them had and they were who mattered. Problem was he was ill equipped to handle the intensity of his attraction to her because nothing like this had ever happened to him before.

Since she'd so boldly asked the question, he decided to answer the best way he could by telling the truth. "I honestly don't know because this is a first for me. You're a beautiful woman and any man would be attracted to you. Now why you're attracted to me, only you can answer that."

She held his gaze as she took another sip of her beer. "Unfortunately, I can't answer that because this is a first for me as well. You, Sawyer Grisham, are a handsome man, but..."

He lifted a brow. "But what?"

"I've been in the presence of handsome men before, and I've never reacted this way from just a mere look from one. I guess the intensity of our attraction to each other will end up in the books as one of those unsolved mysteries."

"I guess so." He wished he could be more conclusive than that but he couldn't. "When do you leave?"

"Tomorrow."

"Morning or evening?" he asked, taking another sip of his beer.

"Evening. Are you rushing me out of town, Sheriff?"

"No, I wouldn't do anything like that." However, he would put plenty of distance between them until her departure. He didn't trust this attraction between them, mysterious or not. Honestly, he was afraid that if given too much time, he could lose his good common sense over it. At least tomorrow he would be in New Orleans with Leesa the better part of the day.

"So, what do you do in New York?"

Now she was the one who lifted a brow. "How do you know I'm from New York?"

"Your driver's license was a dead giveaway."

She chuckled. "Yes, that ticket. I intend to pay it before I leave."

He smiled. "Good. I would hate to have to come all the way to New York to arrest you." Almost immediately he regretted saying that. Did it sound like he would find just about any excuse to go to New York to see her? He hoped she wouldn't get that impression because that's not what he meant.

"I would hate for that as well. But the ticket will get paid before I leave town, and to answer your question, I'm in the hotel industry. I'm employed by a major hotel there as executive manager."

"Like your job?"

Vashti's eyes slid away and she didn't say anything as she took another sip of her beer. "Yes, I like my job. Do you like yours?"

There was more to the story, he could tell, but he decided not to challenge her on it. "Pretty much. Catalina Cove is a nice town. However, ultra-conservative in a number of ways." He chuckled. "At the moment my daughter is not. She wanted that tennis resort to come here. Most of the young people did. She told me the other night she plans to grow up and become mayor one day."

Vashti smiled. "Good for her. I would come back to town and help her campaign for change."

He chuckled again. "That will definitely be her platform."

She smiled back at him and asked, "Tell me about her."

"Who?"

"Your daughter."

She seemed genuinely interested so he told her. "Her name is Jadelyn but prefers Jade, and she's sixteen. Already she wants a summer job and a car…not necessarily in that order and I'm not crazy about her getting either. She's a good kid. Respectful. Has good manners. And not only does she keep her room clean but the entire house. She convinced me that the money I paid for a housekeeper I could pass on to her so she will have a larger allowance. I took her up on it and figured she wouldn't last a week. She proved me wrong. Came up with this system for cleaning and was quick to tell me how to correct my old ways that had become bad habits. Like not picking up after myself."

Vashti grinned. "I love her. Boy, I wished I could have deprogrammed my parents' bad habits, like not scraping food off the plates before putting them in the sink. Especially when my father refused to buy a dishwasher. I was it. Their live-in dishwasher."

They both turned when Kaegan called out to get everyone's attention. "Thanks for coming tonight to help celebrate a successful two years," Kaegan said, smiling. "Roll up your sleeves and get ready to dig in. All the shrimp, crabs and oysters you can eat."

"I hope you're hungry because Kaegan has prepared a feast," Sawyer said as he gazed down at the woman walking beside him as they headed toward the area where tables were set up. Even with his long strides Vashti was keeping up with him, her steps almost in sync with his. More than once her thigh brushed against him and each time he drew in sharp breaths.

Most would consider him a big man at six-three

and weighing close to two hundred pounds. However, thanks to a vigorous workout routine he was all muscles no fat. But next to her he seemed larger because of her small frame. But then there were all those curves she had in all the right places. Curves he liked looking at. Curves he enjoyed brushing against.

"Grab us a place to sit and I'll fill our plates," he suggested and then asked, "Anything you don't want to eat?"

She smiled up at him. "Nope, I'm hungry and want it all."

Sawyer watched her walk toward one of the tables. The food line moved quickly, and he was handed a huge container that he packed with steamed shrimp, crabs, raw oysters and grilled fish. After taking the container to the table Vashti had claimed, he went back to fill smaller bowls with seafood gumbo.

Moments later they were diving into their meal. Bryce, Ray Sullivan and several others were sharing their table. While engaging in lively conversation, the men used the utensils to break open the crab claws, making it easier for the women to pick out the meat.

An hour or two later everyone had eaten their fill, and warm scented hand towels were passed out for cleanup, followed by more beer. At some point someone turned up the music. Vashti tried urging him into a line dance, but he declined, preferring to sit and watch. And he did enjoy watching, namely her. As he sat there, he wondered how he could manage to get her alone. Each and every time she smiled at him with those gorgeous full lips, hot sparks of desire would cause a yearning so intense it felt close to pain. His mouth ached to kiss her, a condition he'd never felt for any woman.

It was much later when he'd been presented with the opportunity for privacy. Kaegan had taken a group on a tour of the home he was building within walking distance of his parents' home. He took them around back to show the view of the bayou and how he'd be able to stand on his porch every night to see the setting sun.

After the tour, when everyone was headed back to the cookout, Sawyer took hold of Vashti's hand, no longer able to ignore the flagrant heat of that carnal attraction between them. "Come with me," he leaned down and whispered close to her ear. His brain nearly faltered when her scent enveloped him.

Without asking where he intended to take her she went with him. He placed his arm around her shoulders as they moved farther away from the group and toward the secluded beach. "I hope you're aware there are alligators that come out at night," she said, smiling up at him.

He chuckled. "I can protect you." Moments later when he stopped she turned to him and their gazes connected. He took in her features illuminated in the moonlight. Even after all she'd eaten, the cherry-red lipstick still shaded her lips, making her mouth that much more delectable.

She glanced around. "What's so special about this spot?" she asked him.

His mouth curved into a smile. "You're here."

She chuckled. "Yes, I am. I guess I should ask you why," she said as an I-already-know look appeared in her eyes.

"Earlier tonight you asked me a bold question."

"I did?"

"Yes. You wanted to know just what was going on with us."

"You got an answer for me, Sawyer?"

"Not really, but I hope this is the first step in trying to find out." Then he lowered his mouth to slant it across hers.

DESIRE RIPPED THROUGH Vashti the moment Sawyer's lips locked to hers. This was crazy. She'd never been this attracted to a man before in her life. And of all people, the sheriff of Catalina Cove. The same man who'd given her a ticket a couple of days ago. But thoughts of his profession and that ticket were fading into oblivion with every stroke of his tongue. And then as smooth as it could get, he changed his technique and began lapping her up like her mouth was the next best thing to blueberry muffins.

Every feminine cell in her body sparked to life, made their presence known and showed just how lusty nearly three years of abstinence had made them. Had it been that long since she'd kissed a man? Been held in one's arms? Felt the hardness of one pressed against her thighs? Been made love to?

Hot sensations from the top of her head to the bottom of her feet began swamping her. They enticed her to lap him back with matching intensity. A flare of heat speared between her legs and her breasts felt full, heavy and sensitive as Sawyer continued to ravage her mouth in a way that no man had ever kissed her before. In a way that should be deemed a criminal offense.

Suddenly, he released her mouth and a soft moan escaped her. That was all the time allowed before he recaptured her mouth. Practically devoured it as their lips fused together again for a long, delicious and intense moment. Sawyer deepened the kiss in a way that made every blissful sensation known to man flare through her. And if that wasn't torturous enough, the tips of his fingers seemed to be tracing erotic designs on the back of her blouse. A deep need she'd never, ever felt before had her senses spinning, had her body feeling like it was on fire to the point where she felt the need to get naked.

Thinking of doing something so outrageous should have shocked some sense into her, and she believed it would have if Sawyer hadn't switched techniques again. Whatever he was doing to her mouth had her practically drowning in the smothering depths of his. Never had she been blindsided by lust, but she was now.

How could any man have the techniques of kissing down to a science? She was doing her best to keep up with him but he'd left her behind several tongue strokes ago. Never had she wanted a kiss not to end but it finally did and she felt so weak that she dropped her head on his chest.

Vashti could tell from the sound of Sawyer's breathing that he'd needed to pull air into his lungs, otherwise there was no telling how much longer they would have continued kissing. She wasn't sure just how long they'd been gone from the party and before Sawyer got any ideas to go for a third round, she lifted her face from his chest, looked up at him and said, although not too convincingly, "It's time for us to go back."

"I could have kissed you all night," he said in a deep, husky voice.

She was tempted to say, *I wish you would have*, but instead she said, "You know what they say, all good things must come to an end."

"I know, but I wish they didn't." After drawing in another deep breath, he said, "And just so you know, I haven't figured out what's going on between us, Vashti. I don't know any more now than I did before. Other than I like the way you taste."

## CHAPTER TEN

"I HAD FUN TONIGHT," Vashti said, coming into the kitchen for a cup of coffee, feeling refreshed after her shower, and for the moment satisfied that she'd gotten the kiss she had wanted. When she and Sawyer had returned to the party that was in full swing, everyone was either dancing or had gone back to the seafood pot for seconds. No one seemed to have noticed them drifting back to rejoin the group.

Not even Bryce. At least if she had, she hadn't mentioned it in the car ride home. Vashti felt stuffed from eating so much food and would admit Catalina Cove had the best seafood in all the world. Bryce grinned over at her as she came to sit down at the table. She'd taken a shower as well. "I guess you would since you had the sheriff's attention most of the night."

So she had noticed. "Umm, he's nice."

Bryce nodded, eyeing her closely. "Anything you want to tell me, Vash?"

She shrugged. "No, nothing that I can think of."

"Okay, keep your lips sealed. Lips that happened to look as if they've been thoroughly kissed."

Vashti laughed. "They don't."

"Oh, yes, they do, trust me. Good thing you're leaving town tomorrow. If any of those women who've been chasing behind our sheriff get wind that you, who haven't been in town but a couple of days, made a home run when they'd been striking out, they will be out for blood."

"Well, you know what they say. You win some and you lose some."

Bryce smiled. "Well, it looks like you came out a winner tonight. I like Sheriff Grisham, but so does everyone in the cove. Even Reid Lacroix. However, I will say tonight was the first time I noticed him paying attention to a woman. Consider yourself lucky."

Vashti smiled, thinking about that kiss and decided yes, tonight she certainly felt that way. "The kiss wasn't planned. It just happened."

"Yeah, right. I guess you two didn't intentionally wander off from the group either."

Vashti took a sip of her coffee. "I can't help that there's an attraction between us."

"Hey, I'm not complaining. You can kiss any man you want."

Deciding to change the subject, Vashti asked, "Who's that guy you were hanging with tonight? He's quite handsome."

"That was Ray Sullivan. He's a pretty nice guy who moved to town last year and works for Kaegan. He keeps to himself most of the time. A real loner. Although that hasn't stopped the women who've given up on the sheriff to turn their attention to him. So far he's managed to stay clear of all the eager beavers. Even when he comes into the café he's by himself, except for those times Kaegan or the sheriff joins him."

"Do you know where he's from?"

"I have no idea, but I overheard Kaegan tell my dad that Ray's a hard worker and a pretty smart guy, which is why he made him his right-hand man in the company. And before you get any ideas, don't. Ray was only being nice to me."

Later that night after Vashti slid between the sheets, she eased on her back and stared up at the ceiling. Even after taking a shower and relaxing with a cup of coffee, her brain was still on overload and her stomach doing somersaults. And all because of Sawyer Grisham's kiss. Yes, while talking to Bryce she had deliberately downplayed all that sexual chemistry flowing between her and Sawyer tonight, mainly because they had tried to themselves. Instead they'd tried to concentrate on all that seafood and the music. Then there was the conversation where he'd told her more about his daughter. The smile on his face when he talked about her was breathtaking. Vashti wondered if her father ever smiled when asked about her. She would hope that one day long ago he had…before she did something her parents could never forgive her for.

She'd managed to get through the meal with him sitting beside her. Afterward, the music was cranked up for line dancing. Kaegan had the perfect patio in his yard and it had been fun. Sawyer hadn't danced. Instead he'd stood on the sidelines drinking a beer while watching everyone. Namely, her.

Just knowing his gaze was on her body's movements while she danced made her feel tingly inside. It had been a while since it had been so obviously clear that she had a man's attention. For the first time in a long time she thought it felt good being a woman and taking the time to flaunt it.

She'd done it with a purpose and he'd taken the bait. She had wanted that kiss as much as he had and a part of her knew that he'd gotten the message. The man had kissed her in a way she'd never been kissed before. He had taken his time. He had been thorough. Her brain waves were still dancing from the impact of how delicious his tongue had tasted in her mouth.

She had noticed Sawyer wasn't the only man in lust with a woman tonight. She doubted Bryce realized it but Kaegan had practically watched her every movement as well. Especially when Bryce seemed to spend a lot of time with Ray Sullivan.

Her thoughts shifted back to Sawyer and that kiss. A part of her regretted she'd probably seen him for the last time tonight since she didn't ever plan to return to the cove. She thought about Bryce's suggestion tonight that she move back to the cove and reopen the inn. What could she be thinking? She would admit when she'd gone to the inn yesterday she had visions of the things she would do if she were to open it up. But just as quickly as the thoughts had entered her mind, she'd dismissed them. The inn was in need of repair and that would take money. It was money she didn't have. She would have to take out a loan and she couldn't do that. She was still paying her student loan for college. And she needed to be careful how she spent her severance pay. Moving back here and running the inn was out of the question. Before leaving she would instruct Bryce to put Shelby by the Sea back on the market. In the meantime, when she returned to New York she would continue to look for a job and hope she found one soon.

"How was the party, Dad?"

Sawyer glanced across the room the minute he closed

the door. Jade was sitting on the sofa in the dark. He turned on a lamp. "Why are you still up?"

"Waiting for you. You're late."

He chuckled as he crossed the room to sit down beside her. "Do I need to remind you who's the parent and who's the child?"

"No, but that doesn't mean I can't worry about you."

He lifted a brow. "Then maybe I need to remind you who's a student and who's the sheriff. I think I can take care of myself."

She leaned into him and he automatically placed his arm around her. "Oh, Daddy, I know you can but that doesn't mean I don't worry sometimes. I was in bed and had a dream. It wasn't a bad one or anything. It was a dream about Mom."

He squeezed her tighter and said, "Tell me about your dream, sweetheart."

She took his hand and held it. "I dreamed the three of us, me, you and Mom, were in Florida again. At Disney World. Remember when we went there?"

He remembered. It was the last vacation they'd taken as a family. "Yes."

"I dreamed about it but this time we did something in my dream that we didn't do in real life."

"And what was that?"

"The three of us rode on Space Mountain."

He chuckled. "Yes, that was definitely in your dream because there's no way I would have gotten on that thing." Johanna and Jade had a penchant for scary and he much preferred keeping his feet on the ground.

"Well, in my dream you were there, flying high with us and loving it."

"It shocked you awake, didn't it?"

"Pretty much. I got up to tell you about it and saw you hadn't come home and it was after midnight."

"Your old man was having fun."

She smiled. "You should. You work hard in this town protecting everyone. You need to enjoy life. Heck, Dad, you don't even have a girlfriend."

Her comment surprised him and he glanced down at his daughter. "Are you throwing out hints?"

She shook her head. "Possibly. I just want you to be happy."

"And that's the same thing I want for you, too, Jade. Your old man wants you to be happy. By the way, I have business in New Orleans tomorrow. I might not be here when you come home from school."

"Okay, Dad, and I know the routine."

"Yes, you do."

An hour or so later, instead of getting in bed Sawyer stood at the window in his room. There was a full moon out tonight in a starlit sky. Someone once said that when there were a lot of stars out that meant your loved ones were smiling down. If that was true then Johanna had a huge smile. Their little girl was everything she would have wanted her to be. By no means had he made her life cushy. He'd taught her responsibility and deep down he believed she would appreciate him for it.

Leaving the window he pushed back the covers to get into bed and once settled he thought about tonight and Vashti Alcindor and the kiss they'd shared. There was no way he could not think of her when the heat of her taste was embedded on his tongue. The woman had a way of unsettling his mind, every part of his body. He wished he could say the kiss hadn't been planned, but it had. After spending all that time with her, getting turned on by her mere scent, by watching her move her body while dancing, he'd sat there while his entire body hardened with desire for her. And then he'd decided to find out for himself what was going on with them, just like she'd asked. Now he knew and at that moment logic was replaced by a need he hadn't felt in years, if ever.

It bothered him that after she left town tomorrow, chances were their paths would never cross again. The very thought of that made a surge of longing and regret fill him.

He pushed those emotions aside. They had no place with him. He didn't get attached to women. Johanna was the only female he'd gotten attached to and he preferred keeping things that way. Vashti was a woman a man could get attached to easily if he wasn't careful. She was the kind of woman who had the ability to take a man's breath away without even trying. The kind of woman a man intent on staying single for the rest of his life should stay away from.

He had studied her a lot tonight, even when she hadn't known she was the object of his intense scrutiny. She had the ability to brighten up an entire yard. Her smile had dazzled him and was contagious. He doubted he had ever smiled so much and her laughter was just as infectious. He had enjoyed getting to know her. At least the part she was willing to share. The former FBI agent in him could sense when he wasn't being told everything. But then he was of the mind that everyone had something they'd rather keep to themselves.

She was a free spirit, someone who enjoyed life and relished the times she could have fun. For some reason he had a feeling she hadn't done either for a long time. But tonight, she had, thanks to Kaegan.

It was easy to see Vashti's friendship with Kaegan was an old one, built on love and trust. She felt comfortable around him and the people he entrusted with his life. It was as if the saying, *a friend of yours is a friend of mine*, applied between the two. And because she trusted Kaegan's judgment when it came to people, she was relaxed and at ease.

Sawyer switched his thoughts to something else he'd observed tonight. He wasn't sure what was going on with Kaegan and Bryce Witherspoon but there was a story there. He believed Kaegan had kept his eyes on Bryce as much as Sawyer had kept his on Vashti tonight. Especially when the two women had been dancing. He had detected something deeper than male interest in the eyes that had stared at Bryce. He had detected a need that was capped by anger. He found that odd since he thought Kaegan was one of the most easygoing men he knew.

Sawyer switched his thoughts back to Vashti. She'd worn jeans tonight and the pair had hugged her hips in a way that reminded him he was a man every time she moved. And whenever he engaged in conversation with her, which had been most of the night, his gaze seemed to zero in on the pair of firm breasts that fit perfectly beneath the pink cotton shirt she'd been wearing.

He recalled those same breasts touching his chest when he'd kissed her. And how his arms had wrapped around her small waist while holding her. And he couldn't forget how their tongues had tangled when he'd kissed her deeply. As deep as he could possibly get.

At some point that night Sawyer fell into a deep sleep and when he began to dream, they were dreams of Vashti Alcindor.

## CHAPTER ELEVEN

SAWYER ENTERED THE hotel suite and glanced around. Normally, they used the same room each time and she'd always ordered a bottle of wine for them. Room service would deliver their meal later. Much later.

Leesa was there, sitting in the chair waiting for him. She was fully clothed since they enjoyed undressing each other. She stood and moved toward him and when she wrapped her arms around his neck a pair of firm breasts pressed against his chest. Immediately, he thought of the breasts that had pressed against this same chest last night. Vashti's.

"How are you, Sawyer?" her soft voice asked.

Instead of answering, he kissed her, but for some reason it wasn't the same and all he could remember was the mouth he'd taken hungrily the night before. Not appreciating the memories or the comparisons his mind was making, he suddenly broke off the kiss.

Leesa lifted a brow as she studied him before asking, "Are you okay?"

"Yeah, I'm fine." He took a step back and began removing his shirt. She took a step back to watch him. After he'd tossed his shirt aside and had moved his hands to the belt of his jeans, she reached out and stopped him.

Sawyer looked at her. "What's wrong?"

She held his gaze. "You tell me." And then as if she fully expected him to do just that, she moved to the lounging chair in the room and eased down on it.

"What makes you think something is wrong, Leesa?"

She smiled over at him. "A number of signs. You weren't kissing me back for starters. Then you began undressing yourself instead of letting me do it."

He didn't say anything at first. Instead he walked across the room to pour a glass of wine. He stared into the dark contents for a minute. Possibly two. He knew her well. Just like she knew him. Leesa was a beautiful woman and he hoped one day she would find someone who could give her the type and degree of love she deserved, although he knew she would fight such a thing tooth and nail. She was highly intelligent and was one of the few women who'd become a marine pilot. He valued their friendship. Always had and always would.

"No rush, Sawyer."

At the sound of her voice, he turned and looked at her as he took a sip of his wine. "Sure you'd rather talk than get naked in that bed with me?"

"The thought is tempting, trust me. However, something is bothering you. I picked up on it the minute you opened the hotel room door and walked in. You've always listened whenever something bothered me, and I want to do the same for you."

She paused a moment and then asked, "Is it about Jade? Is she okay?"

He shook his head. "Jade's fine, although last night she did throw out a hint that I needed a girlfriend."

Leesa smiled. "Did she?"

"Yes."

"Well, at least she's open to the idea. Nelson would

have a hissy if I were to even mention anything about dating. My son wants me to remain single forever."

"Boys are different. They are protective of their mothers," he told her.

"And there're some girls who are protective of their fathers. They don't like sharing. Now tell me, Sawyer, what's bothering you?"

With his wineglass in hand, he moved to sit on the edge of the bed. "It doesn't bother me as much as it mystifies me, Leesa."

"What does?"

He took a drink and then said, "I met someone a few days ago. A woman. I pulled her over for speeding and gave her a ticket." He smiled. "I think she got a little miffed that I didn't give her a warning ticket."

A smile curved Leesa's lips. "I'm sure you told her that you don't give out warning tickets."

He returned her smile. "Yes, I did." Then his smile slowly faded. "There's something about her, Leesa, that I can't put my finger on. I was attracted to her from the first. I ran into her a couple of times in Catalina Cove and it's like I'm totally mesmerized. Thoroughly captivated."

Leesa nodded. "Any reason you can't get something started with her? I hope you don't think I'd object to us ending things. We agreed that if either of us met someone or just wanted to end things, we would, without any questions asked."

He shook his head. "No, that's not it. She's from New York and was only in town for a few days visiting."

"So? There is such a thing as a long-distance love affair. There are flights out of New Orleans to New York practically every hour. Straight flights. Trust me I know. Nelson's grandparents live in Harlem."

"A long-distance affair?" Sawyer asked, omitting saying "love affair" because love wouldn't have anything to do with it. He was sexually attracted to Vashti and nothing more. He was convinced that love was not part of the equation.

"Yes, and don't make it sound so distasteful. While in the military Todd's and my long-distance love affair lasted for two years before we decided to tie the knot. It was kind of fun. It was like a firestorm of passion every time we hooked up."

A firestorm of passion sounded nice, he thought. "I don't want to get serious about a woman. Now or ever. That's why it mystifies me that—"

"She might be the one who could change your mind about that?"

Sawyer stood and began pacing. After several moments he stopped and turned to Leesa. "I have responsibilities. Jade for one. She should be my main concern."

"She *is* your main concern and will always be. But didn't you say earlier that Jade threw hints that you should be thinking about a girlfriend? Remember, pretty soon Jade will have a life of her own, Sawyer. In two years she will be a senior in high school and it won't be long before she starts dating and hanging out with her friends more. It's obvious that Jade cares about how you feel and what you think. You don't want her to feel guilty when she decides to do those things and you don't have a life. She would want you to be happy."

Sawyer didn't say anything for a long moment while thinking. Hadn't that been what Jade had said last night? She wanted him to be happy. He shoved his hands into the pockets of his jeans. "In a way it doesn't matter even if I wanted to pursue this woman for a long-distance anything. She's leaving the cove to return to New York today."

"What time is her flight?"

He shrugged. "Around six I think."

"Good. That will give you time."

He lifted a brow. "Time for what?"

"To intercept her when she leaves Catalina Cove. If she's like most people, she plans to arrive at the airport at least two hours ahead of time." Leesa glanced at her watch. "That means she'll probably leave the cove in about an hour. There is only one way out of the cove to New Orleans. You can intercept her."

Stunned at what Leesa was suggesting, he just stared at her. "Do you hear what you're saying? We still have two more hours in this room."

She laughed. "Now, do you hear what you're saying? Honestly, Sawyer, do you think I care about that after what you've told me? There hasn't been any woman you've been even remotely interested in since Johanna. To me that's more important than our occasional rounds of recreational sex. Put your shirt back on and leave. I bet you can head her off before she gets to the airport."

He stared at Leesa for a full minute before grabbing his shirt and putting it on. He moved to where she sat and extended his hand to pull her out of the chair and give her a fierce hug. "Thanks for everything, Leesa."

She leaned back and smiled up at him. "No, thank you, Sawyer. It's been an enjoyable experience. Goodbye."

At that moment he knew she was really telling him goodbye. Not goodbye until next time, but goodbye because what they'd shared for the past year had run its course. If she believed that, then she had more confidence in his abilities to win a certain woman over than he did. "Goodbye, Leesa." And then he crossed the room and was out the door.

As he rushed out of the hotel he asked himself what he was thinking. For all he knew, Vashti might have changed her mind and gotten an earlier flight out. But still a part of him pushed his steps forward into a full run to his SUV.

Since this was his official day off, he drove his personal vehicle. No way would he have his police cruiser parked outside a hotel for four hours on a Friday afternoon. That meant he couldn't speed to get where he was going even if he wanted to. Otherwise, he would be giving himself a ticket.

It seemed to take him longer than usual to get out of New Orleans traffic and hit the interstate. From there it was smooth sailing on the open road. Here he was racing back, at the speed limit, mind you, to hopefully say goodbye to a woman who might not even want to give him the time of day. Although he would have to admit she didn't seem to mind him dominating her time last night. In fact, she seemed to enjoy his company as much as he'd enjoyed hers.

He had driven for twenty minutes when he saw her car, that red Corvette. And when she passed him she had the top down with her hair blowing in the wind. Making sure it was safe to do so, he quickly made a U-turn on the highway and headed after her.

Reaching under his seat he pulled out his portable flashing red-and-blue light and placed it on the dashboard of his car. He used it only in extreme cases when his personal vehicle needed to be used for official business. At the moment this was his very own official business and it was definitely, in his book, an extreme case.

VASHTI DROVE WHILE rocking to the sound of Bruno Mars. She hated admitting that although she wasn't returning to New York ten million dollars richer, she felt good about her visit back to Catalina Cove. More than she thought she ever would. It had been good seeing Bryce's family and Ms. Gertie, even though on both days she'd gone to see her Ms. Gertie hadn't known who she was.

Her visit to Shelby by the Sea had brought out pleasant memories and very unpleasant ones as well. It was hard to believe Aunt Shelby was no longer there with her hugs like in the good old days. Seeing Kaegan had been a plus and she'd had so much fun at the gathering at his place last night. Like she'd told Bryce, she would not make any promises she would be back. Chances were, she wouldn't.

Then there was Sheriff Sawyer Grisham. The man who…

Vashti glanced back in her rearview mirror and saw the flashing red-and-blue light behind her. What was going on? She knew for certain she wasn't speeding because she had adjusted the cruise control on the Corvette to three miles under the speed limit.

She pulled to the side of the road, incensed that she would be pulled over when she was not speeding. She was getting her license out of her purse when she felt a presence beside the car. "You weren't speeding, Vashti. I don't need to see your driver's license."

Her head jerked up and she looked into a pair of dark

brown eyes. She drew in a deep breath and was about to give him her sexiest smile, when she got a whiff of his scent. Instead she gave him a stony glare. "Then why was I stopped?"

She tried not to notice how good he looked. Today must be his day off because he was wearing a pair of jeans and a nice black collared shirt. But she knew that scent that was all over him, and it could mean only one thing.

"I just wanted to say goodbye and I hope you have a safe trip. I was off today and spent some time in New Orleans. I rushed back, hoping to see you before you left."

Hadn't Bryce mentioned he was seeing some woman living in New Orleans? Evidently today had been their hookup day. "Why were you hoping to see me before I left, Sheriff?"

He leaned down in the open window and she wished he hadn't done that. The scent was even more potent. "I wanted to ask if perhaps I could fly to New York to see you in a couple of weeks," he said.

Vashti pushed her hair back and removed the sunglasses from her eyes to make sure they had direct eye contact. "Let me get this straight. You pulled me over to say goodbye and to ask if you can come see me in New York?"

"Yes."

She became furiously offended. "You have the nerve to ask me that after just getting out of some woman's bed?"

The look that appeared on his face immediately spelled guilty. He straightened to his full height and his jaw tightened. "And what makes you think I just got out of a woman's bed?"

He hadn't denied it probably because he couldn't, she thought. "Because her scent is all over you. Unless you've decided to make Loveswept your personal perfume now."

He didn't say anything. He just stood there and stared at her for a long moment. She could tell from his expression that he hadn't liked what she'd said, but she didn't care a royal flip. Then he said, "If I was in a woman's bed, yet I got out of it to come say goodbye to you, Vashti, and to let you know I want to see you again, what does that tell you?"

Without waiting for her to answer, he walked back to his SUV, got in and drove off.

## CHAPTER TWELVE

"CALM DOWN, VASH."

"I don't want to calm down, Bryce. Can you believe what he did yesterday? I'm still mad about it."

"Obviously."

Vashti was incensed as she paced her living room. The only reason she hadn't called Bryce when she'd gotten in last night was because by the time she'd gotten home from the airport it was late. She would have called from the airport, but her battery had died.

"Sounds like the sheriff ruffled a few of your feathers."

"He most certainly did. I feel sorry for the woman whose bed he was in. If he would treat one woman so shabbily then what does that say for me?"

"Whoa, don't you think you're going overboard? Why don't you do what he suggested and figure out why he did it? If he really did do what you're accusing him of. Sounds like he didn't really admit to anything."

"He did it. Guilt was all over his face and her scent was all over him. Men can be such asses."

"Umm, wasn't it just the other night that you said you thought he was nice?"

"I was wrong."

"He *is* nice and if you want my honest opinion, I don't think things are all that serious between him and this woman. Like I told you, he's never brought her to any social functions in town."

"Although he might not think things are serious, the woman might think otherwise. There might be another reason he doesn't bring her around. What if she's married?"

"Honestly, Vashti. Not all men are like Scott. Sheriff Grisham has never come across as a man who wouldn't honor marriage vows. His or anyone else's. And I believe he knows how to treat a woman because I've seen how he operates. He opens doors for all the ladies, young and old. He stands when one enters a room and always shows respect. He has a daughter, so I wouldn't expect anything less."

Bryce paused a minute then asked, "So will you let him come see you in New York?"

"Why would I?"

"So you can hear his side of things."

Vashti rolled her eyes. "What is there to hear? He chased after me after being in bed with another woman. Her perfume was all over him."

"What if it was? Did he betray you by sleeping with the woman?"

Vashti thought about the kiss they'd shared. The one that had caused her knees to buckle. The one she still couldn't get out of her mind. "No."

"Are you jealous that he was sleeping with someone?"

Yes, she was jealous at the thought he was kissing other women the way he'd kissed her. But she wouldn't admit it. "Of course I'm not jealous."

"Then don't act like you are. If anything, let him visit you in New York and ask why he would leave another woman and chase you down. Only he can answer that."

"I don't want to know, Bryce."

"If you say so. Oh, and by the way, someone called me yesterday looking for you."

"Who?"

"Reid Lacroix. He didn't know you were leaving so soon. He thought you would be staying awhile."

Vashti eased down in her kitchen chair. "Why would Mr. Lacroix call looking for me?"

"He said he needed to talk to you, but didn't say what it was about. I told him I couldn't give out your number without your permission. So, do you want him to have it?"

Vashti nibbled on her bottom lip. "He knows."

"You don't know that for certain, Vash."

"What other reason would he want to talk to me for, Bryce?"

"I don't know. I suggest you give me permission to give him your phone number and find out."

Vashti didn't know how she felt about the possibility Reid Lacroix knew her deepest secret, but she found herself saying, "Okay, fine. Give Mr. Lacroix my phone number." When she hung up the phone after talking with Bryce, Vashti hoped she wasn't making a mistake.

"How are things going?" Kaegan asked Sawyer as he slid in the booth seat across from him.

"Not bad for a Saturday morning. Quiet, and that's good. Did you take the day off yesterday?"

"Nope. But I did give everyone a half day and told them not to come in until noon. Of course Ray was there like it was a regular work day. His work ethics are astounding."

Sawyer nodded. "Still no sign of his memory returning?" He and Kaegan were the only people in town who knew that Ray Sullivan, who had moved to Catalina Cove a year ago, had retrograde amnesia.

"So far, no. I can't imagine living for the present and not knowing what life you might have lived in the past."

At that moment the waitress brought over Kaegan's food. He had ordered the same thing Sawyer was eating: a juicy hamburger and fries. There were plenty of other things on the menu, but Sawyer was convinced Witherspoon Café hamburgers were the best anywhere.

He waited until the waitress had served Kaegan his food and he'd said grace before saying, "And speaking of a past, what you can tell me about Vashti Alcindor's?"

Kaegan looked at him as if he was trying to decide just how much to reveal. "You mean you didn't interrogate her at the party? You seemed to have held her captive most of the evening. It looked like the two of you talked a lot. And I happened to notice that you and Vashti got lost after the tour."

Sawyer heard the edge in Kaegan's voice. He was surprised Kaegan had noticed how much time he'd spent with Vashti. His gaze had been on Bryce Witherspoon most of the night, so Sawyer knew it wasn't a jealous edge he heard in Kaegan's voice. It was a protective edge. "Do you think you have to protect her from me, Kaegan?"

Silence hung suspended between them for a few seconds and then Kaegan shook his head. "No. It's just that she's been through a lot."

"In the past?"

"That, too, but closer to the present as well. She and her husband divorced a month ago, although they've been separated for over a year. I heard he was a real bastard. Cheated on her with another woman."

Sawyer nodded. No wonder she was so accusing. Had she smelled another woman's scent on her ex-husband like she'd done on him? If that was true then he could see why she'd gotten upset. Now he wished he had known her history. But still, it wasn't like he and Vashti were an item, although they had kissed. Did she think that one kiss gave her territorial rights? "She told you about her husband?"

"Yes. That night of the zoning board meeting when I walked her to her car. I'd heard she'd gotten married but noticed she wasn't wearing a ring. I asked her about it and she told me why." Kaegan's eyes narrowed. "Is your interest in her for real?"

Sawyer met his gaze. "Depends on what you mean by *for real*. I don't ever intend to marry again, Kaegan, if that's what you want to know. My prime goal is to get Jade through school and into college. After that then I'll even consider retirement as a sheriff."

Kaegan smiled. "You want to play the role of grand-daddy full-time then?"

"Let's not rush things with Jade please. It's a chore getting her through high school. I don't want to think beyond college, especially to marriage."

"It's going to happen one day, so you better be pre-pared, Sawyer. You're going to need a life. Would you want to be alone?"

Sawyer decided not to answer that because it was pretty much what Leesa had said. Whenever he thought of the future his daughter was a key element. "Would you want to be alone? I don't see you dating anyone around here seriously."

At that moment Bryce came from out back. Evidently she was helping her parents out today with the lunch hour weekend crowd. He watched as Kaegan looked at her with the same intensity in his gaze as the night of the party. And before Bryce could detect she was being watched, Kaegan glanced back over at Sawyer and said, "No, I don't date anyone around here seriously. At least not anymore."

ON SATURDAY EVENING Vashti had come home from the gym and was about to take a shower when her phone rang. She didn't recognize the number, but she knew the area code. The call was coming from Catalina Cove.

She clicked on. "Hello?"

"Ms. Alcindor, this is Reid Lacroix. Thanks for taking my call."

Vashti sat down at her kitchen table. "Yes, Mr. Lacroix? Is there a reason you wanted to talk to me?"

No need to beat around the bush. And of course, there was a reason. Otherwise, why would he be calling? Did Julius tell his parents about them before he died?

"Yes, there is. I plan to be in New York in two weeks on business. Is it possible for us to meet for lunch? I'd rather not discuss anything over the phone." He sounded unsure of himself, and that was unlike Reid Lacroix.

And she'd rather not discuss anything at all. If he had to say what she thought he had to say, then it was better left unsaid. What happened between her and his son was sixteen years ago. Julius had shown her that although it had been love on her part, it hadn't been on his.

"Ms. Alcindor?"

When he said her name she realized she hadn't responded to him. She wanted to say no, that she preferred if they didn't meet for lunch or for any other meal. That she saw no reason why they should. However, she knew if she went that way, there would never be closure. She would always wonder why he'd wanted to meet with her. What he had to say.

"Yes, Mr. Lacroix. I'll meet with you for lunch."

"Good." He sounded relieved. She could only hope that's how she felt after they met.

## CHAPTER THIRTEEN

"You're leaving, Nana?" Kia asked her grandmother who'd just announced at the dinner table she was going back to her home in Philadelphia next week.

Gloria Harris smiled at her granddaughter. "I have my home in Philly, Kia. I need to go there and check on it. I've been here for two months and it's time for me to go home."

"But Gramps is not there," Kia said in a sad voice. She missed her grandfather and found it hard to believe he was gone, although it had been two years.

"I know, sweetie, and it's been hard but I've accepted that as my new normal."

Kia wasn't sure she could accept it as her new normal. Other than her father, Gramps had been the most important male in her life. She always looked forward to spending the summers with her grandparents, and Gramps had been so cool.

"You sound like your grandmother won't come back to visit us," Percelli Harris said to his daughter as he cut into his pork chop.

Kia glanced over at her father. "I know, Dad, but…"

"But what?" Alma Harris asked her daughter.

"Nothing. I'm just going to miss her."

Gloria reached out and took her granddaughter's

hand. "And I will miss you. But remember, we have our trip to Barcelona in July. I can't wait to tour Spain."

Kia couldn't wait either and the thought made her smile. She had taken another Spanish class to be ready for it. It would be the first trip abroad she and her grandmother would take without Gramps. She intended to make it fun and wondered if she was the only one who noticed how sad her grandmother looked around the eyes.

Hours later as Kia was getting ready for bed she felt a pain in her stomach. It was different than the cramps she got every month, sharper. Drawing in a deep breath she sat on the side of her bed. This wasn't the first time this had happened. It happened last weekend, but it went away, like it was doing now.

Easing into bed she wondered if she should mention it to her mom, but quickly dismissed the idea. The first thing her mother would do would be to haul her to the doctor and she hated being seen by doctors. There were too many things going on in her life to be sick, especially with majorette camp around the corner. Now that she'd made the majorette squad, a number of the older girls had promised to help her perfect the dance routines and she couldn't miss out on that.

She rested on her side and hoped the pain in her stomach wouldn't come back.

"DON'T GET ANY crazy ideas," Vashti muttered to herself as she lay on her back in bed and gazed up at the ceiling. By rights she should be concerned with what Reid Lacroix wanted to meet with her about next week. Instead she was thinking of Sawyer Grisham. If she was honest with herself, she would admit to thinking about him all day, all weekend. Quite a lot since seeing him last and engaging in their one and only kiss that she couldn't forget.

On top of that, his parting words were eating at her. Forcing her to not only think about their kiss but what he'd meant by what he'd said. Bryce thought he was letting her know he held her in high regard. Did she care how he held her? What bothered her more than anything was that she was spending time thinking about it, was affected by it. And she knew the only person who could explain his words was him.

She shifted in bed to lie on her side, the way she preferred to sleep. Now she was staring at the wall while thinking of him, remembering how she'd felt when they had kissed. It had been years since she'd gone to bed thinking about a man. Definitely not since her teen years and Julius. During those times her days and nights had been filled with thoughts of them and what she hoped would be their future. She didn't have a future with the sheriff so why was she thinking about him so much?

She tried to think of something else and decided her state of unemployment was something she should be concentrating on. When she'd assumed that she would be ten million dollars richer, she hadn't much thought about not having a job and not using the skills she'd not only gone to college for, but had worked ten years perfecting. She'd been good at what she did, had received a number of bonuses over the years as employee of the month, had received promotions and raises in a timely manner. Everything had been on point regarding her career goals. Then all of it had come to a screeching halt because of Mr. Nunes's decision to sell his hotels.

Even with that she was sure some other hotel chain would have contacted her by now. The job site that was posting her résumé said it was impressive. But over a month later and still no job offer was a cause to be concerned, although the agency she was using tried assuring her that it wasn't. But she knew her severance package, no matter how generous, could only last for so long. She had some time and had curtailed her spending, but the bottom line was that she needed a job. She wasn't used to spending her time every day doing practically nothing.

She hoped a job opportunity came her way and that it came soon. But what if it didn't? And did she really want to start at the bottom of a company and work her way back up the corporate ladder? What choice did she have? *You could do as Bryce suggested and go back to the cove and reopen your aunt's inn.*

Vashti wished Bryce hadn't planted that seed in her head. More than once since returning home the possibility had flowed through her mind and more than anything, she wished it hadn't.

SAWYER EASED OUT of bed and sat on the side of it. Glancing at the clock he saw it was close to two in the morning. The house was quiet and it should be. It was a school night so Jade had gone to bed long ago. He'd stayed up past eleven to watch his favorite cop show and then he'd gone to bed himself. Now he was awake and thinking about Vashti Alcindor. In fact, he'd just awakened from a dream he'd been having of her, which was probably why his pulse was rapid and he was in an aroused state.

Hell, he wasn't some randy teenager but a thirty-six-year-old man. But that hadn't stopped him from getting an out-of-this-world pleasure kick thinking about her. He needed to cool down since heat was swirling through his blood in a way it had never done before. She had appeared in his dream dressed in a way that had made his imagination go wild.

She'd been wearing a dress that had been so short it had barely covered her thighs, and her long gorgeous legs had been encased in a pair of sexy-strappy high-heel sandals. Her hair had cascaded in a mass of waves over her shoulders. At least he had seen her in that hairstyle, the day he had stopped her for speeding. The first time he had looked into her face.

And tonight in his dream, he had held that very beautiful face between his hands just moments before closing his lips over hers. His tongue coming into play had been automatic. So had hers as they had proceeded to kiss each other with an intense greed like the last time. A greed that filled him with a gigantic sexual need. It was only when he was about to strip her naked had he awakened.

He stood and walked over to the window and glanced out. Maybe it was a good thing his dream had ended when it had. Vashti Alcindor had become his fantasy girl and it seemed she would remain that. Just a fantasy. For a crazy moment last week he'd thought she could be more, thanks to Leesa for putting the idea in his head that a long-distance romance might work for them.

He'd even figured the time Jade was away visiting her godmother in Texas next month during spring break would have been the perfect time to visit New York. But it seemed that was not going to happen. Vashti had let him know that as far as she was concerned, no time was the perfect time. Chances were he wouldn't ever see her again. If that was the case, then why was she constantly on his mind, even during some of the oddest times? How could one kiss do that to a man? There had to be more.

Sawyer knew he had never been a man easily swayed by a beautiful face. It took a lot to capture his interest. There had to be substance in her character and from the little time he had spent with Vashti at Kaegan's party, he'd known there was more to her than met the eye. There had to be a reason he'd been so strongly drawn to her from the first. His attraction to her just wasn't normal. At least with a man like him it wasn't. A man known to hold tight rein on his emotions, except when it came to Jade.

After the pain of losing Johanna he'd been determined that no other woman would be the mainstay of his life, but for a short while Vashti Alcindor, a woman he barely knew, had threatened that decree. So maybe it was a good thing she was gone and their paths wouldn't be crossing again.

Johanna's death had taught him that everything happened for a reason. That had been a hard and bitter pill to swallow but over time, he had. In that same vein he had to believe not getting anything started with Vashti Alcindor was for the best as well.

## CHAPTER FOURTEEN

SAWYER READ OVER the Miller file again. Vaughn Miller lived in Catalina Cove years ago and after college he never returned. Five years ago he was accused of a white-collar crime in which he claimed he was innocent, yet he'd served time but had gotten released after a couple of years for good behavior. Now he wanted to return to the town where he was born. Under normal circumstances Sawyer would not even be looking at a file such as this; however, he'd gotten a call from a friend, a former FBI agent, who knew Miller personally, believed in his innocence and wanted to make Miller's return to the cove as easy as possible. There would be people who were aware that Miller had served time and there were some who wouldn't. Sawyer didn't expect trouble and he couldn't stop people from talking. However, he would make sure the man was treated fairly. One thing he discovered about the people of Catalina Cove was that if they liked you, they liked you. If they didn't like you, then they didn't like you. And if Reid Lacroix liked you, they loved you.

He had closed the file and was putting it in his out tray so Trudy could refile it when the intercom on his desk buzzed. "Yes, Trudy?"

"You have a call, Sheriff. A woman who didn't give her name."

It wasn't Leesa. She would have called his cell number. Could it be Vashti calling him? She didn't have his private number so if she wanted to reach him she would have to call him here. "Put her through."

The moment the connection was made, he said, "This is Sheriff Grisham. May I help you?"

The person did not begin speaking immediately. It was as if she'd taken a pause once she heard his voice. Would she hang up without identifying herself?

He was about to restate his greeting when she said, "Yes."

He raised a brow. "Yes?"

"This is Vashti and yes, you can visit me in New York if you still want to, but there is a stipulation."

He drew in a deep breath, imagining he could smell her luscious aroma through the phone. "Name it."

"I want you to explain your actions on the day I left, when you chased me down with the scent of another woman all over you."

He could do that, or at least try. "Okay. I'll try to explain my actions. I'm looking to be up your way in a couple of weeks," he said, knowing he hadn't planned a trip to New York until now. "May I have your number so I can let you know when that will be?" He reached for his cell phone on his desk.

"Yes, you can have my number." She gave it to him and he keyed it into his phone's contact list.

"And I want you to have mine," he said, not waiting for her to ask for it. "I'm sending you a text now so you'll have it. As soon as I know the date, I will call you."

"That's fine. Goodbye, Sawyer."

"Goodbye, Vashti."

He smiled when he hung up the phone. Why was he feeling all cheerful? Hadn't it been just a few nights ago when he'd concluded that not getting involved with her was for the best? That was then and this was now. For the first time in seventeen years he was going out on a date. A real date.

VASHTI CLICKED OFF her phone thinking, yes, she was crazy. Of all the idiotic things she'd ever done, calling Sheriff Grisham probably headed the list. However, it was either that or endure more sleepless nights.

Why was she allowing herself to get pulled into anything related to Catalina Cove? She and Reid Lacroix would be meeting for lunch next week. His secretary had called and everything was set.

The way she figured things would go down, she and Sawyer would meet for dinner and that would be it. She didn't indulge in long-distance romances, no matter how tempting. And the thought would be tempting. The degree of sexual chemistry she shared with Sawyer still boggled her mind. Would it be that way when they saw each other again? If it was, then what?

She was about to go into her kitchen when her phone rang. It was the ringtone she'd given her parents. "Yes, Mom?" She figured it was her mother since her father never initiated a call to her.

"I spoke to Lottie this morning and she said you've been to Catalina Cove. You didn't mention to me or your father that you had plans to go there."

Vashti drew in a deep breath. Lottie Mercer had been her mother's best friend for years. She'd spoken to Lottie at the zoning meeting and figured the older woman would let her mother know she'd seen her. As for telling her parents that she was going to Catalina Cove, it wasn't as if she and her parents talked often. They didn't. If they exchanged calls once every other month that was fine. A part of her wished things were different, but they weren't. It was only when she got older did she accept her parents had a controlling streak. She hadn't been able to do anything about it when she'd been younger, but as an adult she had. Putting distance between them had been a decision she'd made and it ended up being for the best.

"I didn't think it was important. Bryce got an offer for the inn and I went there to meet with the developer."

"You sold it? That's great!"

She could hear the happiness in her mother's voice and truly didn't understand it when that inn had meant the world to her mother's sister. When her parents left Catalina Cove to move away, it was as if they'd expected Aunt Shelby to pack up and move as well. Vashti was convinced it bothered her mother to discover her aunt had a life that didn't cling to them.

"No, I didn't sell it. The zoning board refused to approve what the developers wanted to do with it."

"Which was?"

"To turn it into a tennis resort."

"That's a pity. A tennis resort would have boosted the cove's economy."

"I know but it was their decision," Vashti said, leaning against her sofa table.

"So what do you plan to do now?" her mother asked.

"Nothing. It's back on the market. Bryce will let me know if another offer comes in."

"Then you'll have to go back there to finalize things?"

Vashti frowned. Why was her mother concerned

about her going to the cove? Was she worried that the townspeople would stir up the old scandal about her, which meant their names would get pulled into it since she was their daughter? She could alleviate her mother's fears and tell her how Reid Lacroix had welcomed her back and everyone had followed his lead. Surprisingly, she had enjoyed the short time she'd been there. Seeing the Witherspoons again, seeing Kaegan and Ms. Gertie, although the older woman hadn't recognized her.

"I got to see Ms. Gertie."

"You did what?"

Vashti frowned again. Was she imagining things or did her mother just ask her that in her freaking-out voice? "I said I got to see Ms. Gertie."

"Lottie said she has dementia."

"She does. She didn't even recognize me."

"Then why did you go to see her?"

Vashti honestly thought that was a stupid question. "I went to see her because I've always liked Ms. Gertie and she was always nice to me." She didn't add that the woman had been nice to her when others, including her parents, had acted rather mean. "I'm sure if you ever return to Catalina Cove that you would drop by and see her as well."

"No, I would not. And I did return there for your aunt's memorial, which you didn't attend. I did not drop in to see Gertie. If you recall she was rather upset with me and your father for sending you away. Gertie thought we were slighting her because she was the cove's midwife."

If Ms. Gertie thought that then she was wrong. There was no way her parents would have let her remain in the cove to have her baby, when they'd done all they could to keep it a secret. She hadn't told her parents until she couldn't hide her pregnancy from them anymore.

"Well, I guess I'll let you get back to work."

Vashti knew now would be a good time to tell her parents she was no longer employed, but decided that would be a conversation she would have with them another time. "Thanks, Mom, and it was good hearing from you."

She said that since she rarely did. Whenever she and her parents talked, she usually would be the one to call first.

"Alright and your dad said hello."

She knew her father had said no such thing, but Vashti's response was, "Tell him hello as well."

When she hung up, Vashti thought the people of Catalina Cove had been more gracious than her own parents were to her. No one even brought up her teenage pregnancy, whereas it felt like her mother never missed an opportunity to use it to put her down.

## CHAPTER FIFTEEN

REID LACROIX CHECKED his watch before taking another sip of his coffee. He was early and would admit to looking forward to this trip since his secretary had made the reservations. He just hoped that he would be able to convince Vashti Alcindor to go along with his plan.

He glanced around the establishment. This restaurant was one he usually frequented whenever he was in New York. He recalled the number of times he'd gotten Roberta to join him in New York on his business trips. She would spend the day shopping while he attended his meetings, and then in the evenings they would take in a play or come here to LeBlanc, the French restaurant known for its fine dishes.

He wondered why being here now didn't strike any specific memories. It might be because he intentionally kept himself busy these days so he wouldn't become dependent on the past. Maybe that had been a bad idea to make such a decision because now he'd become a lonely old man heading into his sixties. Losing both his son and wife in the same year had hit hard and was something proving impossible to move beyond.

Trying to get a new lease on life was something he did whenever he came to New York. He would attend the plays and have great meals but since he hadn't been interested in another woman since Roberta, he would attend alone. It was times like these that he often felt hollow inside, which was one of the reasons he hoped Ms. Alcindor would accept his offer. She wasn't a relative per se, but was the woman his son had taken his last breath loving. Julius's death-bed confession had made it clear how much he'd loved her. Although it might sound crazy to some, since she was the woman his one and only son had died loving, that meant a lot to him.

"Reid?"

He glanced up and at first there was no recognition. And then, "Glo?" He smiled as he stood. "Gloria Latham?"

The woman smiled back. "I haven't been called that in years. I got married not long after leaving Yale."

The two of them had been in the same study groups and activities while on campus. "If I recall you were dating a guy name Martin Harris."

"Yes, you have a good memory. Martin and I were married for close to thirty-eight years."

"Were?"

"Yes, Martin died from a heart attack two years ago. What about you? I remember you were dating someone attending Brown University."

"Yes, and you have a good memory as well. She was the former Roberta Ashford. We didn't get married until I finished law school and we were married for close to thirty-two years. Roberta passed away seven years ago from cancer."

"Oh, no, I'm sorry to hear that. You have my condolences."

"Thanks and you have mine. Do you live here in New York?"

"No, Martin and I moved to Philly after we got married. I have friends who live here, and we get together on occasion to go shopping. What about you? I recall you were from a seaside town somewhere in Louisiana."

"Yes, Catalina Cove. I moved back there after law school to take over the running of my family's blueberry plant."

"Hmm, I recall how you would return to school from spring break with blueberries for all of us. They were the best."

He couldn't believe she remembered something like that. "Thanks."

"What about kids?"

Pain suddenly flared in his heart. "Roberta and I had a son but he was killed in a car accident a few months before Roberta passed away."

"Oh no," she said, placing a hand to her upper chest as if she felt his pain. "How awful for you."

"Yes, it was."

"You have my condolences again. Martin and I also had a son. He lives in Sacramento. I just came from visiting with him and his family. I have a beautiful granddaughter but of course I'm biased when it comes to her."

"You have every right to be. Unfortunately, my only grandchild died at birth years ago."

This was the first time he'd ever acknowledged that to anyone. Ever since he'd discovered the child Vashti Alcindor had lost had been his grandchild he'd wanted to claim the child he hadn't known existed. Staking a claim would have caused tongues to wag in Catalina Cove, and he felt the young woman his son had loved but failed had endured enough.

Sympathy shown in Gloria's eyes. He saw it and wished he didn't. "Oh, my goodness, I almost forgot," she said, glancing at her watch. "I'm supposed to meet my friends on the ground floor of Macy's at exactly one o'clock."

He was glad she didn't respond to what he'd said about losing his grandchild on top of everything else. It wasn't his intent to garner anyone's pity, but his life was as it was. He had lost everyone who had meant anything to him. "You only have a few minutes to get there, so you need to be going."

"Yes, I do. I'm so glad I ran into you, Reid. Seeing you brought back pleasant memories."

"I feel the same way, Glo."

"Thanks. Goodbye, Reid."

"Goodbye."

He watched her walk off while thinking she was still a very attractive woman and recalled she'd been Miss Yale in their senior year. She'd been well liked and popular on campus. Everyone had known that Gloria and Martin Harris had been the perfect couple, and she said they'd been married for nearly thirty-eight years. What a blessing.

He was about to sit back down in his chair when his name was called again. This time he turned and came face-to-face with Vashti Alcindor.

EVEN FROM ACROSS the room Vashti had been able to tell Reid Lacroix was a man of wealth. It wasn't just the clothes he wore, although the smooth designer suit and shoes were the sharpest male attire she'd seen in a long time. It had a lot to do with the way he'd been standing. Tall. Ultra-sophisticated with a lot of debonair.

She wondered if Julius would have been a chip off the old block. Probably. However, with her he could be himself and shed some of the rich stuffiness some wealthy people wore. She wanted to believe around her, Julius had been himself.

"Again, I want to thank you for agreeing to see me, Ms. Alcindor," he said, pulling out the chair for her.

"Thank you. I will admit I'm a bit confused as to why you wanted to meet with me, though."

He didn't say anything when a waitress came and opened their table napkins and placed them in their laps, filled their water glasses before handing them both menus. Then she left. It was only then that he looked at her and said, "I want to make you an offer that I hope you will consider."

Vashti raised a brow. "What kind of an offer?"

He smiled at her. "Let's order and we can discuss everything over lunch."

Vashti wondered why everything seemed rather mysterious to her, but she would do as he asked. "I take it you've been here before," she said.

"Yes, several times."

"Then what do you suggest?" she asked him.

"I like their lobster bisque as an appetizer and you can't go wrong with their rib eye."

She nodded. "Okay, Mr. Lacroix, I will take your suggestions."

"And please call me Reid."

She nodded. "Okay and you can call me Vashti."

While eating her steak Vashti tried not to stare across the table at Julius's father, but this was the first time she'd ever been alone with him and the only time she'd been close enough to really study his features. She could see Julius in them. They had the same dark eyes and sculpted jaw. She knew she was looking at what would have been an older Julius had he lived.

At that moment he glanced up and caught her staring. "Sorry. I was thinking how much Julius looked like you."

He smiled and she decided he and Julius shared similar smiles as well. "A lot of people thought so," he said.

She pushed aside her plate and he did as well. "Thanks for lunch, Mr. Lacroix, I mean Reid. Although I enjoyed dining with you, I'm aware you invited me here for a reason. Why?"

Reid Lacroix met her gaze. "It's about Shelby by the Sea."

Vashti should have known. More than likely he had blocked the sale of Shelby from the developers because he wanted the inn for himself. He knew that couldn't happen since it was clearly stated in Hawthorne Barlowe's will when her aunt had inherited the mansion. She didn't know the entire story but when old man Barlowe left his home to her aunt, he had made two stipulations. The Barlowe land could not be sold to any member of the Lacroix family. Evidently at some time in the past there was a disagreement between the Barlowes and Lacroixes that was never resolved. The other stipulation was that although the mansion was known as a historical landmark since it had once been the summer home of President Theodore Roosevelt before it had been sold to the Barlowe family, her aunt could not donate the inn to the historical society. It had to be either sold or passed on to her aunt's offspring or a family member.

"Reid, if you're about to say that you want to purchase the inn, there's no way I can sell it to you. I think you're well aware of that."

"Yes, I'm aware of it, but that's not why I asked to meet with you."

"Then what's the reason?"

"To ask you not to sell Shelby by the Sea. It's your legacy. I'm sure your aunt would not want you to sell it."

Vashti frowned, wondering why he thought he knew what her aunt would have wanted. They may have been neighbors but they didn't run in the same circles. The Lacroixes were the wealthiest family in the cove. She'd made the mistake when she fell in love with Julius to think money didn't matter, but in the end he'd shown her that it did.

"If that was my aunt's desire then she could have easily stated it in her will, but she didn't. Therefore since I inherited the inn, I can do with it what I please."

"Yes, but do you really want to sell it? It's your aunt's legacy…and yours."

Her frown deepened. What made him think he knew so much about her? As if he read the question in her features, he asked, "Did you know your aunt and my wife became friends?"

Vashti looked skeptical. "Aunt Shelby and your wife?"

"Yes."

If this was true then it was news to her. "When?"

"When Roberta discovered she had cancer. Your aunt used to be a nurse and was reputed to know how to mix herbs into a tea that could cure just about anything. Everyone claimed that's why old man Barlowe lived as long as he did, thanks to your aunt. Without even asking her to, Shelby made the tea. Not saying your aunt was a miracle woman, but Roberta did live two years longer than the doctors had given her." He paused a minute and then added, "I'm convinced she would have lived even longer but Julius's death destroyed her will to live. He was her heart."

That was something Vashti knew to be true. Julius loved his mother deeply and she loved him. "So, they became friends. What of it?"

"She told my wife that if anything happened to her that the inn would go to you because she believed you would never sell it, because you loved the inn as much as she did."

Vashti drew in a deep breath. There was a time she had. "Why are you telling me this when you know I have to sell it? It can't just sit there." There was no way she would tell him she didn't have a job and needed the income.

"I'm hoping that you'd consider moving back to Catalina Cove and running it yourself."

Vashti was convinced if she hadn't been sitting firmly in her chair she would have fallen out of it. It was a thought that had been running through her mind lately. Since she didn't have the funds to do such a thing it had merely been a thought. Now she was surprised in addition to Bryce, he'd had a similar idea. "Why would I want to do something like that?" she asked, needing to know why he would suggest such a thing.

"Why wouldn't you? You have a hotel and tourism degree from NYU. That says a lot."

She'd thought the same thing until she'd gotten laid off. And now she couldn't get a job in her chosen field. Not in New York anyway. Competition was fierce. And then there was the issue of her starting salary. She'd been earning six figures at the Grand Nunes Luxury Hotel-Manhattan. The only job offer she'd gotten wanted to start her off with half of what she'd been making.

"I love living in New York and have no reason to give it up to return to Catalina Cove."

Reid didn't say anything but just looked at her with those eyes and with the same expression Julius would when he was about to spring a surprise on her. Julius's surprises had been playful and fun. She had a feeling his father's would not.

He took a sip of his wine and then said, "I would think there's nothing to hold you here any longer since you're no longer employed with the Nunes Hotel Corporation."

FROM THE EXPRESSION on Vashti's face Reid could only assume her unemployment was supposed to have been a closely guarded secret. It was at times like these that Reid wished he wasn't so direct, so matter-of-fact. But he was. Besides, he needed to make sure she fully understood why returning to Catalina Cove and taking over the inn made good sense. He could have easily voted her way at that zoning board meeting. If he had, the other board members would have done so as well, and Vashti would have left Catalina Cove a very rich woman. But he knew money wasn't everything and believed in his heart that Shelby by the Sea was her legacy and it was time she returned to the cove and claimed it.

"How do you know I'm unemployed?"

At least she didn't deny it. "My blueberry plant supplies blueberries for a number of hotels in this city. The Grand Nunes is one of them. I was advised by my sales manager over a month ago that the hotel had changed ownership and that we would have to submit a new bid. It was then I discovered the new owner was letting every top management person go. I knew from talking to Shelby that you were a top employee there."

She lifted a chin. "And what makes you think I haven't found another job?"

He took another sip of his wine. "Have you?"

"No, but what business is it of yours?"

"Because I want to make you an offer about the inn."

"And I told you I can't sell it to you."

He nodded. "That's not the kind of offer I want to make."

He saw the confusion in her features. "What kind of offer are you talking about, Reid?"

He declined the waitress's offer to refill his wine-glass. When she walked off he said, "I need you to keep an open mind at what I'm about to say and consider the possibilities."

"I can't make any promises but I'll try."

He smiled. He could see why his son had fallen in love with her. Although he was certain her attitude had changed a lot over the years, for Julius to love her so long and so deep meant she'd been special to him.

"And that's all I ask." He paused a moment and then he said, "When your aunt Shelby was alive, the inn was one of the most sought out places in Catalina Cove by tourists. It was booked months in advance. I'm aware there has been a decline over recent years. Shelby wouldn't take my advice about using another market-ing strategy to promote the inn and it cost her potential customers. New customers. It's okay that she had the old ones, but in order to grow, the inn needed to attract new ones. She needed to add Wi-Fi to the rooms and offer other amenities."

She nodded. "Yes, I know. She had a magical touch with the place but she refused to move into the new age of media advertising."

"I believe you can have that same touch and at the same time know that the right advertising and marketing plan will work wonders and put the inn back on the map."

He paused a minute then said, "When I suggested that you consider returning to the cove to bring life back to the inn I was deadly serious. You have the perfect experience for it. You used to spend a lot of time there with your aunt so you know what works and what doesn't. And you get the chance to be your own boss. You'll build your own legacy."

"Whoa, what you're suggesting will require a lot of work."

"Are you saying a little work scares you?"

"No. However, there is the issue of what all it will take to get the inn up to snuff. I visited the inn while in town and noticed a lot of repairs are needed and a number of upgrades that need to be done. That will require the use of funds I don't have."

"And that's where I'll step in."

She gazed at him suspiciously. "What do you mean?"

"Because I know repairs are needed to bring the inn not only up to standards but to get it in the digital age, like providing Wi-Fi to every room and also adding a business center, I'm willing to give you a low-interest loan to do whatever you need to do to bring the place up to par."

"Why would you do that?"

"Mainly because it would mean the small businesses in the cove will remain family-owned."

She stared at him for a long moment before asking, "You do have a problem with others moving into the cove and taking over, don't you?"

"Not with everyone. Take Sheriff Grisham for instance. Although we don't always agree on everything, I know he's fallen in love with the town and will do what's right. Besides, it's boring when everybody agrees with me. The sheriff and Kaegan keep me on my toes. Nothing like a good argument every now and then." And he had a feeling if she ever returned to the cove that she would keep him on his toes as well.

"And what happens if something happens to me before the loan is repaid? Does that mean you would expect to take the deed to the inn?"

"No. I will require you to carry an insurance policy that stipulates the balance would be paid in full if anything were to happen to you."

Vashti wasn't sure why she was asking all these questions when she had no intention of doing what he suggested. There was no way she would move to the cove and reopen the inn. But still… "You said it would be a low-interest loan. How low are we talking?"

He quoted her an amount that was simply ridiculous. "You're kidding, right?"

He chuckled. "No. I'm deadly serious. You aren't the only person I've offered such a deal to. I've lured back a number of others. Like Kaegan."

She lifted a brow. "Kaegan?"

"Yes, and I'm only telling you about him because he gave me permission to do so. Before coming here today, I talked to him on the phone and told him about the offer I would make to you. He said to tell you that if you doubted my sincerity or trustworthiness, to give him a call."

Vashti didn't say anything. Although she hadn't asked Kaegan about it, she'd wondered how he could afford all those new boats and where he'd gotten the money to turn his father's floundering business into a profitable one. "Any penalty for early repayment?"

"None."

"I'd basically get the same terms you offered Kaegan?"

She was aware of his long silence before he answered. "No, not quite."

She lifted a brow. Okay something was going on here. She could feel it. "What's going to be different?" she asked in a cool and calm voice.

"Kaegan's contract stipulates that if anything happens to me before the loan is repaid, payments will continue to be paid to my estate." He paused a moment and then said, "I lost my only son and my wife, and since I was an only child, I don't have family. The Lacroix line ends with me."

She felt that same lump in her throat that she always felt when she remembered Julius's death. "I'm sure I'll have to do the same. Continue making payments to your estate."

"You can if you wish, but that won't be necessary."

What he said didn't make sense. "Why not?"

"Because if anything happens to me, Vashti, you become my heir."

## CHAPTER SIXTEEN

VASHTI WAS CERTAIN she misunderstood what Reid Lacroix had said. "Excuse me. Could you repeat that?"

He nodded. "If anything happens to me, you will become my heir."

Vashti's head began spinning. What he said didn't make sense. "Why would you make me your heir? We aren't related." Were they? She hoped not since she'd gotten pregnant from his son. Was that why her baby had died? Had she and Julius been related and not known it. Was she somebody's secret baby? Was she—

"You look like you're about to pass out, Vashti. Whatever reason you're assuming isn't it."

He had no idea what she was assuming. Or did he? "It's not?"

"No. You and Julius were not related."

She let out a deep sigh. For him to tell her that pretty much confirmed her suspicions. He knew. "Why would you make me your heir?"

Instead of answering her, he motioned for the waitress to refill his wineglass and asked Vashti if she would like hers filled as well. Since she had an idea what he was about to tell her, she figured she needed to drink something stronger than iced tea.

After both glasses were filled and the waitress had

left, he said, "Before answering your question, I need to tell you this. Hopefully it will explain a few things."

He took a sip of his wine and then said, "After graduating from high school Julius left for Connecticut to attend Yale. Roberta and I detected something was bothering him but had no idea what. Whenever we asked he would clam up and say it was nothing, but we knew there had to be a reason for him to start acting withdrawn and anti-sociable. It was during college he developed a drinking problem."

She lifted a brow. "A drinking problem?"

"Yes. We hoped it was just a phase he was going through and things would be better when he returned home from college. But things got worse, not better. We tried to get him help but he refused. He erected a wall between him and us. That hurt us deeply because we'd always had a close relationship. Especially him and his mother. Then when Roberta got cancer, his drinking got worse. It was as if he couldn't cope with knowing she had the disease. We didn't even tell him it was terminal, but I believe somehow he knew."

He got silent for a moment and Vashti knew he was trying to keep his emotions in check. It was hard to believe they were talking about the same guy. Julius never drank. Whenever they would steal away and meet in the woods between the two properties, he would bring a picnic basket with sandwiches and sodas. He'd once told her he didn't like the taste of alcohol. When had that changed?

"I will never forget the day I got that call saying he was in that accident. He'd been drinking."

She sucked in a deep breath. She hadn't known that. She would always remember the day Bryce had called and told her about the car accident that had killed Julius. All she'd heard was that he had lost control of his car while driving at a high rate of speed. Nothing had been said about him driving while under the influence. "I didn't know that."

"Nobody did. The accident happened near Shreveport, and he was airlifted there. He wasn't brought to the hospital in Catalina Cove, and I had his medical records sealed."

"Airlifted? I thought he died at the scene."

Reid shook his head. "No. He died at the hospital. In fact I saw him before he died. We were able to talk. That's when he told me."

"Told you what?"

"That he had been the father of your child and the reason he'd started drinking was because he thought he failed you."

Vashti didn't say anything because honestly she'd felt he had failed her, too. He had been the first person she'd told about being pregnant. He had held her. Told her everything would be alright and that he would stick by her side. He'd claimed he had wanted the baby as much as she did. That she didn't have to worry about anything. Then he hadn't shown up at their next secret meeting or the next. When he began avoiding her at school she'd known he was turning his back on her. The pain of his desertion had hurt, but she was determined to not let him know how much. Even when everyone found out about her pregnancy and all but demanded to know the father's identity, Julius had remained in the shadows and not admitted to his part in her pregnancy. Yet she had still loved him.

Vashti met Reid's gaze. "He did what he believed he had to do."

"No," Reid said with strong conviction in his voice. "He failed you like he said. I reached that conclusion after he told me everything. The promises he'd made to you and didn't keep. A part of me feels responsible."

Vashti took a sip of her wine, her throat suddenly dry. "And why do you feel responsible?"

"Because from the time he learned to walk and talk, I instilled in him that he was a Lacroix and what that meant. It was a name to uphold. Pride. Certain standards to live by. And more than anything a scandal-free existence. The latter is the reason he did what he did by putting the sanctity of the family's name above his love for you. You and Julius engaged in a secret love affair and at sixteen you got pregnant. He saw the scandal that would cause. So he kept quiet and eventually guilt began setting in. He couldn't handle letting you down. He loved you."

Anger thickened her throat as she shook her head. "Julius did not love me. A guy who loves a girl would not have let her go through what I went through alone. He couldn't even look at me. Yet that night I went into labor, he was the one I wanted with me. Not strangers and not my parents. I wanted the guy I loved."

Vashti felt tears that threatened to fall from her eyes. After all these years she swore she would not cry again over Julius's treatment of her, yet here she was doing just that. And in front of his father.

"Trust me, Vashti. He died loving you and knowing he'd failed you. I'm convinced that's why he started drinking. The timeline indicates as much. He failed you and I failed him. I failed him by drilling into him the importance of family duty over love. I thought it was perfectly okay for him to one day marry a woman that I chose for him the way my parents chose Roberta for me."

Vashti lifted a brow. "Your parents forced you to marry your wife?" She'd heard of wealthy families having such ideas but to hear him admit such a thing was unexpected.

"I didn't consider it as being forced. I saw it as doing my duty to keep the Lacroix's line moving. Roberta and I were friends and by the time our son was born I had fallen in love with my wife. I was willing to accept that same fate for Julius. I was wrong to do that and I told him that before he died. He gave up on love, happiness and life because of me."

Vashti didn't say anything. Although she didn't know Reid Lacroix she'd known Julius loved his father. She'd always seen him as a man who was wealthy, polite, dignified and coolly controlled. Now she saw him as a man with regrets.

"By the time I got to the hospital Julius knew there was nothing the doctors could do, so with his last breath he made a request of me. He wanted me to tell you, if you ever returned to Catalina Cove and I saw you, that he loved you and that he loved the child the two of you made together. He wanted me to let you know that he did mourn the loss of his child and regretted not being strong enough to stand by your side."

Reid Lacroix got quiet and then he said, "Because of that weakness he went through his own hell that was filled with guilt. That's the reason he'd turned to alcohol. I hadn't known."

Vashti wondered why he was telling her this and

what any of it had to do with him wanting to make her his heir. "I'm sorry, Reid. I loved Julius and I loved our baby as well. Even when my parents tried forcing me to give my child up for adoption, I refused to do so. I intended to raise my baby alone if I had to. Even if it meant leaving Catalina Cove."

She paused a moment and then continued, "I'd figured out everything you told me, except Julius's drinking problem. I hadn't known. And I hadn't known he loved me and wanted our baby. What I had known was that I was not the woman his family would have wanted for him to marry and in the end he'd made a decision about us."

Vashti took a sip of her drink to alleviate the thickness she felt in her throat as a moment of sadness tried overtaking her. Not for the first time she wondered how different things would have been if her child had lived. Had she brought her son back with her, she wondered if her secret would have finally gotten out when he got older and began looking like his father? Or would Julius have denied her child as his son? She glanced at Reid. She was getting to know a side of him that she hadn't before. It was obvious that he was a father who had loved his son. The final analysis was that he believed he had failed him like Julius believed he had failed her.

"Julius died seven years ago. Why are you just telling me this now?" she asked.

He met her gaze. "I had to deal with Roberta's grief. She took Julius's death hard and refused to take any more chemo treatments. I finally got her to start them again but by then it was too late. The cancer had spread and she died less than a year later. Losing both my son and wife within months of each other was hard for me. I underwent grief counseling, and several trips abroad to pull myself together. By the time I did and hired some-one to seek you, I discovered you'd gotten married the week before. I knew what I had to tell you would be the last thing a newlywed wanted to hear so I decided to wait and tell you at another time. And then I heard you'd returned to town for the sale of the inn and that you were now divorced. I knew it would be the oppor-tunity to tell you. Before I got a chance to request a private meeting with you, you'd left the cove. I hadn't figured you would leave so soon."

She nodded. "Honestly, I stayed longer than I had intended. Thanks for keeping your word to Julius and telling me what he'd said, Reid. But that still doesn't explain why you'd want to make me your heir."

He had been looking down, studying the contents of his wine. When he looked back up at her again, his eyes were watery. "I don't have anyone now. My son and my wife are gone. You are the woman my son loved until the moment he died. In fact, your name was the last word off his lips. I see you as the woman my son loved and the woman who carried my grandchild before giving birth to it. It pains me to know I lost my one and only grandchild. A grandchild that would have come from you had it lived. That means a lot to me."

He swallowed once, twice. "Had Julius lived, every-thing I possess would have gone to him. Knowing that, I have no problem leaving it all to the woman he loved. The mother of my grandchild. Losing the baby at birth doesn't matter to me."

It was hard for Vashti to swallow. "I didn't lose the baby at birth."

Reid lifted a brow. "You didn't?"

"No. My baby was born alive. However, he didn't live but a few hours. My parents were there and took care of all the arrangements."

"He?"

"Yes. I gave birth to a boy." Julius hadn't even known he'd had a son because he never asked. When she'd returned to town he avoided her and hadn't asked her anything and she'd reached the conclusion he hadn't wanted to know.

"There were complications during labor and delivery. The doctor explained them to me, but I didn't want to hear anything that he or anyone had to say. All I knew was that I'd lost my child and I grieved for him." There was no need saying that she still grieved for him now, that she thought about him on what would have been his birthday every year. He was buried in a cemetery in Little Rock and she'd gone there several times to visit his grave.

"Did you get to see him? Hold him?"

She shook her head. "No. Because I had a difficult labor and delivery, I don't remember any of it. I recall waking up hours after my delivery and being told that although my child had been born alive he only lived a few hours and eventually died of a collapsed lung."

She watched him pick up his wineglass again to take another sip. She still saw a man filled with regrets. But at that moment she also saw a man filled with loneliness. Although she didn't have a close relationship with her parents, they were still alive, well and living in Pensacola, Florida. Then she had Bryce and Bryce's family who years ago had made her one of their own. But Reid had no one. Why should she care? Because she realized something. Just like she'd been the mother of his grandchild, he was the grandfather of her child. Regardless of whether she was ready to accept it or not, they did have that connection. That bond.

And it was that bond that was inspiring him to make her his heir. He also wanted her to return to Catalina Cove and reopen Shelby by the Sea. Return the inn to being the beautiful place it had once been. Even though her aunt never requested her to do that, a part of Vashti knew she would have wanted that. But it wasn't just the inn that she found significant. Everything he'd told her today was overwhelming, especially what Julius had wanted her to know before he'd died.

"Will you consider returning to Catalina Cove to live and run the inn, Vashti?"

She took a deep breath, knowing she was not ready to give him her answer. Surprised that she would even entertain any thoughts of doing what he'd suggested. "I need time to think about it, Reid."

He nodded. "Alright. Take all the time you need. And just so you know, becoming my heir does not hinge on whether you return to Catalina Cove or not, Vashti. You will become my heir regardless."

# CHAPTER SEVENTEEN

"EVERYTHING IS ALL SET," Erin said. "I got Jade a straight flight from New Orleans to Waco and she will be with me for two weeks for spring break. I can't wait. The boys, Damon and I are excited about her coming. I tried to get three weeks out of her this summer, but she said something about getting a job."

Sawyer shook his head. "That's not a definite. We've talked about it but I'm not sure I want her to work. She'll have plenty of time to do that. I would like her to use her time to volunteer at the hospital again this year."

"And what about that car my goddaughter wants?" Erin asked.

Sawyer smiled. "She'll get one eventually. I'm in no hurry to see her behind the wheel of one. Besides, she just got her license a few months ago."

"I know. They grow up fast."

"Tell me about it. I regret not being here when she was born. I would have been right there in the delivery room with Johanna. I hate she did it alone."

When Erin didn't say anything, Sawyer said, "Erin? You still there?"

"Yes, I'm still here. Sorry about that. Damon stuck his head in the door to let me know he and the boys are going for ice cream," she said. "And Johanna understood why you weren't there. You were in Afghanistan serving our country and could not be with her."

"Glad you were there."

"Thanks. Well, I need to talk to Damon before he leaves and remind him that Lil' Damon can't eat all flavors of ice cream. He and chocolate aren't best buddies."

"And how are Damon and the boys?"

"Fine. Damon has a new toy. A Harley-Davidson. And the boys are growing like weeds. It's hard to believe Lil' Damon is five and Lonnie is three. Damon hints about having a third child. He still wants a daughter."

"Daughters are nice," Sawyer said.

"You don't regret never having a son?"

"No. Although I wanted more children, I knew because of all the problems Johanna had in delivering Jade, she would be our only child."

"Think you'll ever remarry? You're still young."

He chuckled. This seemed to be a theme with the women in his life these days. "No. I have no plans to remarry and father more kids. Jade is my one and only."

When Trudy gave her signature knock on the door, he called out, "Come in."

Then to Erin, he said, "Time to get back to work. I'll let Jade know things are all set for her trip."

"Okay, Sawyer. I will talk to you later."

"Same here. Tell Damon I said hello and I'm going to have to try out that Harley-Davidson when I come get Jade." He would usually drive to Waco and pick her up instead of putting her back on a plane to return home. That way he got to spend time with her on a road trip that usually included returning to their neighborhood in Reno so she could visit with her old friends.

"Will do. Goodbye."

"Goodbye, Erin."

When he clicked off the phone he looked up at Trudy. "I'm leaving for lunch, Sheriff. Rosalyn will be handling things out front until I get back."

He nodded. "Taking a late lunch, aren't you?" It was almost three.

"Yes, but I'm getting my nails done so it works out fine. I'll be back in an hour."

"Okay. I'll see you in an hour."

When Trudy left he picked up the calendar on his desk and marked off the dates Jade would be in Texas. Now that he knew when his daughter would be gone, he could figure out when would be a good time to visit New York. Hopefully whatever dates worked for him would work for Vashti as well.

He stood and walked over to the window and looked out. He couldn't wait to see her again and had stopped resenting his inability to push her to the back of his mind or to not think of her at all. He'd begun accepting that there was a reason he'd been uniquely drawn to her the way he had. And she was also drawn to him, regardless of whether she wanted to be or not. They had acknowledged that attraction between them at Kaegan's party. But even if she hadn't boldly called him out on it, he had known. One of the reasons he'd quickly moved up the ranks in the FBI was his ability to read people. Body language was something he specialized in. People didn't know just how telling it was. For Vashti it had been obvious in the eyes that looked at him and the tilt of her head when she did so. And he knew from the tightening of her lips that last day, the way her forehead had bunched and the way her hands had tightened on her steering wheel that she'd been mad at him and figured she had a reason to be so.

At first, he had rebuffed her anger, thinking she had no right to get mad at him. They didn't have a relationship. However, as the days went by he could understand her anger and felt she deserved an explanation, especially if he wanted to take their association to the next level. The first step was admitting to himself that he did.

It could very well be something he wanted and she didn't, but still he needed to know why he did. There had to be a reason that he was drawn to her in a way he'd never been drawn to another woman since Johanna. Other women had come on to him. Some he'd noticed before they'd noticed him, but other than a fleeting attraction, he had felt nothing. Definitely not the urge to get to know them better, take them out on dates and introduce them to his daughter. Definitely not the latter. That's why he'd been so open to and accepting of the type of affair Leesa had proposed. He hadn't wanted a relationship full of conjectures and wanted to take the guesswork out of it. He and Leesa had known what they wanted and what they hadn't wanted. He'd had rules he didn't intend to bend. So why was he so willing to break his rules now? Why was a woman he'd known only a few days enticing him to do so?

He walked back to his desk and sat down. When he met with Vashti he intended to be honest and open about the extent of his affair with Leesa. If she couldn't get beyond that then he knew he was wasting his time trying to get something going with her. His relationship with Leesa was something he refused to regret and if

Vashti had a problem with what he did before meeting her, then he would move on.

Then there was the issue of Jade. He'd mentioned he had a teenage daughter to her the night of Kaegan's party. She asked a few questions, just the routine cursory questions and comments. He would have to make sure any woman he accepted in his life also accepted his daughter. He wouldn't have it any other way since he would never put anyone before his daughter.

For the first time since Johanna, he knew he could get real serious about a woman and he needed to make sure pursuing her was worth the effort. He picked up his cell phone to call her.

VASHTI SAT ON her rooftop patio and enjoyed the April breeze while thinking about her lunch meeting with Reid Lacroix. What he'd told her had been an emotional drainer and when she'd gotten home she'd gone straight to her bedroom, thrown herself on the bed and had a good cry.

Julius *had* loved her. Now she knew the truth and appreciated Reid for keeping his word to Julius and telling her. If only she'd known. More than once she'd been tempted to reach out to Julius and make him look her in the eye and say he didn't love her. But she never did. Now just like Reid thought he'd failed him, a part of her felt she'd failed Julius as well. And to think he'd become an alcoholic because of the decision to turn his back on her and the baby she carried.

For years after leaving Catalina Cove she had hated him, regretted ever loving him and had called herself all kinds of fool for believing he'd loved her. That was probably why she'd fallen so quickly for Scott. Words of love, and more importantly commitment, had flowed easily from his lips and she'd believed he'd proven his love by asking her to marry him.

However, even that was a lie. The more she thought about it, the more she was convinced that Scott only married her for the convenience of a cover-up. There was a possibility his boss had begun suspecting something was going on between Scott and his wife. She would not have put it past Scott to decide the best thing to do was to get married to deflect that suspicion. Now that Scott was divorced she wondered how that would play out with his boss. She sighed, deciding that was Scott's problem and not hers.

What was her problem was Julius's father's proposal. He wanted to make her his heir, which was an issue within itself. No doubt any other woman would jump at the chance to inherit the Lacroix billions, but she wasn't one of them. Greed had never been a part of her makeup. She earned a living for herself.

She wouldn't lose sleep over Reid's proposal, though. He was lonely, but felt certain that eventually he would get over it. Remarrying wasn't outside the realm of possibility for him and if that were to happen, then he could leave everything to his new wife, his legitimate heir.

What really concerned her was the suggestion he'd made about her moving back to Catalina Cove to reopen Shelby by the Sea. She stood and began pacing around her patio. He had certainly made the offer tempting. Even the low-interest loan. She would call Kaegan later tonight and verify what Reid had told her. As she continued pacing she decided to break down the pros and cons of it. The pros were that yes, she believed she could return the inn to the splendor it once held and make it one of the most sought-after bed-and-breakfasts in the cove. Bookings for weddings and honeymoons had always been full a year or two in advance.

However, that was when her aunt had a full staff that consisted of a full-time cook, a receptionist, a maintenance crew, housekeeping, an accountant and several others who were needed to make the inn run successfully. And Vashti had managed that same type of staff while working for the Grand Nunes. Doing so again for the inn would be a piece of cake.

Another pro was that it would be hers, so working her butt off to make it successful would be to her benefit. Unlike when she worked for Nunes, where all her hard work hadn't helped her keep her job after ten years. Another pro was that her aunt would be proud of her and deep down Reid was right. It would have been something her aunt would have wanted her to do, although she hadn't stipulated as such in her will.

She stopped pacing and drew in a deep, slow breath to curtail the excitement she was beginning to feel. Okay, she would admit that the thought of owning her own business had its perks, but the main question she needed to ask herself was whether she really wanted to leave New York and move back to Catalina Cove after all these years.

She loved New York. Loved the shopping and the Broadway plays. There was so much to do here. However, like she used to tell Bryce, it was a short flight from New Orleans so she could still enjoy those things. But then she also loved the area where she lived, especially her condo. It was costly but while working she could afford it. Without a job, paying for it would take a big chunk out of her savings. She would love to keep it as rental property if she decided to return to Louisiana. That might be a good idea just in case things didn't work out and she failed…

No, she refused to think of failing. She'd never failed at anything. *Except for love.*

She eased back down in her chair, accepting that as the truth. First Julius and then Scott. She had decided after Scott that she had no intentions of ever giving her heart to another man. Heartbreak was a killer and she refused to become a victim for a third time. Deep down a part of her wanted to brush off all the hurt and anger and live again. But this time in a different way. She was never one to engage in meaningless, casual affairs, but now she saw them as viable options to enjoying life again.

She stood and was about to go inside when her cell phone rang. She glanced at the caller ID and felt the pull in her stomach.

Picking up the phone from the table, she said, "Hello?"

"Hi, Vashti."

The deep husky sound of his voice did things to her. Made her legs feel wobbly to the point she sat back down. If he could have this affect on her with the distance separating them, how would it be when they saw each other again? "Hello, Sawyer."

"How are you doing?"

"I'm fine. What about you?"

"Gearing up for the summer. Kids will be out of school soon. They will have way more time on their hands than they'll know what to do with."

"I can imagine. I don't envy you one bit."

"Well, the reason I'm calling is because I know the week I'd be able to visit New York. You can tell me what day will work for you. I know you work every day and I can do a Saturday if you prefer."

Now would be the perfect time to tell him she had changed her mind and he shouldn't come but instead she was clicking on her phone's calendar. "What dates will work for you?" No need to tell him any day would work for her since she didn't have a job.

"What about Friday, two weeks from now? I'd like to take you out to dinner and to a Broadway show."

It sounded like a date and it had been a while since she'd gone on one of those. Even before their divorce when she and Scott had separated, she hadn't dated anyone. "That sounds nice."

"You decide where you want to go for dinner and what play you'd like to see and let me know. We can do dinner first."

She nodded. "Fine and I can meet you at the restaurant."

"Sorry, that won't work for me."

Vashti lifted a brow. "Excuse me? What won't work for you?"

"For us to meet at the restaurant. I prefer picking you up from your home."

"Why?"

"That's just the way I do things."

It was on the tip of her tongue to say tough luck, because that wasn't the way she did things.

"Besides, we need to talk. Remember that stipulation?"

Yes, she remembered it. "I thought we would discuss it over dinner."

"And I prefer that we get it out of the way before dinner."

She thought about that and decided maybe he was right. They should get it out of the way before dinner since there was a possibility, depending on what he said, she might not want to go out with him at all.

"Alright, Sawyer. I will text you my address." And just like that, she had a date.

## CHAPTER EIGHTEEN

SAWYER GLANCED ACROSS the dinner table at Jade. She was quiet and had been all evening. That wasn't like her. "Okay, Jade, what's bothering you?"

"I hate leaving you alone, Dad. I was just wondering what you're going to do those two weeks without me."

He immediately thought of the trip he had planned to New York. "Don't worry about your old man. I'll think of something to do."

She began eating her food again or rather picking around at it. He knew okra and tomatoes and baked chicken were her favorite so that meant something else besides him being lonely while she was gone was on her mind. "Is there anything else we need to talk about, Jade?"

She shrugged her shoulders. "Not sure it's something I have a right to ask you about."

Sawyer lifted a brow. This sounded serious, especially since his daughter knew she could always ask him about anything. "What is it? Go ahead and ask me."

She placed her fork down. "Do you have a girlfriend who lives in New Orleans?"

Of all the things he figured she would ask him, that wasn't it. He wondered how in the world she'd found out about Leesa. "What makes you think that I do?"

She shrugged her shoulders again. "I overheard a group of girls talking in the locker room at school."

Girls' locker room at school? Why would he be the topic of conversation among a bunch of teenage girls? "What were they saying?" he asked, while reaching for the pepper shaker to sprinkle pepper on his chicken.

"They thought I had left already and they were saying the sheriff was hot."

"Hot?"

"Yes, you know. Good to look at. Eye candy and all that. I didn't need them to say it because I know my daddy is handsome."

He would think sixteen-year-old girls would be noticing boys their ages, not a man old enough to be their father. "Thanks, I guess. And what else was said?"

Jade leaned closer toward the table. "Karen Libby is Rachel Libby's niece. Well, she said her aunt wanted you as her boyfriend, but that you already had a girlfriend who lived in New Orleans. Do you, Dad? Do you have a girlfriend who lives in New Orleans?"

First thing Sawyer wondered about was how in the hell Rachel knew his business. Then he knew his daughter deserved an answer but he had to choose his words carefully. Jade was no longer a child. She was a teenager, and to him there was a difference. They'd had in-depth discussions of the birds and the bees, even during times he hadn't wanted to discuss it. But thanks to Leesa's suggestions, he had discussed it with her so she would always feel comfortable coming to him about the topic anytime.

"Yes, I was seeing someone in New Orleans."

Her eyes widened like she'd expected him to deny what that girl had said. "And you never told me?" she all but accused and he saw the hurt look that flared in her eyes.

"The woman I was seeing wasn't my girlfriend. She was just a friend."

"A friend?"

"Yes. She and I met years ago when I first entered the Marines. She was already engaged to someone and I was single and dating around. We were friends. When I moved here I heard she was living in New Orleans and reached out to her on Facebook. I'd heard her husband had gotten killed in a car accident a few years ago and wanted to extend my condolences. Like me, she hadn't started officially dating again and wasn't ready to do so. We discovered we had a lot in common and decided to meet up for dinner and a movie every once in a while. She has a thirteen-year-old son who keeps her busy since he's active in a lot of sports in school."

What he'd just told her was the truth. In the beginning he and Leesa had just met up for dinner and a movie. "Leesa is a nice person but not anyone I'd ever get serious about. Like I said, I just consider her a friend and vice versa." He then picked up his glass to finish drinking his tea.

"So the two of you are friends with benefits?"

*What the hell!* Sawyer nearly choked on the liquid that went down his throat the wrong way. Jade had quickly gotten out of the chair to give him a hard whack on his back. He held up his hand to stop her from hitting him again. "Are you trying to kill me?" he asked, catching his breath and clearing his throat.

"No. I thought you were choking."

"I wasn't. I'm fine," he said, seeing the stricken look

of panic on her face. "Honestly, Jade. I'm fine," he said, picking up his tea to take a small sip.

When she went back to sit in her chair, he asked, "And just what do you know about friends with benefits, young lady?"

She rolled her eyes. "Daddy, pleeze. I am not a child."

He frowned. It was okay if he thought that, but she had no right to do so. "Just answer my question," he said in a stern voice.

"I read about it."

*She'd read about friends with benefits?* "When? How?"

"Romance novels."

He was sure his mouth dropped open. "Romance novels?"

"Yes." And she picked up her fork to begin eating again.

If she thought that was the end of it, then she was wrong. "What are you doing with romance novels?"

"Reading them."

She was trying his patience and he wondered if it was intentional. "What time do you have to read romance novels and where are you getting them from?"

Before she was picking around at her food, but now she was eating in earnest like she was starving. "I read a little every night before going to bed. You know, to clear my mind of math, science and all that stuff."

He hadn't known that and as far as he was concerned "all that stuff" was the only thing she needed consuming her mind. He didn't recall the last time he'd gone into her bedroom. She kept her room tidy and that was all that mattered. He'd had no reason to suspect she had romance novels somewhere in there. "You haven't said just where these novels are coming from."

"Oh. We get them from Karen Libby. Her aunt Rachel reads them all the time. Then she passes them on to Karen. Karen brings us a big grocery bag full each month and we split them up. When we're finished, we rotate them around."

"We? Who are *we*?"

"Hmm, just me and four other girls. There are five of us in our reading club."

*A reading club consisting of teenage girls reading romance novels?* Now he'd heard everything. "Why do you feel the need to read those books? You aren't even dating yet."

"I know but I will be. I guess you can say I'm curious about relationships. The romance novels show me how women should be treated."

*Women?* She was just a kid. "Do you think reading those books is a good idea, Jade?"

She smiled. "Yes. So far I've turned down three guys who asked me out."

*Asked her out? Who told her she could even go out?* "Why?"

"Because they acted like jerks. Behaving as if for them to ask me out was an honor. From this particular romance novel I've been reading it shows that if a girl thinks she's worth a guy's attention and respect, then don't jump for the first one who comes along."

Smart advice, Sawyer thought. But he knew what else was in those novels. "What about the sex scenes in those books?"

At least she had the decency to blush. "Oh those. They are okay. Interesting but nothing I'm ready to indulge in yet. I plan to wait until I have a ring on my finger."

He was glad to hear that. A wedding ring he hoped. "Good for you."

"I like reading about the romance stuff," Jade added. "I like the guys who bring the lady flowers. Take her to dinner. Open her door. Take off his jacket and wrap it around her shoulders when it gets cold."

She took a sip of her iced tea. "So, are you and your *friend* still seeing each other?"

"No."

"Why not?"

"We're just not," he said with no intentions of elaborating.

"Well, I hope that doesn't mean Karen Libby's aunt has a chance with you now. Ms. Rachel is a lot older than you, and I've heard some not-so-nice things about her."

He'd heard some not-so-nice things about Rachel himself. "You can't believe everything you hear, Jade."

"I know, but the first time I saw her when I went into her drugstore, she wasn't nice. She acted like she thought I'd pick up something and leave without paying for it. Then weeks later when she found out I was your daughter, she began acting extra nice to me. Now I know why. It's because she wants you."

He frowned. "She wants me?"

Jade smiled. "Yes, to be a friend with benefits."

He didn't like the way this discussion was going and decided it was best they ended it. He stood to take his plate to the kitchen. "Rest assured that won't be happening."

"Well, Bryce, there you have it."

Vashti had just finished telling her best friend the nature of Reid Lacroix's luncheon meeting with her. She had shared everything he'd said, including his wanting to make her his heir. She'd included that she had spoken to Kaegan earlier and he had verified what Reid had told her about the low-interest loan and that it had been a blessing for his company.

"Just think of all the money you'll get being his heir."

Vashti shook her head. "I'm thinking he'll eventually remarry one day. Maybe a young woman and he can start another family."

"Possibly, but I doubt it. I heard Rachel Libby tried to get his attention."

Vashti wondered if there was any eligible man in town that Ms. Libby hadn't gone after. "I can't see the two of them together."

"Me either. At least now you have confirmation that he's privy to your secret."

"Yes. I just wished I'd known what Julius was going through."

"No guilt trips, Vash. I still think he should have manned up and stood by you regardless of how he thought his parents would handle it. You didn't make that baby by yourself."

Vashti knew that Julius's actions toward her had been a sore spot with Bryce for years. It had been with Kaegan as well, although she'd never revealed the identity of her baby's father to him. It didn't matter. He hadn't liked that she'd gone through that alone. A lot of people hadn't thought she'd done the right thing by protecting the baby's father.

"I guess the huge question, Vash, is whether you

would consider moving back here," Bryce said, interrupting her thoughts. "I suggested the same thing to you, and I'm glad others think it's a great idea as well. You can be your own boss and can bring back Shelby in the way your aunt would have wanted. Why not take all your training, talent and experience and build a business for yourself?"

Vashti would admit on that day she'd visited Shelby by the Sea, she'd felt a longing, an even deeper affection than before. She knew where she would make improvements to bring the place up to snuff, and Reid Lacroix was right when he mentioned the right marketing plan would be key. Shelby by the Sea could be known internationally.

"Are you considering it, Vash?"

She drew in a deep breath. "Yes. I'll even admit I'd thought about it since you first planted the idea in my head, but the issue of funds always brought me back to reality. Mr. Lacroix's offer handles that concern now. I admit the thought of leaving New York bothers me, but you are so right about everything I could accomplish with Shelby by the Sea. And you're there. Your family. Kaegan. People I love and trust." Her thoughts shifted to Sheriff Sawyer Grisham. He was there as well. Could she handle living in the same town as a man she thought was desire personified? A man she discovered could arouse her as no other man could? She would admit that. Vashti would also admit she was having second thoughts about his coming to New York and spending any amount of time with her.

"I also talked to Sawyer today," she finally said. "He's coming to New York in two weeks."

"The two of you are going out on a date?" Bryce asked with excitement in her voice.

"We're doing dinner and a play. But first he has to explain about the other woman."

"You do know that he really doesn't owe you an explanation, Vash? It wasn't like the two of you were seeing each other and he did something behind your back or anything."

"That's true, but I still want to know why a man would do something like that, Bryce."

"Well, now you will get your chance to ask him."

## CHAPTER NINETEEN

IT WAS HARD to believe the day had arrived when Sawyer was coming to New York. Bryce had told her school got out last week and she'd heard that he put his daughter on a plane to visit her godmother in Waco, Texas—for two weeks.

She glanced over at the clock. If Sawyer was on time, he would be arriving in less than thirty minutes. She had texted him last week to let him know her choice of restaurant and Broadway play. He had texted her back a day later to say reservations to both had been made.

Vashti drew in a deep breath. It hadn't been an easy decision, but she'd decided to move back to Catalina Cove. It had taken a lot of soul-searching, not to mention a real serious look at her bank account.

The thought of being a CEO appealed to her and once Mr. Lacroix had planted that seed it had taken root. The only people she'd told of her decision were Bryce and Kaegan. Both were happy that she was returning to the cove. Already her and Lacroix's attorneys were working on the terms of the contract. Terms that even her attorney had stated were too good to be true.

Vashti finished getting ready, and a short while later her doorbell rang and she checked her appearance in the full-length mirror one last time. She'd decided to wear the blue pencil skirt and flowered peasant blouse she'd purchased while shopping a few months ago. The saleslady had given her all kinds of compliments about how she looked in them and she would agree that the outfit did enhance her figure somewhat.

She nibbled at her bottom lip as she headed for the door. Just knowing it was Sawyer had her nerves dancing all over the place. When she reached the door she drew in a deep breath before glancing out her peephole to make sure it was him. As if the law enforcement officer in him expected her to take such precautions, he stared at the peephole. The moment their gazes connected her entire insides lit up like a Christmas tree. Why did the man have to look so yummy?

Drawing in another deep breath she opened the door and there he stood, looking sexier than the last time she'd seen him. He was dressed in a pair of dark dress slacks and a white shirt. His look radiated power she wasn't prepared for. Sensual power, she thought, as her gaze traveled down his chest all the way to the black leather shoes he was wearing. Her gaze traveled back up to his face. "Hello, Sawyer." And because it had been obvious she'd checked him out, she said, "You look nice."

"Hello, Vashti, and so do you."

"Thanks." She stared at his lips when he spoke her name. His mouth had been one of the first things she'd noticed about him that day he'd pulled her over to give her a ticket. He had such a sensual pair of lips.

"Are you going to invite me in or will we have our discussion out here?"

He'd caught her staring again. Little did he know she'd been doing more than just staring. She'd been fantasizing while remembering the highly vivid dreams she'd been having of him. And it was quite obvious the sexual chemistry between them was still there. Sizzling between them and they were both holding it in check. But all she had to do was look into his eyes to feel the heat, see the desire. He was smiling, letting her know his words had been meant to tease. She doubted he knew that his smile could easily arouse her.

"I'm inviting you in," she said stepping back so he could enter.

SAWYER FOUGHT THE pangs of desire that nearly over-whelmed him as he stepped into Vashti's condo. He'd wondered if that strong attraction between them had been nothing more than a fluke. Now he knew that it hadn't. Even before she opened the door, sexual aware-ness had consumed him and had nearly twisted his guts. The first time he'd felt ill equipped to handle the in-tensity of his attraction since nothing like it had ever happened to him before. Now he would accept it as the way things were for them.

He glanced around, liking the layout, design and fur-nishings in her home. She lived on the eighteenth floor and her floor-to-ceiling living room window provided a beautiful view of the Manhattan skyline. An eight-piece stainless steel wall unit provided plenty of cabinet and shelving space as well as a wide platform surface for her huge flat-screen television. The stainless steel accented the appliances in her kitchen. Everything looked mod-ern, including the artwork on the wall. He knew Jade would love the decor since she had a thing for modern furnishing and had several such pieces in her bedroom.

He turned and looked at Vashti. She stood a few feet away while leaning against the closed door. At that moment he thought she looked even better than she had when he'd seen her in Catalina Cove. He doubted that he could eloquently put into words just how good she looked. To him there was nothing sexier than a woman in an outfit that showed her luscious curves. Her hair was piled on top of her head in a twisted bun with a few curly strands dangling along the sides of her face. That particular hairstyle emphasized her oval face. A face with features he thought were perfect.

He shoved his hands into his pockets. Otherwise, he would be tempted to cross the room and touch her. To kiss her. However, until they talked, reached an understanding, he had to refrain from such temptation. "Nice place, Vashti."

"Thank you," she said moving away from the door, and he watched her every movement as his pulse flickered. Whether she was aware of it or not, her sensual aura was so strong it transformed into a feminine power with the ability to overwhelm him.

"You've lived here long?"

"Close to two years. I moved in after separating from my husband. He's my ex now."

"How long have you been divorced?"

"A couple of months. We originally agreed to a clean-cut, no-drama divorce. We would only take what we came into the marriage with. However, when he heard I'd inherited Shelby by the Sea he decided he wanted what he considered as his half. That's when things got ugly."

He was surprised she'd just shared as much as she had. He'd known some of it. At least what Kaegan had shared with him. He appreciated her feeling comfortable enough to tell him the rest.

"Are you ready for us to talk now?" he asked and could tell by her expression she hadn't expected him to immediately dive into anything. He figured there was no reason to put it off. It was either concentrate on something other than the sexual energy flowing in the room or let it consume them.

"Sure. What would you like to drink?"

"Water is fine. I figured we'd have wine at dinner."

She nodded. "A bottled water coming up. I'll be back in a second."

He watched her walk off, feeling heat flow all through his body. Now that he'd seen her again, experienced that effect she had on him, he wasn't sure how he should proceed. Sexual attraction was good but it couldn't be the only thing that held a relationship together.

*Relationship.*

Was that what he wanted to share with her? Was she someone he wanted to spend time with? Obviously, the answer was yes, otherwise, he wouldn't be here. He wanted to get to know her. Spend time with her. Only then could he determine if a serious relationship was possible.

The conversation he'd had with Jade a few weeks ago opened his eyes about a few things. He didn't want his daughter to assume her father was a man who preferred only female friends with benefits. He wanted to set an example for her. A good one.

One thing in his favor was that if he and Vashti continued to see each other after tonight, because she didn't live in the cove and had no plans to relocate there, there really wouldn't be much change in his life in the cove. What he would do was rack up quite a few flying miles.

He much preferred keeping his affairs private and didn't fancy the townsfolk knowing his business. Once he'd thought about it, he decided that a long-distance romance didn't bother him and he would have no problem telling Jade about Vashti. He would even admit the thought of bringing Jade to New York someday to meet Vashti was a pleasant one.

He strolled to the window and looked out. It was a nice view and he figured this kind of view came with a hefty price tag. But then, he was of the mind that you live only once so you might as well enjoy those things in life that made you happy. If you had to work you might as well spend your money on what you wanted to spend it on.

He heard a sound behind him and turned. Vashti had returned and handed him the water bottle. Their hands touched in the process and he felt his pulse throb. "Thanks."

"No problem. Let's sit so I won't have to strain my neck to look up at you."

He smiled. "You are rather short."

"I'm five-eight so I think just the opposite, Sawyer. You're rather tall."

She smiled, and he liked her smile. Taking the cap off the bottle he took a sip. It tasted so refreshing he ended up tilting his head back to drain the entire bottle. When he finished he licked his lips and glanced over at her. She was standing there staring. "Is anything wrong?"

She shook her head. "No. I guess you were pretty thirsty."

He chuckled. "I guess I was."

She eased down on her sectional sofa and he liked

the way she did that. He enjoyed seeing the way her skirt smoothed over her curves and how she looked sitting with her legs crossed. A very nice pair of legs. Following her lead, he sat down in a chair opposite her.

"I meant to ask how was your flight?"

"Uneventful. I watched a movie that took my mind off things."

"I take it like most people you don't like to fly."

"Just the opposite—I love flying. I got used to it while in the Marines and even have my pilot's license. What made me nervous was the age of the pilot. He looked like a schoolkid but I have to hand it to him that he was good at the controls. We had a smooth landing."

She nodded. "How is your daughter?"

"Jade is fine. Thanks for asking."

"I understand school's out for spring break."

"Yes. I put her on a plane a few days ago to spend two weeks in Texas with her godparents. I talked to her this morning and she's enjoying herself as usual. Having a ball."

"That's good. It's important that kids get to enjoy their breaks from school."

She'd said it in a way that made him wonder if perhaps she hadn't enjoyed hers while growing up. "I agree, which is why I usually take a couple weeks off in June to take Jade anywhere she wants to go, within reason. Our father and daughter time." He chuckled. "I scratched Paris, Australia and Johannesburg off the list several times. There's too many places here in the states I want her to see before we start traveling abroad. We have taken a couple of cruises out of the country, though."

"That's good. I could tell when you told me about

her at Kaegan's party that the two of you have a good relationship."

"We do. She's the most important person in my life."

"And she should be. There should never be any question regarding that."

He was glad she felt that way. "So let's talk, Vashti."

She shook her head. "No, you talk, Sawyer, and I will listen. I asked how you could leave another woman's bed and chase after me, and you all but told me to figure it out. Well, I don't want to figure it out. I want you to tell me."

He nodded. Deciding to take the words from his daughter's playbook, he said, "First of all, let's get something straight. I didn't sleep with another woman that day, but she and I had been together for a short while, which is why her scent was on me. All we did was talk. Leesa is a huggy person."

"Leesa?"

"Yes, Leesa." He would give her a first name but there was no reason to give her Leesa's full name. "I think I need to explain Leesa's and my relationship," he said, easing back in the chair.

"She and I met years ago while in boot camp and became nothing more than friends. She was already engaged to marry a guy, another marine, and I was just getting a taste of freedom. I joined the Marines the day after graduating from high school.

"After moving to the cove, I discovered Leesa lived close by in New Orleans and that like me, she had lost her spouse. He was killed in a car accident. I reached out to her on Facebook and we arranged to have dinner together, to catch up on old times. For us it wasn't a date. Just dinner with an old friend. She's always been someone easy to talk to and we discovered after several more planned dinners that we had a lot in common. We were two people who were trying to cope with the loss of our spouses and weren't ready for any type of serious relationship. However, we were two people who had sexual needs. By mutual consent we decided to become—"

"Friends with benefits."

He blinked. She'd defined his relationship with Leesa the same way Jade had. "Yes, friends with benefits. It worked out for us. She has a thirteen-year old son and I have a sixteen-year-old daughter. I've been able to help her through the growing pains of raising a son without a man around and she's helped me understand the ins and outs of having a teenage daughter. Our *friends with benefits* relationship worked.

"Then I met you and there was something about you that I couldn't explain. You even asked me that night at Kaegan's cookout what was going on between us, and I hadn't a clue. All I knew was that for the first time since losing my wife, I desired a woman."

"I'm sure you desired Leesa."

He shook his head. "Not in the same way. There are different levels of desire. My relationship with Leesa was about fulfilling a physical need. The desire and attraction I felt for you was more than physical. I was so confused by the depth of my desire for you that I told Leesa about it."

"You actually told her about me?"

"Yes. Like I said, Leesa and I have that kind of relationship. We discuss things and we help each other figure out things, too. She could tell I wasn't myself and had a lot on my mind. I did. I knew you were leaving the cove that day. Instead of sleeping together, Leesa and I talked. She helped me to realize that I wanted to see you again and suggested I do something about it before it was too late."

"She did?"

"Yes. I was rushing back to the cove hoping to see you and ask if I could visit you in New York."

"So, you left her and came directly after me?"

"Yes, but like I said, Leesa and I didn't sleep together and I rushed back to the cove with her blessings, trust me."

Vashti didn't say anything for a minute and then she asked, "Are you and Leesa still friends with benefits?"

Sawyer shook his head. "No. I haven't seen or talked to her since that day. We both knew when we parted ways it was final."

"Because of me?"

"Because of what I was hoping I could have with you."

She held his gaze. "Which is?"

"The first serious relationship with a woman since Johanna died close to five years ago. You've placed me in a position that I honestly figured I'd never be in, Vashti. You've made me realize something."

"What?"

"That I'm a man with more than just physical needs. I'm also a man who wants to live again and enjoy life."

# CHAPTER TWENTY

*I'M ALSO A man who wants to live again and enjoy life...*

Vashti suddenly felt her throat getting dry at the words Sawyer had just spoken. "I think I need a bottle of water. Do you want another?" she asked, easing off the sofa.

"Yes. I'd love to have another," he said.

What she truly needed at that moment was space. Whether he knew it or not, what he'd just said was similar to how she'd been thinking lately; however with one major difference. He equated living again and enjoying life with building in a serious relationship. Whereas for her, living and enjoying life meant just the opposite. The last thing she wanted was to share a serious relationship with a man.

She walked briskly from the room and entered her kitchen where she released a deep breath. How could she explain to him that she wasn't ready for anything serious and being friends with benefits sounded pretty darn good to her right now? As she opened the refrigerator and grabbed two bottles of water, she had to believe there was a middle ground where they could meet. Because the one thing they did want was each other. It was there when he'd been sitting there talking and looking at her. She'd listened attentively to his words yet she had felt a throbbing need between them. It had evolved from the dark heat she'd seen in his eyes and she was certain he'd seen a similar heat in hers. Every time he looked at her, her body felt warm, aching for his touch. How could any one man stir such physical desire in a woman? A woman who'd never felt such stimulations before? When she'd first met him and experienced the sexual chemistry between them, she thought it totally confusing and irrational. Now she could accept it as sexual energy the two of them could easily generate together. She still found it confusing in some ways, but no longer irrational.

What he'd said about Leesa explained things. She could understand his not wanting to get involved in a serious relationship after his wife died. At the same time, she could accept he was a man with physical needs. He exuded a prominent sexual power she'd never felt from a man before. Her heart skipped a beat just thinking about all that male testosterone being unleashed in her living room.

He'd had the perfect arrangement with this Leesa woman, but because of Vashti he'd walked away, hoping their intense attraction to each other would lead to something more. Unfortunately, she didn't want more. She wasn't ready to be serious about any man.

Returning to the living room she found him standing at the window with his back to her. While she wasn't ready to get serious about any man she could see herself falling for him if she wasn't careful. It could be because he was four years older and more mature. He had a teenage daughter, so he cared about appearances and respect. Julius and Scott had been her age—give or take a few months—and as far as she was concerned, immature. And she'd thought she had loved them both and ended up getting hurt.

"Here you are, Sawyer," she said, getting his attention.

He turned around and the minute their gazes connected a sensuous force ripped through her body. All he had to do was look at her and she burned from the inside out. But then it was easy to see the attraction wasn't one-sided. Staring into his eyes she could see desire that was thick and unrelenting.

He took the bottle and their hands brushed, which only fueled the hungry throb within her. They had another hour before they had to leave for dinner and she felt she needed to do something to curb all the sexual energy flowing in the room.

Unlike before when he drank his water, this time he took a sip as if he needed to savor it. She did so as well.

"Now that I've told you about Leesa, have I cleared my name and character? Do you no longer see me as this horrible person?" he asked, holding her gaze.

"I never saw you as a horrible person, Sawyer. Just another man without scruples."

"Same thing. Just a polite way of saying it."

"You've explained things to me, and I appreciate it. I no longer question your character."

"I'm glad."

It seemed the amount of sexual energy flowing between them was escalating. She moved back to the sofa and sat down to put distance between them as a way of calming the sensual waters they seemed to be floating on. Wanting to get to know him better, she said, "Tell me about your wife, Sawyer."

SAWYER TOOK ANOTHER sip of water to buy some time and collect his thoughts. The only woman he'd ever talked about Johanna to was Leesa. Talking about her to Leesa had helped him appreciate what he'd been given and grieve what had been taken away from him. A part of him didn't want to talk about Johanna, but then he knew he needed to if he wanted to build a relationship with Vashti.

"I met Johanna when I was twenty. I had been in the Marines for two years and had returned home to Waco to bury my foster-dad. I'd been given up for adoption and over my lifetime had been shifted from foster home to foster home. The last couple I was placed with at sixteen had been an elderly childless Christian couple in their sixties, the Fairchilds. They were good people and I was determined to show my gratitude by not getting into trouble. I had only two more years left in school and then I'd planned to join the military. Ms. Edith died the year after I joined the military and a year later Mr. John passed away."

He took another sip of water. "When I came home for Mr. John's funeral, I was surprised to learn he'd left me their home and a number of other belongings. But Mr. John's brother, who he hadn't spoken to in years, blocked my inheritance claiming I shouldn't have a right to anything since I was not a blood relative."

"Did you take him to court?"

"No. I just wanted to attend the services and get the hell out of town. I was a soldier and would eventually earn everything that was being taken away from me. Things I hadn't expected to get anyway. My flight wasn't to leave until the next day so that night I went to a bar to drown my sorrows. Johanna was there working as a waitress. Although she had remembered me from high school I honestly didn't remember her. We talked and I waited until she got off work and invited her back to my hotel room."

"For a one-night stand?" Vashti asked.

"Yes. The next morning I realized the condom had broken and told her to contact me if she got pregnant. She contacted me six weeks later and I came home to marry her."

"A woman you'd had a one-night stand with?"

"Yes. It didn't matter. She was pregnant with my baby and I wanted to do the right thing."

"The honorable thing," Vashti said.

Sawyer wondered if she was thinking about her own pregnancy and how her baby's father hadn't done the right or honorable thing. "During the early years of our marriage both Johanna and I knew why we'd married. It wasn't for love but for a child that hadn't asked to be born. A child that was mine and hers. The love had come later. My love for Johanna had grown from my love of my child. To do the right thing by her. In my mind there was no way to love my child without loving my baby's mother. Some men can separate the two but I couldn't."

Although Sawyer didn't say, he strongly felt one of the reasons he and Johanna got along so well during those first five years of their marriage was because he was gone most of the time. Whenever he came home from fighting battles abroad she provided the welcome he had always needed. She had made him feel loved, important and desired. Things no one had ever made him feel before. Years later, after he'd told her that he loved her for the first time, in a teary confession she had admitted to always loving him. She'd said even in high school, when he hadn't known she existed. That she'd had a crush on him and had loved him from afar. It had touched him that someone had actually loved him during a time in his life when he had felt the most unloved.

"I took military leave so I was able to stay with her during the first four months after our marriage," he said. "I was there when we heard our baby's heartbeat for the first time, and I was there to get her settled into the house I bought with my own money for her and our baby. Then I got orders for a year in Afghanistan."

"You had to leave?"

"Yes. Johanna was almost four months along when I was shipped out, but Johanna sent me pictures. Her best friend stood in as birthing coach in my absence."

"Did you know you were having a girl?"

"No. We didn't want to know. You'll never know how happy I was when she called me overseas to let me know we had a daughter."

He paused a minute and then said, "Although my marriage to Johanna was the result of an unexpected pregnancy, I never regretted marrying her. She was the best wife I could have asked for. She never complained about anything, even when I got out of the Marines and wanted to leave Waco. I got my BA degree while enlisted but wanted my master's. She supported me in doing that as well. I worked during the day as a policeman and attended night classes at the university. Then I applied to be an FBI agent and was assigned to Reno. We'd been married a little over twelve years when she died of cancer. Losing her was hard on me and Jade. She was our rock."

He took another sip of water, feeling both lighter

and heavier after saying all that. "Anything else you want to know?"

She shook her head, her eyes soft. "No." She then glanced at her watch. "It's time for us to leave."

"Okay, but don't think you're getting a pass," he said, standing to his feet.

She did likewise. "What do you mean?"

"I have questions for you."

She lifted a brow. "What kind of questions?"

"About your ex-husband."

"Not much to tell. Scott and I were married for only three years and he was an ass. An unfaithful one. He was sleeping with his boss's wife when we met and continued to sleep with her after we married. I discovered he was having an affair but didn't know with whom. Honestly, at the time I didn't care. All I knew was that the man I loved had betrayed me."

"How did you find out the details of his affair?"

"Not long after I filed for a divorce, Aunt Shelby died. When Scott heard I'd inherited the inn, he got greedy and wanted half of my inheritance. That's when I hired a private detective. By then I figured whomever he was involved with, it was important that he keep her a secret. I just didn't know why. Scott has this high position at a firm on Wall Street and the last thing he wanted was for his boss to find out any details of the affair he'd been having with the man's wife over the past eight years. He only married me for a front and I had all the proof to prove it. I used that as leverage in my divorce. He didn't have a choice but to back off and take nothing from our marriage."

"I'm sorry," Sawyer felt the need to say. He just

couldn't understand a man not being faithful to his wife. "You deserved better."

"Yes, I did. But that's too late now. I'm two and through."

"Two and through?"

"Yes. Scott isn't the only guy I've loved that let me down. Therefore I can't be one and done. I'm two and through."

He figured that guy number one had been the one who'd gotten her pregnant at sixteen and didn't have her back when it counted. Was *two and through* her way of letting him know she didn't want to try again? He hoped she wouldn't give up, believing all men were like the two who'd disappointed her.

He crossed the room to where she stood, fighting the urge to pull her into his arms. "Since I've cleared my name and character, what about repairing our friendship?"

"Repairing our friendship?"

"Yes. Similar to repairing one's relationship."

"And how is that done?"

"Same way. Kiss and make up." He watched her eyes darken and the heat in them nearly seared him. There was no doubt in his mind that she was remembering their last kiss. If she had any idea how she made him feel, just what she did to him, when she looked at him that way, she wouldn't.

"What about a handshake or hug?"

"I'd rather get a kiss. Do you have a problem with that, Vashti?"

No, Vashti thought, she didn't have a problem with it. Nor did she have a problem with the little ball of fire burning in her stomach, or the sexual desire consuming her. Sawyer had the ability to do this. Make her want things she'd never wanted before. At that moment, total awareness was shooting through her and was even in the very air she was breathing.

Sawyer took another step forward and she felt even more heat, and an abundance of chemistry that had intensified to a degree where the muscles in her feminine core tightened. He stood there looking so darn sexy, that there was no way she could deny what he wanted. What they both wanted. "No, I don't have a problem with it."

"Good, because I don't think you have any idea just how much I want to kiss you. I haven't gotten over the last kiss, although I tried to tell myself you were the last person I needed to yearn for. I had a teenage daughter to raise and that was enough."

She was tempted to tell him it should be enough and once she told him of her plans to return to the cove that he had no other choice but to make it enough. There was no way they could become involved when she moved back to Catalina Cove. The reason she'd stayed away from the cove for all these years was because of the scandal she had left behind. She refused to return and start tongues wagging as the sheriff's lover.

"Talk time is over, Sawyer. I'm ready for that kiss." She reached up and wrapped her arms around his neck. Leaning up on tiptoes, she connected her mouth with his.

The way Sawyer all but plunged his tongue inside her mouth told her he was ready for the kiss as well. Immediately, memories of their last kiss, a kiss she hadn't been able to forget, mixed with the reality of this one.

The result was combustion so explosive that she felt ready to detonate.

Sensations she felt in his arms escalated all through her body. Locking her tongue around his rambunctious one fired her blood, made her just as greedy for him as he seemed to be for her.

Like before, he was proving that he was a master at kissing. A man who could give just as good as he could take. A man who knew how to make a woman purr. She was moaning and purring all over the place as he greedily mated with her mouth. He wasn't just kissing her with his mouth—he was kissing her with his entire body by putting everything he had into it.

How could his mouth and tongue be so firm and strong, while his lips felt so gentle? He was reintroducing her to the power of passion and she loved every second. The moment he'd walked into her home he had brought an overload of sexual chemistry with him. She had felt it then and she was feeling it now.

SAWYER'S MIND WAS filled with the thoughts of just how many nights he had dreamed of kissing her again. How many times had he sat in his office daydreaming of having her body pressed so closed to his this way? Her taste was all woman, sexy and delicious all rolled into one. And she was kissing him back in a way that had his stomach rumbling in need.

He had convinced himself that their last kiss hadn't been as captivating as he remembered, but now he saw that it had been. He also saw this kiss was just as hot and invigorating—everything he had imagined it would be again and more. When she broke off the kiss he released a moan of protest deep in his throat. He missed her mouth already.

"I think we need to get out of here before we get into trouble," she whispered against his moist lips.

"I know you're right, but I don't want to stop yet," he said, taking his tongue and licking around her lips.

"You're not playing fair. You're a cop. Where's your sense of honor?"

He chuckled. "I left it in Catalina Cove."

"Hmm, are you trying to tell me you're going to be a badass in New York?"

"I'll let you decide."

He took her hand and led her toward the door.

# CHAPTER TWENTY-ONE

"I HOPE YOU enjoyed yourself tonight."

Vashti glanced up at the man walking by her side and smiled. "I did." And she truly had. Dinner had been wonderful and the Broadway play awesome. Over dinner he'd told her about his life in the Marines and as an FBI agent.

When he'd asked her about her job, she finally told him the truth about her unemployment status. He tried bolstering her spirits by saying he was certain another job would come up and then told her about his anxiety after making the decision to accept the sheriff's job in the cove. It meant leaving a career job with the FBI and Jade leaving her friends.

With the kiss they'd shared before leaving for dinner, it was no surprise that the sexual chemistry between them was still in full force. She was convinced even inhaling his scent was a turn-on for her.

"What are your plans for tomorrow?" he asked when they reached her door.

"I don't have any. Why?"

"I've never been to Coney Island and figured it might be somewhere I'd want to take Jade this summer. I was wondering if you'd like to go there with me tomorrow when I check it out."

She smiled. "Jade would love Coney Island. It's such

a nice place." She paused a moment and said, "I'd love to go to Coney Island with you."

"Great. You mentioned on the drive back here that you had something to tell me."

Yes, she needed to tell him of her decision to move back to Catalina Cove. "Yes, I have something to tell you."

After she opened the door, he followed her in. As soon as she closed the door behind him, hot sparks of desire seemed to bounce off every wall in her condo, filling the space with raw carnal energy. Even the sound of the heels of her shoes on the tile floor didn't break the aura.

"Would you like something to drink or do you prefer water again?" she asked, needing to give them space. Hopefully by the time she returned from the kitchen things would have cooled down.

"I'll take a beer if you have one."

"I do. One cold beer coming up."

She'd turned to walk off when he reached out and touched her shoulder. At the feel of him touching her, desire clawed at her. After drawing in a sharp breath, she turned back to him. "Yes? What's wrong? Want something else?"

"No, nothing is wrong. And yes, I want something else."

Vashti knew Sawyer didn't have to tell her what that something else was. The need and desire were there in his eyes for her to see and for her to feel. If only she didn't see him as a very sexy, very handsome man. Granted, he was only four years older, but already he'd shown her that he had more maturity in his little finger than Scott had in his entire body.

And he'd definitely been more responsible than Julius. When Sawyer had found out he'd gotten a woman pregnant, a woman who'd been a one-night stand and not even a girlfriend, he hadn't hesitated to give her and their child his name. Something Julius hadn't done. Okay, he might have loved her but he hadn't shown her that love when it counted. When she and her baby had needed it. His father had been right when he said Julius had been weak. It didn't matter to Vashti the reason behind his weakness, all she knew was that weakness had let her down.

Standing before her was a strong man. He would be any woman's hero. Too bad they hadn't met when she'd been wearing rose-colored glasses. He would have been a good husband. The best. And she would have been a good wife. Funny how things turned out. Unlucky in love. Some parts of their lives had to deal with crushing blows. Whereas Sawyer was willing to throw his hat back into the ring, she wasn't.

"Aren't you going to ask me what I want, Vashti?"

His question invaded her thoughts and she smiled up at him. "Don't have to. I feel you."

"You feel me?"

She inched closer to him, intentionally letting his aroused body press against her. His erection was so thick, hard and solid, it was poking her between the legs. A kiss wouldn't be enough tonight and the big question was whether she was ready to make such a move. Yes, she was, but first she needed to tell him about her decision to move back to the cove.

"Yes, I definitely feel you, but I need to tell you something."

"Hmm," he said, wrapping his arms around her waist and bringing her body even closer to his and his mouth barely inches from hers. He leaned in and brushed his lips against hers. "I suggest we talk later."

"I suggest we talk now," she said, knowing what she told him might change his mind about taking things further. But then maybe not if he could see anything they shared tonight as one and done. Could he? Could she?

"Do you?" he asked, exerting more seductive pressure on the kisses he was placing on her mouth.

"Yes," she said in a shaky voice. Didn't she? When he began exploiting her mouth for all it was worth with the tip of his tongue, she became dizzy in lust. She closed her eyes and moaned when suddenly he began gently sucking her lower lip. Sawyer was too much of an expert kisser and she was putty in his arms.

"Yes?" he asked, as he continued to make love to her mouth. If he was this thorough with her lips she could just imagine, if given the chance, how he would make love to her body.

When she didn't answer, or open her eyes, he said, "Tell me what you want, sweetheart."

That one word of endearment made her open her eyes and she stared into the dark chocolate ones looking at her. She couldn't remember a time any man had called her sweetheart. Scott might have called her baby once or twice, but never sweetheart. She had truly never been any man's sweetheart. In a way she knew she wasn't even Sawyer's. But still…

"I want you, Sawyer." The words flowed easily from her lips as she stared into his eyes. "I want you."

As if her words unleashed some degree of passion he'd been holding back, he suddenly captured her mouth in a kiss that made her head spin. And then he proceeded to make love to her mouth in a way that had bone-melting fire spreading through her. Never had she been kissed so thoroughly and possessively before.

Then there were his hands that he was using to touch her everywhere, as if to make sure she was really here, and not a figment of his imagination. She wasn't and to make sure he knew it, she began touching him as well, loving the feel of his muscled shoulders beneath her hands.

Suddenly, she felt herself being lifted in his arms and she didn't have to ask where he was carrying her. She knew and as far as she was concerned, he wasn't getting there fast enough to suit her.

As Sawyer placed Vashti on the bed, he was convinced he'd never wanted a woman like he wanted her. In no way did that take away from anything he'd shared with Johanna. He merely assumed the reason he felt this way was because he was older and his desire level had changed or something. He wasn't sure. All he knew was that he did.

He quickly began unbuttoning his shirt and saw she was easing her blouse over her head. He was glad that she decided whatever she had to tell him could wait. This was what they both wanted and needed now. There would be time to talk later.

"You're slacking, Sheriff."

He tossed his shirt to land on a chair in her room and glanced over at her and paused. She was sitting in the middle of her bed naked. Totally naked. And she looked absolutely gorgeous. Her beauty literally took his breath away. He swallowed hard before asking, "Am I?"

She smiled. "What do you think? I'm naked and you're not."

"That can be remedied," he said, easing his slacks down his thighs. Followed by his briefs.

"Wow! You are definitely packing."

He threw his head back and laughed. No woman had ever complimented him on his penis size before. "Thanks."

He pulled a condom packet out of his wallet and tossed it on the bed. "You only have one?" she asked grinning.

He grinned back. "No. Will I need more than one?"

She shrugged a pair of beautiful naked shoulders. "Possibly. It's been a while for me. Although Scott and I had been separated for only a year, we stopped sleeping together a year before that. Unlike you, I didn't have a friend with benefits."

He studied her to see if resentment was in her words and didn't see any. She had accepted his explanation as to the nature of his relationship with Leesa and he appreciated that. "I hope I have a sufficient supply."

"If not, I have you covered. No pun intended."

"You do?"

"Yes. For a quick minute after my divorce I decided to become the liberated woman and bought some to be on the safe side, to complement my own form of birth control. There's nothing like extra protection. I guess you can say I learned from my mistakes."

She hadn't yet told him about her teenage pregnancy, but he suspected that's what her words referred to. Why it was important that she told him herself, he wasn't sure. But it was, so he would wait.

VASHTI WASN'T SURE why she almost mentioned her pregnancy. She would tell him, but right now, the passion burning between them was in control. He leaned down and was kissing her in a way that was curling her toes.

When he finally broke off the kiss, he gave her just enough time to draw in a deep breath of air through her lungs and then he was back, slanting his mouth over hers. It seemed his hands were everywhere, stroking, touching, caressing. And when they eased between her legs, she moaned in her throat. He broke off the kiss and before she could stop him, he leaned down and began placing soft, feathery kisses on her belly.

"Sawyer."

And then she felt his tongue, placing provocative licks around her navel. He was building a need within her that had her groaning aloud. And when he began moving his tongue to her inner thighs, she nearly jerked off the bed. It seemed every inch of her body was sensitive to his touch. Especially his mouth.

Vashti wasn't sure what she expected, but it wasn't him settling his mouth between her legs and kissing her there with the same intensity he'd kissed her mouth. She reached down and ran her fingers over his head. Never had she been kissed this way. It was as if Sawyer was making up for all that and using all his mastery to bring her pleasure.

Pressure began building in the area where his tongue was. It was as if her clit was on fire and then suddenly her body exploded in a gigantic orgasm. But he didn't let up until the last spasm left her body. It was only then that he eased up to settle his body over hers. Leaning down he kissed her and she tasted herself on his tongue.

He broke off the kiss at the same time he used his

knee to nudge her legs apart. And then she felt him, taking his time to gently ease inside of her. "Wrap your legs around me, sweetheart."

She did as he requested and as soon as she did so, he began moving, thrusting inside of her, stroking her to a feverish pitch. The sensations overtaking her were so strong, so powerful, she moved her head from right to left while saying words encouraging him to go harder, deeper and not to stop.

He didn't. Picking up the pace his thrusts became harder, more rapid while moving in and out of her. Naked body against a naked body. Skin to skin. Passion to passion. The sensations that had originated between her legs were spreading to other parts of her body, over-loading her senses. She had wrapped her mind around the fact that his magnificent male body was making love to her with an intensity that could become addictive.

That thought should have given her pause. But she didn't have time for an intermission. The only thing she had time for was to go crazy in lust while he satisfied the throb between her legs.

It happened again when she suddenly saw not only stars but the entire friggin' universe. Stars not only aligned—she was convinced the moon even tilted a lit-tle. She screamed out his name and when he screamed hers while pumping fast and furious within her, she knew she had finally gotten a taste of real passion. Pas-sion you could sink your teeth in and then on instinct, as if to brand him, she sank her teeth into his shoulder as another orgasm tore into her.

"Vashti!"

She heard him call her name as his body jerked, jerked again and then jerked some more. He continued to thrust hard into her while it did so and she enjoyed every single moment.

He went after her mouth and she gave it to him, as greedily as she pleased. And later when spasms left their bodies, he leaned up and captured her mouth with his again. The only word she could think to describe what they'd done was *amazing*. Simply amazing.

## CHAPTER TWENTY-TWO

EVEN BEFORE SAWYER opened his eyes, he inhaled the drugging scent of woman. At least one particular woman. Heat infiltrated his body when he slid his eyes open and stared at her, sleeping in his arms. The early-morning sun was shining bright and coming in through her bedroom window and highlighted her features. He wondered if she knew how beautiful she looked, even when asleep.

Glancing over at the clock on her nightstand, he saw it was past eight in the morning. Usually he got up at five, an hour before he had to wake Jade for school. He couldn't recall the last time he'd slept to eight. He was up early even on the weekends.

He glanced back at Vashti and recalled every single detail about last night. Especially how they had driven each other over the edge, time and time again. The magnitude of sexual energy that had flowed between them had made every cell in him erupt with need every time he'd entered her body. Thrust hard into her. Mated nonstop with her. He closed his eyes as more sensual memories flowed through his mind.

It had not been his intent to spend the night but when she'd invited him to stay, he'd been unable to turn her down—hadn't wanted to turn her down. He looked forward to spending the day together at Coney Island. Afterward, dinner and another night with her, this time in his hotel room sounded nice. Yes, he liked the idea of that.

"There better be a good reason you're smiling with your eyes closed."

He lifted his lids to stare into a pair of beautiful brown eyes. "There is. I'm here in this bed with you. We made love last night, quite a few times, and I'm still having aftershocks of pleasure."

She snuggled closer to him. "So am I. Aftershocks. That's unnatural, right?"

"Not sure but I like them," he said, leaning in to place a kiss on her lips. "I hadn't planned for this to happen, Vashti." He felt he needed to tell her that. The last thing he wanted was for her to feel his sole intent for coming to New York had been to sleep with her.

"I know. But…"

"But what?" he asked her, reaching out and circling a strand of her hair around his finger.

"But I guess we couldn't help ourselves. There's this strong sexual chemistry between us. It was there from the beginning. Neither of us has tried to hide it or deny it. If you remember, I approached you about it at Kaegan's cookout."

Yes, she had. "And if you remember, that's the night we shared out first kiss. To see if we could solve the mystery."

A serious expression appeared on her features. "I've thought about that kiss a lot lately."

"Umm, so have I."

"You have?" she asked him, sitting up, and as if for modesty's sake, she carefully tucked part of the bed-covering under her arms. He was tempted to tell her there was no need to do that since he'd seen all of her last night. Had touched her. Tasted her.

"Yes."

She seemed pleased with his admission. "You ready to get up and go grab breakfast before my stomach starts growling?" he asked, tempted to pull the bedcovering away from her. He loved looking at her breasts.

"That sounds like a plan. But first I need to tell you something."

He pulled up in bed beside her, remembering that's the reason she had invited him inside last night. They'd gotten sidetracked. "Whatever you have to tell me must really be important to you."

"It is. Afterward, you might want to renege on us spending time together today."

He chuckled. "Sweetheart, unless you're about to confess to being a foreign spy, serial killer or something guaranteed to get you jail time, there's nothing you can tell me that will make me withdraw my invitation to Coney Island today."

"We'll see."

Now she had him more than a little curious. "Okay, Vashti, what do you have to tell me?"

She didn't say anything for a minute and then she said, "I've decided to move back to Catalina Cove and reopen Shelby by the Sea."

VASHTI STARED AT Sawyer, needing to see every nuance of his features when her words sank in. The room was quiet as he stared back at her. He'd comprehended what she'd said and she figured that now the wheels were turning in his head. She knew his rule about not dating anyone living in the cove, which meant what they shared last night and in the wee hours of this morning were now a no repeat.

She understood and needed to assure him that she was okay with it because she had no intentions of them continuing anything beyond this weekend anyway. Doing so would invite complications they didn't need. However, she had entertained the thought of them becoming friends with benefits, but that would require sneaking around. She'd done that once before in Catalina Cove and didn't plan to do it again.

She was about to suggest that they just enjoy today together and leave it at that, when the smile that suddenly touched his lips stopped her. Surprised, she asked, "Why are you smiling?"

"Because of your good news. I think returning to Catalina Cove and running that inn would be great. I can definitely see you being a success at it. I'm just confused as to why you thought I would renege on my invitation just because you're moving back to the cove."

Vashti thought she was the one confused. "Because I assumed you wouldn't want for us to start something we'd have to end."

Now he looked confused. "Why would we have to end anything just because you're moving back to the cove?"

Vashti couldn't believe he would ask such a thing. "For starters, you have a rule about not dating anyone in town."

"I do?"

"Yes, don't you?"

"No. I never dated anyone in Catalina Cove for a number of reasons. I wasn't ready to date anyone and there wasn't anyone in town I was interested in dating.

And I never wanted townspeople in my business. But now I am ready to date, I'm interested in you and if I have to get anyone out my business, I can do that real fast." He raised a brow. "Evidently you're the one with misgivings about dating someone in town."

Vashti could feel her face get hot. "Well, yes. I'll be busy getting the inn ready to be reopened. Too busy for any involvement."

"If you're concerned about me getting underfoot, Vashti, don't be. I promise that I won't make a pest of myself." He leaned over and kissed her on the lips. "There, you have nothing to worry about." He eased out of bed. "Let's get dressed for breakfast."

Vashti stared at him, not believing the turn their conversation had taken. "Hey, wait."

He glanced at her when he reached for his pants off the back of the chair. "What's wrong?"

"We will not continue seeing each other after I move to Catalina Cove, Sawyer."

He frowned. "Any reason we won't?"

"Yes. You're the sheriff with a teenage daughter. Imagine the scandal if anyone discovers we're sneaking around."

"Sneaking around? We won't be sneaking around. And if you're concerned about Jade, don't be. She's been throwing out hints that I need a girlfriend anyway. I think she's worried that I won't have anyone when she leaves for college in a few years. Excuse me, I need to go to the bathroom. I'll be back in a second."

As soon as he left the bedroom, Vashti got out of bed and quickly slid the caftan she usually wore around the house over her head. Evidently she hadn't made things clear with Sawyer. She had no intentions of them seeing each other once she moved back to the cove. She needed to make him understand why she couldn't risk a scandal.

He walked out of the bathroom and glanced over at her and smiled. "Do you have any extra toiletries? I left my stuff at the hotel."

"Yes, I have extra toiletries, but I don't think you understand."

"About what?"

"Evidently you're under the impression that I want to continue this."

That got his attention. "And you don't?"

"No."

He stared at her. "You want to tell me why?"

"I have told you, but you haven't been listening. You might be ready to live again and enjoy life but I'm not. I tried it. Twice. I have no reason to do it a third time. Not only will I not have time to be involved with you, I don't want to. You and I are just a scandal waiting to happen. I heard that women in the cove want to date you, yet you refuse to date any one of them."

"I told you why."

"Yes, but think how it will look when I return to town and we hook up. They won't like it."

He frowned. "You think I give a royal damn about what they won't like? My life is my life, Vashti. Like I said, I never dated any woman in the cove because I didn't want to. Wasn't interested. That's why I dated Leesa. But I want a different relationship with you than I had with Leesa. I don't want a friend with benefits. I want someone I can have a future with."

"Then I'm not your girl because I'm not interested

in a future with any man. Been there, done that. Twice. Remember I told you two and through, well I meant it."

He looked ready to argue, but she shook her head. "I can't, Sawyer. I left Catalina Cove and stayed away because of a scandal over my head. I'm not returning for another scandal. When I return to the cove it will be for Shelby by the Sea and not for anyone or anything else." She took a deep breath. "When I was sixteen, I got pregnant."

He stilled, but she couldn't gauge his reaction.

"The guy didn't marry me and I lost the baby. My son died an hour after he was born. Complications."

"I'm sorry."

"Thank you. My getting pregnant at sixteen was a mistake but the baby I carried wasn't. I grew to love him."

His face softened when she said that. She knew he'd experienced the same with Jade.

"Of course you would. You were a mother. It was a natural instinct."

"Yes. My parents wanted me to abort and I refused. They wanted me to give my baby up for adoption and I refused that, too. They never forgave me for defying them."

"I'm sure they've gotten over it."

"No, they haven't. Not really."

He didn't say anything as he stood there and looked at her for a long moment. And then he said, "I'm sorry you went through that. But you have nothing to be ashamed of. And I meant what I said. I want a relationship with you. I don't want a friend with benefits. I'm just asking you to try, Vashti. Get to know me and take a chance."

His eyes implored her to say yes. For a second she wanted to.

"I can't, Sawyer."

She then watched as he began dressing, putting on his shirt and buttoning it up. When he was completely dressed, he glanced over at her. "I wish you the best, Vashti. See you around."

He then left.

# *Part 2*

"We must let go of the life we have planned, so as to accept the one that is waiting for us."

—Joseph Campbell

# CHAPTER TWENTY-THREE

*Six weeks later*

"AND YOU HONESTLY think the inn will be ready for occupancy in four months?" Bryce asked, glancing around.

"Sooner I hope," Vashti said, while following Bryce's gaze around the room. All the furniture was covered since the painters would soon start on the inside, now that the outside structure had been pressure washed and painted.

It was hard to believe she'd moved back to the Catalina Cove a few weeks ago and had hit the ground running. One of the first things she did was personally contact members of the staff who'd worked for her aunt to see if they were interested in coming to work for her. Some had found new employment and were happy where they were. A few of them who'd worked at Shelby for years were more than glad to return and she was grateful to have them back.

Instead of hiring an interior decorator, Vashti had brought on Juanita Beckett, the older woman who'd been the cove's seamstress for years. Juanita had been commissioned to make new custom drapes for every window in the inn.

Albert Rogers, one of the town's carpenters, would

do all the woodwork needed. She was excited to restore the inn to the level of stately beauty it had once had.

Before leaving New York she had posted employment opportunities for the inn. By doing that early, she had essentially announced Shelby by the Sea would be reopening for business and who would be running things. She figured any discussion by the townsfolk would take place before she moved back to the cove and would be old news.

It seemed the residents of Catalina Cove were just happy the inn was reopening because it would put some of them to work. Kaegan's company would be supplying all her fresh seafood, Harold's market all the fresh fruits and vegetables, and Linda's Florist would provide all the fresh flowers for the inn's huge foyer.

Other than Bryce and Kaegan, no one knew about the loan from Mr. Lacroix, and she intended to keep it that way. Since hiring a marketing firm for all the promotions, the announcement of the inn's reopening would appear in a number of tourist magazines around the country. She anticipated reservations would start rolling in. Some people had already gotten the word. A number of those were people who had stayed at Shelby before, either on their honeymoon or for a vacation and wanted to return.

Reid Lacroix had been right. Reopening the inn was the best thing she could have done. She had the perfect experience for it, and since she'd spent a lot of time here with Aunt Shelby she knew what worked and what didn't. She also knew how implementing an aggressive marketing campaign could give the inn exposure on an international scale. She enjoyed being her own boss and continuing the legacy her aunt had started.

"Once the painters finish, Mr. Rogers will come in and take care of all the woodwork and repair the cabinets and tables before Ms. Juanita hangs the drapes. So far everything is on schedule," she told Bryce.

Vashti had stayed with Bryce the first week she had returned, just long enough to get the electricity turned on and most of the things she would need to live at the inn operational. She had moved into her aunt's bedroom and being there had brought her a lot of comfort, although she'd felt alone living in the huge house by herself.

"I heard you go visit Ms. Gertie pretty regularly," Bryce said, reclaiming her attention.

"I don't go see her every day, but at least two to three times a week. I'm hoping that one of those days she will recognize me, and if she doesn't that's fine. What's important to me is that I recognize her. I know who she is and what part she played in my life."

Not only had Ms. Gertie stood with Aunt Shelby against her parents when they tried to force Vashti to give her baby up for adoption, but when they said they wouldn't pay any of the baby's delivery fees if she didn't, Ms. Gertie had countered and said in that case, she would deliver Vashti's baby for free. Vashti thought about the last conversation she'd had with her parents, when she'd told them of her decision to move back to the cove and reopen Shelby by the Sea. They'd literally blown a gasket. She couldn't understand why. It was as if they assumed since they no longer lived in Catalina Cove that she had no reason to live there either. She had told them as politely and respectfully as she could that where she decided to live was her decision and not theirs. They hadn't liked that and hadn't talked to her since, although she'd tried calling them. Their behavior, as far as she was concerned, was ridiculous.

She returned her attention to Bryce. "Hey, I got an idea. Let's go to a movie later."

"A movie?" Bryce asked, raising her brow.

"Yes. I have nothing else to do tonight. Do you?"

"No."

"Then let's go. I've been going full speed since moving back and I feel the need to unwind."

Bryce smiled. "Okay, I'll go. I need to unwind as well. I'm going home to shower and change. Let's meet at the theater in a couple of hours."

"WELCOME BACK, SHERIFF. Did you and Jade enjoy your vacation in the mountains?" Deputy Burney Fowler asked as he walked into Sawyer's office.

"Thanks and yes, we did."

"When did you get back in town?"

"Earlier today. I figured I'll get a head start on paperwork after being gone two weeks. Besides, Jade's at a sleepover tonight." No need to add the house seemed empty. Lonely. On top of that, he felt edgy. Horny. He hadn't felt that way in years. Even after Johanna's death, sex hadn't consumed his mind. Trying to make a life without Johanna for Jade had. It was only later when he'd gotten a sexual itch did he and Leesa hook up. Now what he was feeling was more than a damn itch. It was a full-blown ache. And he knew the woman responsible.

It didn't take much to recall his time in New York. It had been one hot night. So hot he still got heated flashes whenever he thought about it. And he'd thought about it a lot. Even though he'd gone to Coney Island without her and had returned to the cove a day earlier than planned, none of that mattered. Nor had it mattered he had been so mad he could have eaten nails. All that mattered was how she'd made him feel when they'd made love.

Now, six weeks later he had a different perspective on things, mainly because he would get madder than hell at how she ended things between them before they could get started. She'd had a lot of nerve saying she hadn't wanted them to continue anything just because she planned to move back to the cove.

When he'd gotten back today, it had taken all his willpower not to drive by Shelby by the Sea. He had eaten dinner at the café and overheard a couple talking at the next table about how excited they were about the inn reopening and Vashti moving back to the cove. They appreciated the fact she was hiring a number of locals instead of outsiders to do most of the work.

Yes, the townsfolk were talking about Vashti, just like she'd predicted. However, what he'd heard was all positive. He had to wonder would it have been if word got out they'd had an affair. Would the townspeople care? She thought so and that's what mattered to her. And as far as those women in town that he refused to date, did she honestly assume he would take them out now? If he hadn't before, why would he now? Nothing had changed.

He tossed a document aside and leaned back in his chair. How could she turn her back on the best love-making there was between two people? People who could generate sexual energy like it was an element of the universe? Did she not understand that degree of passionate power between them wasn't something they could turn on or off at whim?

After leaving her place that morning in New York,

he had discovered it had been more than sex between them on his part. For the first time in almost seventeen years, he had felt something for a woman. What he felt in his gut whenever he saw Vashti, whenever he thought about her, was more than just sexual. He was now convinced more than ever that she was a woman he could fall in love with, share his life with. Unfortunately, a forever kind of love was not what she wanted. She'd made it damn clear she didn't want love of any kind.

Drawing in a deep, frustrated breath he picked the papers on his desk back up, determined to get work done and keep Vashti Alcindor out of his mind.

A NOISE WOKE VASHTI. Jerking upright in bed, she glanced around. She heard it again and knew the sound was just outside her window. When she'd come home from the movies she had checked to make sure all the doors were locked before getting ready for bed. What if someone was outside trying to get in? It didn't help that the movie she'd seen had been a thriller. She *had* heard something.

Catalina Cove had a reputation for low crime, mainly because most people knew each other and worked hard to make the town safe. But what if someone had driven in from someplace else? The inn was on an isolated street and there were no security gates surrounding it. It backed up against the gulf. A trespasser could come by boat just as easily by car.

When she heard the sound again she told herself not to panic as she quickly reached for her cell phone to call 911.

# CHAPTER TWENTY-FOUR

SAWYER HAD BEEN on his way home when he'd heard the call from the dispatcher. *A possible intruder at Shelby by the Sea.* He didn't waste any time radioing in that he would take the call. He'd heard from Kaegan that Vashti had decided to move in while repairs were being done.

He sped through the streets of Catalina Cove with red-and-blue lights flashing. Reaching Buccaneer Lane, he quickly pulled into the long driveway. The large historic mansion turned bed-and-breakfast inn could barely be seen in the pitch-black night. Had Vashti not installed floodlights yet?

Sprinting up to the steps he glanced around as he made his way toward the door. Knocking, he said, "This is Sheriff Grisham of the Catalina Cove Police Department."

The porch light came on the minute she opened the door. His breath automatically caught in his lungs when he saw Vashti standing there in the doorway, captured by the glow of a light from the foyer. The surprise on her face was obvious. "What are you doing here?"

He frowned. "Did you not call for the police?"

"Yes, but I mean…"

He knew what she meant. She was probably wondering why of all the people on the Catalina Cove police force he was the one who got the call. Not that he owed her an explanation, but given the nature of their history, he said, "I was on my way home when I heard the call. I figured I was closer and would take it." What he said was partly true. He would have taken the call regardless.

"I thought you were out of town."

He wondered how she'd heard that. Had she asked about him? If she had, he wondered why when she'd made it clear she hadn't wanted to have anything to do with him when she moved back to the cove. "I just got back today. I'm sure there's a reason you called the police."

She frowned at him. "Of course there's a reason. I heard a noise outside my bedroom window."

He nodded. "Lock the door. I'll check things out."

And then he turned and sprinted back down the steps.

VASHTI RELEASED A deep whoosh of air through her lungs as she closed and locked the door. She hadn't seen Sawyer since moving back. According to Bryce he'd been on a two-week vacation with his daughter. If there had been any doubt in her mind about the masculine power of Sheriff Sawyer Grisham, she'd been reminded when she had opened the door. She had been very aware of his strength, and how good he looked in his police uniform. While looking at him she was vividly aware of six-plus feet of solid muscle—the breadth of heavy shoulders, masculine arms, broad chest and rippling six-pack abs. It didn't help matters that she'd once seen that "make you drool" body naked. And of course she didn't want to remember the time that same body had made love to hers.

She had been unprepared to see him, especially tonight. When she'd been awakened from her sleep she had been dreaming about him. And it was quite obvious the minute she opened the door and saw him that the sexual chemistry between them hadn't dimmed any. The air shimmering around them had been full of it. It was also quite obvious that he was still mad with her for making the decision she had about them.

"You can reopen the door now, Vashti."

His voice broke into her thoughts and she quickly moved toward the door to open it, and then moved aside when he entered. While standing in the lamplight he looked even more impressive, ruggedly handsome and solidly built. He had a body designed purely to pleasure a woman. She of all people should know. "Did you see anything?" she asked him.

"Yes. There were several trash cans knocked down. I saw animal tracks and not that of a human. I believe your intruders were a bunch of raccoons. Do you have any security cameras around this place?"

"No. Aunt Shelby had them for a while but decided to have them removed."

"Why?"

He would have to ask, she thought. "More than once she caught some of the inn's occupants naked on camera after they decided to either go skinny-dipping at night or make out under the stars near the gazebo."

"Oh." He didn't say anything else for a minute and then he cleared his throat and said, "You might want to have the security cameras reinstalled because you do need them. I suggest you give anyone who checks into the inn fair warning that cameras are located around the property."

He was right. The property was too vast and too isolated not to have security cameras. "Do you suggest anything else? In the way of security?" she quickly tacked on. Not wanting him to get the wrong idea about anything.

"Floodlights. This place looked pitch-dark when I pulled up."

"Your vehicle should have triggered the motion lights."

"Well, it didn't," he said, a little too harsh to suit her.

"Fine. I will have them checked."

He rubbed the top of his head and she could tell he was more than a little agitated. She was proven right when he asked, "Why are you staying out here alone?"

Bryce and Kaegan had asked her the same thing. "This is my home now. There's no reason for me not to." She held back from telling him where she decided to stay was no concern of his.

"Aren't repairs being done?"

"Yes, and it makes more sense for me to stay here while they are."

"Just consider those security measures I suggested and if you hear any other sounds, any at all, call the police again."

"I will."

He headed for the door. A part of her wanted to call him back, but she couldn't do that. Her decision not to get involved with him had been made and she refused to go back on it.

He opened the door and glanced back at her. It seemed for the longest moment he stood there staring without saying anything. She felt herself grow warm under his regard. After calling the police, she had quickly changed into a pair of shorts and a top. Could he tell she wasn't wearing bra or panties? She hadn't thought about leaving them off…until now.

"Any more security suggestions, Sheriff?"

His frown lines deepened. "No."

"Then good night."

She watched him draw in a deep breath before saying, "Lock the door behind me and if you think you hear anything again call the police."

He'd told her that already, but she nodded anyway and said, "Okay."

As if he was satisfied she understood, he said, "Good night."

He pulled the door shut behind him and she quickly locked it before moving to the window to peep out. Thanks to the porch lights she could see him stroll toward his car. The man was walking testosterone and embodied everything male. When he backed out of the driveway she moved away from the window wishing she hadn't noticed that. But then the memory of him standing in her living room was just as bad. Sexual tension between them had been an undercurrent they'd both tried keeping at bay and failed. Now she would have to go back to bed and resume her dreams. All about him.

THE MINUTE SAWYER walked into the house he quickly stored his gun before heading to the kitchen for a beer. Although he was still officially on vacation, he had decided to go into the office tomorrow. Otherwise, he would indulge in something stronger than beer. His senses were just that fried.

Grabbing a beer out of the fridge, he popped the tab and took a long gulp. Seeing Vashti tonight was the last thing he needed, but had to admit it had been everything he'd wanted. When he'd first arrived it had taken all his control not to pull her into his arms and assure her that everything was alright.

He had been more relieved than anything to find animal tracks instead of prints made by a human. The thought of anyone doing her harm unnerved him. He took another long gulp at the mere thought.

At least she was open to those security suggestions he'd made. And when she'd explained the reason her aunt had uninstalled those security cameras, a quick image of naked bodies making out under the stars had flashed through his mind. The image of the naked bodies had been theirs.

Finishing off the rest of the beer, he tossed the can in the trash and left the kitchen, still feeling edgy and horny. He could call Leesa and reinstate his friends with benefits privileges, but he didn't want to do that. The only woman he wanted didn't want him.

He had thought about Vashti, even while vacationing in the Great Smoky Mountains with Jade. His daughter had kept him busy during the day when they'd done a number of activities like canoeing and hiking. But at night while Jade slept off that day's exhaustion, he'd had to deal with dreams that wouldn't go away.

One thing was obvious tonight. They were still extremely attracted to each other. Sleeping together that one time hadn't helped. Now he knew how she tasted, how it felt to be inside her and make love to her until every cell in his body was satisfied. To sleep with her and awake holding her in his arms.

She had looked sexy as hell tonight in those shorts and top. And he knew she hadn't been wearing a bra.

He had seen the imprint of her nipples pressing against that tank top.

He drew in a deep breath and sighed loudly. At present it was the only sound in the room. He should be grateful for her decision for them not to get involved. He'd never wanted any of the townsfolk in his business anyway. He had a reputation to protect and an occupation for others to respect. But then what did either have to do with him as a man who had needs and wants like any other male?

He'd had the perfect arrangement with Leesa, but was it wrong for him to want more? Was it a crime for him to want to finally get serious about a woman after five years? During their two weeks in the mountains Jade had brought up the subject of his needing a girlfriend again. That made him wonder why. Did she miss having a female around?

He rubbed a hand down his face. Maybe he was overthinking things. Turning toward the stairs, he glanced at the clock on the wall. It was close to two in the morning. He had a feeling after seeing Vashti tonight, sleep wouldn't come easy for him.

# CHAPTER TWENTY-FIVE

"GOOD MORNING, VASHTI, you're early."

Vashti smiled over at Charlette Hansberry. "I had a meeting this morning and thought I'd drop by to see Ms. Gertie before I head back to the inn."

"How are things going with that?" Charlette asked as they walked down the corridor that led to Ms. Gertie's room.

"So far so good, although there's still a lot more to do. However, I'm still holding to my October fifteen grand opening date."

No need to mention that the reason she had gotten out so early this morning was to visit with Mason Connolly, the man who had both installed and disengaged the security cameras around the premises of the inn. He was known to go fishing on Friday mornings bright and early, and she'd been at the bait shop when he'd arrived. Mr. Connolly was notorious for not returning calls. She would continue to do business with him, but she had low tolerance for business people who didn't act like they were in business.

She had also called her electrician to come recheck the outside motion lighting and he tried putting her off until Monday. She had made it clear that she wanted something done today. The last thing she needed was to call the police again in the middle of the night only to have Sheriff Sawyer Grisham show up.

"Well, enjoy your visit with Ms. Gertie. I checked in on her earlier and she was still sleeping, but Mavis mentioned she was up, dressed and eating breakfast in her room."

"Thanks. I'll see you later."

Opening the door to Ms. Gertie's room, she saw the older woman sitting at the small table in her room eating what looked like oatmeal while occasionally looking out the window. She was dressed in a pretty yellow dress today and her hair was combed differently. She looked lovely.

Vashti gave her usual greeting. "Good morning, Ms. Gertie. How are you today?"

Ms. Gertie turned and smiled. "Well, aren't you a sight for sore eyes. Vashti Alcindor, when on earth did you return to Catalina Cove?"

The coffee cup Vashti had been holding nearly slipped from her hands. She had to pull herself together. "You remember me?"

Ms. Gertie looked at her like she'd asked a totally stupid question. "Of course I remember you. I remember every baby I brought into this world."

"Yes, but…" Vashti stopped. There was no way she would bring up the woman's condition with her. Instead she said, "You look pretty today."

"Thanks and you look pretty yourself. You always were a pretty girl. You were even a pretty baby. And speaking of babies, did you ever find out the truth about yours?"

*The truth about hers?* She wondered what Ms. Gertie was talking about, but then considering Ms. Gertie's condition, the older woman probably didn't know herself, but Vashti decided to play along.

"I think I found out some of it. You want to tell me the rest?"

Ms. Gertie shrugged. "Not much to tell. Your parents wanted me to go along with their plan and when I refused that's when they sent you to that home for unwed girls. When they came back and told everyone your baby died, I knew it was a lie. They somehow got that place in Arkansas to do the very thing I refused to do. They got that place to go along with their plan."

Although Vashti knew Ms. Gertie was not talking rationally, she was inclined to ask. "What plan?"

"The plan was to tell you that your baby died when it actually had been given away for adoption. I tried to make them understand that doing such a thing, regardless of the fact you were a minor, was illegal."

This time the coffee cup Vashti was holding did fall from her hand and spilled all the contents on the floor. She quickly grabbed a nearby roll of paper towels and made short work of cleaning the mess she'd made while convincing herself Ms. Gertie really didn't know what she was talking about. But still…

"Why would my parents want to give my baby up for adoption when they knew I wanted to keep it?"

Ms. Gertie shook her head sadly. "They didn't care what you wanted, dear. Your getting pregnant at sixteen was an embarrassment to them. There was no way they were going to let you keep a baby they thought would ruin your life."

Vashti was about to ask Ms. Gertie another question when the room door opened and it was the lab technician. "I need to check her vitals for today. Could you step out for a minute?"

Vashti really didn't want to step out. She wanted Ms. Gertie to continue talking. Whether what she was saying was fact or fiction, it had shaken up Vashti. She had known how her parents had felt about her being pregnant. They had constantly tried getting her to agree to an abortion and when it was too late for that, they tried convincing her that she needed to give her child up for adoption. She had refused to do that as well. But there was no way her parents would have gone so far as to do what Ms. Gertie claimed they did. Would they?

While outside Ms. Gertie's room Vashti paced. For heaven's sake, this was the first time the woman had even recognized her in all the weeks she'd been coming here to visit her. She was hard-pressed to believe anything Ms. Gertie was saying now. Everyone knew she had dementia.

"You can go back in now."

Vashti glanced over at the lab technician who was leaving Ms. Gertie room. "Thanks."

Vashti quickly went into Ms. Gertie's room. The older woman was still sitting at the table eating. "I'm back, Ms. Gertie. I had to step out a minute."

Ms. Gertie glanced over at her and smiled and asked. "You're awfully friendly this morning. Who are you?"

"CALM DOWN, VASH. I can't believe you're even taking what Ms. Gertie said seriously. You know about her condition," Bryce whispered as she poured coffee into several cups. "When you walked in here you were shaking to the bones. Even now your voice is breaking. Think about it. Ms. Gertie has dementia and people with that condition say things they don't mean. She remembered who you were one minute and then she didn't know you the next. I remember my grandmother and what we all went through with her."

Vashti drew in a deep breath, appreciating the voice of reason. Bryce was right. When she'd arrived at the café, she'd been an emotional mess, not knowing whether what Ms. Gertie had said was true or not. "Maybe you're right."

"Of course I'm right. Your parents might not be the greatest, but I refuse to believe they could do something like that and keep a straight face around you."

Vashti nodded. "I hate to say it, but you're probably right again."

"There's no 'probably' in it. And if you're going to interrupt me at rush hour you might as well make yourself useful," she added, handing Vashti an apron. "Wash your hands in the back." Bryce walked off to serve the table of eight men who looked like they planned to spend the day fishing.

Vashti knew her friend was right about not taking what Ms. Gertie said seriously, but the ninety-six-year-old woman had recognized her and seemed to have her wits fully about her in that moment.

"You're still standing here?" Bryce asked, returning.

Vashti snapped out of her reverie and glanced around the café. The place was busy. Swarming with customers who couldn't start their day without Ms. Witherspoon's blueberry muffins, or her blueberry pancakes and a cup of the best coffee in the cove. Vashti suddenly felt guilty knowing she was in the way.

"Sorry," she said. Since she wasn't expecting her workers at the inn for at least a couple of hours, there was no reason not to help out here for a while. She put on the apron Bryce had given her. Doing so felt like the old days when as teens both she and Bryce would pitch in and help out at the café on the weekends.

"Hey, Vash," Bryce's mother, father and brothers called out to her when she washed her hands at the sink.

"Good morning."

"You're helping out?" Mr. Witherspoon asked.

"Yes, I've been drafted, thanks to Bryce," she said, smiling over her shoulder.

The bell above the door rang. "That means there's a new customer," Mr. Witherspoon said, grinning. "Go get 'em, tiger."

"Will do," she said, drying her hands and grabbing a pad off the counter. Pasting a smile on her face she turned to the new customer only to look into the face of Sawyer Grisham. He seemed just as surprised to see her as she was to see him.

"GOOD MORNING, VASHTI."

"Good morning, Sheriff."

Sawyer lifted a brow. Did she think calling him sheriff instead of his given name would stop the flow of sexual chemistry they could generate so easily? And had he picked up on something else with her? It seemed she was flustered about something. Had she not been able to get a good night's sleep last night after he'd assured her she was safe? If that wasn't it, then what? It was obvious to him that something was bothering her.

"You need a table for one?" she asked, keeping that smile pasted on her face,

"No, I'm expecting someone so I'll need a table for two."

He saw the curious glint in her eyes before she said, "Okay. Table for two, please follow me."

He followed her and enjoyed doing so. There was just something about seeing a nice-looking backside in a pair of jeans. And to know that he'd once touched that backside, kissed it, had pressed hard against it while skin to skin with it. Had made love to it and for that one night, had claimed her and every part of her as his.

"Will this table work?" she asked, reclaiming his attention.

"Yes, thanks," he said, sliding into a booth.

She handed him a menu. "How's your daughter?" she asked.

"Fine. She's at a weekend sleepover. I don't expect her back home until after church tomorrow."

"Sounds like fun."

"I'm sure it is." He handed her back the menu. "I already know what I want. I got a taste for blueberry pancakes this morning, but I'll wait on the pancakes until Kaegan gets here. I'll take coffee for now."

She wrote down his order on the pad and then glanced at him. He was looking at her and for a minute she didn't say anything. Then she forced her gaze away when she put the pad into her pocket. "I appreciate your coming by last night."

He nodded. "Just doing my job."

"Yes. Of course. And I've taken care of the things you suggested. I've already talked with my electrician and I paid my security expert a visit this morning."

"It's not even ten o'clock yet. You've been busy."

"I figured I didn't have time to waste. I headed Mr. Connolly off at the bait shop and called Summersville Electrics to check the outside lights."

"You don't mess around do you?" She smiled and he felt his stomach tighten. Nothing new there.

"I try not to. I'll be back with your coffee."

She walked away and he watched her. He couldn't force himself not to.

Vashti returned with his coffee at the same time Kaegan showed up. Sawyer watched as they hugged liked the good friends they were, but still he couldn't help the tinge of jealousy he felt.

"Hey, man, you okay?" Kaegan asked, sliding into the seat across from him.

He took a sip of his coffee. "Yeah, I'm okay." Residing in the same town as Vashti was testing restraint and control.

"I'm going out on the boat today. Cruising over to New Orleans to check out a commercial boat I'm thinking about buying. You want to come along?"

"What time?"

"Within an hour."

Sawyer glanced over at Vashti and as if she felt his gaze on her, she looked over at him. It seemed a blaze of desire had their eyes transfixed. When Kaegan touched his arm he looked at him. "What?"

Kaegan smiled. "I was talking to you but it seems your attention was drawn elsewhere."

Yes, it definitely had been. "What were you saying?"

"You never did say whether you wanted to go to New Orleans with me on the boat."

He had planned to go into the office for a little while today, but going with Kaegan away from the cove for a spell sounded like a good idea. "Sure, I'll go," Sawyer said, taking another sip of his coffee.

## CHAPTER TWENTY-SIX

VASHTI GOT UP from behind her desk, stretched her muscles a few times before walking over to the window to look out at the gulf. Doing so always relaxed her and today had been a hectic day. She'd gone through over twenty résumés for a chef.

So far everything was moving forward with the inn. The painters had finished, and the woodwork and floors had been repaired and replaced. The new bedcoverings she'd ordered had arrived and the drapes would be hung next week. She had hired a gardener, maintenance staff and a housekeeping crew. Altogether there would be a total of twenty-five people employed by her. That included the kitchen staff which she was yet to find.

Two weeks had passed since that day Ms. Gertie had recognized her. So far she hadn't again, but that hadn't stopped Vashti from thinking about what she'd said. Vashti had put it off as long as she could but this week she had called and asked her parents about it.

Her mother had denied everything and said she couldn't believe Vashti would believe such foolishness. Vashti might be wrong, but she could swear she heard desperation in her mother's voice. Her father, as usual, had pretty much refused to talk to her, so nothing had changed there.

Then there was the issue of the sheriff she had to deal with. She'd run into him today when his patrol car had come to a stop at a traffic light next to her. She had glanced over at him and the minute their gazes connected intense heat had surged through her. She hadn't looked away. Neither had he, until the car behind her had honked their horn to let her know the light had changed. At the next intersection she had turned right and he'd turned left. However, for one sinful minute she had wanted him to turn right and follow her. To where, she wasn't sure. All she knew was it was getting harder and harder to keep him out of her nightly dreams. Nearly impossible not to think of him every waking moment. And then there were the memories of their one night together. How it felt to rub her hands across his naked chest. How she'd clung to his shoulders while they'd made love. The way he would grip her hips just seconds before thrusting inside of her and how she would lift her thighs for him to penetrate even deeper.

Drawing in a deep sigh, she was about to go back and sit down at her desk when the doorbell sounded. She didn't have any more interviews today so she wondered who would be visiting her. She had talked to Bryce earlier and knew her friend was pretty much in for the evening, studying for a real estate test she would be taking next week.

Going to the door she glanced out the peephole to see a teenaged girl standing there. She wondered if she was part of a group of teens who were going around getting a petition signed for the city council to consider bringing a McDonald's to town. Although she admired their desire to implement change, she knew they had a gigantic struggle on their hands. She opened the door.

"Hi," the girl said in a bubbly tone with a huge smile on her face.

Vashti smiled back. "Hi. I've already signed the petition."

"The petition?"

"Yes, the one to bring a McDonald's to town."

"Oh that. Thanks for signing it, but that's not why I'm here."

"I see. Then what are you selling?"

The girl shrugged, which made a wave of dark brown curly hair fall past her shoulders before another smile touched her lips. "I guess you can say I'm selling myself because I need a job."

Vashti leaned in the doorway finding the teenager's approach amusing. "You need a job?"

"Yes."

"And what job are you applying for?"

"Miscellaneous duties for the summer. I figured you would need someone who can do most of anything."

"And you can?"

"Yes. I'm a wiz on a computer and familiar with a number of software applications."

The one thing Vashti did know was that when it came to being computer experts, these teens had it in the bag. "You have piqued my interest and I would love to interview you. I'm Vashti Alcindor, the owner of the inn. What's your name?"

The girl's smile widened even more and she knew enough about protocol to extend out her hand to Vashti. "Thanks for the interview, Ms. Alcindor, and my name is Jade. Jade Grisham."

SO THIS WAS Sawyer's daughter, Vashti thought as she studied the girl sitting across from her at the kitchen table. Instead of using her office, she suggested they go into the kitchen where she served lemonade and cookies…but only after Jade had assured her she'd eaten dinner already. Vashti certainly didn't want to ruin the girl's appetite.

She recalled Sawyer telling her that his daughter wanted a summer job. At the time he hadn't seemed thrilled with the idea. Evidently he'd changed his mind. However, just to be on the safe side she would make sure. "So, Jade, are your parents okay with your working this summer?"

Jade nodded as she bit into a cookie. "Yes, but it's just my dad and me. Mom died a few years ago."

"I'm sorry to hear that." She saw no reason to let Jade know that she knew her father, especially not the depth of their friendship.

"Thanks. And yes, he knows. He wasn't happy about it but I kept pressing him and he finally gave in since it's just for the summer. I want a car by my seventeenth birthday and I want to feel like I've contributed toward it."

Vashti recalled Sawyer wasn't crazy about her getting a car either. Would hiring her cause a family conflict? She would only do an informal interview as a courtesy. "So tell me why you think you would be a good fit here over the summer."

"Well…"

As she talked Vashti listened. She also found herself studying the young woman and remembering herself when she was that age. She had worked here at the inn with her aunt, doing basically the same things Jade was saying she could do. Simple things like answering the phones, taking reservations, keeping her calendar and other miscellaneous duties. Vashti was also impressed with how articulate Jade was. How poised and self-assured. Jade had yet to mention her father was the sheriff. Some young people would have used that to their advantage. But so far Jade was selling herself on her own merits and not on her father's occupation.

"I promise if you hire me you won't regret it, Ms. Alcindor."

Vashti cringed. Every time Jade called her that she felt old. "It's okay for you to call me Vashti."

"You sure? My dad says it's important to always be respectful."

"I'm sure and you have. I have no problem with your calling me Vashti."

"Would it be okay to call you Ms. Vashti?"

Vashti smiled, nodding. "Yes, that's fine." She bit into her cookie and took a sip of her lemonade and then said casually, "Your last name is Grisham. Our sheriff's last name is Grisham. Are the two of you related?"

A huge smile touched Jade's lips. "Yes, he's my dad and he's the greatest."

It suddenly occurred to Vashti that at no point had she ever thought her dad was the greatest. Vashti asked Jade a few more questions and then said, "I admit I am impressed with you, Jade. Give me a few days to get back with you if I determine you would be good fit for the inn."

Jade's smile grew even larger. "Thank you, Ms. Alcindor…I mean Ms. Vashti."

SAWYER LOOKED UP when his cell phone went off and lifted a brow in surprise when he saw it was Vashti.

Tossing the papers he'd been reading aside, he quickly answered, wondering why Vashti would be calling him. He'd seen her that morning on the way in to work. It had been the first time in almost two weeks. He'd kept busy all that day, not wanting to remember his reaction. And now she was calling. Why? "Yes, Vashti? What can I do for you?"

He swallowed after asking her that, especially when he heard how the sound of her breathing had changed. It was crazy, but even through the phone sexual energy was consuming them. He felt it and knew chances were she felt it as well.

"I met Jade today."

He lifted a brow. "You did?"

"Yes. She came here looking for a summer job and I interviewed her."

Sawyer nodded. He knew Jade had gone to several places to apply for work, but he hadn't known the inn would be one of them. "How did she do?"

"Great. You should be proud of her. It's obvious she's a smart kid who's been well raised. She's very respectful."

The smile of a proud father touched his lips. "Thanks. I do my best."

"And it shows."

Vashti paused again and then she said, "I want to hire her, Sawyer. I can think of a number of things she can help me with over the summer. But I don't want to hire her if it will cause friction in your home."

He shifted in his chair. "Why would it cause friction in my home?"

"I recall you once hinted that you prefer she not have a job."

He released a deep sigh. For a minute he thought she would say because of their past affair, refusing to think of it as a one-night stand. "I gave up that fight when she returned from visiting her godmother in Waco for spring break. I gave her permission to get a job for the summer but *only* for the summer. I have no issue with your hiring Jade if that's what you want to do, Vashti. I think she can learn a lot from you. I can tell you have a strong work ethic and you're a professional."

"Thank you."

"And I appreciate your caring enough to check with me first. You didn't have to and I want to thank you for doing so."

"You don't have to thank me, Sawyer." She paused again before saying. "Well, I'll let you get back to work."

If only she knew. He would rather sit here and talk to her, listen to the sound of her voice. "Okay. Goodbye, Vashti."

"Goodbye, Sawyer."

He sat there and held the phone in his hand for a minute after she'd clicked off the line.

# CHAPTER TWENTY-SEVEN

VASHTI HEARD THE click of her heels on the tiled floor as she made her way to Ms. Gertie's room. It was a beautiful Tuesday morning and it wasn't ten o'clock yet, but already it promised to be a scorcher of a day.

Jade's first couple of weeks at the inn had gotten off to a good start. She had taken inventory of all the linens and bedcoverings so additional sets could be ordered. Not only had she finished the task in a couple of days but had put the results in a spreadsheet in the categories of single, queen and king beds. Then she'd proactively researched several linen outlets for Vashti's consideration. She'd also worked closely with the housekeeping staff to take inventory of what household items needed to be ordered to keep the inn running on a daily basis.

She discovered Jade wasn't as chatty as some teens and you only had to explain things once. And her mastery of technology was amazing. Usually they ate lunch together and it was during those times when they would talk about Jade's plans beyond high school. Jade had told her of her desire to return to Reno to attend the university there.

Jade's work hours were from ten to five and she rode her bike to work every day. Like most sixteen-year-old girls she was into hair, nails and clothes and looked forward to going on her first date. Vashti wondered how Sawyer would feel about that.

Vashti had stopped by the café to grab some blueberry muffins, which were Ms. Gertie's favorites. She would enjoy one with her and then leave to get to the inn before Jade arrived. She saw Mavis Green was coming out Ms. Gertie's room when she rounded the corner. "Hi, Mavis, is everything okay?"

"Yes, everything is fine. Today is one of those rare days Ms. Gertie might remember you. She definitely remembered me," Mavis said, laughing. "Right down to that mole on my backside. After delivering all those babies in town how on earth can she remember my birthmark is beyond me."

Vashti's lips curved into a smile. "That's great that she's herself today."

Still haunted by what Ms. Gertie had said about her baby, Vashti had done research on dementia patients and discovered that although their recognition might return, facts regarding certain things might still be rather clouded. Vashti figured that day had been one of Ms. Gertie's clouded moments.

After saying goodbye to Mavis she entered Ms. Gertie's room to find her sitting in a chair and looking out the window like she usually did. She was wearing a lovely blue dress and her hair had been combed with a cute blue bow keeping it back from her face. Vashti thought she looked extra pretty today. She turned when she heard Vashti and smiled at her.

"Vashti, it's good to see you today, dear."

Vashti smiled back. "Hi, Ms. Gertie, and how are you?" Something else she discovered from her research was that on those days when a dementia patient recognized you, to not make a huge deal of it because most never knew they slipped from one state to the other. And when you told them, they either wouldn't believe you or became overwhelmed by your accusation.

"I'm fine and what about you?"

"I'm doing okay. I brought you some blueberry muffins. I know how much you like them."

"Thank you. You were always a thoughtful child. Now come and sit a spell. You never did tell me what I asked you about before."

Vashti wondered if Ms. Gertie remembered their last conversation. There was only one way to find out. "I can't remember what you asked me the last time."

The older woman shook her head. "I swear you young people are so forgetful. The last time you were here I asked you if you found out the truth about your baby."

Vashti wondered if she should lie and say yes, she had found out the truth and quickly change the subject. But for some reason she couldn't. It was like the game you played as a child when you were compelled to tell the truth. "We ended our conversation before you could tell me everything about that."

"Wasn't much more to tell," the older woman said as if she'd recalled every bit of that conversation. "I probably told you too much anyway."

Vashti thought about what she said and asked, "Did you ever tell my Aunt Shelby?"

"No. I had no actual proof that your parents carried out their plan, although deep down I always had a gut feeling they had."

Vashti recalled running into Ms. Gertie several times after she'd returned to town after losing her baby. "In that case why didn't you tell me what you suspected since I'd been your patient for a short while?"

A regretful expression appeared on the older woman's face. "I didn't tell you for the same reason I didn't tell Shelby anything. I had no proof since I wasn't in that delivery room. But I think you have a right to know just in case my suspicions are true."

Once again Vashti knew she should end this conversation, but for the life of her she couldn't. Instead she asked, "And they wanted you to do it first, to go along with their plan? Before sending me away?"

"Yes, and like I told you, I wouldn't do it because it would have been illegal."

"But how do you know someone at the place in Arkansas really did it and that my baby really didn't die but was adopted out? That would have made what they did illegal as well."

"Yes, however, I had no proof but since it was the same plan to the letter, I questioned them about it."

"And they admitted it?"

"No, but they had guilt written all over their faces."

Vashti didn't say anything as she told herself the key word was *plan*. Her parents might have planned to do something devious but in the end, they hadn't. Even Ms. Gertie admitted she had no proof that they had. But still, just the thought they had planned to do it didn't sit well with Vashti. Drawing in a deep breath, another thought flowed through her mind. What if everything Ms. Gertie was telling her was a figment of her imagination and not true? But what if it was true? Just the thought was sending all kinds of emotions through her. Emptions she didn't want to get worked up about if they were false. Just the thought that she could have a child somewhere out there was too much to think about. Deep down she'd known about the loneliness Reid Lacroix had talked about because she'd endured some herself. Maybe not to the same degree but she knew how it felt to be a loner. She'd always wanted another child, and had hoped her marriage to Scott would lead to making a family. But it hadn't. So for her, her marriage had failed on many levels. Here she was at thirty-two and chances were she would not marry again and be a mother. However, right now, more than anything, she needed to know if what Ms. Gertie was saying had any legitimacy. There had to be a way to be certain.

"When are you going to give me my blueberry muffin?" Ms. Gertie asked, snapping Vashti out of her reverie.

"Oh." Vashti had forgotten she was still holding the bag and quickly crossed the room to the older woman. A smile touched Ms. Gertie lips when she pulled out the muffin.

She was about to ask Ms. Gertie a few more questions when the door opened and Ms. Gertie's fortysomething grandson walked in carrying flowers. He smiled at Vashti. "Hello, Ms. Alcindor. I'd called to check on my grandmother and the lady at the front told me she was in her right mind so I rushed over here to see her."

She was glad one of Ms. Gertie's relatives had come to visit and wished they would do so more often. It was sad they only wanted to see her when she was in her right frame of mind. "Hello, Mr. Landers."

"What are you talking about Charles?" Ms. Gertie demanded. "I'm always in my right mind."

Charles Landers placed the vase of flowers on the

table, ignoring what his grandmother said as he turned to Vashti. "I heard you're reopening the inn."

"Yes, I am."

Vashti watched as the man settled his huge frame in a chair that looked like it might collapse under his weight. She knew the chance for her and Ms. Gertie to continue their conversation in private was no longer an option. It was apparent Mr. Landers intended to visit awhile.

She glanced at her watch. She had less than twenty minutes to get back to the inn before Jade arrived. "Well, I'll be going, Ms. Gertie," Vashti said, brushing a kiss on the older woman's cheek like she always did.

"Alright, baby," Ms. Gertie said. "Thanks for the muffin and remember what I told you. Trust me. I know what I'm talking about. We'll talk some more tomorrow."

Vashti nodded. There was no guarantee what state Ms. Gertie's mind would be in tomorrow. It might be a good idea for her to swing back by later today. "Goodbye, Mr. Landers."

"See you later, Ms. Alcindor. If you ever need your windows replaced, remember my business. I'll give you a good price."

Vashti smiled. "I'll keep that in mind."

As she drove to Shelby by the Sea she recalled the look she'd seen in Ms. Gertie's eyes when she'd said, *Remember what I told you. Trust me. I know what I'm talking about...*

Did Ms. Gertie know what she was talking about? She couldn't wait to visit her later.

"WHAT DO YOU think of this dress, Kia?"

Kia forced a smiled when her mother held a pretty

red dress out in front of her. She really liked the dress and hated that she was feeling too lousy to appreciate it. She had awakened this morning with stomach pains and they were getting worse by the minute. She hoped her mom would cut their shopping trip short so she could go home and take a couple of aspirins and go to bed.

"It's nice, Mom. Are you going to buy it?" *And if you are, please do, so we can get out of here because I don't feel well.* Of course she wouldn't admit such a thing, which was why she hadn't told her parents about the same pain she'd felt in her abdomen for the past few months. The aches would come and go; however, lately they came more often and stayed a lot longer.

Her mother winked at her. "I think so. I can wear it to your dad's high school class reunion. I can't wait."

Kia couldn't either. During the same time her parents were going back to Philly for her father's high school reunion, she and her grandmother would be going on a cruise for a week. Nana would be arriving in a couple of weeks and she couldn't wait to see her grandmother again.

When another pain sliced across her lower belly Kia sucked in a deep breath, glad her mother was too busy looking through the rack of clothes to notice her clutching her stomach. Feeling her legs getting weak, she said, "Mom, I'm going to go sit over there and wait on you."

"Sure, honey," her mother said, without glancing up. "I just need to find another dress then we'll go grab lunch."

Kia drew in a deep breath. She didn't want to grab lunch—she wanted to go home. Turning to walk the few feet to where a set of bench seats were, she suddenly felt another sharp pain in her lower belly at the same time the room began spinning.

She lost her balance and cried out when things began turning black. The last thing she remembered was hearing the sound of her mother screaming her name.

VASHTI LEANED BACK in her chair, smiling. Her interview with Rhonda Livingstone had gone well and the woman's recommendations and credentials were outstanding. If everything worked out okay then she had found the perfect chef for Shelby by the Sea. She had narrowed her selection down to three people and it looked like Ms. Livingstone outshined them all.

After stretching her arms over her head, she glanced at her watch. Jade would be leaving in a few minutes and as soon as she did Vashti intended to revisit with Ms. Gertie. More than once today she'd been tempted to call her parents again, but decided against it.

She was about to get up from her desk and tell Jade she could leave a few minutes early when her cell phone rang. Reaching across her desk, she picked it up. "Shelby by the Sea, this is Vashti Alcindor."

"Vashti, this is Charlette Hansberry."

Vashti smiled. "Charlette, I was just about to head your way to visit with Ms. Gertie again today."

"Mavis mentioned you had planned on coming back this evening, and I wanted to call so you wouldn't come."

Vashti lifted a brow. "Oh? Why?" A funny feeling settled in her stomach when Charlette didn't answer her right away. "Charlette? Why shouldn't I come?"

"Ms. Gertie passed away in her sleep a little more

than an hour ago. She took a nap and never woke up. I'm sorry. I know how close the two of you were."

Vashti sat there in shock. Ms. Gertie was gone? But she had seen her that morning. Talked to her. Had looked forward to seeing her again this evening.

"Vashti?"

Tears she couldn't control flowed unheeded down Vashti's face. "Yes?"

"Are you okay?"

Vashti swiped at her eyes. No, she wasn't okay. Ms. Gertie had been there for her, had defended her and had given her hugs when she'd needed them most.

"I'm fine, Charlette. Was anyone with her?"

"No. Mr. Landers had left. Mavis went in to check on her and found her unresponsive and the doctor was summoned. We called Ms. Gertie's family and they are on the way here."

Vashti drew in a broken breath. "Thank you for calling and for letting me know."

"Of course I was going to let you know. You came to visit Ms. Gertie no matter what. More often than her own family. I know she enjoyed your visits, even when she didn't recognize you. She would tell me and Mavis how nice it was that someone she didn't know would come spend time with her and bring her blueberry muffins."

More tears fell from Vashti's eyes. "Thank you for telling me that."

After ending her call with Charlette, Vashti just sat there, still not believing Ms. Gertie was gone. Leaning forward she propped her elbows on her desk, buried her forehead in her hands and cried.

"Ms. Vashti, are you alright?"

Vashti lifted her head, glanced across the room at Jade as she swiped tears from her eyes. She sat up in her chair. "Yes, I'm fine. I just got a call that someone I care about passed away."

"Oh, I'm sorry."

"Thanks. I know it's time for you to leave. Be careful on your bike ride home."

"I will. And I'll see you tomorrow, Ms. Vashti."

JADE MADE IT to the living room and pulled out her cell phone. She released a deep sigh when the person picked up. "Yes, Jade?"

"Oh, Dad."

"Jade, what's wrong?"

"It's not me, Dad. It's Ms. Vashti."

"What's wrong with her?"

"Someone she knows died and she's crying something awful. I remember when Mom died and how I cried, and you said good words to me and all. I know you don't know Ms. Vashti, but she's a nice lady and she probably could use some good words right now to make her feel better."

"I'm on my way."

SAWYER FOUND HIS daughter sitting outside on the steps when he pulled into the driveway of Shelby by the Sea. Today had been his off day and he'd worked in the yard most of it. He had taken a shower and was about to grab a beer out of the refrigerator and sit outside in the shade to enjoy the view of his freshly cut lawn when Jade had called. He hadn't wasted any time getting there.

"Where is she?"

"Inside," Jade said, standing. "I hope she doesn't get

mad that I called you, but I didn't know who else to call and she looked so sad."

Sawyer placed an assuring hand on his daughter's shoulder. "You did the right thing by calling me."

"I need to introduce you and tell her why you're here."

"Alright," he said, following his daughter inside the house. There was no way he was going to tell Jade that he knew Vashti a lot better than she would ever know. A lot better than she needed to know.

He followed his daughter to the room Vashti used as an office. She was sitting at her desk with her head buried in her hands. "Ms. Vashti. I called my Dad to come talk to you. He knows what to say when someone has lost a person they love."

Vashti jerked her head up and looked at them, surprised. He saw her tearstained eyes and the way her lips were trembling, as if she would break into more tears at any moment.

He turned to his daughter. "You can go on home now, Jade. I'll take it from here. Be careful on that bike."

Jade nodded as if confident things would be alright now that her father was there. "Alright, Dad." She then looked over a Vashti. "My dad's really nice, Ms. Vashti. Honest. And I'll see you tomorrow."

Jade left. Sawyer didn't move until he heard the front door close shut behind his daughter. That's when he crossed the room and pulled Vashti into his arms and she wept into his chest.

## CHAPTER TWENTY-EIGHT

"MR. AND MRS. HARRIS?"

Both Percelli and Alma stood as the doctor approached. An ambulance had rushed Kia to the hospital from the mall. Alma had called her husband immediately and she wasn't sure how it was possible, but he'd driven up within moments of the ambulance arriving. The hospital staff had rushed through the emergency doors immediately, and Alma and Percelli had to provide the necessary insurance information.

"Yes, we are the Harrises. What's wrong with our daughter? How is she?"

The doctor, an older man who appeared to be in his late fifties smiled. "I'm Dr. Telfair. Your daughter is resting now and fully conscious. We're running several tests. She did admit to us that she's been having sharp pains in her stomach for a while. For at least a couple of months."

"She never told us that," Alma said.

"She said the reason she didn't tell you is because she was hoping they would go away."

"When can we see our daughter?" Alma asked, holding tight to her husband's hand.

"You can see her now but we really want her to rest. We have her sedated."

"Sedated?" Percelli asked, alarmed.

"Only because she's still experiencing stomach pains. We're trying to find out why."

A few minutes later Percelli and Alma were led to a room where their daughter lay hooked up to a number of machines. It took all Alma had not to cry out seeing Kia looking so weak and frail. Other than an occasional cold, she had never been sick.

Fighting back tears Alma went immediately to the bed and took hold of Kia's hand. "Why didn't you tell us you hadn't been feeling well, Kia?"

Tears filled Kia's eyes. "I didn't want you guys to worry about me, and I thought I would get better. I'm sorry. Now because of me, you'll miss Dad's class reunion."

"You're more important to us than any class reunion," Percelli said, wanting to make sure his daughter knew that. "The most important thing is getting you well. The doctors said they'll be running a lot of tests. As soon as they find out what's wrong, they can treat you for it and get you back home. You'll be feeling good as new in no time."

"I hope so. I don't like hospitals."

Percelli brushed a curl back from his daughter's forehead. "We don't like them either, but we want you to get better. We love you."

A faint smile touched Kia's lips. "I love you, too, Mom and Dad."

SAWYER CONTINUED TO hold Vashti in his arms while she cried. He had no idea who'd died, but he would get that information later. Right now he just wanted to hold her while she purged her grief.

She finally lifted her head and looked at him and he

reached up and using the pad of his thumb, he wiped tears from around her eyes. It was then that she said, "I lost Ms. Gertie."

He knew of the older woman she'd often visited at the senior citizen home. The wife of one of his deputies worked at the home and was complimentary of how dedicated Vashti was in visiting with the woman, who'd once been the cove's midwife.

"I just saw her this morning," she continued in a broken voice. "And was going back to see her this evening. She was doing so good today and she even knew who I was. That didn't happen often, but it happened today."

He encouraged her to continue speaking. A lot of times that helped. "The two of you had a good conversation?"

She nodded. "Yes. It was a good conversation." She paused and then said, "I guess you think it's silly for me to waste all these tears over a woman who was so old. I should have expected it."

He shook his head. "No, I don't think that. Tears can never be wasted when you lose someone you care about. There's nothing silly about it. And age has nothing to do with it. No matter the circumstances, even if death is a foregone conclusion, you can never be ready for it when it happens to someone who means a lot to you."

She seemed to absorb his words and after drawing in a deep breath she pulled herself together enough to pull out of his arms. Taking another deep breath, she said, "I'm sorry I got Jade upset to the point where she called you."

"Don't apologize, Vashti. You were crying and she cares about you. Unfortunately, my daughter thinks I'm a superhero when it comes to making things right and knowing the words to say in given situations, especially grief. I was that for her when we lost Johanna. In all honestly, we lifted each other up."

Vashti nodded and said, "Ms. Gertie shared some things with me, things I didn't know. Things that even now I'm not sure were real or fiction. But with her last words to me before I left her this morning, she implored me to trust her and believe that she knew what she was talking about."

"It sounds like you have decisions to make and I'm certain in the end you'll make the right one."

"You think so?"

"Yes. I've discovered you're someone with a level head." *Except for when it involves any decisions about me. About us*, he came close to adding.

"I don't feel levelheaded now," she said softly. "I feel if I don't believe her, believe in what she told me, that I will be letting her down. For some reason, I think she died believing I would follow through with what she told me. I don't know what to do, Sawyer."

Hearing her say his name did something to him to the point where he swallowed twice. But then her saying his name seemed fitting. It seemed personal. And between them, considering all they'd shared, it seemed right.

"You want to talk about it?"

He knew what he was doing. He was inviting her to talk to him, share her private thoughts with him—something she might not want to share with anyone, especially with a man she'd spent one night with making love. But a part of him felt they'd done more than just make love that night. They had connected in a way that still had him baffled as to how sexual energy between two people could be so powerful. He wanted it to be meaningful.

"I don't know if I can."

*Can or should?* At that moment it was important to him that she trust him. "You can."

Making a decision he swept her off her feet into his arms. Ignoring her gasp of surprise, he headed for the loveseat in her office. Holding her firmly in his arms he sat down, settling her in his arms in a way to look into her face. The same face he envisioned every night before falling asleep. "Okay, Vashti. Let's talk about it."

VASHTI LOOKED UP at Sawyer and a part of her couldn't believe he was here. His daughter had called and he'd come. Not to make a police call, but as a friend—former lover—the one man she knew she could fall in love with if she let her guard down. But she was finding it difficult to keep that guard up around him.

Sawyer had a way with people. He was a straightforward, to-the-point, no-nonsense, tough-as-nails cop. Yet he could also be kind, tenderhearted, thoughtful and considerate. She had seen all those sides of him and it was that compassionate side he was displaying now. She couldn't fight it, nor could she deny it.

To open herself up to him would be a game changer between them. She knew it and was aware he knew it as well. He'd made it known he wasn't looking for another friend with benefits. He wanted someone he could get to know, become involved with. Not behind closed doors but out in the open. Out in front of prying eyes and uncensored comments.

But then, what would happen if she discovered what Ms. Gertie told her was true? Would she be strong enough to face the lies, the hurt and the betrayal? She didn't want to consider the possibility that her parents had not only outright lied to her, but they had taken her child away. A child who was alive out there somewhere.

Thinking about it was almost too much, and she buried her face in his chest again as she fought back tears. Not only tears for Ms. Gertie, but tears at the thought that the two people a child should trust most, their parents, could outright betray them.

"Vashti?"

She lifted her face from his chest and gazed into the dark depths of a pair of concerned eyes. When he pushed a curl of hair back from her face, she said, "When I was sixteen and pregnant, my parents took me to a home for unwed mothers in Arkansas to have my baby. They took me there, dropped me off and turned around and left. I think they came to see me a couple of times and that was it. Aunt Shelby and Ms. Gertie came to see me often. Then to punish me, my parents restricted their visits. I didn't find that out until I wrote my aunt and questioned why they weren't visiting me anymore. That's when she told me why."

Pausing a minute, she remembered that time. "I was furious with my parents and called them, but they refused my calls. So I had to stay there at that place alone without any connections to my family. They wouldn't even tell Bryce or Kaegan where they had taken me."

"That was awful for a child to endure," Sawyer said.

"Yes, I felt I was in prison. But being alone helped me bond with my baby even more. I felt it was us against the world. The people at the home were nice, but I still felt alone and ostracized."

She stopped talking and swiped at tears, remembering that time and how alone she'd felt. "Then I delivered my baby. I went into labor a day or two earlier than expected. They called my parents and they rushed there. I remember seeing them before I was given something for pain. I remember hearing my baby cry and then nothing. When I came to hours later my parents were there. They told that although my baby had been born alive, it had died within hours because his lungs were weak and had collapsed."

She remembered all the tears she had shed that day for the baby she'd lost. The baby she had never gotten to see. "I asked to see him, but they said he'd already been taken away. I didn't get to name him or anything. I never got to hold him."

She had to stop and breathe or the tears would come again. "My parents, namely my mother, said my baby's death had been for the best, and that I could get on with my life and return to the cove like nothing had ever happened. They just didn't understand that a lot had happened. At least to me it had.

"On two occasions since returning to the cove and visiting Ms. Gertie, she told me something. The first time I just thought she was talking out of her mind and what she was saying couldn't possibly be true—after all she did have dementia. But she told me the same thing again today. I'm beginning to think there might have been some truth in what she said and it scares me, Sawyer. The thought that it could be true really scares me."

He frowned as if the thought of anything frightening her bothered him. "And what did she tell you?" he asked as if he had every right to know, and in a way, he did. Whether he knew it or not, Sawyer Grisham had crossed over the threshold into her heart. She hadn't wanted him to and had fought it, but in the end love had won.

"Ms. Gertie said while she was the midwife taking care of me during the early months of my pregnancy, my parents came up with this plan that she refused to go along with."

Sawyer lifted a brow. "What was the plan?"

Vashti then told him exactly what Ms. Gertie had told her. The arms holding her tightened. The eyes staring down at her were deadly sharp. "Are you saying Ms. Gertie suspected your parents lied to you about your baby dying?"

She nodded. "Yes. She believes they got that home in Arkansas to do what Ms. Gertie refused to do."

"Did you confront your parents about it?"

"Yes. I asked them about it the first time Ms. Gertie told me and they denied it. They got upset that I would even ask such a thing. But now I can see them doing that, Sawyer."

"How? Why?"

"They didn't want me to keep my baby and I hadn't planned to give it up for adoption. I can see them coming up with this plan to suit their purpose. I was a minor, but they couldn't make any decisions for me regarding my own child. Although they knew how much I wanted my baby, I could see them tricking me into signing papers I thought was about my medical care and then putting my baby up for adoption and hoping I never found out."

He asked. "I know you said that you and your parents didn't have a real close relationship, but do you honestly think they would do such a thing?"

"I don't want to believe it, but yes, I honestly think

they would. What I have to do is to find out if they did. I owe it to myself to know the truth."

"Keep in mind, Vashti, even if Ms. Gertie believed what she told you, she had no proof, so in essence it's her words against your parents."

"I know."

"Do you think your aunt knew of Ms. Gertie's suspicions?"

Vashti shook her head. "I asked Ms. Gertie and she said no, she didn't tell Aunt Shelby because she had no proof of anything. The only reason she said she was telling me after all this time was because she'd wondered if over the years I'd found out whether her suspicions were true."

He was quiet for a moment and then said, "As a cop I operate on the side of facts and not just suspicions. But usually my suspicions turn into facts. Not saying that's how things will be in your case, though. You also need to consider the possibility that Ms. Gertie, because of the dementia, was not giving you full facts, Vashti."

"I know, but I can't live my life not knowing one way or the other."

"So what are you going to do?"

"I don't know yet. I have a lot to think about."

"Yes, you do." He eased up from the sofa and placed her on her feet. "Come on, let's go for a walk."

She lifted her brow. "A walk?"

"Yes, on the beach."

## CHAPTER TWENTY-NINE

SAWYER TOOK VASHTI'S hand in his and led her toward the back of the inn. The moment they stepped out the French doors she breathed in a deep breath of ocean air. It had been a hot day but the sun had gone down and a cool breeze was coming off the water.

With him holding her hand Vashti felt a sense of comfort she associated only with Sawyer. They'd made it to the boardwalk before he spoke. "I envy you with this in your backyard."

She glanced up at him. "I don't think I truly appreciated it until after I moved to New York. That's when I truly missed it."

"But you never came back."

She shook her head knowing his words had been a statement and not a question. "No, I never came back, although I was tempted to. My parents moved away a year after I left for college, but Aunt Shelby was here. She knew why I stayed away."

They had reached the steps off the boardwalk that led to the beach. The lanterns located in the marsh had come on and provided a golden glow to the overgrown marsh and wet prairie grass that were growing on both sides of the boardwalk. The sound of shorebirds, waders and ducks could be heard as they headed in to roost at dusk.

"Let's take our shoes off and leave them here," Sawyer suggested and she followed his lead to remove her sandals. She glanced over at him when they were both in their bare feet. "You don't look like a walk-on-the-beach sort of guy."

He threw his head back and laughed. "Typically, I'm not, but I could tell you needed this."

She tilted her head and looked at him. "How could you tell?"

"Men's intuition. Don't think for a minute it belongs only to women."

She smiled. "I won't."

Reclaiming her hand they walked down the steps and the moment her feet touched the sand an exhilarating feeling spread through her. This was her first walk on the beach since she'd been back. She'd told herself she was too busy to do something so frivolous. Now she didn't see it as frivolous at all, but therapeutic.

Sawyer held firmly on to her hand and she loved the feel of his jean-clad thigh brushing against the part of her thigh not covered by her shorts. Although neither said anything, their breathing pattern said it all. Deciding they needed conversation between them, she said, "You were off today?"

He nodded. "Yes. I don't have designated days off. It depends on when my guys want off. Most are young with little ones, so I know weekends mean a lot to them, and I try to accommodate their needs. Being home today worked out because I had yard work that needed to be done."

"And I pulled you away from it?"

"No. I got up early to beat the sun and was finished

before noon. Then I decided to bring some sort of organization to the detached garage in the back."

"Did you finish?"

"Let's say I did as much as I wanted to do today. Then I went inside, showered and was about to grab a beer to sit on the patio a spell. That's when I got Jade's call."

"I'm sorry."

He stopped walking and since he was holding firm to her hand, she stopped as well. He turned to her and stared into her eyes. "You've already given me an apology that's not needed. Jade did the right thing and she didn't interrupt anything. I came because I wanted to come. I'm still here because there's no place else I'd rather be."

She knew this should not be happening, but there was no way to stop it. She'd tried that morning in New York when she'd told him why they couldn't be together once she moved back to Catalina Cove. At the time what she'd told him had made sense to her. Now, none of it mattered.

"Are you sure there's no place you'd rather be right now?" she asked him.

"Positive."

"That's good because there's no place I'd rather be as well than walking on the beach with you." He gave her a skeptical look and she understood, after all she'd said in New York.

He moved closer. "You sure?"

"Yes, I'm sure."

He pulled his hand from hers and reached up and cupped her chin. "I'm going to take you at your word, Vashti."

At that moment, her pulse raced and her heart began pounding in her chest. The eyes staring down at her were filled with a need she felt in every part of her body. She wasn't sure how one man could have so much sexual power over her, but at that moment she didn't care. It was such a heady feeling she felt like she was floating.

And then he lowered his mouth to hers.

WARNINGS SIGNS FLASHED through Sawyer's mind. When he'd arrived at Shelby by the Sea he should have kept his hands to himself. Then he would not have touched her. He'd been a goner the moment he'd done so. And now he should not be kissing her but he was driven to do so.

He'd gone over two months without her taste and it had been hard. He had kept the memories of their one night together, although he had tried forgetting it. But he'd discovered that he couldn't. He went to bed thinking about her and woke up thinking about her.

And now he was tasting her in a way that should be outlawed. It was one of those deep-down, rack-your-brain, locked-lips sort of kiss. And she was kissing him back with equal fervor. They were standing so close he could feel the heat from her body being transmitted to his.

And then she did something he hadn't expected. While their mouths were still locked she tugged at his T-shirt then slid her hands beneath it to stroke his stomach before moving upward. The feel of her fingers running through the hair on his chest shot sensations all through him. Made him moan in their kiss and tighten his hold on her.

He deepened the kiss as emotions he couldn't control took over his mind, body and senses. A shudder of intense desire rushed through him and he moaned so loud he was certain the sound carried across the gulf.

When he felt her fingers working at his zipper he knew he had to stop her. Grief made people do things they hadn't planned on doing. He of all people should know. He had gotten Johanna pregnant the night of his foster-father's funeral.

He reached down for her hand and then broke the kiss. Releasing her hand he took a step back as his gaze held hers. He saw the look of confusion in her eyes. "Why did you stop me when you know I want you? When I know you want me?" she asked him.

If only she knew just how bad he did want her. "Because I'm not a man to take advantage of a grieving woman, Vashti. No matter how much I want her. Besides," he said. "No condoms."

She lifted her chin. "I'm on birth control. I told you that in New York."

He remembered. "Yes, but I'm not about to roll around in the sand with you. You deserve better. And before you offer your bed, I'm sticking to what I said earlier. I'm not a man who would take advantage of a grieving woman, so come on, let's walk." He took her hand again and they continued their stroll on the beach.

"SO, WHAT DO you suggest I do, Sawyer?" she asked a short while later as they continued their stroll.

"About what?" he asked glancing down at her.

The moment she gazed into his dark eyes she had to recall what she'd asked him and why. She forced herself to remember. "How do I find out the truth as to whether my baby lived or died?"

"The law enforcement side of me would go into an

investigative mode. I'd check records. Do you know if that home for unwed mothers is still in business?"

"The first time Ms. Gertie mentioned it to me, I checked. It closed down ten years ago."

"That might be the case, but the law requires birth records be kept indefinitely. Probably the best thing to do is hire a private investigator."

*A private investigator...*

She recalled her divorce attorney had suggested the same thing when Scott had tried being difficult. The guy he'd recommended had been good. Costly but good. But as far as she was concerned, any amount of money she paid to get the truth would be worth it.

"I think hiring a private investigator is a good idea and I have one in mind. I could use the same guy I hired for my divorce. He was thorough."

"Then I suggest you use him."

She smiled. "I think I will. I'll give him a call tomorrow." They headed back toward the inn. When she almost stumbled in a low spot in the sand, he caught her. "Thanks."

"Don't mention it."

Instead of letting her go, he gently pulled her into his arms and kissed her again. She needed the kiss. But deep down she knew it wasn't just the kiss. She needed Sawyer and not just physically. How could she tell him that after what she'd said to him in New York?

He broke off the kiss and rested his forehead against hers and drew in a long, deep breath. "Come on, sweetheart, let's get back before we get into trouble."

She didn't say anything as they walked back toward the inn, pausing briefly to put back on their shoes.

When they stepped off the boardwalk they could see the headlights of a car coming up the driveway.

"Expecting anyone?" Sawyer asked her.

She shook her head. "No."

By the time they made it to the gazebo Vashti saw it was Bryce rushing toward them. "Hello, Sawyer," Bryce said, with a bemused look on her face before turning her full attention to Vashti. "I just heard about Ms. Gertie and immediately thought about you. Are you okay?"

Vashti nodded. "Yes, I'm fine. Sawyer suggested a walk on the beach."

"Oh."

Vashti could see how Bryce would be confused. After all, the last time they talked she'd made it clear to her best friend that there could never be anything personal between her and Sawyer.

"I'm sure you two have a lot to talk about, so I'll leave you now," Sawyer said.

"Thanks for everything, Sawyer. I appreciate your being here."

He gave her one hell of a sexy smile. "Don't mention it." He then turned to Bryce. "Good seeing you again, Bryce." Then to both, he said, "Good night, ladies."

He sauntered off toward his SUV and Vashti watched him. When he stopped in front of his vehicle, he glanced back at her and his gaze practically burned into her. "Excuse me a minute, Bryce."

"Oh. Sure."

Vashti strolled to where Sawyer stood and when she reached him, she said, "I think you forgot something."

"Did I?" Sawyer asked her.

"Yes."

Holding her gaze, he asked. "And what did I forget?"

"This."

She wrapped her arms around his neck and then on tiptoe, she leaned up and pressed her mouth against his. She thought she was doing a pretty good job kissing him, but then he took over. Tightening his arms around her and deepening the kiss, as if they didn't have an audience of one.

Vashti wasn't sure how long they kissed, but when he finally pulled his mouth away, he drew in a long breath and smiled at her. Against her moist lips he whispered. "Only you know where all this is going, Vashti. Think about it before you make your move because when you do, there's no turning back for us. Understood?"

She looked up at him and nodded. "I understand."

Sawyer nodded back at her and then opened the door, got into his SUV and backed out of the driveway. Vashti stood there and watched him go.

"Hey, remember me?"

Vashti turned and smiled at Bryce who was waving her hands in the air. "Yes, I remember you. Doubt I can forget you."

As she strolled back to where Bryce stood with one of those you-better-tell-me-everything looks on her face, there was no doubt in Vashti's mind she had a lot of explaining to do.

# CHAPTER THIRTY

JADE POUNCED ON Sawyer the moment he entered the house. He had expected it, which was why he'd driven around town for thirty minutes after leaving Vashti's place. That kiss she'd laid on him hadn't just knocked around his senses, it had aroused his body to the point it had taken just that long for his erection to go down. The last thing he'd wanted to do was to walk into his house with a hard-on.

"How is she, Dad? Were you able to calm her down?"

"Whoa," he said as he headed to the kitchen for a beer. He leaned against the counter after popping the tab on his beer. "She's fine now, Jade. Yes, I was able to calm her down." No need to go into details of the technique he'd used to do so. "You can go to bed since you have work tomorrow," he said. He needed time alone right now.

"It's still early, Dad, and I'm not sleepy."

He gave her a brief smile. Evidently she didn't take the hint when she moved to sit down at the table. "I'm glad you called me," he told her, joining her.

"I'm glad I called you, too. It's sad about that Ms. Gertie lady."

He lifted a brow. "How do you know the name of the lady who died? You didn't earlier."

His daughter smiled brightly. "I called Karen Libby."

He recalled that name. She was Rachel's niece. The same girl who'd shared romance novels with his daughter. "And how did Karen Libby know who died?"

"Not sure, probably from her aunt Rachel. Karen said that back in the day this Ms. Gertie lady was a midwife and delivered all the babies born here. She was well liked by most people, but she had dementia."

Sawyer figured there was more. "And?"

"And Karen said her aunt couldn't understand why Ms. Vashti was always visiting Ms. Gertie at the nursing home when she wasn't in her right mind most of the time."

Sawyer took a sip of his beer and glanced at his daughter. "And what do you think of that comment?" he asked, always wanting to keep abreast of his daughter's thought processes.

Jade made a face like she couldn't believe someone would think that way. "Only an uncaring person would wonder why. I'm glad Ms. Vashti did care enough to visit her. I would have had I known her. But then, just from the weeks I've been working for Ms. Vashti, I see what a nice person she is. I'm sure you saw that for yourself, didn't you?"

He nodded, appreciating her thought process and also recognizing his daughter's tactic on a certain thing. She liked Vashti and it was important to her that he liked her, too. What his daughter didn't know was that he was already there in such a big way, that even his beer couldn't eradicate her taste from his mouth. "Yes, it's easy to see Vashti Alcindor is a real nice person."

"And she's pretty," Jade said. Sawyer figured the compliment was for his benefit in case he hadn't noticed.

"Yes, she is pretty." His daughter was trying her hand at matchmaking and he figured he was supposed to be too dense to figure it out. So for good measure he decided to tack on, "She's very pretty."

His daughter beamed. If her smile was any brighter it would blind him. "I'm glad you noticed, Dad."

He decided not to ask why she was glad, but he thought knowing she was was a good thing. Especially if Vashti had meant what she said about them moving forward and not backward. That meant they would have to change their mode of doing things. Both were private people and when they began dating it would cause talk. It was talk he could handle and hoped she could as well. As long as his daughter was all in, then to hell with anyone else.

He glanced at his watch as he stood. "You might not be sleepy, young lady, but I am. I'm going out on the boat with Kaegan tomorrow."

"Okay, have fun, Dad. Love you."

"I love you, too."

As he headed for the stairs his mind was consumed with thoughts of Vashti.

VASHTI TOOK A sip of her wine. After walking on the beach with Sawyer she thought it was too beautiful a night to go inside, so she had convinced Bryce to sit on the patio and enjoy the breeze off the gulf.

Since moving back to the cove this was the first time she'd really had to unwind. Her days had been so busy that when night came all she could do was welcome sleep. Tonight was different. She and Bryce decided to enjoy a bottle of wine while swapping Ms. Gertie stories. It was their way to pay tribute to a woman whose hands had delivered them into the world, and who for the longest time had fought for social change in the cove.

Before moving away Vashti had recalled Ms. Gertie had been in a never-ending battle with Mayor Proctor about the need for housing for the homeless as well as improvements needed for the boating docks. Ms. Gertie would also butt heads all the time with Sheriff Phillips, all generations of them, and was quick to remind them that she delivered them into the world and would have given them an extra whack on their rear end if she'd known they would grow up to be power-grabbing men. Needless to say, Ms. Gertie was known to call people out when they were wrong.

Even Vashti's parents…

Knowing that made her think about what Ms. Gertie had told her that morning, which she took the time to share with Bryce. "I need to know the truth, Bryce. What if Ms. Gertie's suspicions are true? I need to know one way or the other."

"So, what are you going to do?" Bryce asked.

Vashti released a deep sigh. "Sawyer suggested I hire a private investigator."

Bryce lifted a brow. "Did he?"

"Yes, and I think it's a good idea. What do you think?"

"I think it's a good idea as well. I also think you've finally realized something."

"What?"

"That you really like Sawyer. It's obvious that the sexual chemistry between the two of you is hot as ever. And tonight it didn't seem like you were holding anything back."

Vashti shrugged. "I've always liked Sawyer. I told you months ago I thought he was a nice guy. I admit I got upset with him when I found out about his New

Orleans affair, but he explained things when he visited me in New York."

"And then you freaked out when he suggested the two of you continue your affair when you moved back here."

Yes, Vashti would admit to freaking out. But since moving back she'd realized the attraction between her and Sawyer hadn't diminished any. If anything, it had increased. "I didn't want to fall for him, Bryce. Lord knows I have lousy judgment when it comes to men, but the thought of falling for Sawyer isn't as scary as it once was."

"And what about the talk? People will have a lot to say at first, but only because that's just the way people in the cove are. They assume your business is their business. Will you be able to handle it?"

"I don't have any choice but to handle it. Sawyer won't sneak around."

"And you shouldn't. The two of you are adults. It's time you stop letting Catalina Cove control your life. Sawyer has already shown that he's a man who won't let them control his."

Vashti was silent for a minute and then she said, "I'm really going to try, Bryce. I want to do this and I want to be all in when I do."

"What changed for you tonight, Vash? What made you decide to make a move?"

Vashti thought about her question. "Seeing first-hand how he handles things and the people he cares about. His daughter didn't hesitate to call him when she thought I needed comforting. And he's good at that. He was here when I needed him and neither Julius nor Scott had ever been there for me."

Later that night after taking her shower, Vashti settled in bed as her last conversation with Ms. Gertie replayed in her mind. It was still hard to believe she was gone. She had called Mr. Landers to offer her condolences and she could tell the man was pretty torn up about it. At least he'd spent some time with his grandmother and had brought her flowers. She felt the lump in her chest get heavier, a sign she was about to cry again and she didn't want to do that.

Vashti wanted to think of something else so she shifted her thoughts to Sawyer. He would never know how much she'd needed someone at that moment when he'd shown up.

She thought about their walk on the beach, their kiss and how she had practically asked him to make love to her, and how he'd refused because he'd known she was grieving. Somehow he'd known about the grief that had filled her heart. Any other man would not have cared and would have gladly taken her, right there on the sand. But Sawyer hadn't because he had cared. He had held her, kissed her, held her hand. It was as if he was willing her pain to become his. Like she'd told Bryce, she believed that had been the turning point. That moment when she realized just what a good man she was denying herself the chance to know because of a past she might regret but couldn't change.

She was about to shift around in the bed to find a more comfortable position when her cell phone rang. When sensations went off inside of her she knew her caller was Sawyer. "Hello."

"Hello, Vashti, I couldn't sleep for thinking about you and wanted to check to make sure you're okay."

She smiled at his thoughtfulness. "I'm fine. Bryce

left an hour ago and I took a shower and got into bed. I take it you're in bed as well."

"Yes, I'm in bed."

She remembered the night they'd spent in bed together. "I tried reading and couldn't stay focused."

"And I tried to get into one of my favorite cop shows on television, but it didn't hold my interest tonight. Thoughts of you took over."

"What kind of thoughts?"

"All kinds. Especially memories of kissing you tonight."

She'd been reliving those same memories. "Seems like we're on the same page." There. She'd just admitted to thinking about kissing him as well.

"Would you go out with me Saturday night, Vashti?"

Vashti knew what he was doing. Propelling them forward with the understanding there would be no turning back. "Yes, Sawyer, I will go out with you."

"How would you like going to the Lighthouse?"

"The Lighthouse? Will we be able to get reservations at this late date?" She knew the exclusive restaurant was usually booked solid weeks in advance.

"I think I can arrange it. I'll pick you up around seven."

"Okay, and thanks for calling, Sawyer. Good night."

"Good night, Vashti. And thanks for agreeing to go out with me."

She smiled, clicking off the phone. The most sought-after single man in the cove was thanking her for agreeing to out with him. She couldn't help but feel good about that.

## CHAPTER THIRTY-ONE

"A KIDNEY DISEASE!" Percelli Harris exclaimed as he, his wife and mother sat across from Dr. Telfair in the physician's hospital office. His mother, Gloria Harris, had arrived yesterday and she had been great in helping to keep Alma calm. Their daughter was sick and now the doctor was saying she had some kind of kidney disease. "Are you sure?"

Dr. Telfair nodded. "For the last seventy hours your daughter has been undergoing a series of tests. Unfortunately, our prognosis is conclusive."

"But how? Kia has always been healthy."

"How the filters in her kidneys got damaged we aren't sure. It could have resulted from a number of things such as a hangover of flu-like symptoms in the body, a urinary tract infection that went untreated or inflammation of organs located near the kidneys."

"How bad is it?" Alma asked in a broken voice. Percelli felt his wife's tears fall on their joined hands.

"The good news is that we've ruled out congenital problems or an inherited condition," Dr. Telfair said. "The bad news is that unless we begin aggressive treatment immediately, we're looking at an end-stage kidney disease which is life-threatening."

"Oh, no," Percelli heard his mother cry out simultaneously with the sound of Alma crying even more. He tightened his hold on Alma's hand and used his other hand to grab hold of his mother's.

"What can be done so she doesn't reach that stage, Dr. Telfair?" he asked, trying to hold it together.

"Ideally, a kidney transplant from a close family member such as a parent or sibling. But you've indicated in her medical records she was adopted so I can only assume you have no way of contacting the biological mother."

"We have no information on her. The adoption documents are sealed. All we know is that the mother was a sixteen-year-old girl who gave her baby up for adoption. We hired a private attorney to handle the adoption for us."

Dr. Telfair nodded. "In life-threatening situations, we usually can get a court order to unseal adoption documents to reach out to the biological parents. It will be up to them to decide if they want to get involved. I've seen it go both ways. There are some biological parents who do and others who won't."

"Who would be that heartless?" Gloria asked.

"A person who has gotten on with their life and doesn't feel any connection to the child they gave up years before," Dr. Telfair answered.

"What are our options?" Alma wanted to know.

"Kia will be placed on the kidney transplant waiting list. Usually it's a two-year wait at least. In this case, it could be longer because your daughter has a rare blood type. While she's waiting for the transplant she has to be on dialysis."

Percelli rubbed his hands down his face. He loved his daughter and would give up his kidney in a heartbeat if doing so would keep her alive. But neither his kidney,

nor that of his wife or his mother was an option since
they had different blood types than Kia.

"We need to explain Kia's condition to her since
we'll be starting dialysis right away. She needs to know
what's going on with her body and what we'll be doing
to make her better."

Percelli nodded. "Okay, and we want to be there
when you tell her."

"MR. BANKS, THANKS for coming to Catalina Cove to
meet with me," Vashti said to the private investigator.

"No problem. I had business in Shreveport today
anyway. This is a nice town and definitely a nice inn
you have here. I can see why you were quick to leave
New York," Jeremy Banks said, easing into the chair
across from her desk.

Vashti figured there was no need to tell him that
moving to Catalina Cove hadn't been her original plan,
but now that she was here, she intended to make not
only the most of it but to reclaim it as her home, something she hadn't thought she would ever do again.

"Now tell me everything you know," he said, taking
out a pad to jot down notes.

She told him her parents' version regarding her son
dying an hour after she'd given birth and how he'd died.
She then told him what Ms. Gertie suspected.

"That was sixteen years ago, right?" Banks asked
her.

"Yes. March would have been sixteen years."

"You said the baby lived for about an hour. The first
thing I'll do is find out if there is a death certificate.
Those are public record in Arkansas. If there's not one,
though, that doesn't necessarily mean the child sur-

vived. Records can go missing or be misfiled, especially when a facility closes. Do you recall any of the other nurses there? What about the teachers?"

"I recall my math teacher was a Rosie Farlow. That's the only one I remember. Why would you ask about my teachers? They would not have been in the delivery room."

"No, but if contacted, they might be able to provide names of individuals who were. The problem we have to face is the possibility the birth records were sealed as requested by the adoption parents, which isn't unusual. If that's the case, we might have to obtain a court order to see them."

After asking her several more questions he closed his pad and looked over at her. "I hope your parents have told you the truth, and I'm being hired to verify their story. However, there is something you need to seriously think about."

"What's that?"

"If they lied to you and Gertie Lander's suspicions are true, then you have a child somewhere who would be sixteen now. What if he was never told that he was adopted only to find out because of your investigation?"

She had thought about that and the one thing she didn't want to do was to disrupt her child's life if he was alive somewhere and doing well. "I would want to know that he's happy and healthy. If he is then I will be satisfied."

Jeremy Banks nodded. "And if he's not?"

She thought about what could bring about an *if he's not* situation. She recalled what Sawyer had told her about his childhood. How his mother had given him up for adoption only for him to be shifted from foster home to foster home, trying to find his way, fit in and belong. Yet in the end, what he'd face was denials, deprivation and rejection. Vashti knew she would not want that for her child when she could offer him better. And that's what her answer to Jeremy Banks was. "If I were to find out that wasn't the case then I would want the opportunity to offer him better."

Banks nodded again as he stood to his feet. "Fair enough. You've given me enough information to get started and I'll contact you when I find out anything."

"I DON'T CARE, Percelli, we need to find Kia's biological mother," Alma implored her husband. "Our child might be dying."

She thought the hardest thing she'd ever had to do was to stand there beside her daughter's bed and hold tight to her hand while Dr. Telfair explained Kia's condition to her. When the doctor left, Kia had cried in her arms first, then her father's, and lastly her grandmother's. The three people who loved her the most.

Alma wanted to twist out of her husband's arms when he wrapped them around her. "Baby, please don't say that. We won't lose her."

She swiped back her tears. "Then we need to find her. I don't care if her mother doesn't want to be found. We're talking about a life or death situation. We're talking about our baby. Our little girl."

They had come out of Kia's hospital room and left her with Gloria. Kia adored her grandmother and Gloria was giving Kia a pep talk. Now it seemed Percelli was giving Alma hers, but she didn't want to have a pep talk. She wanted their daughter well and back home where she belonged.

"I've taken care of it."

She pulled out of his arms, swiping at the tears she'd tried not to shed in front of Kia, but couldn't stop from flowing elsewhere. "What are you saying, Percelli?"

He reached out and caressed her chin. "I contacted our family attorney this morning and told him to work with Dr. Telfair based on a life-threatening situation and obtain a court order to unseal those adoption documents. My only prayer is that the biological mother cares enough to want to help save Kia."

SAWYER WALKED INTO his home and caught a nice scent from his kitchen. He followed the aroma and found his daughter busy at work at the stove. He had only one question to ask her for now. "Hey, Jade, whatever you're cooking smells good. Did you follow the recipe?"

She smiled at him. "Hey, Dad, and yes, I followed the recipe explicitly."

In that case he felt it was safe enough for him to ask, "What are you making?"

"Pizza Porcupines and a tossed salad."

Maybe it wasn't safe to ask after all. "Pizza Porcupines?"

"Yes."

The name was a turnoff but the aroma in the kitchen was definitely a turn-on. "You got the recipe from Trudy?"

"No, I got it from Ms. Vashti."

"Oh." The mere mention of Vashti's name sent pleasurable shivers up his spine and made him remember sand beneath his feet, the sound of waves crashing onto the shore and a kiss that he hadn't wanted to end.

"She made us some for lunch yesterday and it was so good. I asked for the recipe. They are easy to make."

"I'll take your word for it." He left to store his gun and a short while later he returned. After crossing the kitchen to the refrigerator he grabbed a beer and sat down at the able. He needed to talk to Jade about his date with Vashti on Saturday night. If nothing else he'd discovered she was tuned in to the town gossip by way of her friend Karen Libby. He wanted her to hear it from him before hearing it from anyone else.

"Just thought I'd tell you that I have a date for Saturday night."

Jade snatched her head up so fast it was a wonder it didn't snap. "A date?"

"Yes."

"With someone living in Catalina Cove?"

"Yes," he said, watching his daughter closely.

"Who?"

"Vashti Alcindor."

A huge smile spread across Jade's face and he was certain if she'd had space in the kitchen she would have been liable to do a cartwheel. Instead she thrust a fist in the air and said, "Yes!"

"I take it that means you don't have a problem with it?"

"Of course not. Ms. Vashti is pretty, she's smart and intelligent, a savvy businesswoman, a great cook, a real nice person, a—"

"I get the picture, Jade."

"Good. And can I add that she treats everyone who works for her with dignity?"

"Dignity?"

"Yes. You know with respect. And she does it in

a way that can bolster your self-esteem, regardless of whether you work inside the inn or outside in the gardens. It's the same. I hope you know I plan to take credit."

He lifted a brow. "Credit for what?"

"For introducing you guys."

If she wanted to take credit for that then he would let her. Besides, to tell her that wasn't true would require a lot of explaining on his part.

"So where do you plan to take her?" Jade asked, intruding on his thoughts.

"The Lighthouse."

"Wow!"

He could tell from his daughter's expression she was impressed. He decided to finish off his beer and take a shower before she started asking him what he planned to wear. "I'm going to take a shower. I'll be back down for dinner in a few."

"Okay, Dad."

He moved to leave the kitchen, glanced over his shoulder and shook his head. His daughter was actually in the middle of his kitchen doing a happy dance.

# CHAPTER THIRTY-TWO

"GOOD EVENING, Sheriff Grisham, Ms. Alcindor. Welcome to the Lighthouse. I'm Samuel, your maître d' tonight and your table is ready. Please follow me."

Vashti felt a spike of heat when Sawyer reached for her hand and tucked it comfortably in his as they followed Samuel. She felt several pairs of eyes on them and figured word would get around town by tomorrow about their date. He didn't seem to care and neither would she.

Ms. Gertie's funeral yesterday had been huge. It seemed like the whole town was there. One of the things she'd taken away from the minister's eulogy was that Ms. Gertie was a person with a big heart who'd live a good life with no regrets. Vashti decided that's what she wanted. To be a person who lived a good life with no regrets. She shouldn't judge Sawyer by how shabbily she was treated by Scott. Julius hadn't treated her shabbily; he just hadn't given her the support she needed when it mattered. Deep down he might have loved her and admitted it in the end, but at that time he hadn't loved her enough.

Once seated, Samuel handed them menus. "Mello is your waiter tonight and he will be with you in a moment."

"Thanks." Sawyer then looked over at her and smiled. "You look nice tonight."

She smiled back. "Thanks. You look nice as well."

She had been ready to leave as soon as she'd opened the door, with wrap and purse in hand. There had been no reason to invite him inside and that had been on purpose. It didn't take much to remember what happened the last time she had invited him inside her home in New York.

She glanced around and saw what a beautiful place the Lighthouse Restaurant was. The architecture, furnishing and design all had an elegant look. They'd been given a window that overlooked the gulf and the beam of light that used to steer ships home now gave a radiant glow to the sea at night. "This is a nice place. No wonder it's hard to get reservations. You've been here before?"

He shook his head. "No, this is my first time. What about you?"

"Years ago when the Bradys owned it, but it wasn't this elegant. The new owners transformed it into a really nice place."

"Last night I told Jade I was taking you on a date," he said.

"Oh? And what was her reaction?"

"A happy dance." He chuckled warmly. "My daughter actually did a happy dance in my kitchen. She likes you."

"And I like her. She's doing a great job completing her assignments and following orders."

"And speaking of following orders, I should thank you for that, too."

"What? Her following orders?"

"Pretty much. But in this case, following a recipe.

She made those Pizza porcupines and they tasted great because she followed the recipe."

Vashti chuckled. "Most people do when cooking something different."

"Not my child. She used to think it was her God-given right to deviate. You would not believe how many recipes she's butchered, destroying great meals."

"Yet, you ate them anyway," she said, knowingly.

He smiled back. "I tried, but eventually we had a little talk. I was on the verge of sending her to cooking school."

Whenever he talked about his daughter Vashti could see that gleam in his eye that was so filled with love she could feel it. Jade was a lucky young lady. She'd told him that before and was about to tell him that again when the waiter appeared.

"Did you hire a private investigator?" Sawyer asked after the waiter had taken their food order and served their wine.

"Yes. He seemed confident that he will be able to tell me something one way or the other."

"If he's good at what he does, he will. It will take a lot of digging, but first he might have legal hurdles to get beyond."

She took a sip of her wine. "I spoke to Kaegan this week and he told me the two of you went out on the water."

He took a sip of his wine as well. "We did. I love going out whenever I can and the fish were really biting that day. Do you like to fish?"

"I'm not going to say I like to fish, but I love going out on the water. I find it relaxing."

He nodded and held her gaze. "Would you go out with me on my boat next Friday?"

There was no escaping the way he was looking at her or the passion his stare was stirring. "You have a boat?"

"Yes, I have a boat. Mine isn't as large as Kaegan's."

Vashti had heard all about Kaegan's huge boat but the one Sawyer owned would definitely work for her. "Yes, I would love to go out on your boat with you."

His face split into a grin and at that moment the waiter returned with their dinner.

"BUT WHAT IF she doesn't come?"

Percelli didn't say anything as his daughter looked at him with her big brown eyes. He had to give her hope. The same hope he'd given his wife and mother earlier before sending them to the cafeteria to grab something to eat. Kia had been in the hospital over a week and the doctors hadn't said when she would be going home. She had started dialysis and hated it.

He had told her that he'd hired a private investigator to find her biological mother, hoping she would agree to be tested to see if there's a match. "If she doesn't come, Kia, then we move to plan B."

"But that could take forever. My life is ruined. No school. No sports. I hate it here. I hate being sick. I hate getting dialysis. I want to go home, Daddy, and sleep in my own bed. I want to go home."

Percelli went to his daughter and held her when she burst into tears. He knew she was having a pity party and she was entitled to it. She'd been pricked and prodded for almost two weeks. He continued to hold her while she cried and it felt as if the weight of the world were on his shoulders. Closing his eyes he sent up a silent prayer for strength and for a miracle. Kia needed her birth mother to come through for her and he prayed that she did.

SAWYER WAS THOROUGHLY enjoying Vashti's company. After dinner they had ordered the Lighthouse's signature blueberry pie with vanilla ice cream. Then later they'd sipped blueberry coffee while she told him of all the things she'd done so far to the inn and the things she had yet to do.

He could tell she was excited about the woman she'd hired who was an amazing chef. She also told him how she had connected with her former college, NYU, to institute an internship program with them next fall.

He in turn had told her about his and Jade's summer adventure and the two weeks they'd spent in the Great Smoky Mountains and the fun they'd had. He told her about their road trip when he'd picked Jade up from her godmother's house in Texas and how they'd spent a week on Galveston Beach.

Later, when he turned his car onto Buccaneer Lane the outside of the inn was lit up like a Christmas tree. Not only had she installed floodlights but there were also lights lining the driveway and flanking several trees in the yard. It had still been daylight when he'd picked her up and now he was seeing just how the placed looked at night.

"I see you took my advice," he said, pulling into her driveway.

"Yes, but I'll probably cringe when I get the first electric bill."

"Maybe, but you can't put a price on safety."

She chuckled. "Spoken like a true cop."

After bringing the car to a stop he turned to her. "I enjoyed myself tonight." The glow from the yard was shining in the car's interior and making her look even more beautiful. He was getting aroused just looking at her, being in close quarters with her and inhaling her scent.

During dinner he'd managed to keep his libido in check thanks to the steady flow of conversation between them. But that didn't mean he hadn't desired her, because he had. What man wouldn't? Tonight she had chosen a pretty pants set that looked good on her and showed just how well-proportioned her body was, especially her curvy hips, shapely breasts and small waist.

He wanted her. The more he was around her the more he remembered how it felt to be inside her, moving in and out of her, skin to skin. He wondered how tonight would end. Would he walk her to the door, say goodnight and leave? Or would she invite him in?

"What are you thinking, Sawyer?"

He grinned sheepishly. "What makes you think I was thinking anything?"

She smiled and his heart raced. "Well for starters, you were staring at me without saying anything."

Yes, he had been. He would admit that. "I couldn't help it."

"Why?"

So, she wanted him to spell it out for her, did she? How could he explain that whenever he was around her he felt hot, smoldering lust? But then, he knew he didn't have to explain anything to her since she could probably feel it with the same intensity that he could. But if she wanted to hear it from him...

"I want you, Vashti."

She didn't seem surprised by his direct honesty. Instead she reached out and with the tip of a polished fingernail she caressed the line of his jaw and said in a voice that was velvety soft, "In that case, I think we need to go inside."

Hell, leave it to her to make his already aroused body that much more stimulated. He quickly reached out and unsnapped her seat belt and then unsnapped his own before opening the door to the SUV to get out.

He all but sprinted around the front of the vehicle to open the door for her. She grinned as she eased out of her seat and he closed the door behind her. "Boy, don't you have a lot of energy tonight," she teased.

"Yeah," he said, taking her hand and leading her toward the steps. "You want me to show you how much?"

"I'm hoping that you do," she said, and at that moment he thought she was simply amazing. She wouldn't be playing games with him and was letting him know that she was all in. He remembered another night she had been all in and the off-the-charts lovemaking that had resulted. Those memories had gotten him through the last few months when he would think of her, want her and had thought he would never have her again. He hoped that things would change tonight.

Holding tight to her hand they walked up the steps. It was a beautiful night and the scent of the sea flowed through his nostrils. She opened the door and he gave her time to turn off the alarm system before following her inside and closing the door behind them.

That was as far as they got before he reached out and pulled her into his arms, claiming her mouth with a degree of passion he felt only with her.

SAWYER HAD A way of turning her life upside down but in a good way. Vashti wanted this and she wanted him. He wasn't the only one with wants. Dinner was great but this was the part of the evening that she'd been anticipating, when he would kiss her in a way that could make her purr.

The moment his tongue tangled with hers, a level of passion she could feel only with him began rushing molten heat through her veins. He was kissing her with an intensity that replaced all of her senses, common and otherwise, with a need that radiated all through her. Something she'd come to expect from a Sawyer Grisham kiss.

He wasn't just taking her mouth—he was making love to it. His tongue was touching every inch of hers. Searing it with wild, undeniable hunger. Then his tongue began moving in circles, driving her crazy with lust. Wrapping her arms around his neck, she hung on, fearful if she didn't the yearning she felt inside would take over and she would become a woman possessed. But then, she was almost there.

It seemed he always had a new and different way to kiss her, whether using a tried and true technique or merely experimenting, it didn't matter. What mattered was that she knew he was getting the intended effect. If it was his aim to push her over the edge with this kiss, make her regret every single day she'd put distance between them and goad her to never make that mistake again, it was working.

He pulled away from her mouth to rain kisses down her neck and to reach out and gently cup her breasts through the material of her top. More sensations rocked her when he touched her there and she could only throw her head back and moan. That gave him more of her neck to lick.

"Sawyer…"

"I love it when you say my name," he crooned, close to her ear before licking along the side of it as well. She thought of making some kind of saucy comeback comment but found she could barely breathe. That meant she needed to leave well enough alone. But well enough in the form of Sawyer Grisham had no intention of leaving her alone, and he showed her how serious he was when he suddenly whipped her top over her head.

She sucked in a quick breath. She hadn't seen it coming but undoubtedly he did and knew his next move. Unsnapping the front clasp of her bra he quickly worked the straps from her shoulders.

"Black lace. Nice."

Vashti had figured the night would end this way. At least she had hoped and decided to be prepared. That's why she'd pulled out her matching bra and panties set. She was a lace woman and he'd told her the last time they'd made love that he was a lace man. She liked colorful lace underthings and he liked black lace. Tonight, for him, she had worn black lace.

Somehow she found her voice to ask, "Shouldn't we take this to the bedroom?"

"In a minute," he said in a deliberate teasing voice.

## CHAPTER THIRTY-THREE

SAWYER EASED A nipple between his lips and began sucking hard. What felt like hot liquid shot through the juncture of Vashti's legs. Was he trying to kill her? She could take only so much. And when he moved to her other breast, she couldn't stop the moan that flowed from her lips. She needed to tell him that his minute was up, but couldn't.

He left one breast to use his mouth, lips and tongue to torture the other. She purred, moaned and nearly screamed, but he refused to let up. Long moments passed before he finally lifted his head to gaze into her eyes. "You liked that?"

Did he really expect an answer? Hadn't all those sounds she'd made been loud enough? It seemed like the good sheriff was in the seduction business tonight.

"Now to strip you naked," he said in a husky voice that sent sensuous shivers all through her. "You're shivering. Are you cold?"

If only he knew just how on fire she was, he would not have asked her that. "No, I'm not cold."

"Good," he said easing away from her. She met his gaze and the eyes looking back at her were filled with an amount of desire that should have frightened her. Instead it stirred more passion to life within her.

"I can't spend the night, Vashti, so you know what that means."

A part of her was afraid to ask, but she did. "No, what does that mean?"

The heat of his gaze nearly scorched her skin and seeped into her body. "It means I plan to make every second, minute and hour count. When I leave here tonight there will be no doubt in your mind or in mine what's ahead for us."

She swallowed. He had an ultra-hungry look in his eyes.

"It's not just sex, Vashti. Get it out of your head if that's the way you're thinking. Like I told you, I don't want another friend with benefits. I want you. Tonight is just the beginning."

"Yes, tonight is just the beginning," she agreed.

Her words must have pleased him, if the smile that appeared on his face was anything to go by.

"I'm holding you to it," he said, strolling back to her in a walk so sexy she was nearly overcome with need.

"And I'm holding you to it as well," was her response as sexual vibes poured between them. Vibes she was certain he felt, too.

He kissed her again and like before, he set off an explosion of pleasure and need within her. Desire began clawing at her, worse than before, and when he finally released her mouth she had to grab hold of him for feeling weak in the knees.

"You're shivering again," he said, leaning in and whispering close to her ear just seconds before his tongue licked a downward trek to her neck. "I would leave my mark here," he said, kissing the side of her neck, "but I would hate for my daughter to see my brand on you."

He was making her feel hotter, even more breathless. "You think she'll make you a suspect?"

"I know she will, baby. Jade is too observant for her own good at times. That means I need to brand you in other places. Places she won't see." With that said, he lowered to his knees in front of her.

SAWYER LEANED BACK on his haunches to look up at Vashti. Standing there topless with the most beautiful pair of breasts any woman could possess. Just seeing them was a wow effect. One that sent an urgent throb of desire through him. He needed to make love to her. To reacquaint his body with hers. To prove he hadn't imagined how good things had been between them that night in New York. He needed to know that reality was a hell of a lot better than any fantasy he'd had of her.

"Sawyer?"

He met her gaze. "Yes, sweetheart?"

"What are you doing down there?"

He gave her a sly grin. She knew what he was doing down here, but since she asked he would tell her. "I'm about to put my tongue to work and get a real good taste of you. I plan on taking licking and sucking to a whole other level tonight." He saw heat flare in her eyes. "Do you want to know why?"

Instead of answering she nodded. "Because the last time," he said, holding her gaze. "The moment I slid my tongue inside of you, I'm convinced I've never tasted anything as sweet, luscious and succulent as you. It was a taste to die for. To cherish. Tasting you only made me want more. Hunger for more. I think I became hung up on you ever since our time together in New York."

He hadn't wanted to bring up that time because they were trying to move beyond it. But he wanted her to know how much he'd been taken with her and the lasting impression she had left on him. "I would lie awake at night remembering you, your taste and everything about you. Your looks, your intelligence, the sexy way you walked, everything about you that made you a woman I wanted to pursue."

Their gazes held and he knew at that moment something, he wasn't sure exactly what, passed between them. An emotion he was ready for but wasn't sure if she was, after reading the sudden panic in her eyes. At that moment he despised the two men she'd loved who had let her down. "I won't ever hurt you, Vashti." It was important to him that she knew that.

Instead of saying anything she bent down to him, cupped his face in her hands and took his mouth in a deep kiss, using her tongue on him the way he'd used his on her earlier. When she straightened and stared down at him he thought he would explode right then and there. Her kiss had been just that powerful.

He then watched as she stepped out of her sandals before pushing her pants down over a pair of curvaceous hips. The lamplight shone on her as she stood there in the middle of her living room clad in only a pair of black lace panties. He'd never seen a woman looking sexier or more beautiful.

Reaching upward he slid his fingers beneath the waistband of her panties and slowly eased them down her hips. He wanted to taste her and couldn't wait any longer. He was tempted to take the lace panties and stuff them into the pockets of his pants as a keepsake, but quickly dismissed doing such a thing. If his daughter ever came across them he would have a lot of explaining to do. But still, doing something like confiscating her undies was such a naughty thought, a total turn-on. Before he was tempted to change his mind he tossed her underwear aside.

He looked back up at her, seeing her totally naked. He marveled at the perfection of her shoulders, the swell of her breasts, the smoothness of her skin, her exquisite hips and thighs. Pure feminine flawlessness on legs.

The area between her gorgeous legs was what was holding his attention. It was simply beautiful. Reaching upward, he traced his fingers down her inner thigh before slipping a finger between the folds of her feminine core. He watched her face, saw the affect his touch had on her and when he used that finger to stroke her, he saw the way her eyes blazed even more with desire.

"Sawyer…"

"Yes, baby. I'm here and don't worry. I plan to finish what I've started." Pulling his finger out of her, he gripped her thighs and placed his mouth where his finger had been and slid his tongue inside of her.

Sawyer groaned as his tongue seemed to have a mind of its own and began lapping her like his life depended on him doing so. She tasted hot, delectable and sensuously yummy. Pleasure surged through him and when he felt her press against him, straining the lower part of her body against his mouth, he knew she wanted as much of his tongue as he could give her. He wanted her to have it all. He changed his technique and began giving her coiled thrusts with his tongue that felt harder and went deeper.

"Sawyer!" she screamed his name and when he tasted her release on his tongue he came close to his own orgasm. He held back, wanting to give her this and needing the full essence of her flavor. At night when he was in his bed and she was a couple of miles away in hers, he would remember this.

He waited until the last spasm had left her body before standing and sweeping her into his arms. He glanced down at her and saw her face was flushed from her recent climax. "Which way?"

"To your left," she said like it took a lot of air to do so.

Nodding he turned left and headed for her bedroom.

VASHTI WAS CONVINCED that rockets were still exploding inside her head when Sawyer placed her in the middle of the bed. After lying in this same bed dreaming of him so many times, it was hard to believe he was here in the flesh and in living color.

"Nice room."

She watched him, where he stood in the middle of the room and began undressing. She was at rapt attention as he removed his shirt and slid it off masculine shoulders. She'd seen him naked before but it didn't matter. Seeing him shed his clothes was doing a number on her.

Next came his pants and then his briefs and when he stood totally naked, all she could do was release a sign of satisfaction as well as of feminine appreciation. She watched him pull a condom out of his wallet and sheath himself.

When he came toward the bed, she raised up on her knees. Reaching out she ran her hands across his massive chest and then after a few gentle caresses she smiled when she heard him moan. "Nice sound," she said, looking up at him.

"I doubt you know what all you do to me, Vashti Alcindor."

She chuckled as her hands continued to stroke him, moving from his chest to his broad shoulders. "I think it rattled us at first to discover what we could do to each other. I've never been attracted to a man this way before."

She began placing kisses on his chest. She was aware of him taking a handful of her hair and running his fingers through it. "You're a beautiful woman, you know that?"

"Only because you tell me. And I think that you, Sawyer Grisham, are a beautiful man."

Vashti was so caught up in planting kisses all over his chest and shoulders, that when he gently pressed her back on the bed she was caught off guard. "Hey, not fair. I'm not through with you yet."

"I need to connect my body with yours, Vashti. In a bad way."

She heard a degree of need in his voice that probably matched her own because she wanted to feel him inside of her, too. In a bad way. She looked up at him when he loomed over her before settling his weight atop her. And then he lowered his mouth to kiss her again.

Wrapping her arms around his neck she was aware of him nudging her legs apart with his knee. Suddenly, he released her mouth and stared down at her. She held her breath when she felt the tip of his erection at the base of her womanly folds. And then he began easing inside of her.

It seemed he'd gotten bigger since the last time and

her body was eagerly expanding to accommodate his size. Their gazes remained locked and she was drawn to the beauty of the dark brown eyes staring down at her.

He pushed farther, he went deeper, and then using his hands he lifted her hips to receive even more of him, going for a more concentrated penetration. When it seemed he couldn't go any farther, her inner muscles begged to differ and clutched him in a firm feminine grip that propelled him to surge forward. She wanted all of him.

He began thrusting inside of her. Gently at first and then hard. Harder and harder still. She arched her hips to take even more of him into her. He established a rhythm and she easily caught on, rotating her hips to meet him stroke for stroke. He was plowing hard inside of her, pushing in and then pulling out. Over and over again.

"Sawyer!"

"Vashti!"

Their worlds exploded into spirals of passionate pleasure. She dug her fingernails in his shoulders as she continued to move her body in unison to his. It was as if her body desperately needed his possession and he was bombarding her with thrust after relentless thrust.

His body jerked again, the same time hers did. She felt totally and complete dazed. Totally and completely fulfilled as her body was consumed by his fire.

Ever so sweetly, he leaned down and kissed her and she couldn't think of a better way to end such a perfect mating. It seemed the kiss lasted forever before he ended it to lift his body off hers. Shifting to hold her in his arms, he whispered against her ear, "You okay, baby?"

She found the strength to nod and say, "Yes, I'm okay."

And then while he held her she drifted off to sleep.

SAWYER DIDN'T WANT to wake her, but knew he had to before leaving. He'd stayed longer than he had intended, but would not have had it any other way. Now he was fully dressed. He had gone into the living room for her clothes scattered there and couldn't resist putting her undies in his pocket.

Placing her bra, blouse and pants across the chair in her room he moved to the bed and touched her shoulder. "Vashti?"

Her eyes flitted open and she smiled at him through sleepy eyes. "Hmm."

"It's time for me to go." He sat on the edge of the bed and pulled her into his lap. "I hate to leave you."

He both felt and heard her yawn against his chest. "You must go. Jade."

"Yes. Jade." He was glad she understood that he could not leave his daughter alone all night.

"I enjoyed my time with you," she said sleepily.

"And I, you. I'm looking forward to taking you boating on Friday."

He kissed her and when he finally released her mouth, he whispered, "Go back to sleep. I'll lock things up and arm your security system."

"Alright."

He lifted her out of his lap to place her back in bed and covered her up. "Oh, and by the way. I brought your clothes in here, but decided to keep your panties."

"Okay," she said, yawning.

He smiled knowing it hadn't registered on her just

what he'd said. He would remind her when they talked tomorrow. Her even breathing let him know she had drifted off to sleep and as he told her he would do, he locked up and left.

When he walked outside her house and headed to his SUV he knew he couldn't wait to see her again.

# CHAPTER THIRTY-FOUR

"You didn't get home until after midnight, Dad."

Sawyer glanced across the breakfast table at his daughter as he was about to bite into the biscuits he'd cooked. "And you know this, how?"

"Because I tried waiting up for you, but I fell asleep."

He nodded, wondering if she knew the actual time he'd gotten in. It was close to three in the morning. "You are aware that I don't have a curfew, right?"

She smiled. "Yes, I know that. I figured you must have been having a good time to stay out so late."

*If only she knew…*and he was going to make sure that she didn't know. But he would confirm what she'd said. "Yes, I had a good time. Dinner was great and I enjoyed Vashti's company."

"I'm glad. Did you make another date?"

She was definitely nosey. "Yes, I did." He glanced at his watch. "If you don't hurry and get dressed you'll be late for church." He didn't care if she thought he was deliberately changing the subject.

"I won't be late. You're taking Ms. Vashti out to dinner again?"

Sawyer saw his daughter was determined to appease her nosiness. "No, I thought next time I'd take her boating."

"Boating? Honestly, Dad, there's nothing romantic about going out on a boat. Surely you can do better than that."

"Excuse me?"

"Taking Ms. Vashti out on a boat should come later. You need to stick with romantic gestures, such as dinner, movies, concerts…you know, those sorts of things. And sending her flowers wouldn't hurt either."

He lifted a brow. Was Jade, who had never been on a date, trying to give him dating tips? It seemed his daughter was reading too many of those romance novels. "I think I know how to impress a woman, Jadelyn Erin Grisham."

"I'm sure you do, but you might be a little rusty since you haven't gone on a date since Mom. At least not a real date. The friend with benefits thing doesn't count."

He tried to change the subject again. "Are you excited about the church outing that's coming up?" She was going away this coming weekend with the church's youth group to Tickfaw State Park.

"Yes, I'm excited and since we leave early Friday morning I got the time off work approved with Ms. Vashti." Jade took a big swallow of her orange juice and asked. "Did you know Ms. Vashti used to be the cove's baton-twirling champion?"

"Yes, I'd heard that."

"Some of her trophies are on display at the high school, and she has a few in a display in a cabinet at the inn. She was national champion. I told her I wanted to be a majorette and try-outs were next month. She offered to give me a few lessons at no charge. Isn't that great?"

"Yes, that was nice of her," he said standing to take

his plate into the kitchen. Jade followed with her plate as well.

He hoped she didn't have any more questions for him about his date last night with Vashti. Honestly, he was still in awe of the entire evening. Nothing could surpass what he thought of his after-dinner enjoyment at her home. The memories alone had made it hard to settle down to a good night's sleep. He'd been too wired up, too sexually satisfied, to close his eyes. By the time he'd finally drifted off to sleep it wasn't long before his alarm had gone off.

"I bet I'll finish dressing for church before you," Jade said, after rinsing her plate and placing it in the dishwasher.

"If you do it will be the first time," he said, grinning.

He glanced over his shoulder to see Jade rush up the stairs.

VASHTI LOOKED AT herself in the mirror and hoped she didn't have that I've-gotten-laid look. Especially when she would be walking out her door in a few minutes heading to church. She had awoken that morning with Sawyer's scent all over her, sore in certain parts of her body yet feeling she would still walk with a spring in her step. What woman wouldn't after spending a night in Sawyer's arms? Well, she hadn't actually spent a night in his arms since he'd left her bed sometime between one and two in the morning, but he had packed a lot of action in during the time he had been in bed with her. And had he told her before leaving that he was taking her undies? She seemed to recall him doing so, which would explain why they weren't with the rest of her clothes he'd picked up and placed over the chair in her room. The thought that he had kept them sent sensuous shivers all through her. Sheriff Grisham had a naughty streak.

Her cell phone rang and she quickly pulled it from her purse. "Hello?"

"Just checking to make sure you're coming to church."

Vashti smiled. It would be the first time she'd gone to church since returning to the cove, and when she'd seen Reverend Castor at Ms. Gertie's funeral he'd made it a point to not only welcome her back to Catalina Cove, but to invite her to church. "Yes, Bryce. I'm coming to church."

"Good. I'm sitting with the folks and will save you a seat."

"Thanks. I'd appreciate that."

"So how was your date last night with Sawyer?" Bryce asked.

"Great and please don't ask for details. I want to keep it all to myself for now. All I'm going to say is that Sawyer is simply amazing."

"Wow, the sheriff has moved from the nice column to the amazing column."

"Yes, and before you asked, yes, we're going on another date. And I'm looking forward to it. I'll see you at church in a few. Goodbye."

Slipping the phone back inside her purse Vashti headed for the door. The Witherspoons had invited her to dinner after church. She figured that she and Bryce would be able to talk privately then.

## CHAPTER THIRTY-FIVE

"It's a BEAUTIFUL day for boating, Sawyer," Vashti said, as he helped her onboard his boat. She noticed all the other boaters taking advantage of the beautiful weather. And his boat, a twenty-eight-foot-long cabin cruiser that was painted metallic blue with splashes of white with a design resembling a bolt of lightning, was beautiful as well. It had a lavish forward berth and wraparound port seating with a table and an integrated swim platform.

"And your boat is stunning. I thought you said it was small." She glanced around thinking there was nothing small about this boat. It was larger than the one her parents had owned and the layout made it twice as roomy.

"Thanks and make yourself at home. I'll give you a tour in a minute. There's a keg of wine coolers over there."

"I think I'll have one now. What about you?"

"I'll get one later, after we select a spot to idle awhile."

She tried not to stare at him while he moved around getting the boat ready. This was the first time she'd ever seen him in a pair of shorts and he had the perfect male physique for them, especially his masculine hairy legs and powerful-looking thighs. She hated giving his body her full attention but temptation got the best of her.

They hadn't spent any time together since Saturday night, although they had seen each other at church on

Sunday, but only at a glance. And it had been a sizzling glance that had tempted her more than once to look across several pews to seek him out. He'd undoubtedly been thinking the same thing because their gazes would automatically connect.

He had called Wednesday evening to finalize plans for their date. Since Jade was to leave this morning for a church outing, he'd suggested they go boating and take in a movie on Saturday.

Like him she was wearing a pair of white shorts, but while he had on a T-shirt, she had a bikini top that matched the bottoms under her shorts. She'd worn a cover-up over her outfit, but since they were now headed out toward the open sea, she decided to take it off. He released an appreciative whistle.

"You look nice, Vashti. Real nice."

"Thanks. So do you." The look he was giving her almost made her weak in the knees.

"I hope you know what you're wearing is a turn-on," he said, roaming his gaze over her.

"Is it?"

"Yes."

If he thought being dressed in an outfit meant to show off his solid muscles wasn't having an effect on her, then he was wrong. Standing there with his legs braced apart with a sailor cap on his head while steering the ship away from shore gave *alluring*, *rock-hard* and *masculine* all new meaning when grouped together.

Their eyes connected and desire lit up his eyes the same time it lit hers. A low moan escaped her lips, a sound she was certain he heard, if the darkening of his pupils was anything to go by. She broke eye contact with him and saw they were not only moving farther from shore but away from other boaters as well.

"I understand you offered baton-twirling lessons to Jade. I appreciate that and I'm willing to pay you."

"Don't you dare consider doing that, Sawyer. First of all, I need to make sure I can still twirl a baton. It's been years. And second, I would love to teach Jade what I know. I guess you already know your daughter is special. You're a lucky dad."

He smiled and she could tell her words pleased him. She was glad because she had told him the truth. "Thanks. Raising a teenager—especially a daughter—isn't easy. Jade and I have a close relationship and I appreciate that. I'm also glad that she has a good head on her shoulders. She's not perfect but I wouldn't trade her for the world."

Vashti thought that was a nice thing for a father to say and figured her own wouldn't think such a thing. She pushed thoughts of her parents out of her mind as she took a sip of her wine cooler. She began talking about how things were going at the inn and the scheduled grand opening.

"I'm glad you hired a full staff. That will make things easy on you," Sawyer said.

"Yes, it will. I'm getting excited about it. I hate I'll be losing Jade in about a month when school starts back. She's been a big help."

When he brought the boat to a stop she saw they were out in the middle of the gulf with no other vessels around. They were alone. Smiling, she thought she liked that.

"Why are you smiling, Vashti?"

"No reason," she said, glancing over at him and again

feeling that magnetic pull that was always there whenever they looked at each other.

"I missed you this week," he said, moving toward her.

"And I missed you, too," she confessed.

He came to a stop in front of her and she knew he intended to kiss her, and she wanted the kiss. Reaching out he caressed her chin with his finger. "I missed you more, Vashti."

His words spoken in a deep, throaty, yet husky voice, sent sensuous shivers down her spine. "That's debatable, Sawyer."

His gaze shifted from her eyes to her lips when he said, "I don't think so, baby."

He then lowered his mouth to hers.

THE MOMENT HIS mouth touched Vashti's, Sawyer felt a fluttering in his chest, too close to his heart for comfort. That knowledge sent a shot of panic through him, tempted him to pull back and end the kiss. However, instead of ending it, he deepened the kiss, needing the taste he was becoming used to. The taste he was constantly craving ever since the first time their mouths had connected that night at Kaegan's cookout.

He cherished these moments with her, whether in the bedroom or out. They were precious to him. Maybe becoming way too precious but he couldn't cease those feelings. The last thing he wanted to do was overwhelm her, especially since she'd been the one against them continuing an affair. Now that they were of one accord, in sync with their wants and desires, he didn't want his greed for her to take over. That's why he had deliberately not seen her this week and had contacted her only on Wednesday to finalize plans for their date. He was trying to slow down and give her time to adjust to them being an item. But just being with her now, the words she'd just spoken and the way she was returning his kiss, tongue stroke for tongue stroke, showed they were past taking things slow.

He finally ended their kiss and licked around her lips with his tongue, something he always enjoyed doing. She was pressed hard to his chest and he could feel her heart beating just as fast and furious as his own. Both were breathing like they'd run a marathon and were gearing up for another race.

Taking her hand, he said, "Now for that tour I promised you."

Sawyer showed her around, pointing out different aspects of the boat topside before leading her down the steps to the cabin where soft music was playing. He knew the moment she saw what he wanted her to see. A table set for two with what appeared to be candlelight. In essence, they were battery operated candles whose flickering flames resembled the real thing. Wineglasses were on the table as well as a bottle of wine. In the center of the table was a beautiful bouquet of flowers.

"The table setting is beautiful, Sawyer," Vashti said looking from the table to him.

"Thanks." He picked up the bouquet of flowers. "These are for you."

"Mine?" she asked, sounding both surprised and excited when he handed them to her.

"Yes. When I told Jade of our plans to go boating, she balked at the idea, saying taking you boating wasn't romantic. So I wanted to make it romantic for you and

figured the flowers, candles, music and a specially prepared picnic lunch from Witherspoon Café should do it."

"It did," she said and he saw the depth of appreciation in her eyes. "I've never been given flowers before."

He lifted a brow, finding that hard to believe.
"Never?"

"Never. I expected flowers my first Valentine's Day
as Scott's wife but it didn't happen. He said sending
flowers was a waste of good money."

The more he heard about her ex-husband the more he
knew how much of an ass the man was. Sawyer would
send flowers to Johanna every Valentine's Day to let her
know how much he loved and appreciated her for taking
good care of him and their daughter. He never thought
about it as wasted money and couldn't imagine any man
being so inconsiderate to the woman he was supposed
to love. Right then and there, he decided this would not
be the last bouquet of flowers she got from him. "Come
on and let me show you the rest of the cabin."

He could tell she was impressed. He showed her how,
by the sliding of a few doors, he could easily convert
his dining area into extra sleeping quarters. She also
seemed amazed how his bed could enlarge from a single to a double with a remote, and the extra hideaway
Murphy bed for Jade with a press of a button. She also
liked the placement of the window near the bed where
you could wake up and view the gulf.

"How often do you go out on the water for long pe-
riods of time?" she asked him, turning from looking
out the window.

He brushed a curl away from her face, needing to
touch her then. "Not often, only because since Kaegan
got his yacht, he invited me to use it when Jade and I

take a trip up the coast. Needless to say, after spending a night in such luxury, it was hard to come back down to earth and take this one out overnight the next time."

A smile touched her lips. "Granted I've never been onboard Kaegan's boat, but I have seen it. However, I would think yours would be perfect. Maybe not for you and Jade because I can see you both needing more space, but if you were to ever invite a friend overnight, the two of you wouldn't mind the limited space."

Sawyer reached out, took the flowers out of her hand to place them behind him on the table. He then wrapped his arms around Vashti. "If I didn't know any better, Ms. Alcindor, I would think you were dropping hints for an invitation."

She grinned. "Yes, you could think that, if you didn't know any better. But just in case you're too slow to read between the lines, Sawyer Grisham, hopefully this will help you somewhat."

Reaching up she wrapped her arms around his neck and on tiptoe, joined her mouth to his.

HOURS LATER, Vashti woke up, loving the feel of having her naked body wrapped in Sawyer's arms with her face buried in his naked chest and their legs entwined. She didn't have to think hard to remember how they managed to get so entangled.

After the tour of his boat she decided she needed to test out his bed and had seized the opportunity to make it happen. And boy, did it happen. It simply amazed her just what a great kisser he was as well as a lovemaking machine. He had more stamina than any man she knew. At least any man she'd ever made love to. One orgasm always led to another and another. She felt weak, probably because they had skipped lunch.

"Hungry, baby?" he asked, lightly running his finger up and down the leg thrown over his. She fought back the moan that threatened to pour from her lips.

She lifted her head to look at him. He gave her a smile like he knew exactly what touching her did to her. "I would love to see what the Witherspoons prepared for our lunch that's turning into dinner," she said.

"Is that a hint that I'm starving you?"

She grinned, thinking of how they'd ended up in this bed. It had been all her doing this time and not his. He had gone along for the ride, so to speak. "No, but I feel like I might be starving you."

"Never. I love you here with me." He leaned closer and then whispered. "And I love whenever I'm inside you."

Vashti fought off the sensations his words caused to flow through her. They had been in bed for at least a couple of hours. For all she knew other boaters might have decided to idle in the area. What if they had and were curious as to what was happening on Sawyer's boat? That thought made her glance out the window.

"Looking for somebody?"

She glanced back at him. "Are you sure we're still out in the area alone?"

He chuckled. "No. The only thing I'm sure about is that I want you again, although I know we should eat to regain our strength."

"Does that mean we won't be fishing today?"

"It means we will do whatever you want to do. Today belongs to you."

She loved it when he said stuff like that. Whenever

he made her feel special. "Then I think we should eat dinner."

"Okay."

They both pulled their naked bodies out of bed. It amazed her how comfortable she felt being nude with him. And she absolutely loved looking at him naked.

"Like what you see?" He'd caught her checking him out again.

No need to lie. "Yes, I like what I see."

And as she slid into her top and shorts she came close to saying she was falling in love with what she saw.

# CHAPTER THIRTY-SIX

VASHTI SMILED WHEN Jade walked into her office. "It's that time already?" she asked, glancing at her watch.

"Yes, I just wanted to let you know I was about to leave and that I finished everything on that list you gave me to do today."

Vashti leaned back in her chair. "You always do. You're very efficient, Jade, and I don't regret hiring you."

Jade laughed. "You need to tell that to my dad. I believe he thinks I'm probably more of a pest to you than a helper."

"Then I will definitely tell him when I see him again." Vashti lowered her head to go back over the papers she'd been reading. When she detected Jade was still there, she lifted her head. "Jade? Is there anything you want to talk about?"

She noticed Jade was nervous, as if she was trying to make up her mind about something. "You look busy. Maybe this isn't a good time."

Vashti wondered what this was about and tossed the documents in the middle of her desk, and set aside her late-afternoon cup of coffee. "This is a great time. Would you like to have a seat and tell me what's wrong?"

Jade took the chair across from Vashti's desk and

nervously rubbed her hands together. "Nothing is wrong, but I would like to talk to you about my dad."

Vashti raised a brow. "What about your dad?"

Jade met her gaze. "He likes you."

A smile touched Vashti's lips. She and Sawyer had been seeing each other for several weeks now. It didn't take much to remember their first official date at the Lighthouse and the lovemaking afterward. Then almost a week later they had spent most of the day out on the gulf in his boat. They were supposed to be fishing and not below deck in bed wrapped in each other's arms. By the time they'd grabbed their fishing poles it had been barely light enough to see. However, they managed to bring in a good catch that day.

Since Jade had gone on that church outing Sawyer had spent the weekend with Vashti. It had been nice waking up both Saturday and Sunday mornings, wrapped in his arms in her bed. Saturday morning they'd had breakfast at the café. She hadn't imagined it when all eyes had gone to them when they walked in. Even Bryce, who'd been helping her folks out, had lifted a brow.

Later Bryce told her the reason she'd done so was because Vashti had walked in wearing a just-made-love look. It was no surprise by Saturday afternoon, anyone living in the cove who hadn't known before was now well aware she and Sawyer were involved. Having others know didn't bother her like she thought it would, and it certainly hadn't bothered Sawyer.

If anyone had thought Sawyer would cool things when his daughter returned to town from the church outing they had been sadly mistaken. Although he hadn't stayed overnight at her place, he did drop by a couple of times during the week to keep her company and usually didn't leave until after midnight.

Her very intense affair with Sawyer had been going on for about three weeks, and now Jade wanted to talk to her about her father. According to Sawyer, Jade was fully aware they were seeing each other, although Jade had never mentioned anything about it to Vashti...until now.

"And I like your dad, too, Jade. Sawyer is a very nice guy."

Vashti knew she could say a lot more than that, but of course she wouldn't.

Jade's smile brightened. "I'm glad. I have a great dad and he means the world to me. I was beginning to worry about him."

Vashti lifted a brow. "Worry about him? Why?"

"Because I knew when I left for college he would be all alone. I know he has friends here like Mr. Kaegan, but he didn't have a girlfriend. Now I'm glad he does."

There was no need to try and explain to Jade that she wasn't exactly Sawyer's girlfriend, just a friend whose company he enjoyed. But then that sounded too much like a friend with benefits. She and Sawyer had talked about it and they thought of themselves as lovers, but Jade didn't need to know that.

"And I like you, Ms. Vashti, a lot. I think you're the type of person my dad needs. He smiles a lot. He no longer looks sad. I want to thank you for making him happy."

Vashti wondered if she'd done that. Made Sawyer happy. He definitely had made her happy in addition to rocking her world. She tried not to think what the future held or didn't hold for them. How could she when she didn't even know what the future held for her? She might have a kid out there somewhere. Being around Jade reminded her of that every day since he and Jade would be close to the same age. The investigation would totally consume her mind if it wasn't for Sawyer. She enjoyed his company and he seemed to enjoy hers. They were both living again.

"Thanks, Jade, and I like you, too," Vashti said, and really meant it. "I tell Sawyer all the time just how lucky he is to have you for a daughter."

"You do?" Jade asked, surprised.

Vashti chuckled. "Yes, I do. The two of you have a strong father-daughter relationship. I like it."

"Thanks and I just wanted you to know I'm glad Dad is dating you and that the two of you are special to me."

Vashti fought back tears, thinking that was a real nice thing for Jade to say. "Ahh, thanks, Jade. I appreciate that."

"I say it and I mean it, Ms. Vashti. You're nice to everyone and you're smart. I like the way you run your business. Very professional, but you don't let anyone run over you. I watch, listen and observe. I like what I see."

And this compliment was coming from a sixteen-year-old? "Thank you."

"Are we still on this weekend for the baton lessons?" Jade asked.

"Yes, I'm looking forward to it. And your dad plans to grill the fish we caught while out boating that day."

"Super! Wait until you taste Dad's grilled fish. You're going to love it."

Vashti chuckled. "That's what he says and I didn't want to believe him, but since you claim it's true, I'll give him credit."

Hours after Jade had left, Vashti got a call from Sawyer asking if he could stop by. One thing she liked about him was that he never assumed anything. He had the decency to ask first, although she made it her business to make time whenever he visited.

She had taken a shower and dressed in a lounging outfit when her phone rang. A part of her was hoping it wasn't Sawyer canceling since she had looked forward to seeing him tonight. "Hello?"

"Ms. Alcindor, this is Jeremy Banks."

Her heart nearly skipped a beat. He'd told her weeks ago that she wouldn't hear from him until he had something. "Yes, Mr. Banks?"

"I'm sorry it's taken this long to check in, but the inquiry into the death certificate is taking a while with the state of Arkansas. Meanwhile, I've been working the adoption angle. I got a court order to review the records of that facility in Arkansas. Because it closed down it's taken a lot of searching to find out who were the keepers of the records."

"And you have now?"

"Yes. Digital records were lost, but paper records were transferred to a hospital in Arkansas for storage. This will be like finding a needle in a haystack, but I'm on it."

Vashti nodded. "Thank you for the update. At least we're making progress, right?"

"Yes, Ms. Alcindor. We are making progress. I'll check in again in a week, or if I have anything before then."

Vashti had just hung up the phone with Jeremy Banks when her doorbell sounded. She quickly moved to the door and opened it. The minute Sawyer walked into

he house he must have detected something was wrong
because he reached out for her. She went straight into
his arms.

"You okay?"

Vashti buried her face into his chest, not ready to talk
yet. Right now the only thing she wanted was to be held
by him. The man she was falling in love with, although
he hadn't meant for such a thing to happen. But right
now, he was the stationary object when everything in
her world seemed to be moving all around her, some
out of place. She was getting confused, befuddled and
tangled, and couldn't operate that way.

He stepped back and lifted her chin for her to look
up at him. "Tell me what's wrong, Vashti," he said, wiping a tear from her eye.

She was crying? She hadn't even known it. Why was
she letting the fear of the unknown get to her? "I just
got a call from my private investigator."

Sawyer's eyes grew intense. He took hold of her hand
to lead her into the living room. "And?"

They sat down on the sofa side by side. He continued
to hold her hand and she appreciated that. She wasn't
sure why Jeremy Banks's phone call had rocked her
world but it had. "He said the request for the death certificate is being processed, but that he tracked down
where the facility's records were sent when it closed."

Sawyer nodded. "So when will he know something?"

"In a week, and it will be the longest week of my
life, Sawyer."

He reached over and pulled her into his lap and
pressed her head down to his chest. "This is what you
wanted, right? To know for sure?"

"Yes, but if I get confirmation my baby did die then

I will relive the pain all over again and berate myself for believing Ms. Gertie when I knew the extent of her condition."

"And if you find out your baby is somewhere alive?" he asked her.

She lifted her head from his chest and met his gaze. "Then my parents have a lot to answer for, Sawyer. I doubt if I could ever forgive them if that's the case. So either way I will be unhappy."

He reached out and lightly ran the tip of his finger around her mouth. "And I'll be here, Vashti, ready and willing to make you happy again. And at some point you'll have to forgive your parents no matter what. Anger, bitterness and animosity are too much baggage to carry around. At some point you have to let it go. Otherwise it will destroy you. And I don't ever intend to let anything destroy you."

He leaned down and kissed her, and then picking her up into his arms, he headed for the bedroom.

HOURS LATER, Sawyer leaned over and kissed her lightly on the lips before carefully easing from her arms. It was time for him to leave. After grabbing his clothes, which he'd tossed earlier on the chair in her bedroom, he began getting dressed. Glancing over his shoulder he saw she was still sleeping soundly and he was glad. Hopefully she was having pleasant dreams and nothing to wake her up until the morning.

He knew she was worried about what that private investigator would report, but like he'd told her, either way, he intended to be there to help her through it. He glanced back at her while he sat down in the chair to put on his socks and shoes. She was mumbling some thing in her sleep and he paused a minute when he recognized his name.

At that moment something stirred to life within him. Something he thought was dead to him forever. Love. He wasn't sure when and how he had fallen in love with her but he had. It might have been the same day he'd pulled her over and given her a ticket. Or it might have been the night at Kaegan's party when he'd kissed her. It didn't matter when it happened; all he knew was that it had happened. That was the reason he couldn't stay away. The reason he thought about her often and why he couldn't wait to see her whenever he could.

He stood and walked to the bed and stared down at her. She had that satisfied look on her face even while sleeping with her hair tousled over the pillow. She looked beautiful. Like a goddess. Like the woman he had fallen in love with.

He leaned down and carefully placed another kiss on her lips. He knew there had to be a reason Vashti had been brought into his life when he had been alone for so long. He had preferred being alone, but now as he moved around her house to recheck the locks before leaving, he knew because of her he didn't want to ever be alone again.

# CHAPTER THIRTY-SEVEN

SAWYER TRIED KEEPING his attention on the fish, shrimp and salmon that were cooking on the grill and not on Vashti, who was giving Jade baton-twirling lessons.

Jade was an eager student and Vashti a worthy instructor. He was amazed at how easily the baton moved through her fingers. It had to be a gift, definitely a special skill and talent. He appreciated her taking the time to share that talent with his daughter.

Both were dressed in shorts and tank tops. This was the first time he'd seen Jade and Vashti interact together and he noticed how similar some of their features were. Jade resembled Vashti more than she had Johanna.

Sawyer figured it had to be the fact Jade and Vashti had the same coloring, where Johanna's had been a shade darker. Then it might have been because both Jade and Vashti had curly dark brown hair that flowed down their shoulders and both had chocolate-colored eyes. Although Jade was a few inches shorter than Vashti, their frames were similar.

He shook his head. Maybe the reason he thought the two favored each other was because unintentionally he was looking for similarities; anything that would give rationale to his desire to make Vashti a permanent part of his family. He knew Jade adored Vashti and she wouldn't have a problem with it.

He turned back to observe Jade and Vashti. He thought his daughter was doing a good job and would ace the try-outs. However, Vashti was letting her know there was more to being a majorette than twirling a baton. There was a certain way you had to march as well. Band music was playing from the stereo speakers, while Vashti and Jade were now marching around his backyard as if they were in a parade. The one thing he discovered about most Louisianans was that they loved parades.

His eyes were glued to Vashti's legs as she moved them around and kicked them out. They were beautiful and she knew just the right precision while stepping to the music. He'd heard her tell Jade that during the next lesson they would go through several majorette dances.

"How do you think I did, Dad?" Jade came over to ask him when she and Vashti finally took a break.

"I think you did awesome."

"Yes, she did," Vashti said, placing her arm around Jade's shoulders. "She's a natural."

"Thanks and I can't believe how easy baton twirling is for you, Ms. Vashti. You're a pro."

"Thank you, Jade, but it took years of practice. I happen to think you're doing a great job."

Sawyer watched Jade's eyes light up. It was as if Vashti's compliment equated to being handed a million dollars. "Thanks, Ms. Vashti."

"Food is ready," Sawyer said. "I thought it would be nice to sit out here and enjoy the breeze for a while."

"That would be great," Vashti said, agreeing. "You have a great view of the cove."

He chuckled. "So says the lady who has the gulf in her backyard. And as far as a view of the cove, you're right, it's there, but look at all the trees you have to get through to find it."

After dinner, which both Vashti and Jade had complimented him on, they began the baton-twirling lessons again.

He was about to start cleaning the grill when he heard the cell phone Vashti had placed on the patio table ring. He knew she couldn't hear it over the music so he picked it up. After getting her attention, he walked it over to her.

"Someone is trying to reach you."

"Thanks, Sawyer."

"You're welcome," he said, handing her the phone before walking off.

"I'll be right back," Jade said, rushing past him to go into the house, evidently in need of a bathroom break.

Sawyer glance back over his shoulder at Vashti in time to see a strange look appear on her face. He stopped walking and turned back around as she clicked off the phone. "Are you okay?" he asked her.

"Not sure. That was my investigator. He has information that he wants to share with me. He wouldn't tell me anything over the phone and wants to fly here tomorrow."

Sawyer lifted a brow. "On a Sunday?"

"Yes. I wonder what he has discovered."

He reached out and took her hand in his. It was shaking. He covered hers with his to let her know things would be alright. "You will know tomorrow, baby."

"DON'T YOU WANT to come sit over here by me for a while, Vashti?"

Vashti stopped pacing to glance at Sawyer who was

sitting on the sofa watching her. He had to work today, which was obvious since he was wearing his uniform. But he had come here anyway, to be with her when Jeremy Banks arrived. She appreciated his thoughtfulness in doing that.

Bryce had wanted to be there with her, but she'd left first thing that morning to attend a week-long real estate seminar in Dallas. They had talked last night and like Vashti, Bryce was wondering why Jeremy couldn't tell her what he'd found over the phone.

"I can't help being nervous." Mr. Banks's plane had landed and he'd texted her that he was on his way. That had been an hour ago.

Sawyer got up and walked over to her and placed his arms around her. "Considering the circumstances, your being nervous is understandable. I just figured being in my arms was a whole lot better than pacing the floor."

She smiled up at him. "Being in your arms is a whole lot better than a lot of things." Sawyer had that natural ability to calm people down, soothe their ruffled feathers, relax their mind. How he did it, she wasn't sure. That night when Ms. Gertie had died and Jade had called him had been a turning point in their relationship. In all honesty, it had been the start of their relationship. She'd already seen the law and order part of him. Even the seduction and sex part of him. But that night she had been exposed to the compassionate and supportive side of Sawyer Grisham. That had been her downfall. That's what had knocked down her guard, picked away at her resolve and ground it into dust.

"In that case," he said, tightening his arms around her. "Let me just stand here and hold you for a while."

She lifted her head to stare up at him. The eyes gazing back at her sent sensuous shivers all through her.

He lowered his head and their mouths were inches from connecting when the doorbell sounded. He pulled back and caressed her cheek. Smiling, he said, "I suggest you get that while I try to get my body in order."

She knew exactly what he meant and smiling, she quickly headed for the door.


"I DON'T UNDERSTAND what you're saying, Mr. Banks."

Sawyer felt Vashti's hand tighten in his. Like her, he was listening to what the private investigator was saying. Since Banks was an ex-FBI agent, Sawyer was doing a good job of following him, although he knew Vashti was not. When it came to sealed documents and records, it wasn't always easy for the courts to comply with requests to unseal such documents. However, Banks had been able to obtain a copy of the adoption agreement, which it appeared that Vashti had signed. It was just like she suspected. Her parents had tricked her into signing the document.

Banks leaned forward and said, "Okay, using the least legal terms as I can, what we do know is that the night you gave birth, there were records of four babies born that night. All females. No males. And I checked forty-eight hours before and forty-eight hours after. The only male child born was to a woman within eight hours following. She kept her baby and didn't give him up for adoption. Her son is now sixteen. I was able to contact her."

"And?" Vashti asked.

"The woman seems to have a good memory. She said she recalled the nurses telling her that her son had finally broken the drought with boy babies being born and that her son had been the first boy baby born in a week's time. The others had been girls. So far my investigation substantiates her claim."

Vashti frowned. "But how can that be when I gave birth to a boy? The only reason I can come up with as to why he wasn't included in the count was because he died within hours of being born."

Banks shook his head. "And that's another thing that doesn't add up. There are no records of any baby dying, male or female. There was one recorded case of a stillbirth two months after you gave birth, but that was a female baby as well."

Vashti released a deep sigh of frustration. Sawyer could hear it and could feel it. And he knew it wouldn't be long before that frustration became borderline annoyance. He decided to step in and ask questions. All intended to be direct and to get them from point A to point B. The man's approach to have Vashti figure some things out on her own without Banks spelling them out for her wasn't working.

"So what are you saying, Banks? That Vashti's got the birthdate of her son confused?"

As he expected, she glared at him. "I didn't get the birthdate wrong, Sawyer. I know the day I went into labor and the day my son was born."

He smiled at her and reached out and brought their joined hands to his lips and kissed them. "I believe you, since that's the sort a thing any mother would remember."

He turned back to Jeremy Banks. "In that case, there can be only one reason for the discrepancy." He was certain that Banks already knew what that reason was.

"Then will someone tell me?" Vashti said in exasperation.

Sawyer turned and looked at her. "That you didn't give birth to a boy but to a girl."

Vashti stared at him, and then tilted her head like he'd suddenly gone bananas on her. "Sawyer, I had a boy," she said, as if she needed to make sure he understood.

He decided to play the role that obviously Banks didn't want to play. That of devil's advocate. "And how do you know that? Did you see the baby? Check out its genitals?"

"No, of course not. By the time I came out of anesthesia, my baby had died and they had taken him away."

"And who told you that you'd given birth to a boy?"

"My parents."

He didn't say anything just gave her time to digest what she'd said. He watched her, saw the wheels beginning to turn in her head. These were the same parents who had tricked her into signing adoption papers. Vashti then asked both him and Banks, "Why would my parents tell me I gave birth to a boy when it was a girl? That doesn't make sense."

"It would if they never wanted you to find out the truth," Banks spoke up. "A blatant cover-up they never intended for you to know about."

Vashti didn't say anything and Banks took that time to continue. "Working on that assumption, I was able to determine that there were four female babies born that day, the same day you are certain is your baby's birthday. What I didn't say is that there are only the names of three women listed as giving birth."

"That means one of the girls had twins, right?"

Vashti asked, and Sawyer saw she was now not only following along but was beginning to think like an investigator.

"That's the only thing I can figure," Banks said, "without seeing any further records. The reason I flew in was to meet with you personally before I continued. I am now working this investigation on the presumption that you gave birth to a girl and not a boy. Or to possible twins."

Vashti waved off the latter. "Trust me, I was not the one who had twins. I would have known. Compared to other girls there, I wasn't that big. There were others with bellies a lot bigger than mine."

Banks nodded. "I will determine that as fact. At this point, given this information, I'm confident the child you gave birth to didn't die that day." He paused to let that sink in.

Vashti nodded, but Sawyer wasn't sure she was processing all the implications of that statement just yet.

"Do you want me to proceed?" Banks asked.

"Yes, although it's going to take some getting used to whether I did have a daughter and not a son. Not that it mattered. I would have been happy with either."

"So what's next, Banks?" Sawyer asked.

"Now that we're confident there was an adoption, I go back to the courts to see if I can get the records unsealed. Since she's not asking for contact with the child, but just inquiring as to the well-being of the child, getting a judge to grant our request might not be too difficult. We won't know until we try."

Vashti turned to Sawyer and said, "Even if my parents lied and my child was adopted, it won't be fair to the adoptive parents to try and lay claim on that child after all this time. They've had sixteen years. For all I know the child might not even know he…she was adopted. I couldn't disrupt its life that way. That's why I made the decision if the child is fine and in a decent home, I will leave matters be."

Sawyer nodded, thinking that decision had been thoughtful of her. "And what if you discover the child has been shifted from foster home to foster home and isn't okay?" He tried to push to the back of his mind that he'd pretty much stated how his life had once been.

"Then I would ask for the court's permission to claim my child and give it the loving home it should get." She paused a moment and then said, "It was never my intent to give my child up for adoption."

She turned to Banks. "Proceed with the investigation. I need to know one way or the other that my daughter is okay."

Jeremy Banks nodded before standing. "I've discovered when it comes to reopening adoption cases, the courts are slow and often not readily accommodating. Look at possibly another four to six weeks before hearing from me again. If you don't want to wait that long, you might consider talking to your parents about the matter again."

## CHAPTER THIRTY-EIGHT

VASHTI SANK DOWN on the sofa and released a painful sigh. How could her parents lie about her baby's death? Not only that, but the sex of her baby? And then trick her into signing adoption papers when they'd known she had wanted to keep her baby? How could they do that to her? And then keep the lie all this time? She never gave birth to a boy but to a girl and her baby hadn't died. Ms. Gertie had been right about that.

"You okay, sweetheart?"

She glanced up and saw Sawyer returning from walking Jeremy Banks to the door. "Yes, for a woman who just discovered how far her parents would go to save face in a community, I guess I am okay."

He dropped down beside her on the sofa to pull her into his arms. She tried resisting but he wouldn't let her. "I'm not good company now, Sawyer."

"Why?"

She jerked around and glared at him. "You know why. My parents lied to me. They lied to me and they tricked me," she said in a louder voice in case he hadn't heard or understood. "I'm mad."

"Be mad. You have every right to be. But what does your being mad have to do with me? With us? With my wanting to be here with you? With my wanting to be here for you?"

Vashti didn't say anything. She couldn't. She doubted she could love him any more than she did at that moment. He was refusing to let her be alone when that's all she'd ever felt since she'd lost her child. Alone. Yes, she'd had Aunt Shelby, but when Vashti had made the decision not to make Catalina Cove her home, she'd known that meant not having the close relationship with her aunt that she'd always had. Although she and Aunt Shelby still managed to do things together, it hadn't been the same.

However, this man, this handsome, sexy man, was letting her be angry, but not alone. She eased up from the sofa and he stood as well. That's when she wrapped her arms around him and all but melted into his embrace. She looked up at him. "Thank you."

He lifted a brow. "For what?"

"For wanting to be here with me when I'm not in a good mood."

He shrugged. "It happens to the best of us at times, Vashti. And like I said, you have a right to be mad. Are you going to call your folks?"

She shook her head. "No, I called them before and they lied. This time I plan to pay them a surprise visit. I want them to look me in my face and tell me I gave birth to a son who died."

She looked at Sawyer and said, "Until then, I refused to let them take away my joy. And right now, Sawyer, you are my joy."

Swallowing deeply, she looked up at him wondering if he knew what she saying. If he had any idea just what she meant. Granted she hadn't come out and told him that she loved him but that was the closest thing to it.

Words of love would come when she was certain, beyond a shadow of a doubt, that he could love her back.

She watched as his expression grew serious and when he reached up and cupped her chin, she felt heat rush through her veins. "And you, Vashti Alcindor, are my joy as well."

She wondered if he was holding back expressing his emotions like she was doing or if he was merely repeating what she'd said. She settled with the latter as she leaned up on tiptoes.

The moment their lips touched she felt slightly off balance with the immediate rush of desire that overtook her. And when he slid his hand to the nape of her neck to claim her mouth greedily, she couldn't fight back a moan. It seemed forever before they broke off the kiss, needing to pull air into their lungs.

"Sawyer?" she whispered close to his neck.

"Yes, baby?"

"Do you have to go back to work?"

He drew back and looked at her and the smile that creased his lips sent flutters off in her stomach. "No. McMillan is covering my shift the rest of the day. I'll do the same for him on Wednesday when he takes his father for an eye appointment. So what do you have in mind, Ms. Alcindor?"

"Come with me and I'll show you, Mr. Grisham."

Taking his hand, she led him toward the bedroom.

"VASHTI! WHAT ON earth are you doing here?"

Vashti wondered how many mothers, who hadn't seen their daughters in close to a year, would open the door and say such a thing, instead of throwing their arms around them to let them know they were glad to see them. She'd been to this house only twice. Neither time had been by invitation.

"I'm glad to see you, too, Mom," she said, entering the house when her mother widened the door and stood aside.

"Of course, I'm glad to see you. It's just that your father and I weren't expecting you."

*When do you ever?* She wanted to say, but didn't. She had followed Sawyer's advice and instead of flying out to see her folks first thing Monday morning, she had waited a couple days, until her anger had subsided some. She was still mad, but the extra time gave her the ability to control it.

She glanced around the spacious living room. When her parents had sold their home in Catalina Cove, they'd made a killing and had then moved to Pensacola for a place that was walking distance to the beach. "Where's Dad?"

"Out back tending his garden. I didn't notice any luggage."

She turned her attention back to her mother. "I don't intend to stay. I came to talk to you and Dad."

"What about?"

She picked up on her mother's nervousness. "I'll let you know when you get Dad in here."

Her mother didn't say anything. She just looked at her oddly, before saying. "I hope you're not here to cause trouble about anything. I didn't want to tell you this, but your father has a bad heart."

"So do I, Mom." *And it breaks even more whenever I look into your face knowing that you and Dad lied,* she almost said, but didn't. "If you go get Dad, I can say what I came here to say and be on my way."

Her mother hesitated a moment before opening the set of French doors to go outside. Vashti paced for a minute, trying to hold her anger in check. Sawyer had offered to come with her. But she knew that meant not only rearranging his schedule, but Jade's as well. He had, however, taken her to the airport and would be there when she arrived back in New Orleans later that day.

"Vashti, what do you want to talk to me and your mother about?"

She turned to find her parents standing side by side as if they were a unified force. There was no doubt in her mind they were.

Since they appeared to be glued to the spot where they were standing, she would cover the distance separating them. She would admit they both looked well. No sign of the heart issues her mother claimed her father had. But she wasn't surprised. Once a liar always a liar.

She came to a stop in front of them. "I want to know why you lied to me about my baby."

When her mother started to speak, Vashti raised her hand for silence. "No, Mom. No more lies. I'm not asking if you lied because I know you did."

"You know nothing but the lie Gertie told you."

"Wrong, Mom. Ms. Gertie might have got me to thinking, but I hired a private investigator who proved everything she said was the truth. I also know the two of you tricked me into signing papers to give my baby up for adoption, so no more lies. I just want to know why you told me I had given birth to a boy when I had a girl? Why you told me my baby had died. And why after all these years when I questioned you about my baby, you still lied? Why, Mom, Dad? Why?"

Her father had the sense to look away, but her mother didn't. "You were sixteen, Vashti. You embarrassed us when you acted like nothing more than a parentless slut. People talk. They talked about us. But you didn't care. All you cared about was yourself and not what being pregnant was doing to me and your father. What people were saying. How our life was changing. So yes, we lied. You didn't need to be a mother. You were only sixteen, for heaven's sake. You wouldn't tell us the name of the guy who got you pregnant. For all we knew you could have gotten raped. All we knew was that you didn't even have a boyfriend. Or you weren't supposed to have one. You acted like you were happy to be pregnant, but for us it was a total embarrassment. People wanted to know the name of your baby's father and thought it was shameful that we didn't even know."

Her mother paused a moment before adding, "As far as I'm concerned, we did the right thing with the adoption, even if we tricked you to do it. You finished school and went to college and made something of your life. If we had to do it over again, we would."

Anger filled Vashti to the brim. "My baby was your grandchild. Did that not mean anything to either of you?"

At first she thought neither would answer and then her father surprised her and said, "Yes. But like your mother said, you were too young to be a mother and we figured you would get married one day and have other babies."

"But what about that one, Dad? My daughter. My little girl."

Her parents quickly glanced at each other as if there was something else. Something Vashti had missed. "Is there something else I need to know? Do you know who adopted my baby?"

"No," her mother quickly said. "There's nothing else and it was a private adoption."

Vashti tightened her hand on her purse straps. The latter meant her parents had no idea who had adopted her child. "Then I have nothing else to say, other than you were wrong for what you did to me. I intend to find my child, to make sure she's okay. So, all you did was done for nothing."

"Why can't you leave well enough alone, Vashti?"

They obviously didn't have a clue what their actions had done to her and it was obvious they didn't care.

"Because I can't leave well enough alone. I guess it's the mother in me, the parental connection in me that can't let go. It's obvious neither of you knows how that feels."

She headed for the door, opened it and walked out.

THE SUN WAS going down over the cove when Vashti unlocked the door to Shelby by the Sea. The moment they were inside Sawyer walked up behind her and drew her into his arms.

From the moment he'd seen her at the airport, he'd known what the outcome of the meeting with her parents had been. The sad look on her face had said it all. Her parents had betrayed her, and she was hurting over it.

"Do you want to take a walk on the beach?" he asked, leaning in to nibble on the underside of her ear. He was somewhat satisfied when he heard her pleasurable purr.

"I'm really tempted, but not now. I just want you to hold me for a while."

He wanted to do that as well and tightened his arms around her. After they stood there for a few moments he whispered. "I'm ready to listen when you're ready to talk about it."

She lifted her head from his chest and he saw pain so sharp in her eyes he felt like someone had hit him in the gut. He also saw the tears that threatened to fall from her eyes. Whatever happened between her parents had hurt. The lies. Their actions. Their ultimate betrayal.

"They admitted to lying, Sawyer. My parents admitted to giving my baby away," she said softly. "Even now they felt they did the right thing." She paused a moment and then said, "I don't think I can ever forgive them for what they did to me."

Sawyer didn't say anything. He knew what her parents had done seemed unforgivable now but one day she had to forgive them. In his line of business he'd seen families torn apart and then refuse to work it out because someone didn't want to forgive. It was like a sore that wouldn't heal and if allowed to fester would only get worse.

"Vashti?"

"Yes?"

"I know your parents have let you down, but I think you need to remember something."

She lifted a brow. "What?"

"They are human and aren't perfect. They made a mistake."

She stared at him for a moment. "I know what you're saying, Sawyer, but do you have any idea how I feel? What they did to me? I have a child out there somewhere who probably thinks I never wanted her. That I didn't love her. A child that I wanted to raise myself but has

been raised by someone else. That's not fair. It's just
not fair. I hate them."

And then she broke down and cried in his arms and
the sobs tore into him. He heard the pain. He swept
her off her feet into his arms and headed for the sofa
to sit down with her in his lap, where he continued to
hold her while she cried. "You're incapable of hating
anyone. You're too full of love. It's takes up too much
time and effort to hate. It's time and effort you can be
putting into love." He wondered if she got what he was
saying. He wished more than anything all that love she
had inside of her could be shared with him.

"I need to go see Reid Lacroix," she said, suddenly
sitting up and pulling out of his arms.

He frowned. "Reid Lacroix? Why?"

"Because now I know for certain that I have a daughter out there somewhere."

Sawyer felt even more confused. "Why would that
matter to him?"

Vashti slowly pulled her hands from his chest, as if
too late she'd realized she had said too much. Breaking
eye contact with him she looked away, and he knew she
was trying to decide what to tell him. Then as if she'd
made up her mind about it, she looked back at him and
placed her hands back on his chest.

"It would matter to him because his son, Julius, was
the father of my child. That means my daughter, where
ever she is, is Mr. Lacroix's granddaughter."

THERE. SHE HAD shared her secret with another person.
Vashti watched as an expression of surprise lined Sawyer's features. "The identity of my baby's father was a
secret," she heard herself say. "The only other person

who knows is Bryce. I never told anyone else. Not even my parents or Aunt Shelby."

"Why?" he asked her, pulling her back into his arms.

"Because no one knew we were even seeing each other. Julius and I were young and sneaking around. We were in love." Vashti knew she could say that now, especially after what Reid Lacroix had shared with her. Julius had loved her—he'd just been too weak to take a stand.

"But Reid knew?"

Vashti shook her head. "Not at first. He only found out at the hospital when Julius was dying. I guess you can say it was Julius's death-bed confession and request." She paused a moment and then said, "He wanted his dad to tell me if he ever saw me again that he was sorry, and that he did love me but lacked a backbone to claim me or his baby. He hadn't wanted to cause a scandal in his family."

Over the next twenty or so minutes, Vashti found herself telling Sawyer everything, including how Mr. Lacroix had paid her a visit in New York and everything he had shared with her, including his proposal that had brought her back to Catalina Cove and that he had made her his heir. "Now he won't have to because a legitimate Lacroix heir is out there somewhere."

"Do you think now is a good time to tell him that?" Sawyer asked her.

Vashti's eyebrows lifted in question. "Why not?"

"Think about it for a minute. I heard what you told Banks. You don't want to disrupt your daughter's life if she's happy and content with the couple who adopted her, right?"

"Yes."

"Do you think Reid will feel that same way? He's a very lonely man right now. A man without any blood connections to a family. From what you've just told me, he's a man who desperately wants to continue the Lacroix legacy. Based on that, I think he will move heaven and earth to make sure he's a part of his granddaughter's life. I'm not saying you should not tell him, I just think you might want to wait and hear the next report Banks gives you before deciding that you do."

Vashti nodded. Sawyer did have a point. She could see Mr. Lacroix demanding a relationship with his granddaughter, regardless of the situation. Even if the adoptive parents refused to allow the courts to unseal the records, he would find a way to do so anyway. He had the money and means. He would feel he had that right.

"You're right. I need to wait."

## CHAPTER THIRTY-NINE

HOLDING VASHTI'S HAND firmly in his, Sawyer entered the high school gymnasium where the majorette try-outs were being held. The place was already packed, which meant a lot of the townsfolk were in attendance. He'd been told by Trudy that the reason a lot of the people of Catalina Cove thought the baton-twirling try-outs were such a big deal was because for years, thanks to Vashti, the cove had been put on the map and everyone was curious to see if perhaps there was another Vashti Alcindor out there who could reclaim the cove's national title.

"Evening, Sheriff, Vashti."

"Hello."

"Hello, Sheriff and Vashti."

"Hello."

Several people spoke, calling out to them as they climbed the bleachers to find a good place to sit. They passed Rachel Libby and a group of others. Everyone had spoken to them; however, Rachel stared straight ahead and ignored them, which was fine with Sawyer.

"This spot will work?" he asked Vashti, releasing her hand.

"Yes. We have a really good view from here."

Sitting down he glanced around. It was obvious the

townsfolk were getting used to seeing them together. Not that it mattered to him one way or the other.

It had been close to three weeks since Vashti had flown to Florida to meet with her parents. So far, they hadn't tried contacting her and she hadn't contacted them. He knew her goal was to stay busy so the inn would be opened as planned. Bryce Witherspoon had signed on as assistant manager at the inn and so far that arrangement was working out nicely. He knew it was important to Vashti to have someone working closely with her who she could trust.

"They're getting started," Vashti leaned over and said when the school's band began performing.

The majorette try-outs started with everyone standing to recite the pledge of allegiance and sing the school's song. Of course, he didn't know it and refused to pretend that he did. It seemed however that Vashti remembered it and was singing at the top of her lungs.

The principal came up to the microphone and said, "Before we get started I'm proud to say we have Catalina Cove's reigning national baton-twirling champion here with us tonight. I want to ask Vashti Alcindor to stand and be recognized."

Sawyer could tell by Vashti's expression that she hadn't expected to be acknowledged this way. She stood and everyone gave her a loud and rowdy round of applause and cheers. The town was letting her know whatever happened in the past could stay there and they had moved on.

When Vashti took her seat, the principal announced the majorette twirling try-outs were about to begin. There were twelve girls trying out and only five would be selected. Sawyer was well aware that Vashti and Jade had been keeping long hours in the evenings and on the weekends to get Jade ready for this day.

A sense of pride filled Sawyer when the opening performance included all twelve girls. His heart swelled when Jade marched out, holding her body and stepping in precision just like Vashti has taught her to do. And the way she was twirling her baton was just short of perfect. He didn't want to brag but she looked like a natural.

*Our baby is out there looking good, Johanna,* he thought to himself and in his heart he believed Johanna had heard him.

WHEN JADE HAD gotten selected as a majorette, Vashti cheered so much she was certain she would lose her voice. Sawyer, she noticed, was on his feet cheering as well, along with others.

"Thanks for helping her reach this goal," Sawyer whispered close to her ear, wrapping his arms around her shoulders. "She could not have done it without you. Her dance routine was awesome."

Vashti beamed. "No need to thank me, Sawyer. Jade was a darling to work with. I am so happy for her."

"We need to celebrate," he said. "I bet the Witherspoon Café will be packed with most of everyone headed over there from here. What do you think about me, you and Jade driving over to New Orleans to eat at Spencer's? That's her favorite restaurant there."

A smile touched Vashti's lips. Spencer's was one of her favorite restaurants as well. It was a fast-food place that served the best hamburgers, french fries and milkshakes. There weren't any Spencer's in New York and she hadn't been to Spencer's since moving back to the cove. "I think it's a wonderful idea."

LATER THAT NIGHT dressed in her pj's, Vashti left her bedroom to open the door for Sawyer. After what she could only think of as a wonderful evening at Spencer's, Jade had fallen asleep on the ride back to the cove. That was understandable, considering the number of hours she'd spent over the past weeks practicing for tonight.

Sawyer had dropped Vashti at home and then taken Jade home to tuck her in. He had called an hour ago to see if she was still up because he wanted to tuck her in as well. Passing through the living room she paused a minute and glanced around. It was hard to believe that in a couple of months this place would be open for business and she was excited about it.

Opening the door, she smiled up at Sawyer. "How's Jade?"

"She woke up long enough to shower and get into her jammies and then she was out again." After closing the door behind him, he leaned against it and his gaze roamed all over her. "Nice jammies."

She glanced down at her blue silk cami-top and shorty-shorts sleepwear and then back at him. "I'm glad you like them."

"I like them a lot. Too much," he said, leaning down to place a kiss on her lips. He had just deepened the kiss when her cell phone rang. Pulling back, he whispered against her moist lips, "You might want to get that so we can finish what we're starting."

Vashti smiled and thought those were her sentiments as well. "It's probably Bryce. I'll be right back," she said, before rushing off to her bedroom.

She picked her phone off the nightstand. "Hello?"

"Ms. Alcindor, this is Jeremy Banks."

Air nearly rushed from her lungs. She hadn't expected to hear from him for another three weeks, possibly more. "Yes, Mr. Banks?"

"Sorry to be calling so late, but I need to meet with you. Immediately."

Her heart began pounding. It sounded urgent. "You have information for me?"

"Yes, and like before, I'd rather not discuss it over the phone. If it's okay, I'm flying in tomorrow."

"Yes, it's okay."

"Good. I will text you my flight itinerary to let you know when to expect me."

"Alright."

After clicking off the phone she left her bedroom and saw that Sawyer was no longer in the living room parlor. "Sawyer?"

"I'm in the kitchen."

She walked to the kitchen and caught her breath when she saw him. He had removed his shirt and was standing in the kitchen by the huge island wearing only a pair of low-hanging jeans. He glanced up at her and smiled. "I thought I'd pour us a glass a wine."

"Thanks. I'm going to need it. That was Jeremy Banks."

Sawyer's hand stilled from pouring the wine. "What did he say?"

"He has information for me and is flying in to see me tomorrow. I wonder what it is."

Sawyer finished pouring the wine and crossed the floor to hand her a glass. "You'll know tomorrow and let's believe whatever he has to tell you is good."

Vashti took a sip of her wine while thinking that more than anything, she wanted to believe that.

## CHAPTER FORTY

"So, Mr. Banks, what information do you have for me?" Vashti asked in a nervous tone. When she felt the hand that was holding hers tighten, she glanced at Sawyer. Like before, he was there, sitting beside her on the sofa and giving her his support. Again, she appreciated him being there.

Jeremy Banks had texted that morning he would be arriving around five. It had taken everything for Vashti to keep busy until then. She had met Bryce for breakfast and had told her best friend the entire story, promising to call her after Banks left.

The man in question stared at her, his expression unreadable. Then he spoke. "I know I told you that you probably wouldn't be hearing from me for at least six weeks and it's been half that time. Mainly because while I was working with the courts for permission to unseal the adoption records, the couple who had adopted your daughter was doing the same thing. They were seeking permission from the courts to open the records as well. It was imperative that they locate you."

Vashti's heart began pounding and the hand holding hers tightened even more. "Why?" she asked, almost too afraid to do so.

"Because their daughter, your daughter, has a life-threatening condition."

Vashti's heart jumped in her chest and leaned forward. "What kind of life-threatening condition?"

"A kidney disease. It developed recently, in fact no more than a few months ago. She's on dialysis and is on a transplant list awaiting a kidney donor. But that could take a while. They were reaching out to see if you would agree to be tested as an eligible donor."

"Yes. Of course I will," Vashti said immediately, standing to her feet. "Oh, my God," she said, drawing in quick breaths of air. "Where are they? When do I need to leave? When do—"

"Calm down, baby," Sawyer said, standing to his feet as well, and pulling her into his arms. "Let Banks finished. I think there's more."

She studied the man and then asked. "Is there more?"

"Yes."

Vashti frowned as she sat back down. Sawyer sat down beside her. "What additional information do you have?"

"The last time I was here I alluded to the fact that one of the girls who had delivered that night had given birth to twins."

Vashti nodded her head. "Yes, I recall you saying that."

"Well, my investigation has concluded that *you* are the one who delivered the twins."

Vashti shook her head. "No, that's not possible. There's no way I could have given birth to twins. The last time you were here I went to see my parents. I confronted them and they admitted to giving my daughter away. But they said nothing about a second baby. There's no way they would not have told me. They had every opportunity to do so if that was true. At that point, they had nothing to hide."

She looked from Banks to Sawyer when neither man said anything. It was obvious these two former FBI agents doubted her words and with good reason. They were probably thinking once a liar always a liar. And a lie of omission was still a lie. However, she wanted to believe her parents could not be that heartless, cruel and merciless to not only deny her one baby but two. But the more she thought about it, the more she knew that yes, they could be, and the sad thing was that they truly believed they had done the right thing.

Tears she couldn't control began streaming down her face and she swiped them away. Sawyer's arms went around her shoulders and he gently pulled her into his side. Too overwhelmed with the emotions to speak, she was grateful when Sawyer took over and began asking the questions.

"How did you discover this?"

"One of the staff members I tracked down returned my call and was willing to talk. She confirmed there were two baby girls born to Ms. Alcindor that night. Identical twins that were born ten minutes apart."

"So my babies were separated," Vashti said quietly, tears shining in her eyes at how hard-hearted her parents truly were.

"Yes, that's my understanding. I found out after the adopted couple contacted me, and I came straight here. I didn't tell them, and I don't believe they know about the twin. I figured that's your call to make."

Sawyer nodded. "What's next, Banks? What does Vashti need to do?"

"Get to Sacramento, California, immediately to be

tested. And if there is some way she could contact the babies' father, then—"

"No, he died a few years ago," Sawyer said.

"Okay. Grandparents on both sides would be a long shot, but it might be a consideration if they are still living," Banks said. "In the meantime, I'm going to work to get a decision about unsealing the other baby's records soon."

Banks handed her a business card. "Here is the name of the adoptive father. He would like you to call him and his wife as soon as you can, if you agree to the test."

"I CAN'T BELIEVE your parents, Vash. How could they do something like that to you?" Bryce asked when Jeremy Banks had left, and Vashti had immediately called her.

"I don't know and right now I don't care. I am so through with them. I'm not even going to call to let them know what I found out. When I visited them a few weeks ago, they could have told me the truth then, all of it, and they chose not to do so."

"When do you leave for Sacramento?"

"I'm trying to get a flight out first thing in the morning. I hate to be deserting you when there's so much to be done for the grand opening."

"Hey, don't worry about it. I'll take care of everything. I just hope you're a perfect donor match for your daughter."

Happiness flowed through Vashti and she felt like she was actually floating on a cloud at the thought she had given birth to twins. Identical twins. Daughters. "I feel like none of this is real. I can't believe I had twins, Bryce. Twins."

"When are you going to tell Reid Lacroix?"

Vashti drew in a deep breath. "I'm calling him after lunch to meet with me. Sawyer's in the kitchen preparing sandwiches and iced tea for us."

"Sawyer's really been there for you a lot during all this time. That must mean something to you, Vash."

"It means everything. After Julius and Scott, I didn't want to fall in love with him or any man, but I have. I love him so much, Bryce."

"I was wondering how long it was going to take you to realize that."

"But I'm afraid he will let me down like the others."

"I don't think he will. Look how he's been lifting you up so far."

"You're right. Then there is this other fear I have."

"What other fear?"

"I'm not sure if he will ever love me back. He adored his wife," Vashti said softly.

"I'm sure she will always have a place in his heart, but that doesn't mean he can't make room in that same heart for someone else. I've seen the two of you together, even with Jade. The three of you would make a beautiful family and I know for a fact that Jade thinks the world of you."

"I think the world of her, too." Vashti paused, then said, "Sawyer's rearranging his schedule to join me in Sacramento. He can't fly in until the day after me, though."

"I think that's wonderful, Vash."

"It means a lot that he wants to be there with me."

"And it should. Let me know how Mr. Lacroix takes the news."

"I will."

A COUPLE OF hours later Vashti sat on the plush sofa in the living room at the Lacroix estate. She had tried reaching Reid Lacroix by his cell phone number and when that had failed, she had tried contacting him at his office, thinking perhaps he'd gone into work on the weekend. When she hadn't gotten in touch with him there either, she decided to take a chance and just go to his home.

She had driven up his long, winding driveway that led to the antebellum-style mansion just moments after he had. It was obvious he had spent the day playing golf. She recalled that Julius had told her that his parents had been members of the New Orleans Country Club and were avid golfers.

Mr. Lacroix had been surprised to see her. When she told him that she needed to speak with him about an urgent matter, she figured he assumed it had something to do with the loan for the inn. There was no other reason for her to seek him out. He had invited her inside and after instructing his housekeeper to make sure she was comfortable, he'd gone upstairs to freshen up.

She glanced around the immaculate room. This was the first time she had ever been inside the Lacroix estate. She remembered those times when Julius would tell her it was more like a museum than a home, and now she could see why. The furniture was antique and probably had been owned by the Lacroix for generations. Even the staircase with its intricate wood carving looked like something out of one of those long ago Southern movies. With a place this huge, it had to be lonely for Mr. Lacroix.

"Sorry to keep you waiting, Vashti. Would you like something to drink?"

She turned when Mr. Lacroix came down the stairs. "That's no problem, and no, I don't want anything to drink. Thanks for asking. And like I told you outside, I tried calling you before coming over, but I had to see you."

"Sorry I missed your calls. Is something wrong?" he asked, sitting on the loveseat across from her.

She shook her head. "Yes. No. At least I'm praying that it's not. In fact, I think what I have to tell you is pretty amazing."

"Really? What is it?"

She tried to compose herself before saying. "My parents lied to me sixteen years ago. I didn't give birth to a boy—I have a girl. Two of them, in fact. And thinking they were doing what was best for me, they put my babies up for adoption without my knowing anything about it."

Reid Lacroix stared at her, as if trying to make sense of the words that had spilled out of her mouth. He leaned forward in his seat to give her his absolute attention. "I think you need to start from the beginning," he said.

It took her a good thirty minutes to explain everything, starting with what Ms. Gertie had told her and her parents blatant denials. It would have taken less time, but understandably, he had a lot of questions, which she took the time to answer.

"And your parents admitted to lying when you went to see them?"

"Partly. They admitted they gave up one baby. I didn't find out I had twins until today, when the PI I hired told me."

"When are you flying to Sacramento?" he asked, not even trying to downplay the excitement in his voice.

"I'm trying to get a flight out in the morning."

"Don't bother," Reid said, smiling broadly. "I'll contact my pilot to have my jet fueled and ready to fly out by eight in the morning. Nothing is going to keep me from seeing my granddaughter. And I intend to get tested as a kidney donor as well."

SAWYER SAT ON the wooden steps of the boardwalk while waiting for the woman he loved to come home. He had made all the arrangements and Trudy would be staying at his place with Jade, something she usually did whenever he was out of town on business. The older woman preferred his house, saying he had a bigger television with a lot more channels than she could afford, and his kitchen was larger, too. That worked out for him since it meant Jade got to stay at her own house.

He drew in a deep breath of ocean air. In another hour or so the sun would be going down and from here it was a beautiful sight. For now he was perfectly content watching strands of sunlight spill across the waves of the gulf. In a way he understood Reid Lacroix's desire to keep parts of the cove natural, uninhabited by outside forces that would eventually destroy the beauty before him.

"I thought I'd find you out here."

He glanced over his shoulder, glad Vashti had returned. He had missed her but knew it was time she told Reid everything. So he'd promised to be here when she returned. As she sank down on the step beside him, he could admit he never thought it would be this way if he ever fell in love again. To love someone to distraction, for their hurt and pain to become yours, and for the desire to make them happy something you constantly thought about.

"Thanks for being here when I got back."

"I told you that I would," he countered.

"Yes, but you didn't have to."

Now that's where she was wrong because he did have to. Loving her the way he did gave him no choice. "How did things go with Reid?"

"He's happy and even offered to fly me to Sacramento on his company jet in the morning. He intends to be tested for a donor as well. I did have to warn him that because of the adoptions, our rights to my daughters, his granddaughters, are limited. God, Sawyer, just listen to what I said. My daughters. Can you believe it?"

Images of her teaching Jade those baton-twirling lessons filtered through his mind. Yes, he could believe it since she'd been a natural with his daughter. "I'm happy for you and I hope things work out the way you want."

She leaned into him. "Thanks, Sawyer. I appreciate it."

He didn't want her appreciation. He much preferred her love. "Come on, let's walk on the beach."

After removing their shoes, they stood. She gave him her hand and he tucked it into his as they strolled down the steps toward the gulf. They walked quietly together as his mind was filled with the thoughts that he'd never met anyone as beautiful, both inside and out, as this woman.

She hadn't wanted a relationship with him when she'd returned to the cove but when they'd met at every turn, neither could fight the attraction between them that had become so powerful. Something neither of them could deny or ignore. But every time they'd come together he had wanted more, and now that more was eating away at him because he knew he didn't want to just give her support today, tomorrow and next week. He wanted to be there for her for the rest of his life. For as long as he had breath in his body.

"You're quiet, Sawyer. What are you thinking?"

Maybe now he should be honest and tell her and let the chips fall where they may. But what if those chips, like this beach sand, got swept away? How would he handle it if she wasn't ready? She was dealing with a lot now already and it wouldn't be fair to add more to her load. Even if it was a load he would happily help her carry.

He looked down at her and smiled. "I was trying to imagine what a mini Vashti would look like."

"How do you think?"

"Not sure since I never knew Reid's son and I'm sure your girls would take on both of your features. But as their mom I would think they were beautiful."

She beamed up at him. "Ahh, you say the nicest things."

"But then, they would probably easily get into a snip if things don't go their way."

"I don't easily get into a snip," she said, before playfully slugging him in the arm.

"You do to. Trust me I know a snip when I see one. Jade does it as well. She could be your daughter since the two of you have the art of snipism down pat."

Vashti threw her head back and laughed. "That's not true and *snipism* is not a word."

"I'm making it one."

They continued walking a bit when Vashti said in a

wishful tone, "Where were you years ago when I needed a Sawyer Grisham in my life?"

He knew he really didn't have to answer that because they both knew the answer. He'd been married to someone else. "Is it enough that I'm here now?"

She stopped walking and turned to him. A smile played around the corners of her lips. "Yes. It's more than enough, Sawyer."

There was something in the tone of her voice that touched him deeply. "Come on, let's head back."

"But not before this," she said, leaning up and placing her lips to his.

VASHTI KNEW SHE wasn't the expert kisser Sawyer was by any means. But the one thing she did know was that more than tongue movement was going on in this kiss. It was filled with something he hadn't counted on, something he probably didn't even detect. Love.

All around her was the sound of the gulf, the gentle tweeting of the birds coming in to roost for the night and the not-so-muted chirping of the crickets in the marshes. But none of that held as much of her attention as the man who was holding her in his arms and allowing her to kiss him the way she wanted.

She heard his moan and it emboldened her to turn up the heat. His response was automatic and she marveled that she could entice him to desire her this way. Then she felt him, his aroused state pressing against the juncture of her legs. She closed her eyes, loving the feel of his erection pressing against her.

Vashti felt him cup her backside, deliberately pressing her even more against the rigid swell of his hardness. Then his hand slowly and erotically began moving to touch her in other places. Like snaking his hand beneath her shirt to gently stroke her back, while her mouth mated greedily with his. Primitive urges that she only experienced with him took over her mind and when he hungrily took over the kiss, she let him, savoring his taste.

He broke off the kiss and she felt naughty and alive. "Tell me, Sheriff. Is it against the law to go skinny-dipping on the beach?"

He stared at her. The desire in his gaze seemed to flame at her question. "On a public beach, yes. A private one, no."

"Just making sure I'm not about to break the law." And then she began stripping off her clothes.

SAWYER WATCHED HER and was about to stop her and then decided not to. It was now dark and there was no indication of a boat idling out in the gulf. It was just the two of them on this private stretch of beach. He looked at her. She had stripped down to her bra and panties—both resembled a bikini.

"Are you going to join me?" she asked.

He realized the craziness of what they were doing. But after today they needed the craziness. She needed the opportunity to let herself go, relinquish her mind and body to sexual desire of the most potent and primitive kind. No telling what the days ahead would mean for her, and he wanted to give her pleasant memories to have when and if she needed them.

He began removing his clothes and by the time he had tossed aside the last piece she had removed her bra and panties and stood before him naked. Under the light of the stars she looked beautiful. He reached out, wanting to touch her everywhere, starting with her breasts and working his hands all the way down her legs.

His breathing thickened in his throat when his hand touched her between the legs. The contact was fiery and sent heated lust all through him. No, not heated lust, but sweltering love. Dropping to his knees in the sand he grabbed a hold of her hips, and buried his face between her legs before sliding his tongue inside of her. He knew what he was doing, what he always enjoyed doing, was incredibly intimate.

He enjoyed loving her this way, branding her his with his mouth and tongue and laying claim to her clit while intentionally driving her wild. It didn't matter her fingernails were digging deep into his shoulders or that she was pushing the lower part of her body against his mouth for deeper penetration. What mattered was that he wanted to love her this way, while savoring her taste.

He knew the moment she came and her body gave him even more of what he wanted while jerking hard against his mouth. Tightening his hold on her hips, he held on while his tongue dove even deeper, lapping her more greedily, more intensely. And when she cried out his name he drank in the very essence of her.

When he finally pulled his tongue out of her and glanced up, he saw half-closed eyes and a satisfied smile on her lips and that did something to him, knowing he was the reason for her state of bliss. He lifted her up in his arms and whispered. "Open your legs and then wrap them around me."

The moment she did, he entered her body with his shaft, going deep. Almost pulling out only to thrust in even deeper. Exerting as much strength while firmly planting his feet into the sand for balance, he made love to her hard. He sank deep into her only to pull almost out and then thrust back hard inside of her again. This was a mating of the most intense kind and he refused to let anything stop him. Even the waves of water that began washing against his legs, nearly making him lose balance. Somehow, he held firm and made love to her upright.

When he felt her inner muscles squeeze him tight, she triggered his explosion and his semen drenched her womb. Too late he recalled what he hadn't done and the thought they were skin to skin made him ejaculate even more inside of her.

"I'm so sorry," he whispered as he eased her down his body to stand back on her feet. "I should have used protection."

"I'm glad you didn't," she said in a soft voice. "I love the feel of you shooting off inside of me. And like I've told you, I'm on birth control. I take injections and I'm safe."

*She loved the feel of him shooting off inside of her? Wow.* "I'm safe as well."

With her standing there naked in front of him after having made love to her the way he had, feeling closer to her than he had to any woman in years…possibly ever, he reached out and caressed the side of her face, which caused her to look at him with those beautiful eyes of hers. At that moment his control snapped and his better judgment went north when he whispered, "I love you, Vashti."

She froze and for a minute he wondered if he'd made a mistake in confessing his feelings to her. Then she threw herself against him and said, "You don't know how much I needed to hear that, Sawyer. I love you, too."

He pulled back and forced her to look at him. "You love me?" he asked to make sure he had heard her correctly.

"Yes, with all my heart. And you love me, right?"

He nodded. "Yes, with all my heart. And you do know that Jade and I come as a package deal?"

"Yes, and I couldn't imagine it being any other way. The same holds true with my daughters…although I'm not sure what part, if any, their adoptive parents will let me play in their lives. It doesn't matter—I still want to think of them as mine."

"And they are yours. We will deal with all that when the time comes. The most important thing is to hopefully be able to help the one who needs you the most right now."

"Thank you for loving me."

"And thank you for loving me." He let out a laugh, so happy and relieved. "We better redress before our clothes get washed out to the sea," he said, picking up hers and handing them to her. "Then we'll shower and make love again before I leave."

"Alright."

He kissed her again before they got dressed. Then when they had their clothes back on, he wrapped his arm around her shoulders as they walked back to the inn.

## CHAPTER FORTY-ONE

"You're not hungry?"

Vashti looked from her plate to Reid Lacroix. The flight from New Orleans to Sacramento was a long one and it seemed as if they'd been in the air for hours. His jet was amazing and the food the attendant had served looked delicious. Only problem was that she was too excited to eat. Jeremy Banks had called her before she'd left Catalina Cove to let her know he would meet her at the hospital. Just the thought that she would come face-to-face with the daughter she'd given birth to had her moving the food around on her plate instead of eating it.

"I'm too wired up to eat," she explained.

"Trust me, I know how you feel. Right now I'm feeling downright ecstatic. However, I have no choice but to eat before taking my medication."

He must have seen the questions in her gaze because he explained, "I've been on antidepressants for a while now."

*Probably since losing his son and wife.* She recalled he had explained in New York how he'd been consumed by grief and loneliness after losing both his son and wife. She understood even more since visiting him yesterday. His house was huge and he lived in it alone. But she needed to make sure he fully comprehended what she had told him yesterday and not build up his hopes about anything in Sacramento. Especially when his eyes were brimming with anticipation and eagerness.

"Mr. Lacroix, you do accept that there's a chance the adoptive parents only want us to be tested for possible donors and nothing else. For all I know, their daughter might not even know she was adopted and they might want to keep it that way."

He nodded slowly. "I hear you, Vashti, but if that's the case, it will be hard for me not to try and persuade them to allow us to be a part of her life."

A part of her was afraid of that. "And if they aren't easily persuaded?"

"Let's just hope that they are. Now if you will excuse me I need to make a few calls to check on things at the plant. I had a management meeting today that I had to cancel."

"Alright."

Vashti watched him unbuckle his seat belt and walk down the aisle of the spacious jet to the room he told her was his in-flight office. Some things never changed and Reid Lacroix was used to having things his way. Now she was questioning whether she should have told him at all. What had she expected when he'd explained to her that day in New York that family meant everything to him? Now there was a child, two of them, with his blood flowing through their veins. He wouldn't easily walk away. No, she hadn't made a mistake in telling him. He'd had a right to know his granddaughters were alive.

Deciding she needed her strength for whatever came her way later, she stopped toying with her food and began eating. The chicken, rice and gravy were good.

She finished then off and then dived into the blueberry pie.

As she sat alone eating, she could not help but think about last night and the confessions she and Sawyer had made to each other. He loved her and she loved him. She chuckled softly while thinking that they both loved Jade. After making out on the beach they had returned to the inn, showered together and then made love again before he had left. He would be flying into Sacramento tomorrow, and she had given him the name of the hotel where she would be staying. She'd even gone so far as to add his name to the registration just in case she was at the hospital when he got in. That way he would not have a problem getting a key to her hotel room.

They'd talked some last night and she knew they would be talking some more while together in California. The most important thing for now was that he had told her no matter what decisions she made or had to make, he supported her one hundred percent. That had meant a lot to her. It had meant everything.

"Are you finished with your meal, Ms. Alcindor?"

She glanced up at the man who was the lone flight attendant. "Yes. Thanks, Karl."

Moments later Mr. Lacroix returned. "My pilot will be signaling for us to buckle up in a minute. We'll be landing soon."

She buckled her seat belt and glanced out the window as butterflies began floating in her stomach. She had to believe in the end everything would be alright. Her daughter would be fine.

"I understand you and Sheriff Grisham are pretty serious about each other."

Vashti was trying to determine if she'd heard censure

in his voice and decided that no, she hadn't. And there was no need to ask how he knew that when probably the entire town knew. There wasn't much that went on in the cove that Reid Lacroix didn't know about. "Yes, we are."

What she felt was a genuine smile touched the older man's lips. "I'm happy for you, Vashti. Considering everything, if anyone deserves happiness, it's you."

As soon as Vashti and Reid walked into the hospital's lobby they were met by Jeremy Banks. She introduced Mr. Lacroix to Banks.

"The Harrises are waiting in a conference room that the hospital was kind enough to let us use," Banks said, leading the way.

They followed him down a wide corridor. The nervous flutters in her stomach increased and as if sensing her nervousness, Mr. Lacroix touched her shoulders reassuringly. She knew he was probably just as nervous and excited as she was, but figured he had years of experience when it came to controlling emotions.

Banks stopped in front of a door, opened it and then stepped aside for Vashti and Reid to enter. Vashti's gaze immediately went to the couple who stood. Both appeared to be in their late thirties or early forties. She thought the guy was handsome and the woman very attractive. This was the couple who had raised her daughter.

"Vashti Alcindor, this is Percelli and Alma Harris. The couple who adopted Kia."

After shaking their hands, Vashti asked. "Kia?"

"Yes," Alma Harris said, smiling. "We named her

Kia after my best friend who'd passed away while we were in college. Thank you for coming."

Vashti returned her smile. "There's no way I could not have." She then said, "And this is Reid Lacroix. His son, Julius, was Kia's biological father. He wants to be tested as a possible donor as well."

Reid shook both Percelli's and Alma's hands. "Thanks for being tested," Percelli said. "Is your son willing to be tested also?"

"My son died seven years ago in an auto accident," Reid said.

"Oh, I'm sorry to hear that," Alma said.

"Thank you."

"Let's sit down so we can discuss any questions any of you have," Jeremy Banks said.

At that moment there was a knock at the door. "That's probably my mother," Percelli said. "She went to my home to freshen up, and I texted her as to where we were."

Banks opened the door and an attractive older woman walked in smiling. "Hello, everyone," she greeted.

"Glo?"

Surprise showed on the woman's face when she saw the person who'd called out her name. "Reid?"

Percelli looked from his mother to Reid. "The two of you know each other?"

"Yes," Glo said, smiling over at her son. "Your father and I attended Yale together with Reid. We graduated from the same class. In fact, Reid and I ran into each other just months ago in New York." She turned back to Reid with a confused look on her face. "What are you doing here?"

"To be tested as a possible kidney donor," he said.

"For Kia?"

"Yes. I take it she's the granddaughter you were all smiles about in New York."

Gloria smiled proudly. "Yes, she's my one and only. Small world." She then asked. "How are you involved?"

"My son, Julius, was her biological father."

A sad look appeared on Gloria's face. "The son you lost. Your one and only."

Reid nodded. "Yes."

"I know I said it before in New York, Reid, but my heart goes out to you for losing your son and wife."

"Thanks, Glo."

Then Gloria Harris, with the grace, style and refinement of someone used to being a hostess, introduced herself to Vashti and Banks and shook their hands. "Kia favors you," she said to Vashti. "Especially around the eyes. And the two of you have the same smiles. You're beautiful, just like my granddaughter."

Vashti appreciated the woman's kind words. "Thank you."

At that moment Banks spoke up. "We were about to sit down so any questions any of you might have can be addressed."

Everyone sat down at the long conference table. Once everyone was seated, Percelli said, "I have a question." He glanced over at Vashti. "Once the doctor apprised us of Kia's condition and we knew we needed to try to locate you, we were surprised when our attorney informed us that you were seeking us out as well. Why? Had you decided to try to reach out to Kia as her biological mother?"

Vashti shook her head. "No. To be quite honest, Mr. Harris—"

"Percelli. I think considering the circumstances, it sounds less formal."

Vashti nodded and said, "I'm definitely okay with that."

The others sitting at the table nodded their agreement as well.

"Like I was saying," Vashti said. "No, I had no intentions of reaching out to her if Mr. Banks informed me she was in a good home." She paused then continued, "I only learned less than a month ago that the child I had delivered that night was alive and it was a girl. My parents had lied to me and told me I had a son who'd died within an hour of being born due to medical complications."

"What!"

"How could they?"

"How awful!"

The responses given by the Harrises were in keeping with the indignation Vashti felt.

"Why would they do such a thing?" Alma said angrily.

Vashti drew in a deep breath. "I've asked myself that same question a number of times since finding out the truth. After talking with them about it, the only reason I could come up with is that they truly believed they were doing the right thing. I was pregnant at sixteen and they felt the last thing I needed to take care of was a baby."

"So, you hadn't even planned to give your child up for adoption?" Percelli asked.

"No, I hadn't planned to do that. I wanted to keep my baby and my parents knew it. However, it appears they tricked me into signing adoption papers when I thought I was signing papers for something else," Vashti said, not trying to hide the bitterness coming through in her voice.

"Well, I'm glad you found out the truth, dear," Gloria said, reaching out and patting her hand.

"I'm glad, too." Vashti looked across the table at Percelli and Alma. "Does Kia know she was adopted?"

They nodded. "Yes. She's known for a while now. Since she was ten," Alma was saying. "My husband and I are both engineers and she began stressing out when she discovered she hated math and science. She couldn't understand why since she was our child. She figured she should love them, too. We decided to tell her the truth."

"How did she take it?" Reid Lacroix wanted to know.

"I think she was upset for a day or two but then she was fine and said since her mother didn't want her, she was glad we had her."

Vashti didn't say anything but the words pierced her heart. Her child had no idea she'd been wanted.

"I apologize for being so insensitive, after what you just told us," Alma said.

Vashti could see genuine regret in her eyes. "No, how Kia feels is understandable, knowing what she believes."

"Well, now you'll be able to tell her differently. She knows we reached out to you and like us, she appreciates your agreeing to be tested. She didn't think you would. To be honest, none of us did. We assumed you'd gotten on with your life."

"I had, but only because of what I'd been told," Vashti then said.

"Well, I'm glad we all found each other," Glo said.

"There is more information the private investigator

discovered that I want to share with you," Vashti said. "It was something I didn't know. Kia is a twin."

Vashti could see the shock on the Harrises' faces. "A twin?" Percelli finally found his voice to ask.

"Yes. I have another daughter out there who is an identical twin to Kia. I don't have any idea where she is now or who the couple who adopted her are. From Mr. Banks's report, the twins were born ten minutes apart with Kia being the youngest."

"And you are trying to find her?" Alma asked.

"Yes. I refuse to give up hope that she will be found."

"Thank you for sharing that with us," Percelli said.

"Considering everything, I felt you had every right to know." Vashti then drew in a deep breath. "So, when can we see Kia?"

"In a minute. But first I want to have Dr. Telfair paged so he can meet you and tell you what to expect."

"Okay," Vashti said.

AN HOUR LATER Vashti and Reid were catching an elevator with the Harrises to Kia's hospital room. The meeting with Dr. Telfair had lasted only twenty minutes, but he told them to take time to relax a minute because Kia had been taken for her dialysis treatment. Everyone went up to the hospital cafeteria to grab a snack while they waited.

The Harrises had agreed that for now they should not mention anything to Kia about her having a twin sister. They would wait for Vashti's private investigator's report to see how to proceed. The last thing they wanted was to get their daughter's hopes up about anything. It was mentioned to Dr. Telfair who'd said a sibling, especially a twin, had a better chance of being an eligible donor. Vashti knew that like her, now more so than ever, in case things didn't work out with her or Mr. Lacroix as possible donors, it would be wonderful if they could find Kia's twin.

Vashti had called Sawyer to let him know she had arrived in Sacramento and how her meeting with the Harrises had gone. She'd even told him that Gloria Harris and Reid Lacroix knew each other from college. Sawyer had given her good news. Since he had made all necessary arrangements to be away from town, including making sure Jade was taken care of, he would be arriving in Sacramento tonight instead of tomorrow. In fact, he was at the airport when she'd called him.

The closer they got to Kia's hospital room the more nervous and excited Vashti got. She had a feeling Mr. Lacroix was nervous as well, but was trying not to show it. She did notice, however, that he'd been looking at Gloria Harris quite a few times...and the woman had been looking at him. Hmm, Gloria a widow and he a widower. Was Vashti detecting interest there?

They stopped in front of room 545 and Vashti's heart began pounding in her chest. In a way she felt like she was about to have an anxiety attack and hoped that wasn't the case. "Wait," she said softly, when Percelli was about to open the door. "I need to compose myself. I can't help it but I'm so excited."

Gloria touched her arm. "Take a couple of deep breaths and it will be okay. Considering what you told us about thinking your child was dead all this time, we can understand." Vashti did as the older woman suggested and breathed in.

"Kia is your typical teenager," Percelli said, grinning. "She likes loud music, video games and shopping. She got a car for her sixteenth birthday and so far no tickets. She recently was chosen as a majorette at school and is looking forward to football season in the fall. She was preparing to practice her baton-twirling dance routines before she got sick."

"I used to be a majorette," Vashti said, appreciating the group of people talking to her in order to calm her nerves. It was working. Still, she wished Sawyer were here beside her. He had become her rock.

"Vashti was national champion in baton-twirling while in high school," Reid Lacroix told everyone proudly. "She's Catalina Cove's celebrity."

Alma smiled. "Congratulations." She then asked with concern, "You're okay now, Vashti?"

Vashti nodded. Her breathing had been coming fast but now it had slowed back down to normal. "Yes, I'm fine now. Sorry."

"Hey, don't apologize. We understand," Percelli said. "Like I said, Kia is your typical teenager, but she's also a loving and caring person. I know you will love her as much as we do."

Vashti believed that to be true and just hoped Kia would like her. Percelli opened the door. When they entered the hospital room Kia's back was to them as she chatted on her cell phone. There was something about the sound of Kia's voice that made the hairs on the back of Vashti's neck stand up.

"Kia, you have company," Gloria said.

The teenager turned around and the minute Vashti looked into Kia's smiling face, her head began spinning and then suddenly, everything went black.

## CHAPTER FORTY-TWO

VASHTI FELT THE warmth of someone's flattened hand on her forehead and realized her temperature was being checked. Slowly opening her eyes, she stared up into the face of Dr. Telfair. It was then she realized she was lying in the bed of an unoccupied hospital room with the doctor hovering over her. Out of the corner of her eyes she saw Alma and Gloria.

"How do you feel?" the doctor asked her.

"Fine." She tried sitting up but the doctor's firm hand on her shoulder stopped her.

"Lie still a minute," he instructed.

She relaxed back down on the bed. "I'm sorry. I didn't mean to be a bother," she said to anyone who cared to listen.

"No need to apologize. The ladies here explained things and said you had what appeared to be an anxiety attack before entering the room. Shock will do that to you."

He could say that again. A barrage of questions was running through her mind. What had her parents done? How? Why? "I guess Kia thinks I'm a basket case for passing out like that," she said to Alma and Gloria when they came to stand beside the doctor.

"She doesn't think that at all. When we told her that

you had assumed your baby had died all those years ago, she understood," Alma said.

"Where is Mr. Lacroix?" Vashti asked.

"He's in the hospital room talking to Kia. Do you need to see him?"

"Yes."

"You can sit up now, Ms. Alcindor, and do it slowly," Dr. Telfair instructed.

As Vashti sat up she heard the hospital room door open and close. She saw both women had left and she and Dr. Telfair were alone. "Where am I?"

"You're in one of the empty hospital rooms down the hall from Kia Harris's room," Dr. Telfair said. "I'll leave you now."

When there was a knock on the door, Dr. Telfair said, "Come in."

Mr. Lacroix entered. "You're okay, Vashti?" he asked her with genuine concern on his face.

"Yes, I'm fine, Reid."

Dr. Telfair said, "A lot of excitement for one day, but she'll be fine." He then left, closing the door shut behind him.

"Glo said you wanted to see me."

Vashti nodded. "You've seen Kia." It was a statement, more so than a question.

He actually beamed. "Yes, and she's something else, too. Friendly and smart as a whip. I can't wait to get to know her better. And Glo was right," the older man added. "She favors you around the eyes and has Julius's nose and mouth."

Vashti nodded again. "Does she remind you of anyone besides me and Julius?"

She could tell from his expression that he was thinking. Real hard. Then he said, "No."

How had he not looked into Kia's face and seen Jade? Their features were identical. Even the smile and voice. She could only assume he hadn't seen Jade very much, which would explain not noticing the similarities. After all, their paths wouldn't cross much.

Vashti reached for her purse, pulled out her cell phone and sweeping her fingertips across the screen, she went to her photo app and tapped to find the photos she was looking for. She then handed her cell phone to him. "Take a look at these photos. These were taken the night of the majorette try-outs."

He looked at them and she saw the moment his mouth dropped open in shock. "H-how can this be?" he asked, lifting his gaze to stare at her. "Sheriff Grisham's daughter is Kia's…"

"Twin."

Mr. Lacroix looked at the photos and then back at her again, still in shock. "This doesn't make sense. I was part of the team that interviewed Grisham for sheriff. He told us his wife died leaving him to raise their daughter. He made it sound as if she was his natural child when he'd mentioned the difficult pregnancy his wife had had."

"As far as he knows, he is her natural father," Vashti defended.

"How could he not know his daughter was adopted?"

Now that was a good question. "He was away, on a tour of duty in Afghanistan when she was born. When he returned home, his daughter was six months old."

Reid shook his head. "You mean to tell me that I had a granddaughter living in Catalina Cove for the

past four years and didn't even know it? Well, now we
know what happened to your other baby."

No, she was far from knowing what happened. How
did Johanna Grisham get Vashti's child to pass off as
hers? And what had happened to the Grishams' baby?
"Sawyer is flying in tonight instead of tomorrow," she
said, remembering their last conversation. "He has to
be told."

"And you're the one who needs to tell him, Vashti.
You need to tell him the truth."

She didn't know what the truth was. How had his
wife been in a position to adopt Vashti's baby? "Yes,
I have to tell him. But how can I do that when I don't
know the full story?" She drew in a deep breath thinking, *What a mess. What a big mess.*

"Yes, but Sawyer is your future now, Vashti. Even if
you don't know the full story, the two of you can discover it together. The one thing I do know is that he
will need your love and support. That is essential when
you're going through difficult times."

She agreed. "You're right and I will be there for Sawyer," she said. *Just like he's been there for me during my
difficult times.* But the question she was asking herself
was how was he going to handle finding out about his
wife's betrayal? How would he handle knowing he was
not Jade's biological father?

"I will tell him when he arrives tonight. But for now
I want to go and meet Kia."

A VOICE IN the back of Vashti's mind was trying to re-
assure her everything would be alright when she stood
beside Reid and knocked on the hospital room door.

"Come in."

Opening the door she stepped inside. Four people looked over at them, specifically at her. But Vashti's gaze was on Kia. "Hello," she said, barely recognizing her own voice.

"Hello. Sorry seeing me made you pass out. I'm glad you're better," the teenager said, smiling. She extended her hand. "I'm Kia Harris. Thanks for coming and being tested to see if your kidney will work for me."

"You're welcome." Like Jade, she figured Kia never met a stranger, at least not one she couldn't charm.

"I think it would be a good idea," Gloria Harris said, "if we gave Vashti and Kia time alone. Reid, I would love to share memories of our days at Yale over a cup of coffee."

"And while you two are doing that," Alma said, "Percelli and I need to make a few calls." She took hold of her husband's hand and led him toward the door. In less than two minutes, Vashti found herself alone with Kia.

"Honestly, could they be any more transparent?" Kia laughed.

Vashti smiled. She had to admit the Harrises were not what she expected, considering the circumstances. They weren't at all threatened by the appearance of Kia's birth mother and grandfather in their daughter's life. She wondered how Jade would handle the truth because like her father, she assumed Johanna was her birth mother.

"You have swell folks and a nice grandmother," Vashti said as she took the chair beside Kia's hospital bed.

"They are the best, although since becoming a teenager they are getting a lot more protective. But I understand. There are a lot of crazy people out there so I try not to make them worry."

"That's mature and thoughtful of you."

The room got quiet for a minute and Vashti knew Kia had questions for her, so she said, "I want you to ask me anything you want, Kia. Anything at all."

"Okay. The guy who got you pregnant at sixteen. My biological father. Mr. Lacroix's son, Julius. Did you love him? I asked Mr. Lacroix if he thought his son loved you and he said yes, that he did, and that he told him he'd loved you before he died."

Vashti nodded. "Yes, I loved Julius. He was my first boyfriend. My parents didn't even know he and I were seeing each other."

"You were sneaking around?" Kia asked.

"Yes." But not to give her daughter any ideas, she said, "That's where we made our first mistake. We should have dated out in the open and supervised."

Kia nodded. "And your parents? Why would they lie to you?"

Evidently Kia's parents had told her the entire story. "They thought I was too young to be a mother and my child would be better off being adopted."

Kia nibbled on her bottom lip, something Vashti had seen Jade do a few times as well. "I don't know what kind of life I would have had with you, Ms. Vashti, but I can't help but be glad my parents adopted me and that my grandparents were my grandparents. I can't imagine growing up around anyone else. I hope that doesn't make you feel sad."

Vashti shook her head. "No, it doesn't." Honestly, in a way it did. She would like to think her daughters would have grown up well-adjusted in Catalina Cove.

But then, what kind of life could she have offered them without a college education? She would have had to kiss college goodbye as a single mother. However, there was the option of taking classes at night. That meant being away from her kids during the day while she worked and then at night while she attended school.

There was no doubt in Vashti's mind that being the only child of two engineers who were in love and respected each other had merits. It was obvious Kia was a well-adjusted child…just like Jade. She hoped the two of them got to meet. It would be essential that they did. There was no guarantee that Vashti or Reid would be a donor match for Kia, which meant Jade would need to be tested. Whether she was or not would be Sawyer's decision.

"You're pretty. Do you have a boyfriend?"

Kia's question pulled Vashti back into reality. "Yes, I'm seeing a guy. He's the sheriff in Catalina Cove."

"A sheriff? I bet he gives out plenty of tickets."

No need to tell her that's how she and Sawyer had met. "I'm sure he does, to speeders."

"Mom says you used to be a national baton-twirling champion. Is that true?"

"Yes, but that was years ago when I was about your age."

"But it's something you don't forget, right?"

Vashti grinned. "Right. It's something you don't forget, although if you don't do it often, you'll get rusty."

"Do you ever want any more kids? You're still young."

Honestly, she hadn't thought about it. She had when she'd married Scott, but when her marriage began turning sour she was glad she hadn't brought a child into it. But she was with Sawyer now—did she want his child? Would he want to start over in fatherhood when he had a teenage daughter? "Yes, if I were to marry I would want a child."

She and Kia talked for a half hour more before everyone returned. Dr. Telfair dropped by to let her and Reid know their tests would be done tomorrow. More than anything Vashti hoped that one of them would be a perfect donor for Kia.

VASHTI WOKE TO the sound of the hotel room door opening. She glanced at the clock on the nightstand and saw it was three in the morning and knew Sawyer had arrived.

Easing out of bed she didn't bother putting on a robe when she left the bedroom to enter the sitting area of the suite. After placing his carry-on luggage aside, he opened his arms and she rushed across the room to be engulfed in his warm embrace.

"I know it's only been a day, but I miss you," he whispered close to her ear before taking her mouth to devour it.

Vashti needed this kiss. She needed him. And she knew after she told him about Kia and Jade that he would need her. When she had left the hospital she'd known what she had to do. There was a chance he probably wouldn't believe her at first, but once he saw Kia he would see for himself.

When Sawyer deepened the kiss even more, every thought suddenly fled from Vashti's mind. A shiver of desire overtook her when the warmth of his body seeped through to hers, and when the hardness of his erection poked at the juncture of her thighs, all she could imagine was being in bed, wrapped in his arms while he made love to her.

He broke the kiss and stared at her moist lips before shifting his gaze to hers. "You're beautiful," he breathed out and then breathed in deeply, as if inhaling her scent. Since being involved with Sawyer she was used to his extreme arousal state, and his unending stamina. But what she loved and admired about him was that he always made satisfying her his top priority. There was never a time they made love that he hadn't made her feel like a woman. A woman he fully desired. And she knew he desired her now and she desired him.

"You're trying to make my head swell?" she asked, smiling up at him.

"I don't see why not," he said, as a sexy, self-assured smile touched his lips. "You've made a certain part of me swell. Turnabout is fair play."

And then he swept her off her feet and carried her into the bedroom.

SAWYER EASED HIS body off Vashti and shifted to hold her in his arms. Their legs were entwined, and her breasts were flattened against his chest while she faced him. Sweat dampened her forehead, and her lips were still moist from his overindulgent kisses.

Over the past few months, he'd told her countless times she was beautiful, and he honestly didn't think she knew just how beautiful she was. He doubted she realized how her smile alone could make a rush of heat flow through him or how just seeing her could make his heart pound. He also doubted she had a clue just how deeply he'd fallen in love with her. He'd told her that he loved her, but he was certain she hadn't grasped just how much. At first it had scared the hell out of him that after Johanna he could love any woman to that degree, or that he could constantly analyze the depth of that love. He hadn't ever done such a thing for Johanna. He'd just accepted over time that he loved her. With Vashti he was convinced he'd begun feeling something for her the minute he'd pulled her over and given her a ticket.

"We need to talk, Sawyer."

He reached up and caressed the side of her face. "Sorry, baby. I should have asked how things went for you today. I'm sure they could not have been easy. But when I saw you standing there, I wanted you so much."

"And I should have asked how your flight was. But then I had wanted you to make love to me, too."

That was one of the things he loved most about her, Sawyer thought. She had no qualms in letting him know she enjoyed their lovemaking as much as he did. She was such a passionate person and he wanted to always be there for her. That's why he hadn't hesitated to move his schedule around to take days off to make sure she had someone to lean on. He could not imagine her dealing with any of this alone. Granted Reid had come, but the man had to be encountering his own emotions as well.

"Tell me, baby. Tell me how things went."

"The doctor doesn't think I can be a donor for my daughter since she has one of those rare blood types. Luckily, Mr. Lacroix has the same blood type so there's still a chance he might be."

Sawyer nodded. He studied her and then as if he could read her mind, he said, "There's more, isn't there?"

She nodded. "Yes. And when I tell you, I doubt you will believe me because I'm having a hard time believing it myself. But I know together you and I will get to the bottom of it."

He lifted a brow as he stared into her eyes. "Get to the bottom of what?"

She nibbled on her bottom lip and Sawyer wondered why she'd suddenly become nervous. "Get to the bottom of what, Vashti?" he asked her again.

She drew in a deep breath and said, "My daughter's name is Kia," she said softly, while holding his gaze.

"That's a pretty name," he said, knowing a name wouldn't have her suddenly acting uneasy.

"I think so, too. And what we need to get to the bottom of, Sawyer, is how Kia and Jade are twins."

# CHAPTER FORTY-THREE

VASHTI WATCHED HIS expression and knew Sawyer hadn't fully comprehended what she'd meant. He proved her right when he said, "What about her reminds you of Jade? Is it the hair, her size, the eyes, the—"

"All of it," she interrupted him to say.

He nodded. "You know what they say. Everybody's got a twin somewhere."

"I mean a *real* twin, Sawyer."

Something in the tone of her voice made him lift a brow. "What do you mean a real twin?"

She swallowed, this had to be one of the most difficult things she'd ever had to do. "You know what Jeremy Banks said about my giving birth to twins that were separated at birth."

"Yes, I heard him, but what does that have to do with Jade?"

Now she could hear signs of irritation in his voice. Detangling their legs, she pulled herself out of his arms to sit up in bed. It was important that he not only heard her but understood what she was telling him. "What I'm trying to tell you, Sawyer, is that Jade is Kia's twin."

He looked up at her like she'd lost her ever-loving mind. And from the sympathetic look in his eyes, he actually thought that she had. Reaching out he ran a sooth ing hand up and down her arm. "I know you've had a rough time dealing with everything, baby. It had to have been hard all these years thinking your baby had died and now finding out you gave birth to twins who are alive. That's enough for any one person to have to deal with. I understand your wanting to find both babies and your eagerness to do so. But, sweetheart, you know as well as I do that there's no way Jade is anyone's twin."

"But she is, Sawyer."

He frowned and pulled his hand away. "Listen to me, Vashti," he said in a stern voice. "There is no way she can be. How in the world can you even think such a thing?"

"Because when I walked into Kia's hospital room, the girl who smiled at me looked identical to Jade."

"I can believe she resembled Jade."

"No, she is Jade's twin."

He reached out for her again to pull her into his arms. "Let's get some sleep. You'll be okay tomorrow. You're so exhausted that—"

"I'm talking crazy?"

"Yes," he said, leaning in and brushing his lips across her forehead.

"I'm not crazy, Sawyer."

"I didn't say you were crazy. I just think you're a little confused and it's understandable."

She wouldn't expect him to believe her, at least until he saw Kia for himself. Even now it was still hard to believe, and she had to periodically convince herself this was reality and not an episode of the *Twilight Zone*. But still...

"None of this is understandable, Sawyer. Can you tell

me how you and your wife adopted one of my daughters?"

In the lines of his face, she could see frustration was turning into anger. "There is nothing to tell, Vashti. Jade is my daughter, not yours. She's my and Johanna's biological daughter."

"You're sure of that?"

His hand reached up and closed around her naked shoulder like he was tempted to shake some sense into her. "Of course, I'm sure of it."

"Why? Were you with Johanna when Jade was born?"

"You know I wasn't." He frowned and pulled his hand off her. "Hey, wait a damn minute," he said, sitting up in bed as well. "Now, you've gone too far. Whether you know it or not, you're all but accusing my wife of deceiving me. Not only does that not make sense, but it's something Johanna wouldn't do."

He got out of bed and slid into his pants. "I'm trying to be understanding, Vashti, but I refuse to let you accuse Johanna of doing something that's not only horrendous but outright dishonest. You didn't know her, but I did."

"I know what I saw, Sawyer. And it's more than a coincidence that Jade and Kia not only look alike, but they share the same birthday."

He put on his shirt. "What you saw is a girl who favors my daughter. As far as them sharing the same birthday, so do a lot of people. For God's sake, Vashti, even you have to know what you're claiming is impossible."

By his words and expression she could tell he was mentally blocking out what she was saying. He had to believe she wasn't making this stuff up. He had to know after spending so much time around Jade that she could tell the difference between someone who looked like her and someone who was her identical twin.

"Where are you going?" she asked him as he got dressed.

"I'm leaving."

"Leaving?"

"Yes, leaving," he said, glancing around as if to make sure he had everything. "You have no right to slander my wife's good name for any reason and I won't allow it. Regardless of what you want to think, she is Jade's mother and I won't stay and let you try and convince me otherwise. I'm flying back to Catalina Cove."

"But wouldn't it make sense to go to the hospital tomorrow to see Kia for yourself? Then you'd know I'm telling the truth. That I am right."

He narrowed his gaze at her. "Nothing you're saying makes sense, Vashti. And I don't need to go to any hospital because there's no way you're right," he said, heading for the bedroom door. When he reached it, he turned around and stared at her with cold, dark eyes. "Goodbye, Vashti."

She recalled another time he'd told her goodbye. She didn't want things to end between them this way. "I thought we would find out the truth together, Sawyer," she said in a soft voice.

He shook his head. "There's no truth in your words. I refuse to accept what you're accusing my wife of doing." He then turned and walked out of the bedroom.

When she heard the hotel room door close behind him, she buried her face in her pillow and cried.

THREE HOURS LATER, Sawyer was still at the airport, waiting on standby, trying to get a flight back home. He bit into a strawberry muffin he'd purchased from the snack machine and had to admit it didn't taste bad, and he wasn't a big fan of strawberries. But then he hadn't been crazy about blueberries either until he'd moved to Catalina Cove, the blueberry capital of the world.

He glanced up when he heard a cry of happiness and watched a young woman who looked to be in her late twenties rush into the open arms of a military man. They probably were being reunited after he'd been gone awhile, Sawyer thought. He remembered those times for him and how every time he returned home, Johanna and Jade would be at the airport to welcome him home. Those had been some of the happiest days of his life.

He shifted his thoughts to what Vashti had said, what she'd all but accused his wife of doing. Obviously, she had gotten overwhelmed by yesterday's events and was going through some kind of emotional shock. He could accept that and considering all she'd had to deal with lately, the stress of reopening the inn and then finding out how her parents had betrayed her, he could understand her feeling pushed somewhat to the limit. But that didn't give her the right to slander his wife's name and make up stuff that simply wasn't true.

However, on the other hand, Vashti was not a woman who gave into dramatics of any kind. In fact, she had to be the most logical person he knew, although from being in law enforcement he knew that even logical people could experience meltdowns. But then being in law enforcement had also taught him not to take anything at face value. Not even the reputation of the wife he'd fully trusted.

Bottom line was that Vashti was right. He hadn't been there when Jade was born. But did that matter when he'd been with Johanna up to her fourth month of pregnancy before deployment? Jade had been born a few weeks early. The cause of the premature birth had been due to placental problems Johanna had encountered during the pregnancy. At least that's what she had told him.

He tightened his hand into a fist. And did it mean anything that Jade also had a rare blood type, something Vashti didn't know? And was it just a coincidence that the two girls shared the same birthday?

Damn it. Why was he questioning any of that? It wasn't fair to Johanna. But then, was it fair to Vashti for him not to question it when she totally believed what she'd seen? Her claim was way too farfetched to make up, even while under the influence of some type of emotional shock.

He lifted his head when the lady at the counter called his name. He walked over to where she stood. "I'm Sawyer Grisham."

"Good news. We can get you on the next flight to New Orleans."

It would have been good news if Sawyer hadn't suddenly made up his mind about something. He knew what he had to do. "Thanks, but I've changed my mind about going to New Orleans. I want a ticket to Waco, Texas, instead."

An hour later he was boarding a plane to Waco. He needed to see Erin. She'd been with Johanna through her entire pregnancy. Erin had even been her birthing coach in his absence. She would know the truth.

"He doesn't believe me, Bryce," Vashti said, trying to hold it together while talking to her best friend on the phone. She'd just finished telling Bryce everything. "You believe me, don't you?"

"Yes, as bizarre as it sounds, I believe you."

"Then why can't Sawyer? Why would he think I'd make something like that up? All he had to do was go to the hospital with me. Once he saw Kia he would have known I was telling the truth."

"Yes, but think about what you were accusing his dead wife of, Vash. A wife he loved, adored and trusted. A woman that he believes is the birth mother of his child, like he is the biological father. You were trying to get him to believe all of that is a lie."

"But it is a lie," she said. "Don't you think I'd thought about it? Wondered how I would break the news to him? What I would say? Maybe I should not have told him anything. Just let him walk into Kia's hospital room to see for himself."

"You did the right thing by telling him whether he wants to believe it or not. Sawyer is a cop and they have suspicious minds. The cop side of him will eventually begin questioning some of those things you pointed out to him."

Vashti drew in a deep breath, not so sure. Bryce hadn't seen the way he'd looked at her before walking out the door. His goodbye had been final.

"How do you think his wife got to adopt your baby?" Bryce interrupted her thoughts to ask.

"I've been thinking about that. It had to have been through the Smithfields, Johanna Grisham's grandparents. They attended our church and were well acquainted with my parents. Mr. Smithfield was a federal judge and he had the money and the means to do it and keep it quiet. Of course, my parents, who were all too eager to rid me of two babies, would have jumped at the chance for him to do so."

"You're probably right. I guess my question is what happened to Johanna Grisham's baby? The one she was pregnant with when Sawyer was deployed? At some point he's going to have to realize and accept that baby isn't Jade. Are you going to tell the Harrises about her?"

"I have no choice. Kia has a life-threatening condition. It won't be fair not to be totally honest with them."

"I agree," Bryce said. "You're no longer an eligible kidney donor for Kia. What if Mr. Lacroix isn't either?"

A lump formed in the back of Vashti's throat. At that moment she didn't want to think about that possibility. She couldn't.

SAWYER KNOCKED ON Erin's front door. He had rented a car at the airport and during the drive here he had contemplated how he would question her. He knew how close Erin and Johanna had been. Best friends since high school and if Johanna had made her promise anything Erin wouldn't break that promise, no matter what. He would have to resort to one of his interrogation techniques. Let them think you knew something when you really didn't.

A surprised look was on Erin's face when she opened the door. "Sawyer? What are you doing here? I wasn't aware you were in Waco," she said, moving aside for him to enter.

"I just flew in from Sacramento."

"Oh," she said, smiling. "You were in California on business?"

"No." He refused to tell her any more than that. Glancing around, he asked. "Where are Damon and the boys?"

"He took them biking in the park. They should be back soon. Would you like something to drink?" she asked, leading him from the foyer into the living room. "Several cans of your favorite beer are still in the fridge from your last visit."

"No, I don't want anything to drink. What I do want, Erin, are answers."

She stopped walking, turned around and lifted a brow. "About what?"

"About how Jade is not my biological child."

# CHAPTER FORTY-FOUR

ERIN DROPPED DOWN in the nearest chair. "How did you find out after all this time?"

Sawyer felt like he'd been punched hard in the gut. His head was beginning to spin. So it was true. Vashti had been right. Jade was not his biological child. Johanna had betrayed him in the worst possible way. He drew in a deep breath, knowing he had to keep the facade going for now to get all the information he could out of Erin, while keeping his pain and anger at bay. She couldn't even look at him. Instead she was studying her hands and speaking in a low tone.

"I found out the truth when I saw Jade's identical twin sister today," he said, lying.

Her head jerked up. "Jade has a twin?"

So, she hadn't known that. Had Johanna known? "Yes, they were separated at birth and adopted by difference couples."

"And they are identical?" she asked, as if making sure she had heard him correctly.

"Yes. Do you think Johanna knew Jade had a twin?" he asked, needing to know.

"No. She would have told me if she had."

Erin went back to staring at her hands again, and then she finally lifted her head and said, "I tried to get Johanna to tell you the truth, especially before she died.

But she refused. I think she was afraid to admit to what she'd done by then. She didn't want to die not knowing what would become of Jade."

Sawyer frowned. "Did she think I wouldn't take care of my daughter?"

"I guess she wasn't sure how you would feel once you discovered the truth, Sawyer. She made me promise if you found out after her death and didn't want Jade anymore that I would take her and raise her as my own."

Sawyer's loud expletive ripped through the room, making Erin jump. "If she actually thought something like that then she really didn't truly know me at all."

He drew in a deep breath, trying not to let more anger overtake him. "Why did she do it?" he asked, needing desperately to know. "Why did she deceive me that way?"

Erin's mouth trembled and he could see tears forming in her eyes. "Johanna lost her baby at five months."

Sawyer swallowed as pain ripped through him. "How?"

"All I know is that during one of her routine doctor's visits, he couldn't pick up a heartbeat. He performed more tests and it was determined the baby had died and they had to induce labor."

"My God! Why didn't she tell me?"

Erin paused a moment and then said, "Because she believed the only reason you married her was because she'd gotten pregnant, and without a pregnancy there was no reason for you to stay married to her."

Sawyer's expression hardened. "How could she think something like that?"

"How could she not?"

Sawyer's eyes narrowed. "What the hell is that supposed to mean?"

Erin stiffened her spine and met his glare. "It means that Johanna never believe you loved her during the first few years of your marriage. The two of you had a one-night stand that resulted in her getting pregnant. You married her because of that pregnancy. When you became deployed and would write or call, the first person you would ask about was the baby. You always asked how the baby was doing before asking how she was doing."

Sawyer's lips formed a grim line. *Had he?* "I don't remember doing that, and if I did it was out of habit and nothing else."

"Well, she didn't see it that way. To her way of thinking, it was an indication of who was more important. She got so distraught over losing the baby that she went into a state of depression fearing you would find out and that she would lose you, too. That's when her grandparents stepped in."

When Erin stopped talking, Sawyer said, "Please continue."

Erin nodded. "They knew a couple whose sixteen-year-old daughter was expecting, and the baby was being put up for adoption. If you recall, Johanna's grandfather was a federal judge. He took extra steps to make sure those adoption papers were sealed and were never to be opened. The baby Johanna lost was a boy, but since—"

"A boy?" he interrupted to ask.

"Yes. Since neither you nor Johanna had wanted to know the sex of your child beforehand," Erin was saying, "the Smithfields figured switching babies would work."

*And it had.* Anger consumed Sawyer in every part of his body. Who gave Johanna and the Smithfields the right to do what they'd done? Deceiving him that way. He held Erin's gaze and asked, "Would you have ever told me the truth?"

She shook her head. "No. I promised Johanna that I wouldn't, and I would have taken her secret to the grave."

Sawyer stood. "Johanna was wrong. I did love her. I might not have in the beginning, but over time I fell in love with her. I honestly thought she knew that."

"She did know it, Sawyer. Johanna died knowing you loved her. By then the two of you had been married over twelve years. She feared telling you the truth at that point. And once she discovered she had cancer, telling you was no longer an option for her."

"There are always options, Erin."

He turned and moved toward her front door but she stopped him. "Wait! You didn't say how you ran into Jade's twin?"

Sawyer stopped and turned around. "The woman I'm seeing gave—"

"I didn't know you were seeing anyone. Jade never mentioned it."

"Well, I am. She recently moved back to Catalina Cove and discovered her parents gave away her babies for adoption when she was sixteen. Instead of telling her the truth, they told her that her lone child, a son, had died at birth. She found out the truth when one of the adoptive parents contacted her because their daughter is in need of a kidney transplant. Imagine her reaction when she arrived at that hospital in California and walked into the room and came face-to-face with a girl who looked identical to Jade. She had wondered what happened to the second child, then she knew—I had her."

Sawyer turned and walked out the door.

LATER THAT NIGHT Sawyer's plane landed in New Orleans. Jade had to be told the truth immediately.

But how was he going to tell her that the woman she thought was her biological mother really wasn't? That the man she assumed all this time was her biological father wasn't either. That the woman she'd come to know first as an employer and then as the woman her old man was dating, was her biological mother? But then the real icing on the cake was that the one man Jade detested, due to his strong opposition to change in the cove, was her grandfather.

He released a frustrated breath, not sure how she would handle any of it. But then Jade was strong and her sense of doing the right thing was astounding. But that was still a lot of crap for any kid to have to deal with. Like him, she would be confused and hurt by Johanna's deceit, but it would be up to him to convince Jade nothing would ever change the dynamics of their relationship.

A part of him wanted to believe that no matter what, Johanna would always be her mother and he would always be her father and that his role in Jade's life wouldn't change. More than once he'd been tempted to call Vashti and tell her that he now knew the truth. But considering all the things he'd said before leaving her, he needed to tell her face-to-face and apologize for not believing her. Right now, his main concern was Jade. Then he would fly back to California to talk to Vashti and hope that she would forgive him for letting her down.

## CHAPTER FORTY-FIVE

"You okay, Vashti?"

She glanced across the table at Mr. Lacroix. They were enjoying breakfast in one of the hotel's restaurants. "Yes, I'm fine." Okay she was lying because she really wasn't fine. How could she be when yesterday the man she loved had walked out on her?

He nodded as he took a sip of his coffee. "I take it you haven't heard from Sawyer."

No, she hadn't and honestly, she hadn't expected to either. "No, I haven't talked to him since he left."

"Have you made a decision as to whether you're going to tell the Harrises about Jade Grisham?"

"Yes, I will tell them when I see them today. It's only fair that they know, although I can't promise them what, if anything, Sawyer will do as long as he's in denial."

Reid took a sip of his coffee. "Sawyer is a good man. As a cop he will begin questioning things. Besides, even if he doesn't, pretty soon it will become obvious you were telling the truth."

She lifted a brow. "How so?"

He leaned back in his chair. "I invited Kia to come visit me in Catalina Cove. Her parents said it would be okay and Glo has agreed to bring her. You know what that means don't you?"

Vashti nodded. There was no doubt in her mind Mr. Lacroix would let everybody know Kia and Jade were his granddaughters and Vashti's daughters. When that happened, the townspeople would finally know the name of the person who fathered her babies.

"Yes, I know what it means. Secrets aren't meant to last forever. I'm not worried about me, but I am about Sawyer and Jade—especially if he refuses to accept me as Jade's biological mother. It will be a brutal awakening for him when he sees Kia."

Deciding to change the subject, she asked, "How did your test go this morning at the hospital?" His test had been scheduled at six that morning.

"Fine. Dr. Telfair said it will be late today or tomorrow before I get the results. I hope I'm a match. Glo was there this morning. She knew because of the test I hadn't eaten anything since midnight, and she had a doughnut and coffee waiting to give me afterward."

"Gloria seems like a nice person." It hadn't gone unnoticed that he and Gloria had been spending a lot of time together for the past couple of days. And now he'd mentioned Gloria would be the one bringing Kia to Catalina Cove.

"Yes, she's a nice person. Always has been." He paused a moment and added, "We have a lot in common and enjoy reminiscing about old times. She loved Martin like I loved Roberta. Losing spouses and being alone at our age is difficult."

Vashti nodded while thinking of her own love life. The one she no longer had since she was back to square one. This time she intended for things to stay that way. It would mean less pain and heartbreak.

"GOOD MORNING, DAD, when did you get back?"

Sawyer glanced up from his coffee to look at Jade when she walked in the kitchen. "Late last night. You were asleep so I decided not to wake you."

He studied his daughter and recalled that day when she and Vashti had been outside practicing her baton twirling. That day when he'd seen them interacting together he had noted their similarities. At the time he thought it was just a coincidence. Now he knew that hadn't been the case.

"How is that person Ms. Vashti went to see in California? The one who is sick?"

He blinked, realizing Jade had asked him a question. Before leaving town he had told her where he was going and why. He just hadn't told her the sick person's identity.

"She's somewhat better."

"I'm glad," Jade said, joining him at the breakfast table with several pancakes loaded on her plate. Trudy had gotten up early and fixed breakfast before leaving. "Ms. Vashti seemed pretty upset about it."

He placed his fork down, knowing Jade had given him the opening he needed. "We need to talk, Jade."

She glanced over at him. "I didn't do it."

He lifted a brow. "You didn't do what?"

She shrugged. "Whatever has you looking so serious, Dad."

A smile curved his lips. He truly did love this child of his, and she was his. "I love you, Jade," he couldn't hold back saying at that moment.

She smiled back at him. "I know you do. If this is where you tell me that you love Ms. Vashti, too, then I already know that you do."

He stared at her. No, that hadn't been what he was going to tell her, but he was curious how she knew that. "Yes, I've fallen in love with Vashti," he admitted. "How do you know that?" he asked her.

She rolled her eyes. "Seriously, Dad, I read romance novels, remember? You always look at her all dreamy-eyed."

"Dreamy-eyed?"

"Yes, like you really like her a lot and can't wait to get her alone. And before you have any spasms from what I said, remember I am a teenager and know about the boy-girl stuff."

Too much to suit him.

"I hope Ms. Vashti knows how you feel," Jade said.

"She knows. At least she used to know."

His daughter's eyes widened. "Did the two of you have a fight or something? Is that why you came back earlier than planned?"

"I guess you can say that."

"Then you need to fix it. I like her, Dad. I like her a lot. In fact, I think you should add her to our family."

"You wouldn't have a problem with that?"

"Heck no. Ms. Vashti is awesome, and I want you to be happy and she makes you happy. I see how you smile around her and I know you make her happy, too."

He hoped so.

"So you need to fix whatever problems the two of you are having." Now it was Jade's face that was all serious.

He shook his head thinking if his daughter ever joined the military she would make a good general. "Trust me, I will try fixing it and I intend to keep Vashti a part of our lives." He wouldn't go so far as to say he would add her to the family, because as far as he was concerned, as Jade's biological mother, she was already part of the family. He knew his daughter was referring to marriage. Once he fixed this problem between them, he would definitely ask her to marry him and he hoped she would say yes.

"That's not what I wanted to talk to you about, Jade."

She lifted a brow as she took a sip of her milk. "It's not?"

"No."

"Then what?"

Drawing in a deep breath he began telling his daughter what he thought she needed to know.

SAWYER WATCHED HIS daughter's facial features as she absorbed what he was telling her. So far, he had covered only a third of what he needed to tell her, which was about the adoption. He hadn't told her Vashti's involvement or the fact Jade was a twin. When the first tear fell from her eye he held his breath, wondering how she would handle what came next. She got out of her seat to come over to give him a big hug.

With her arms wrapped around his neck, she said, "I'm sorry, Daddy, that Mommy lied to you. I'm sorry that she lost the baby. I'm so sorry you are unhappy today. But I am not sorry I am your daughter and that you are my dad."

The words his daughter had spoken meant everything to him. She was comforting him, and the fact she was adopted didn't seem to faze her and he knew why. She felt secure in his love. But he did have more to tell her.

"Thanks, sweetheart, and I'm glad you're my daughter and that I'm your dad. So glad. But there is more."

"Okay," she said, wiping a tear from her face and giving him a kiss on the cheek before returning to her chair. She sat down and looked at him expectantly.

"It's about your birth mother."

"What about her? She didn't want me, right?"

"Wrong. She did want you, but her parents didn't think she was ready to raise a baby so they lied and told her that her baby had died at birth."

Jade shook her head sadly. "I hate to say it, but adults tend to lie a lot."

Sawyer quickly picked up his coffee cup to take a sip to keep from grinning. Unfortunately, she was right. Some of them did. Placing his cup back down, he cleared his throat. "Yes, there are some who do."

"I'm glad you aren't one of them."

He was glad, too. "Your biological mother found out the truth that you are alive."

Jade rolled her eyes. "Please don't tell me she's coming here to make trouble for us. I'm no longer a child, you know. I am a teenager and old enough to tell a judge who I want to be with."

"That's not the issue."

"Oh? What is the issue then?"

"I think you should know who she is."

Jade nodded. "Okay, who is she?"

He hesitated a moment. "Vashti Alcindor."

She stared at him for a minute like she was trying to let what he said penetrate her brain. He knew it had when a huge smile touched her lips. "My Ms. Vashti? Your Vashti?"

He nodded, watching her closely.

"OMG! I'm the baby she had at sixteen? The one she wouldn't tell anyone who her baby's daddy was?"

He wondered how she knew all that, certain Vashti never told her. He figured she'd heard from one of her gossipy friends who'd heard it from their gossipy mothers. "Yes."

"All righty now." Her smile then faded. "She knows?"

"Yes, she knows now."

Jade nodded. "And is she okay with it?"

He smiled. "It was a shock. Learning what her parents had done hurt her, but learning you were alive made her so happy, so yes, she's okay with it. But there is more."

"More?"

"Yes." Deciding not to keep her in suspense any longer, he said, "Vashti discovered there were two babies instead of one. Two girls. That means you have a twin."

"A twin?" she asked, leaning over the table to stare at him as if to make sure he was serious.

"Yes, a twin. An identical twin and her name is Kia."

## CHAPTER FORTY-SIX

"COME ON, DAD, we're going to miss our plane."

Sawyer shook his head. If his daughter had any idea how many flights he'd been on over the last seventy-two hours, she wouldn't be rushing him. But it was okay because more than anything he wanted to see Vashti, apologize and hope like hell she forgave him for not believing what she'd tried telling him.

After telling Jade about her twin, she'd had a lot of questions that he couldn't fully answer since he hadn't met Kia. And when Jade discovered that Kia was the person in the hospital who Vashti had gone to see and why, she immediately decided that they needed to pack and go to Sacramento because "my sister might need me." Those had been Jade's exact words. He doubted he could have been any prouder to be her father than at that minute.

The only part of the information that hadn't made her smile was when he revealed the identity of her paternal grandfather. She did admit she was willing to give Lacroix a chance, but that he had to put forth an effort as well. He honestly didn't think Reid would have a problem doing that.

Five hours later after a layover in Houston, their plane landed at the Sacramento Airport. He rented a ar and upon Jade's insistence, they headed straight to the hospital. "Do you think Kia will like me, Dad?"

He glanced over at Jade when he brought the car to a top at the traffic light and smiled. "Of course, she will."

"And Ms. Vashti?"

He reached out and playfully tweaked her nose. "I hink you already know how she feels about you."

Jade nodded, smiling. "Yes, she loves me," she said onfidently.

As Sawyer pulled into the hospital's parking lot, he wished he had the same level of confidence regarding Vashti's feelings for him. When he had walked out on her two days ago, he had done the same thing the other two men in her life had done. He had let her down.

DR. TELFAIR SAID I can go home this weekend if my fever tays down. That means the infection is cleared up," Kia said happily as she looked at the five people in the oom who were standing around her hospital bed. Her parents, grandmother, biological mother and biological aternal grandfather.

"That's wonderful," Percelli said. "Let's just hope it loesn't come back."

"And while we're all here together, we have something to tell you," Alma said, smiling.

"What?"

Vashti took a step closer to the bed. "When I found out about you, I found out something else."

"What?"

"That you are a twin."

Kia's mouth literarily dropped open. "A twin?"

"Yes. You have a twin sister. Right now there's not a lot I can tell you about her, but—"

"Hello, everyone. Look who I ran into on the elevator," Dr. Telfair cut in to say. He moved away from the door to let two people enter the room. Sawyer and Jade.

The moment Jade and Kia saw each other, they released loud screams. First from shock, then excitement and elation.

DR. TELFAIR TOOK it all in while smiling broadly. Sawyer, who stood frozen in place, stared at the girl in the hospital bed who was an absolute replica of Jade...or vice versa. The Harrises had the same reaction as Sawyer. It was evident that Reid was astounded. Tears formed in Vashti's eyes.

The reason Dr. Telfair had come to see Kia and her family was to deliver the not-so-good news that Reid Lacroix's lab results indicated he would not be an eligible donor for Kia. But there was more than an eighty percent chance her identical twin sister would be.

Dr. Telfair had the good sense to move out of the way when Jade finally rushed past him to give her sister a hug. He had to admit it was a touching moment with the two girls meeting for the first time, and the biological mother seeing both her babies together. They weren't babies anymore, but two sixteen-year-olds. From the look of things, they had a lot more in common than just the mother who was trying real hard not to get too emotional.

Dr. Telfair watched with keen interest as the man who just moments ago had introduced himself as Sawyer Grisham, moved past him to walk over to Vashti Alcindor to hand her a tissue. He was certain there was a story with those two. You didn't have to be a romantic to figure that out. Right now Dr. Telfair's main concern

was his patient who seemed to be in very good spirits
and surrounded by people who cared about her.

He eased out the door, deciding he would return to
check on Kia Harris later.

AFTER HE HAD showered and shaved, Sawyer caught the
hotel's elevator down to Vashti's floor. It was almost
ten at night and he hoped she hadn't gone to bed yet.
He didn't get the chance to talk to her at the hospital.
Jade and Kia had taken center stage and refused to relinquish it one iota. Introductions were made and then
Jade and Kia decided, and quite determinedly, that they
needed to spend more time together to get to know each
other. They announced the only way that could be ac-
complished was for Jade to spend the night. Dr. Telfair
was all for it and a few minutes before visiting hours
ended a cot was wheeled in for Jade to use. Sawyer had
left to get Jade's things out of the car and when he returned Vashti had left with Reid to return to the hotel.

He still had the passkey to Vashti's hotel room in his
wallet but had enough sense not to use it. There was a
strong chance she was still upset with him. For her not
to wait around for him to offer her a ride to the hotel
instead of leaving with Reid had been a pretty good
indication.

He knocked on her hotel room door and knew the
exact moment she stood on the other side looking out
the peephole. He could actually feel her body's heat
through the metal door. He could inhale her seductive
scent.

Sawyer knew at that moment that he would do whatever it took to get her back. Grovel if he had to, and at
this stage, he would even beg.

VASHTI DREW IN a deep breath after looking through the peephole. It was Sawyer. Taking the chain off the door, she opened it, trying not to stare. He had that just-showered look and he smelled good. Like aftershave and cologne. He'd changed clothes and was wearing a pair of jeans and a polo shirt and as usual, both looked good on him. Hot + denim = Sawyer.

She had showered and put on a shorts set. The California weather was beautiful this time of the year and she'd intended to take full advantage of it.

She wished her gaze hadn't automatically roamed over him, and she wished he wasn't aware it had done so. But then he was checking her out as well. Her heart began beating very fast like it did whenever he looked at her that way, with male interest that he alone could take to an unprecedented level.

"Vashti."

She refused to allow the deep, throaty sound of his voice to weaken her defense. But Lordy it was difficult. The moment he'd said her name thrills of desire raced all the way down to her toes. "Sawyer. Any reason you're here?" Other than to get me all turned on from the sight of you? It had been bad enough at the hospital and now here he stood at her hotel room door.

Then he had the nerve to shove his hands into the back pockets of his jeans. Whether he'd wanted to or not, doing so tightened the denim on a pair of masculine thighs. Thighs she remembered all too well.

"I'd like to talk to you."

Hadn't he said enough the last time before telling her goodbye? Yet she was giving in to his request and stepping aside to let him in. At some point he'd discov-

red she was telling the truth. Otherwise he would not
have brought Jade.

Closing the door behind him she moved to the loveseat in the room and sat down. "Okay, you can talk."

He moved to sit in a chair opposite her. Then as if
he wasn't satisfied with that, he stood and walked over
to her, which made her tilt her head all the way back to
stare up at him. "I'm sorry, Vashti. I did the one thing
I said I would not do. And that was to let you down. I
proved to be no better than the last two men in your
life."

Vashti wouldn't go that far, but he was right, when
he'd walked out that door he had let her down.

"I'm truly sorry."

Vashti didn't say anything. She scooted around him
and walked over to the door. Before opening it she
turned to him and said, "Apology accepted. You can
leave now."

He shoved his hands into his pockets again. "I love
you, Vashti. Will you give us another chance?"

She shook her head. "I can't. A lot is going on in
my life right now, Sawyer, and I don't need a man who
doesn't believe in me. A man who thinks I would stoop
so low as to accuse his deceased wife of things just for
the hell of it. I gave you my heart, my soul and my body.
I gave you my love."

"And I gave you mine. You're going to end things
because of one screwup on my part?"

"I didn't end things—you did, when you thought I
had slandered your wife's name. You're the one who
said goodbye."

"And I'm admitting I made a mistake."

She couldn't handle the riot of emotions inside her

so she changed the subject. "How did you confirm
was telling the truth?"

"When I was at the airport on standby, I was able to
think rationally, and the more I thought about it, there
were too many coincidences to suit me. I knew I had
to find out the truth."

Vashti recalled that both Bryce and Reid had said he
would eventually do that.

"Instead of flying back to Catalina Cove," he continued, "I caught a flight to Waco to see Johanna's best
friend, Erin. When I questioned her about it, she told
me the truth."

Vashti leaned against the door. "And what is the
truth?"

He told her of his conversation with Jade's godmother.

"Your wife lost your son?" she asked, her stomach
tightening in sorrow.

"Yes. At five months."

To be honest, Vashti had begun wondering if his wife
had been pregnant at all, although he had said he'd been
with her until her fourth month. "And with the Smithfields' help she replaced your baby with mine?"

"Yes."

Vashti could only imagine how he must have felt
finding out the depth of his wife's betrayal. Even while
telling her she'd seen the pain in his eyes. "I'm sorry."
And she was. For years Vashti had thought she was the
one who'd lost a son, when it had been him.

"Johanna had no right to do what she did," he said.
"When I returned from my tour of duty I had no idea
Jade wasn't my biological child."

"Did Erin say why she did it?"

"Yes. Johanna didn't believe I would stay married to her without the baby."

"Why would she think such a thing?"

He inhaled deeply before saying, "I married her because of the pregnancy, and whenever I called or wrote to her, I would ask about the baby before her."

Vashti moved away from the door to go back to the loveseat. His wife hadn't believed he loved her?

"Erin said Johanna knew I had grown to love her. However, by then she didn't want to tell me the truth and risk losing me anyway."

He paused a moment and then added, "I didn't get to mourn my son. She took that chance away from me. I'm not sure I can ever forgive her for that."

"You're going to have to."

He lifted a brow and stared at her. "Why?"

"Because I was told that anger, bitterness and animosity are too much baggage for anyone to carry around. At some point you have to let it go. Otherwise it will destroy you."

He remembered giving her that advice. "It's hard when you love someone and find out they aren't perfect like you thought, isn't it?"

She looked away and thought about what he'd asked her. She'd never thought he was perfect. She'd just expected… What? That he would be different from Julius and Scott. But then, hadn't he been different? Unlike Julius, he'd publicly acknowledged their relationship; and unlike Scott, he hadn't been unfaithful to her.

And now he was asking her for another chance. Hadn't he given her another chance when she'd pushed him away that night in New York? Her decision had been final, yet when Jade had called him because she had needed him, he had come and had been with her since, giving her support in ways Julius and Scott never had.

"It's hard when you love someone and find out they aren't perfect like you thought, isn't it?" Sawyer asked, repeating the question.

She looked back at him. "Yes, it's hard."

He nodded and then without saying anything else, he turned, went to the door and walked out, closing it behind him.

The moment Vashti heard the door closed she leaped to her feet. He hadn't said goodbye. She rushed to the door and snatched it open. The hall was clear. Where had he gone? The elevator!

She stepped out into the hall and too late, when her hotel room door closed behind her, she remembered she didn't have her key. She would worry about that later. Right now she had to stop Sawyer.

Rounding the corner, she saw him standing at the elevator about five feet away with his back to her. "Sawyer?"

He turned and stared at her. "Yes?"

"You didn't say goodbye."

When he didn't say anything but stood there staring at her, roaming his gaze over her, she said, "Well?"

He lifted a brow as he met her gaze. "Well, what?"

She felt heat from his gaze. "Why didn't you say goodbye?"

He shoved his hands in his pockets, ignoring the elevator door when it opened. "I've decided to never tell you goodbye again. For some reason you think good-

ye is the same thing as *the end*, and there won't ever
e an ending for us, Vashti."

"Why not?"

He leaned against the wall. "Because I won't let there
e. Neither will Jade. I told you once that my daugh-
er and I were a package deal. Nothing has changed regarding that. You want her, then you have to take her
ld man, too."

Out of the corner of her eye Vashti saw one of the
otel room doors slowly open. Someone must have
eard voices out in the hall and was now trying to eaves-
drop on their conversation.

"Well?" Sawyer asked, grabbing her attention again.

"Well, what?"

He began walking toward her and came to a stop in
front of her. "Are you going to take the package deal?"

She swallowed back a lump as she stared up at him.
he saw the movement out of the corner of her eye again
nd knew this time he'd seen it, too. "I think we need
o talk privately, but now I'm locked out of my hotel
oom," she whispered.

"We tried talking privately already, and I have a key
o your hotel room," he whispered back, pulling his
vallet out of his back pocket and fishing out the extra
asskey to hand to her.

"You kept it?"

"I must have had every intention of coming back,
Vashti."

She smiled up at him. "Thank you and I'm taking
he package deal."

"Smart choice." He placed his arm around her shoul-
ers. "Now we need to go back to your hotel room and
vork out the details."

VASHTI FUMBLED WITH the passkey and Sawyer eased it from her fingers and opened the door for her.

Once inside she handed the key to him. "You can have this back."

Sawyer's heart lurched. Was this her way of telling him he could use his key to her hotel room? He was ready to hash out those details now more than ever. When she made a move to walk away, he reached out and grabbed her wrist. "Not so fast."

"Then what about slow, Sawyer? Do you prefer slow to fast?"

He smiled as he leaned toward her. "I prefer Vashti any way I can have her. Will you forgive me?"

"Yes, I told you I accepted your apology. It's time we put it behind us." She took a step back. "You know all about following bread crumbs, right?"

He lifted a brow. "As a cop, I'm more into following leads."

She smiled. "Then follow these leads, Sheriff Grisham. We can finish our discussion in the bedroom."

She turned and began walking. First off were her sandals. Then her top. Then he watched her bra dropped, all without breaking a stride. By the time she reached the bedroom door, she had shimmied out of her shorts. Only thing left were her panties. He already had a pair in a very private place in his bedroom at home. He didn't have a problem confiscating another.

He blinked out of his reverie when the bedroom door closed shut. She was a lousy criminal for leaving so many leads and he followed each one, collecting them as he went. Missing one. The panties. That meant...

Without knocking he opened the bedroom door to find her naked on the bed. He dropped the clothes she'd scattered in a chair. He recalled the last time he'd been in this room and how he'd left before morning. With Jade spending the night at the hospital, there would be no rush to leave when morning came. But they were yet to finish those details.

He sat in the chair to remove his shoes and watched her while he did so. His blood began to sizzle. "About that package deal, Vashti."

"What about it?" she said, easing over toward him, wrapping her arms around him from the back and burying her face in his back, using her nose to sniff him through the material of his shirt. "I love the way you smell."

"Evidently."

"And I love you."

Those were the words he'd been waiting for her to say. Reaching behind him he gently pulled her down and she tumbled into his lap. He met her startled gaze. "And I love you. The only thing I ask is for you to remember I'm not perfect."

"I will remember and you need to remember that about me, too."

He nodded. "Now back to those details."

She was playing with the hem of his polo shirt, sneaking her hand underneath to rub his chest.

"I want something permanent."

Her hand went still. "Do you?"

"I'm getting too old to be leaving your bed before sunrise. You don't have to give me an answer this minute, but think about it."

She nodded. "I will."

"And I promise in the future, Vashti, whenever there's an issue, you and I will get to the bottom of it together. I have a feeling we're going to have to stick together now more so than ever. We won't have one teenaged daughter to worry about, but two. I have a feeling Kia will be visiting us a lot."

A huge smile touched Vashti's lips. "I think so, too. And I don't have to think about anything, Sawyer. I want a permanent package deal, too. Now off with your clothes."

He gently placed her back on the bed to finish undressing. She watched his every moment. "You're enjoying this, aren't you? Seeing me get naked."

"Yes."

He threw his head back and laughed. "I love you, Vashti."

"And I love you."

"I hope you know we're going to give Catalina Cove a lot to talk about for a while."

"Yes, but just until Reid Lacroix makes a statement. Jade and Kia are his granddaughters and you better believe he's going to protect them at all costs," Vashti said smiling, knowing how that worked.

"And am I assuming there might be interest between Reid and Kia's grandmother, Gloria?"

"Hmm, possibly. They went to college together and both lost spouses. I'm glad if there's interest. Everybody needs somebody and he's been alone for a while."

"Well, I hope he doesn't give in to his granddaughters' every whim. If he's not careful they will have him wrapped around their fingers," Sawyer said, easing down his jeans.

Vashti chuckled. "I think Kia is halfway there and I heard Jade telling him why the cove needed a Spencer's and McDonald's. You want to take bets on how soon we'll get them?"

He heard her sharp intake of breath when he slid out of his briefs. He loved her reaction to seeing him naked. When he joined her on the bed she leaned up and captured his mouth in a kiss whose purpose was to make his head spin.

No matter how often he kissed her, he would always want more. And he proved just how much more by exerting a degree of provocative pressure to her mouth. When he heard a satisfied purr, he knew for them there was no turning back. It would always be about moving forward.

"One day. No time soon, mind you, after we go permanent, I want a baby, Sawyer."

He froze and after sucking in an audible gasp, he gazed down at her. "A baby?"

"Yes. Your baby. Our baby. I'm only thirty-two and I'd like at least two before turning thirty-five and before you hit forty. Think you can manage it?"

Sawyer was stunned by the intensity of emotions he felt at that moment. He eased his body between her open legs and stared down at her, never knowing the degree of happiness he felt at that moment was possible.

"Yes, I can manage it. It's about time we make babies in a way that won't have tongues wagging. Born to our union. You plan the wedding, sweetheart, because I am all in and impatiently waiting."

He leaned down and kissed her, making love to her mouth in a way that had him savoring her taste in the most urgent way. When he released her mouth he stared down at her while easing his body into hers. The feel of his shaft sliding between her wet womanly folds and going deep, and then deeper, sent sensuous shudders through him. And when her inner muscles clenched him and she arched her back for better penetration, every nerve ending in his body was primed for an explosion of the most gigantic kind.

He fought for total control, knowing from here on out, whatever he and Vashti did, they would do together. They were a team in this and everything, and they would need to be a team more than ever in the days ahead. "Love me hard, Sawyer."

He didn't have to be told twice, and he began moving—all the way in and then pulling all the way out, and then starting the process all over again. He loved making love to her as his fiancée and would love making love to her as his wife.

Over and over he brought them to the edge and back, not ready to soar to the stars. She was so damn responsive to his every touch, his every thrust, and when he felt her body start spasming, he joined her, bonding them in a way that he knew in his heart was meant to be.

Always.

## *EPILOGUE*

*A month later*

VASHTI STOOD IN the gazebo and took it all in. It was grand opening day at Shelby by the Sea. Couples were already checking in and by tonight, the inn would be filled to capacity. In fact, there were no vacancies until spring. Already there were seven weddings planned between the months of March and June, including her own. She hadn't expected to book so many and had hired a woman whose job would be just to help coordinate weddings and receptions.

What she loved about today was that so many of the townspeople had come to help her celebrate. Reid had suggested she set up an old-fashioned Catalina Cove picnic on adjacent Lacroix land. He even offered for his company to foot the bill for all the food and entertainment. That was kind of him, although she knew there was an ulterior motive for the generous offer. The Harris family had arrived yesterday and so far the only thing any of the townsfolk had approached her to say was that she had beautiful daughters.

In Reid Lacroix fashion he had squashed rumors before they could begin. After Sawyer and the Harrises had given their permission, upon returning to Catalina Cove from California, Reid had called a press conference to announce that he'd recently discovered he had twin granddaughters. One, who was already living in the cove. Namely, Jade Grisham. And the other who lived in California. He even went further to say their biological mother was Vashti Alcindor, who had given birth to them at sixteen and who'd thought they'd died at birth. The secret was out and now everyone knew it had been Julius Lacroix who'd fathered her babies.

Reid had also told them that he would appreciate it if everyone was respectful of the privacy of all parties involved. In other words, whatever thoughts they might have, he better not hear about them. So far the people had taken his words seriously, although Vashti was certain some were trying to piece together all the components to the puzzle. Especially today when Reid appeared at the picnic with his identical twin granddaughters on each arm. Vashti was certain she had never, ever seen the man so happy. And she noted, as she was certain others had, too, that he kept Gloria Harris close by his side as well.

Vashti glanced to her right and saw Bryce talking with the man named Ray Sullivan. She knew what Bryce had said about the man just being friendly, but she wondered, especially when Ray was such a good-looking man.

She noticed that Kaegan, who was in charge of cooking all the seafood, seemed to be keeping his eyes on the couple. Hmm, interesting.

"Here you are."

She smiled at Sawyer when he returned with a bag of cotton candy. Reid had rented a huge cotton candy machine and had hired an attendant to man it. Since there was always a line, it was obviously one of the most popular booths at the picnic. At times Vashti had to pinch herself when she thought of how things had turned out. She, Sawyer and the Harrises were getting along great and it was like a huge extended family.

As Dr. Telfair had predicted, Jade had been a perfect donor match for Kia and was excited about giving her twin one of her kidneys. The procedure would be done over the Christmas holidays so the girls could miss minimum school days. So far Kia hadn't had another kidney infection and her dialysis had been reduced from three times a week to two. Of course, everyone was looking forward to when she wouldn't have to get them at all.

Trying to move toward forgiveness with her parents like Sawyer said, she had called to invite them to the grand opening, and they had surprised her by coming. The reunion had been bittersweet and her parents had actually cried when they'd seen Jade and Kia together.

"Thanks," she said to Sawyer, taking the bag of cotton candy from him.

"You're welcome. Reid's idea of using this land for a picnic was a good one. All you can see from the road is woods. I never knew all this was back here. It's nature's paradise on the sea."

Vashti had thought the same thing the first time Julius had brought her here. No need to tell Sawyer that this had been their secret hideaway, and that her daughters had been conceived in a spot not far from here.

"I have something to ask you about, Sawyer. Something I observed."

"What?"

"Ray Sullivan? Does Kaegan have competition?"

Sawyer followed her gaze to where Bryce and Ray stood talking. "Nah. There's nothing going on there."

She lifted a brow. That's what Bryce had told her the last time. But still… "How can you be so sure?"

He took a sip of iced tea. Then he said, "Ray is a victim of retrograde amnesia and made a decision not to get involved with anyone."

Vashti gasped. "Amnesia? How?"

"From a head injury a few years back. He was in a coma for a few weeks and when he came out of it, he'd been robbed of his memory. Totally. He couldn't even tell the authorities who he was. Ray Sullivan isn't even his name."

"How did he end up in Catalina Cove?"

"The doctor who'd treated him was a college roommate of Kaegan's who was practicing medicine in Ohio. He reached out to Kaegan because, although Ray had no memory of his former life, he did know he had a love for boats and the ocean. Ray needed a job and Kaegan's doctor friend asked him to hire Ray."

Sawyer took another sip of his tea then said, "There's a chance his memory might come back and there's a chance it never will."

Vashti looked over to where Ray and Bryce were still talking. "The townspeople know about his amnesia?"

"No. So far it's just me and Kaegan. And now you. Ray's a loner and usually doesn't socialize with anyone in town other than me and Kaegan. He prefers being by himself. I guess he likes Bryce, but not the way you might think. Ray knows Bryce used to be Kaegan's girl and he won't cross that line."

Sawyer chuckled before adding. "But I guess Ray feels there's nothing wrong with stirring Kaegan's jealousy every now and then."

Later that day Sawyer talked Vashti into taking a

walk on the beach. Holding hands they walked in their bare feet in the sand as they made more plans for their future. "I'm glad I came back to Catalina Cove. If I hadn't then I might not have ever found my girls."

"Yes, but now you've found them."

She stopped walking. "Yes, I found them. And I found you, too."

Leaning up on tiptoes, she gave her future husband a huge kiss. Happy that they had found love in Catalina Cove.

\* \* \* \* \*

*Fall in love with Catalina Cove all over again in*
Forget Me Not,
*the story of Ray Sullivan,*
*from* New York Times *bestselling author*
*Brenda Jackson and HQN Books.*

*In Royal, Texas, two best friends are in for
the night of their lives!*

*When shy beauty Tessa Noble gets a makeover and
steps in for her brother at a bachelor auction,
she doesn't expect her best friend,
rancher Ryan Bateman, to outbid everyone.
But Ryan's attempt to protect her ignites a desire
that changes everything...*

*Turn the page for a sneak peek at*
His Until Midnight *by Reese Ryan!*

Tessa Noble stared at the configuration of high and low balls scattered on the billiard table.

"I'm completely screwed," she muttered, sizing up her next move. After a particularly bad break and distracted play, she was losing badly.

But how on earth could she be expected to concentrate on billiards when her best friend, Ryan Bateman, was wearing a fitted performance T-shirt that highlighted every single pectoral muscle and his impressive biceps? He could have, at the very least, worn a shirt that fit, instead of one that was a size too small, as a way to purposely enhance his muscles. And the view when he bent over the table in a pair of broken-in jeans that hugged his firm ass like they were made for it...

How in the hell was she expected to play her best?

"You're not screwed," Ryan said in a deep, husky voice that was as soothing as a warm bath. Three parts sex-in-a-glass and one part confidence out the wazoo.

Tessa's cheeks heated, inexplicably. Like she was a middle schooler giggling over double entendres and sexual innuendo.

"Maybe not, but you'd sure as hell like to be screwed by your best friend over there," Gail Walker whispered in her ear before taking another sip of her beer.

Tessa elbowed her friend in the ribs, and the woman giggled, nearly shooting beer out of her nose.

Gail, always a little too direct, lacked a filter after a second drink.

Tessa walked around the billiard table, pool cue in hand, assessing her options again while her opponent huffed restlessly. Finally, she shook her head and sighed. "You obviously see something I don't, because I don't see a single makeable shot."

Ryan sidled closer, his movements reminiscent of a powerful jungle cat stalking prey. His green eyes gleamed even in the dim light of the bar.

"You're underestimating yourself, Tess," Ryan murmured. "Just shut out all the noise, all the doubts, and focus."

She studied the table again, tugging her lower lip between her teeth, before turning back to him. "Ryan, I clearly don't have a shot."

"Go for the four ball." He nodded toward the purple ball wedged between two of her opponent's balls.

Tessa sucked in a deep breath and gripped the pool cue with one hand. She pressed her other hand to the table, formed a bridge and positioned the stick between her thumb and forefinger, gliding it back and forth.

But the shot just wasn't there.

"I can't make this shot." She turned to look at him. "Maybe you could, but I can't."

"That's because you're too tight, and your stance is all wrong." Ryan studied her for a moment, then placed his hands on either side of her waist and shifted her a few inches. "Now you're lined up with the ball. That should give you a better sight line."

Tessa's eyes drifted closed momentarily as she tried

to focus on the four ball, rather than the lingering heat from Ryan's hands. Or his nearness as he hovered over her.

She opened them again and slid the cue back and forth between her fingers, deliberating the position and pace of her shot.

"Wait." Ryan leaned over beside her. He slipped an arm around her waist and gripped the stick a few inches above where she clenched it. He stared straight ahead at the ball, his face inches from hers. "Loosen your grip on the cue. This is a finesse shot, so don't try to muscle it. Just take it easy and smack the cue ball right in the center, and you've got this. Okay?"

"Okay." Tessa nodded, staring at the center of the white ball. She released a long breath, pulled back the cue and hit the cue ball dead in the center, nice and easy.

The cue ball connected with the four ball with a smack. The purple ball rolled toward the corner pocket and slowed, teetering on the edge. But it had just enough momentum to carry it over into the pocket.

"Yes!" Tessa squealed, smacking Ryan's raised palm to give him a high five. "You're amazing. You actually talked me through it."

"You did all the work. I was just your cheering section." He winked in that way that made her tummy flutter.

"Well, thank you." She smiled. "I appreciate it."

"What are best friends for?" He shrugged, picking up his beer and taking a sip from the bottle.

"Dammit!" Roy banged his pool cue on the wooden floor, drawing their attention to him. He'd scratched on the eight ball.

Tessa grinned. "I won."

"Because I scratched." Roy's tone made it clear tha he felt winning by default was nothing to be proud of.

"A win's a win, Jensen." She wriggled her fingers her palm open. "Pay up."

"You won? Way to go, Tess. I told you that you had this game in the bag." Ryan, suddenly beside her wrapped a big, muscular arm around her shoulder and pulled her into a half hug.

"Well, at least one of us believed in me." Tessa counted the four wrinkled five-dollar bills Roy stuffed in her palm begrudgingly.

"Always have, always will." He beamed at her and took another swig of his beer.

Tessa tried to ignore the warmth in her chest that fil tered down her spine and fanned into areas she didn' want to acknowledge.

Because they were friends. And friends didn't ge all…whatever it was she was feeling…over one another Not even when they looked and smelled good enough to eat.

Tessa Noble always smelled like citrus and sunshine Reminded him of warm summer picnics at the lake Ryan couldn't peel an orange or slice a lemon withou thinking of her and smiling.

There was no reason for his arm to still be wrappe around her shoulder other than the sense of comfort he derived from being this close to her.

"Take your hands off my sister, Bateman." Tessa' brother Tripp's expression was stony as he entered the bar. As if he was about five minutes away from kick ing Ryan's ass.

"Tessa just beat your man, Roy, here." Ryan didn't move. Nor did he acknowledge Tripp's veiled threat.

The three of them had been friends forever, though it was Tessa who was his best friend. According to their parents, their friendship was born the moment they first met. Their bond had only gotten stronger over the years. Still, he'd had to assure Tripp on more than one occasion that his relationship with Tess was purely platonic.

Relationships weren't his gift. He'd made peace with that, particularly since the dissolution of his engagement to Sabrina Calhoun little more than a year ago. Tripp had made it clear, in a joking-not-joking manner, that despite their longtime friendship, he'd punch his lights out if Ryan ever hurt his sister.

He couldn't blame the guy. Tess definitely deserved better.

"Way to go, Tess." A wide grin spread across Tripp's face. He gave his sister a fist bump, followed by a simulated explosion.

The Nobles' signature celebratory handshake.

"Thanks, Tripp." Tessa casually stepped away from him.

Ryan drank his beer, captivated by her delectable scent, which still lingered in the air around him.

"You look particularly proud of yourself today, big brother." Tessa raised an eyebrow, her arms folded.

The move inadvertently framed and lifted Tessa's rather impressive breasts. Another feature he tried hard, as her best friend, to not notice. But then again, he was a guy, with guy parts and a guy brain.

Ryan quickly shifted his gaze to Tripp's. "You still pumped about being a bachelor in the Texas Cattleman's Club charity auction?"

Tripp grinned like a prize hog in the county fair, his light brown eyes—identical to his sister's—twinkling merrily. "Alexis Slade says I'll fetch a mint."

"Hmm…" Ryan grinned. "Tess, what do you think your brother here will command on the auction block?"

"Oh, I'd say four maybe even five…dollars." Tessa, Ryan, Gail and Roy laughed hysterically, much to Tripp's chagrin.

Tripp folded his arms over his chest. "I see you all have jokes tonight."

"You know we're just kidding." Ryan, who had called next, picked up a pool cue as Roy gathered the balls and racked them. "After all, I'm the one who suggested you to Alexis."

"And I may never forgive you for creating this monster." Tessa scowled at Ryan playfully.

"My bad, I wasn't thinking." He chuckled.

"What I want to know is why on earth you didn't volunteer yourself?" Gail asked. "You're a moderately good-looking guy, if you like that sort of thing." She laughed.

She was teasing him, not flirting. Though with Gail it was often hard to tell.

Ryan shrugged. "I'm not interested in parading across the stage for a bunch of desperate women to bid on, like I'm a side of beef." He glanced apologetically at his friend Tripp. "No offense, man."

"None taken." Tripp grinned proudly, poking a thumb into his chest. "This 'side of beef' is chomping at the bit to be taken for a spin by one of the lovely ladies."

Tessa elbowed Ryan in the gut, and an involuntary "oomph" sound escaped. "Watch it, Bateman. We aren't *desperate*. We're civic-minded women whose only interest is the betterment of our community."

There was silence for a beat before Tessa and Gail dissolved into laughter.

Tessa was utterly adorable, giggling like a schoolgirl. The sound—rooted in his earliest memories of her—instantly conjured a smile that began deep down in his gut.

He studied her briefly. Her curly, dark brown hair was pulled into a low ponytail and her smooth, golden-brown skin practically glowed. She was wearing her typical winter attire: a long-sleeved plaid shirt, jeans that hid her curvy frame rather than highlighting it and the newest addition to her ever-growing sneaker collection.

"You're a brave man." Ryan shifted his attention to Tripp as he leaned down and lined his stick up with the cue ball. He drew it back and forth between his forefinger and thumb. "If these two are any indication—" he nodded toward Tess and Gail "—those women at the auction are gonna eat you alive."

"One can only hope." Tripp wriggled his brows and held up his beer, one corner of his mouth curled in a smirk.

Ryan shook his head, then struck the white cue ball hard. He relished the loud cracking sound that indicated a solid break. The cue ball smashed through the triangular formation of colorful balls, and they rolled or spun across the table. A high and a low ball dropped into the pockets.

"Your choice." Ryan nodded toward Tessa.

"Low." Hardly a surprise. Tessa always chose low balls whenever she had first choice. She walked around the table, her sneakers squeaking against the floor, as she sized up her first shot.

"You know I'm only teasing you, Tripp. I think it's pretty brave of you to put yourself out there like that. I'd be mortified by the thought of anyone bidding on me." She leaned over the table, her sights on the blue two ball before glancing up at her brother momentarily. "In fact, I'm proud of you. The money you'll help raise for the Pancreatic Cancer Research Foundation will do a world of good."

She made her shot and sank the ball before lining up for the next one.

"Would you bid on a bachelor?" Ryan leaned against his stick, awaiting his turn.

He realized that Tess was attending the bachelor auction, but the possibility that she'd be bidding on one of them hadn't occurred to him until just now. And the prospect of his best friend going on a date with some guy whose company she'd paid for didn't sit well with him.

The protective instinct that had his hackles up was perfectly natural. He, Tripp and Tessa had had each others' backs since they were kids. They weren't just friends—they were family. Though Tess was less like a little sister and more like a really hot distant cousin three times removed.

"Of course I'm bidding on a bachelor." She sank another ball, then paced around the table and shrugged. "That's kind of the point of the entire evening."

"Doesn't mean you have to. After all, not every woman attending will be bidding on a bachelor," Ryan reminded her.

"They will be if they aren't married or engaged,"

Gail said resolutely, folding her arms and cocking an eyebrow his way. "Why, Ryan Bateman, sounds to me like you're jealous."

"Don't be ridiculous." His cheeks heated as he returned his gaze to the table. "I'm just looking out for my best friend. She shouldn't be pressured to participate in something that makes her feel uncomfortable."

Tessa was sweet, smart, funny and a hell of a lot of fun to hang out with. But she wasn't the kind of woman he envisioned with a paddle in her hand, bidding on men as if she were purchasing steers at auction.

"Doesn't sound like Tess to me. That's all I'm saying." He realized he sounded defensive.

"*Good.* It's about time I do something unexpected. I'm too predictable...too boring." Tessa cursed under her breath when she missed her shot.

"Also known as consistent and reliable," Ryan interjected.

Things were good the way they were. He liked that Tessa followed a routine he could count on. His best friend's need for order balanced out his spontaneity.

"I know, but lately I've been feeling... I don't know... stifled. Like I need to take some risks in my personal life. Stop playing it so safe all the time." She sighed in response to his wide-eyed, slack-jawed stare. "Relax, Rye. It's not like I'm paying for a male escort."

"I believe they prefer the term *gigolo*," Gail, always helpful, interjected then took another sip of her drink.

Ryan narrowed his gaze at Gail, which only made the woman laugh hysterically. He shifted his attention back to Tessa, who'd just missed her shot.

"Who will you be bidding on?"

Tessa shrugged. "I don't know. No one in particular

in mind, just yet. The programs go out in a few days. Maybe I'll decide then. Or... I don't know...maybe I'll wait and see who tickles my fancy when I get there."

"Who *tickles your fancy*?" Ryan repeated the words incredulously. His grip on the pool cue tightened.

He didn't like the sound of that at all.

# SPECIAL EXCERPT FROM

.wyer took them around back to show the view of the
.you and how he'd be able to stand on his porch every
.ght to see the setting sun. He took hold of Vashti's
.nd, no longer able to ignore the flagrant heat of that
.rnal attraction between them. He leaned down and
.hispered close to her ear, "Come with me." His brain
.arly faltered when her scent enveloped him.

Without asking where he intended to take her, she went
.ith him. He placed his arms around her shoulders as
.ey moved farther away from the group and toward the
.cluded beach. "I hope you're aware there are alligators
.at come out at night," she said, smiling up at him.

He chuckled. "I can protect you." Moments later, when
. stopped, she turned to him and their gazes connected.
.e took in her features illuminated in the moonlight. Even
.ter all she'd eaten, the cherry-red lipstick still shaded
.r lips, making her mouth that much more delectable.

She glanced around. "What's so special about this
.ot?" she asked him.

His mouth curved into a smile. "You're here."

She chuckled. "Yes, I am. I guess I should ask y
why," she said as an "I already know" look appeared
her eyes.

"Earlier tonight you asked me a bold question."

"I did?"

"Yes. You wanted to know just what was going
with us."

"You got an answer for me, Sawyer?"

"Not really, but I hope this is the first step in trying
find out." Then he lowered his mouth to slant it across he

\* \* \*

# Get 4 FREE REWARDS!

**We'll send you 2 FREE Books plus 2 FREE Mystery Gifts.**

Both the **Romance** and **Suspense** collections feature compelling novels written by many of today's best-selling authors.